I0592757

RUBY HEART

Cry Havoc Book 1

DONNA MAREE HANSON

Copyright Information

Ruby Heart first published by Donna Maree Hanson 2018

Copyright © Donna Maree Hanson 2018

The moral right of the author has been asserted.

All rights reserved. This publication (or any part of it) may not be reproduced or transmitted, copied, stored, distributed or otherwise made available by any person or entity (including Google, Amazon or similar organizations) in any form (electronic, digital, optical, mechanical, audio) or by any means (photocopying, recording, scanning or otherwise) without the prior written permission of the author.

ISBN978-0-6482795-9-4 (ebook)

ISBN (print on demand) 978-0-9876381-0-6

Cover design by www.crocodesigns.com

Proofread by Maxine McArthur

This book is written in Australian/British English, which means the spelling conventions differ from the USA. For example, colour, not color, apologise not apologize and so on.

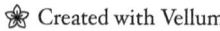 Created with Vellum

This one is for my writer retreat buddies
Thank you for the inspiration and support over the years
Matthew, Trudi, Russell, Kylie, Nicole, Cat, Robert, Joanne, Alan, Ian, Shauna
and Kim

PROLOGUE

1858 EAST SUSSEX, UNITED KINGDOM

The wheels of the extractor's machinery ground against the gears, vibrating the timber floor. The Executioner looked on, eyes greedy for every tremor of pain, every cry of anguish. Heat and steam rolled against his skin as the great piston shoved and tugged, turning the large wheel. The sight of Wilbur Hardcastle, recalcitrant magician, struggling feebly against the restraints as the extractor sucked out his life force, stirred no pity, only curiosity. The process of death never ceased to fascinate the Executioner. Wilbur emitted a hoarse-voiced cry steeped in agony and still he sighed at the wonder of it.

A ripple of power brushed up against his skin. Turning slightly, he saw Brother Wilfred materialise and then stride forward. The tall, gaunt magician, his features hidden by shadow, whispered urgently. "Did he reveal the location of the texts?"

"No. Only that they are hidden. If you want to question him, do so now. Within minutes, he will be drained and beyond redemption."

"I have completed the search. He hid them well. I can find no trace. Has he said anything since the interrogation?"

The Executioner shook his head. An idea for one final attempt to extract an answer caused him lift an eyebrow. "Was not there a child?"

Brother Wilfred's mouth dropped open. "A small talent and a

female. Oh you mean as leverage?" His eyes widened as he caught on to the Executioner's idea. "This execution was sanctioned. The child is thus protected."

The Executioner shrugged. Wilfred had no imagination and was too limited by the rules. Lucky, not all the brothers in the *societas magicae* were as inhibited. "No use to us then. Shall I end it?"

Wilbur Hardcastle's skin was pale, his cheeks concaved, and his darkened sockets feebly clutched bloodshot orbs. He looked as if his body had been wasted by disease for many months. Only the last stubborn spark of life remained in his eyes. The Executioner increased the machine's speed and watched that spark fade.

The powerful machine was useful for harnessing life energy and efficacious in murder. Brother Hardcastle's life force now resided in the machine to be used as the brotherhood saw fit. Stepping back, Brother Wilfred performed the spell that would send the machine back to their sanctum and bowed a farewell before he conjured himself away.

The Executioner began the task of arranging the body of Wilbur Hardcastle on the bed, setting all that was awry to rights. Evidence that his life had been unnaturally taken was quietly removed and his death would remain forever a mystery to the local coroner.

❦

With the hum of industrious bees in his ears, Edward Hardcastle Huntington strode through the grounds of Willow Park, his newly inherited estate. Garden beds brimmed with summer flowers, the kitchen garden swelled with vegetables and the orchards with ripe fruit. Amazed at what fortune had bestowed on him, Edward continued his excursion, trying not to gape at every wonder that passed his eye—an Italian garden, a yew maze and a water maze, a well-stocked lake with pretty willows casting dappled shade on a row of punts.

Tall, with a good bearing and curling dark locks, he was at home with his surroundings. He was dressed finely in a new morning coat, offset with a dark blue silk cravat. His long legs ate up the distance between the lawn and the pleasure gardens, with the estate's solicitor, Mr Stradbroke, trailing behind him, huffing and wheezing as he struggled to keep up.

"I am flabbergasted," Edward remarked more to himself than his companion.

Mr Stradbroke took a few, hasty breaths and wiped a handkerchief across his brow. "Yes, a most worthy estate unencumbered by debt. Your cousin had modest tastes and has managed to deliver your inheritance to you in very good shape, indeed."

Edward rubbed his chin, his gaze eating up the vista. Situated in East Sussex, the estate was within easy distance of London. How different his life would be, what wonders were his, what opportunities to indulge his passion for science. No more dark, rat-infested rooms and scrounged equipment.

Stradbroke cleared his throat and wiped perspiration from his brow with a large handkerchief. "So, Mr Huntington, is the estate to your liking? Do you have any particular directions for me?"

"I like it very well." He had yet to come to terms with his inheritance and had no particular plans to change arrangements. He turned to Mr Stradbroke, taking note of the solicitor's eager posture. "As for directions—"

A loud scream interrupted him. The solicitor started, his long moustache twitching at the ends.

"What the devil?" Edward uttered as he peered around, searching for the source of the disturbance.

More screams and two children erupted from some nearby bushes and, without a care for those around them, bounded down the path toward the lake's edge before disappearing into the yew maze, where more screams emitted. One was a girl with hair flying in a tangle, wearing a stained apron over a dress rimmed in mud along the hem. The other was a blond youth of about sixteen, dressed in nothing but trousers and ripped shirt and equally smeared in dirt.

"Children of the servants, I expect," he remarked to Mr Stradbroke.

The solicitor went pink around the ears. "I err...Yes, quite right. I'll speak to the housekeeper about them." They walked together in a slow circuit that would return them to the house. "Ehem..."

"What is it?" Edward asked, still distracted by the radical changes in his circumstances. He was now the owner of a splendid house and the generous income that came with it.

"I was wondering, sir, whether you had read all the terms of the will and the papers you have signed this morning."

Edward's left eyebrow rose. "Of course, I read them all. What are you suggesting?"

He turned and left the garden perimeter, his boots crunching up the gravel drive as he strode towards the front door. A cup of tea was in order and perhaps a few sandwiches. The housekeeper, Mrs Eddington, seemed a competent woman. Hopefully, she was able to predict that her new master needed refreshment on this very warm day. His mind was busily contemplating his afternoon tea when Mr Stradbroke coughed in his fisted hand to clear his throat. "I don't mean to imply any insult, Mr Huntington, but you have yet to enquire after your ward." He gazed up at Edward, his moustache dropping along the sides of his frown.

"My ward?" Edward stopped in his tracks, his heartbeat rather lumpy all of sudden.

The solicitor nodded vigorously. "Yes, sir. Mr Hardcastle left you the guardianship of his daughter, Miss Jemima Lily Hardcastle."

"My lord, did he?" Edward suddenly faint, inserted a finger into his cravat to let some air onto his skin, and hurried through the front door and across the hall into the cool confines of the library.

"Well, yes, sir. The papers...this morning?" Mr Stradbroke said as he followed along behind.

"What the devil did he do that for? I have only just come of age myself." Edward threw himself into a chair, sighing as his eyes ranged over shelves that housed an impressive collection of books. He recollected himself and sat up to face the unctuous solicitor. "A girl you say? How old is she?"

Mr Stradbroke stood before him, wiping the edge of his moustache with a forefinger. "Well, sir, she is an interesting young girl of about thirteen or fourteen."

"I see…" A knock on the door heralded the arrival of the butler, hefting a loaded tea tray. The housekeeper had anticipated his needs precisely. Edward found his estimation of Mrs Eddington climbed even higher as he bent forward to inspect the tray. Feeling quite peckish, he took a plate of sandwiches and began to gnaw on them, while offering the solicitor to partake himself with a careless wave of his hand. After a sip of tea and a large swallow, he instructed Mr Stradbroke to tell him more.

The solicitor nestled his tea cup and saucer on his knee. The butler had served him with a moustache cup, with inbuilt guard to protect his waxed and pampered facial hair. Edward's estimation of the butler, Cobb, rose also.

"She has her own legacy. One from her mother, who died when she was an infant, a heart condition, I understand, and one from the estate so she would not be a financial burden to you. There is the issue of her education."

Edward reached for a generous portion of rich fruit cake and offered the plate to Mr Stradbroke, eyebrows raised. "Education? She's at school then?" he asked with an optimistic air.

Mr Stradbroke placed his cup on the table, refusing the cake offered him with a shake of his head. "Ah no, not quite. You may not have heard about your second cousin, Wilbur Hardcastle, in great detail." The solicitor coughed. "I am not sure how to say this with discretion. I will own he was a portion eccentric and spent much of his time in his laboratory performing experiments, most of which I could not comprehend. After his wife died, he brought the girl up at home, educated her himself."

The butler poured another cup of tea, while Edward helped himself to a jam tart. All that walking had excited his appetite. "What is so eccentric about that? Next you will say he taught her Greek, Latin, logic and philosophy, with a smattering of modern science. A man's classical education rather than how to read, write and do her sums." He chuckled at his own wit.

"That's exactly what he did."

Edward coughed, choking on tart and tea. The solicitor hurried over and slapped him soundly on the back.

"There, there sir. Nothing to be upset about. I'm sure when you meet her you'll know what to do."

When the tea tray was taken away, Edward left the solicitor in the library to go over the accounts and prepare a list of the various investments for further discussion, while he inspected his newly acquired laboratory. It was such a luxury to have his own space instead of sharing rented rooms. Down in the converted basements, he found the most interesting array of animals—some stuffed, some preserved in jars. In journals, he found copious notes as to their habitat and sketches of the creatures from conception, birth and death.

In another part of the laboratory, he found a section devoted to plants, leaves, herbs, flowers in various stages of preservation—dried, chopped, pickled. Again, there was the same meticulous attention to detail in the naming of the plant, its properties, its propagation and culture. On the centre laboratory table, he saw the beginnings of a machine, the pieces not quite assembled. Cousin Wilbur had indeed been a man of science. A noise from the depths of the laboratory startled him. He swung around; he was not alone. As he strode down the aisle between the long workbenches, he saw a girl, the dirty urchin from that morning, putting away glass beakers in a cupboard.

"What the devil are you doing?"

The girl gasped and spun around. "Ah! You must be Uncle Edward." She edged a pail to the side with her foot, then curtseyed. "I am Jemima Hardcastle. How do you do."

"How do you do." He responded automatically. "And what are you doing down here?"

She looked around at the bench. "Making sure my things were put away. Papa always made sure everything was put exactly where it should be."

Edward jerked his chin at the pail. "What have you got in there?"

"Tadpoles," she held up the pail, then lowered it to peer inside. "They will grow into common frogs, unfortunately—not pool frogs. Found them by the lake." She shrugged and lifted her face to stare at him. "I want to try them on a new diet to see if it affects their rate of growth and colour." He studied her as she rattled on about her frogs. Her face had a good bone structure, slight freckling across the nose, which might fade in time with the right application of creams. She was reasonably tall for her age, he supposed, but only time would tell. He had no idea what shade her hair was under the layer of grime. She looked as if she had been the object of a fox hunt. It just wouldn't do, he thought sourly, realising that he was now responsible for this girl. This was a great responsibility, one that terrified him.

"Please dispose of them this minute and then meet me in the library."

"But..."

"Now, if you please. This is my laboratory, and I won't have a little chit of a girl getting under my feet."

Jemima jerked the pail, spilling pungent water as she stormed out.

Edward rubbed his chin, considering what he was to do with his ward. She could not remain there—a most unsuitable arrangement. If she was to be a useful member of society, she had to go to school or have a governess.

෨෪ඁ

In the library stood Jemima still adorned in all her muck, not even having deigned to wash her face. Stradbroke stared at the ceiling, probably trying to keep his gaze from this feral child, who was meant to be a young lady. The solicitor was probably embarrassed, too, because he had withheld important details when Edward had been signing all the paperwork, thus landing him with the responsibility for Miss Hardcastle. Edward felt bad for what he must do to this wild, orphan girl. It was his duty to see that she was raised properly. Heavens forbid, but he had to assert some authority, some discipline into her life.

"Mrs Eddington!" Edward called out.

The housekeeper, a pleasant and rounded middle-aged woman, with hair under her cap and rosy cheeks, immediately put her head around the door. "Yes, sir?"

"Please escort Miss Hardcastle upstairs and make sure she is bathed and properly dressed in time for dinner."

Jemima in turn stood there gaping at him as if he was some kind of apparition. Obviously, she had been running wild for months while the estate confirmed him as next heir in the entailment. Certainly, the servants had not taken charge of her. She was too old by halves to be running with a young man without a chaperone.

Shrugging off the guiding hand of Mrs Eddington, she blurted out. "How dare you, sir! Who are you to tell me what to do in my own home? Why we have only just been introduced." Her gaze went pleadingly to Mr Stradbroke. "Please, sir, tell me what is to do here?"

Edward raised himself up, puffing out his chest as his own erstwhile father was wont to do. At twenty-one, he did not have much fatherly experience himself and had not supervised anything except maybe the care of his cocker spaniel, Turnip, before being sent to school.

"I will tell you what is happening. You are going to school. Tomorrow. A proper school for young ladies, where you will learn deportment, drawing, elocution, sewing and, most importantly, manners. You will leave first thing in the morning."

"What?" was all the girl could manage. Despite her unseemly upbringing, she had tears in her eyes. The feminine in her had not been totally obliterated. This gave Edward some hope that she was not lost, not destined to be a blue-stockinged spinster forever an outcast in society.

"Stradbroke, you will ride to London this evening. I have an acquaintance who runs a school for young ladies. You will take my letter to her. I am sure she will oblige us by taking on Miss Hardcastle in on short notice. You will, of course, access the necessary funds to set up her wardrobe and other essentials. Miss Blake will take it all in hand."

"No! You cannot send me away from my home. This is all I have left of my father, of my life. And what about David? You cannot send me away without letting me say goodbye to him."

The torn look on her face, shredded his heart. He tried not to buckle so he frowned at her, adding some theatre to his posture. "I can send you away young lady. Your father made me your guardian, therefore, I make the important decisions in your life and control your money until you come of age or marry. I am sorry for your loss, but this is my home now and you must bear it as best as possible. If your young friend can read, you have my leave to dispatch a note to him so that one of the servants can deliver it. However, you will not be able to visit him in person. Now, I suggest you accompany the good Mrs Eddington upstairs and see to your toilet. I will see you again at dinner."

The young lady turned on her muddy heel, lifted her ragged and stained skirts and stormed out after the housekeeper, slamming the door. After a moment of shocked silence, the butler brought in some wine. "Sherry, sir?"

"Most certainly," Edward replied, reaching for the glass. He was relieved to see Mr Stradbroke partake because it convinced him that the solicitor had found the scene taxing also. He fought the guilt and won. He knew he was doing what was best for her in the end.

Miss Hardcastle did not make an appearance at dinner but rather ate in her room. According to the housekeeper, the young lady was feeling out of sorts. From what he had heard while changing for dinner, he thought it likely that she had ruptured some organ or other while screaming blue murder in her room and tossing about a few items of furniture. He smiled to himself as he tucked into his roast beef. His friend, Miss Blake, ran a very strict school. He cut into the crispy Yorkshire pudding. All of Miss Hardcastle's wayward habits would be curbed and a nice marriageable young lady would be produced at the end of four years or so. By the time he finished off the baked potato and soaked up the last of the gravy, he considered his role of guardian well in hand. Later, he sat by the hearth, sipping some very nice port, smoking a cheroot and told himself that she would get over her grief and thrive in her new environment. It was for the best.

His ward had departed by the time he arose in the morning. He had to admit that he was glad he had missed the farewells and the tears. He might have buckled and that would not do. A young man could not have charge of a young girl, particularly one as wayward as she. Mrs Eddington's tears did give him pause as she saw her dart into her room. The butler guided him to the breakfast room before he could ask after the cause of her distress. After a leisurely repast, he made his way to the laboratory to become acquainted with the most treasured part of his inheritance.

He lit a few lamps and investigated a number of under-bench cupboards. Everything was placed precisely and with much care. After wandering down the aisles, he came once again to the partially assembled machine. There he stood examining the pieces, when he felt a tingling sensation against his skin, more like the soft caress of a feather. He looked behind him, wondering if there was a breeze, but the several small windows high in the wall were shut. Turning back, he noticed a sealed white envelope, sitting on top of a pile of journals. These were shut up tight with rather sturdy locks and no key was visible anywhere. After trying to pry them open for a few minutes, he once again stared at the letter and turned it over. It was odd that it was addressed to him by name. Wilbur Hardcastle must have known who his next heir was, which seemed strange as it took the trustees an age to decide. Edward was sure his cousin had died unexpectedly.

On opening it, his eyebrows went north as he read the neat script. His cousin had indeed been eccentric, for the letter contained the most extraordinary communication. Then looking about him, he could see nothing but order and logic, which was contrary to the bizarre assertions in the letter. With a shrug, he picked up the uppermost journal and touched the lock saying 'open' as instructed. To his surprise, it sprang open as if by magic. Immediately, he dropped it and, with trembling hands, picked up the letter to read it again.

"Could it be true?" Edward let the letter fall from his hands and reached for the next locked journal. Again, it sprang open at his command.

A vibration in the air tingled the skin on the back of his neck. Turning slowly to peer behind him, he saw a weathered, wooden chest. He had not noticed it before. Kneeling in front of it, he ran his hands over the once fine wood and along the partially rusted, iron straps. The huge lock, he cradled in his hand, shaking his head in disbelief.

"Open," he said, and the mechanism clicked. Lifting the lid, he inspected the contents—three, large leather-bound tomes, reeking of age. When he reached in, the tips of his fingers brushed a number of innocuous looking stones. He hesitated at the vibration emanating from them. The scientist in him wanted to reject the thought of magic, of inexplicable power, yet he had felt it, used it. He had always known there were things that could not be explained. He stood and picked up the letter, re-reading the last lines—this is your true inheritance, your heritage, your destiny...you have magic. Use it well. He frowned though at the warning hastily scrawled along the bottom of the page...tell no one of what you have.

CHAPTER 1
FOUR YEARS LATER— KENT, UNITED KINGDOM

The sound of Sylvia Horton's familiar laugh drew Jemima Hardcastle to the rear garden of Primrose Manor, where the large party of house guests lounged on chairs and sipped cool lemonade. Under the shade of her parasol, Jemima walked with a light step. Last night's introductions had been rather blurred as both Sylvia and Jemima had been tired, arriving well after dinner. Despite their fatigue, they spent half the night discussing the people they had met. One young man had already attracted Sylvia's interest—Mr Jasper Heaton, who was a dashing medical man with dark hair, hazel eyes and a ready smile. Sylvia's parents had assembled an assortment of young people for their daughter's entertainment, the goal being a good marriage. Jemima had no such inclination for matrimony but had to admit the attention of the handsome and intelligent members of the opposite sex was diverting and flattering.

With a wave to Sylvia, who was dressed in pale pink, with her white blonde hair curled into tight ringlets, Jemima walked up to the party, not too ashamed of her own turnout. She was wearing a pale green day dress, trimmed in braid, with flattering sleeves. Her own strawberry blonde hair was swept up in a tall bun, with one trailing ringlet draped over her neck. Sylvia's maid had dressed it for her and she felt so mature. No more school ringlets and pigtails.

A deep laugh drew her attention, a newly arrived guest, she surmised. Her gaze darted to the tall figure of a man, with a well-tailored morning coat hugging his broad shoulders. When he turned around, she saw dark, curly hair trimmed to frame his somewhat olive-toned face. Their eyes met. Her heart thumped, and she had to lock her knees before she collapsed. Sucking in a breath, she did her best to hide her trembling hands. How odious that he should be here. No glint of recognition flashed in his deep blue eyes, allowing her to relax somewhat. She smiled to hide her discomfiture and hoped she did not perspire too much. Had she changed that much in four years?

He stepped forward and bowed slightly. Sylvia performed the introductions. "Oh, Mr Huntington, please meet my friend, Jemima H Castle."

"Pleased to meet you, Mr Huntington." Jemima blushed, terrified to her heart at the out and out lie of her name. Sylvia had no trouble calling her by her school nickname, Jemima "H", for Hard, Castle. And Sylvia knew she was using the name to avoid the notice of her guardian. The Hortons had accepted the name, swallowing the story that she was an orphan of no particular breeding, which meant of course, she was a nobody and less likely to compete with Sylvia in the marriage stakes. But now, what could she do? If she announced she was Jemima Hardcastle and that Mr Huntington was her guardian, there would be no end to the uproar. His was the exact circle she wished to avoid.

"A pleasure, Miss Castle." He bowed over her hand, which quivered in his grip. A slight flicker of his eyelids betrayed that he noticed her reaction.

"The pleasure is all mine," Jemima replied, while thinking she could not bear him calling her by that counterfeit name. Glancing about, she was in want of a seat before her trembling knees failed her completely.

"Will you not join us?" he asked pleasantly.

With a sigh, she relaxed as she was in no immediate danger. "With pleasure. Thank you." Jemima gracefully lifted her skirt and sat down on the garden chair he held for her. She placed her parasol beside her leg and smiled nicely at everyone. She had no idea how long she would get away with it. When she was found out, all hell was going to break loose. At that odious thought, she began to look optimistically on her predicament. It was a good joke to play on him—mixing in society in front of his nose. That thought made her arch her eyebrow and consider her situation some fine fun, provided she had the nerve for it. Of that she was not convinced. Her smile widened. Those who dare win, they say.

❦

Sylvia's brother Roderick, who was as every bit as blond as his sister, joined them, swelling the party of young people to twelve. Beside Huntington and his friend Heaton, there was their school friend, Genevieve Preston, who suffered from lack of spirits, and her unfortunate brother, Eustace, who had a stutter and a weepy skin condition, a set of twins from the neighbourhood, Winifred and Oliver Luton, who had interesting country manners and did not resemble each other at all. Oliver paid a lot of attention to Sylvia, which her friend accepted with ease. Roderick Horton was accompanied by his fiancé, Catherine Catch-pole, her poet brother, Gideon and rather effeminate cousin, Julian Beldere, who often embroidered his conversation with French. Another family friend, who Sylvia confessed she did not know well and neither did Jemima, was Penelope Winters and her rather handsome cousin William Littleton, who were modest people brought up by a vicar.

There was enough variety of company to avoid boredom, provide interest and inspire humorous private commentary. The young folk spent the morning in desultory conversation. It was hot, and no one seemed to mind whiling away the hours doing nothing in particular. Jemima found her guardian's gaze often on her. When she caught him at it, she smiled. Not too flirty, she hoped. Was that speculation in his gaze a titillating memory of a screaming, muddy girl in the library?

Gideon Catchpole's poetry was amusing, not intentionally, Jemima guessed. It was not quite riveting either and she found she had to shut her mouth so as not to tease the young gentleman. Terribly bad mannered of her to even think of doing so. While Catchpole recited rhyming couplets, her eyes danced over the assembled party, avoiding Mr Huntington the best she could. The others though were all too polite, though she did notice William Littleton's eyebrows jerk a few times when a mismatched metaphor was expounded by the budding poet.

With interest, Jemima watched Heaton skilfully monopolise her friend after Gideon ran out of poetry to recite. Heaton was rather deft at seeking out things of interest to say to Sylvia, compliments on her clothes, hair, manners and taste and Sylvia had a great deal of trouble keeping the admiration from her gaze. Jemima recollected the object of her own childish admiration and dropped out of the conversation going on around her.

Penelope Winters was urgently whispering to her cousin William—no doubt advising on tactics to outwit Heaton's play for Sylvia. Sylvia had a good dowry, that Mr Littleton could not ignore. Jemima thought he had lost his chance as Sylvia looked smitten with Heaton already.

Genevieve Preston had begun to extol all of her brother's virtues to an unspecified audience in a loud but flat voice. Eustace Preston blushed, thus emphasising the deplorable state of his skin. Looking away to preserve the man's dignity, Jemima found herself in the past, reliving her departure from Willow Park and the wrench of leaving David Longhurst, the vicar's son, without saying goodbye. David Longhurst had corresponded with her for a year or two while his father was the local vicar. Then he had stopped writing to her. He had been her childhood friend, perhaps her first love. That night she had cried over her farewell note. What a silly girl she had been and how angry had she been at her uncle.

"It grows chilly," her guardian's voice cut through her thoughts. The others were gathering shawls and heading inside, away from the evening chill. "Shall I escort you indoors, Miss Jemima? I believe there is tea and sandwiches being served at present."

Jemima looked up, startled that Huntington was addressing her as she had been day dreaming about the past. "I do beg your pardon. Have I been ignoring you?"

"Not at all," he said, holding out his elbow for her to hold. "I must confess I have been watching you from afar."

Jemima blushed and looked away. Goodness, she thought. He was flirting with her. She glanced sideways at him, seeing a smile curve his lips, then she shook herself. What a horrible fate it would be to be attracted to the very man she had hated all these years.

There was a rustle in the bushes behind them. Mr Huntington frowned. "I wonder what that could be."

He stopped, moving her gently behind him as he scanned the lawn and the hedge. He lifted his hand as if to salute and spoke under his breath and then drew it down in a slash.

"Is there something wrong?" she asked, her gaze travelling over the lawn bathed in the afternoon sun. She thought she heard something: a faint gasp. Her gaze narrowed. What was he doing?

He turned back to her, once again securing her hand in the crook of his elbow. "No, it is nothing. I thought I saw someone there, crouching in the bushes. Did you see anyone?"

"No, only you." She laughed and smiled up at him.

That response brought a sparkle to his remarkable blue eyes. He led her on, pausing slightly to look over his shoulder, a slight frown marring his brow. She glanced behind her and saw nothing. Catching her look, his expression cleared, letting her precede him into the drawing room.

Visitors mingled, and the room was quite full. Jemima took a place next to Lady Arbunkle, who sat like a sultana on the sofa. She was a baroness by marriage and wore outrageous jewellery at all times. Currently, a sizeable emerald hung around her neck, nestled between her ample bosoms. It was so remarkable that even Mr Huntington commented on it.

"My, that is a great beauty of a stone, Lady Arbuckle. Is it a new acquisition or a family heirloom?"

"Why it is from India. My husband gave it to me along with some lovely rubies and a collection of sapphires. I am so fortunate in my choice of husband, am I not? He sends me so many pretty things silks, shawls, jewels, servants...I want for nothing."

"Why certainly," Edward replied, before turning his gaze back to Jemima. While she suppressed a smile, she believed he winked at her.

Sylvia had gossiped to her that Lady Arbunke's husband was a bit of a libertine. The baron had many mistresses but kept his wife's silence by showering her with jewels and expensive gifts. Such a situation made Jemima angry. It smacked of inequality and although Lady Arbunkle seemed happy with the arrangement, why should she accept jewels instead of fidelity in marriage? It confirmed her dislike of the married state.

Edward Huntington brought her a cup of tea, passed her sandwiches, begged her to take some cake. Was he playing with her? Surely, he was not so absent minded that he failed to remember the letter and the name of the family she had requested to visit. Jemima swallowed the offered cake, feeling it stick in her throat, remembering that letter. Her face began to heat as she recalled the details of the alterations she had made to his letter to Miss Blake that ended up providing permission for her to travel with Sylvia. All she could envisage was a sticky end to this situation. The overload of her nerves would lead her into error, she was sure.

After dinner that night, where luckily Mr Huntington had been seated too far away from her to engage in conversation, the group gathered together in the large drawing room. The folding doors opened to the music room where Eustace Preston played a concerto, thereby elevating himself in her esteem. A few of the older guests gathered there talking quietly, some listening to the music.

Mr Heaton, Mr Huntington and Sylvia, along with Jemima and a few others lounged on the sofas, discussing trivial things when suddenly someone introduced the topic of burial practices.

"As a doctor, indeed as a man of science, I think it is deplorable in this day and age that people who commit suicide are buried at the crossroads and staked through the heart to prevent them from becoming the walking dead. Why it's utter rubbish." This was from Mr Heaton.

Mr Huntington leaned forward in his chair, his posture giving every sign of keen interest in the topic. "I do agree with you, Heaton. It is not very scientific at all but not everything has a logical explanation. Customs like that have some basis in historical events."

"Barbaric practice! Next you will be saying that there is such thing as the walking dead and...and vampires."

Mr Huntington smiled, his shoulders lifting in a small shrug. "All I am saying is that some customs and superstitions derive from some real fear or real event. Not everything can be explained by scientific means. There are mysteries that defy the scientific method."

Jemima found the conversation extremely interesting. "I read about vampires in some countries in Eastern Europe. Surely there is some truth to those stories."

Mr Heaton scoffed, and Mr Huntington nodded. "Perhaps," he said warmly.

Encouraged by that smile, she continued the topic. "So, Mr Heaton, have you not come across some curious things in your work? For instance, unexplained blood adorning the mouths of cadavers on your dissecting table?"

"Jemima!" Sylvia and a few others blurted in shock.

Conscious that she may have overstepped the mark, she turned to them all and said, "Oh I beg your pardon. Was that a portion too explicit?"

"Really, Jemima, we are not at school now. No point in trying to prank anyone here."

Jemima laughed lightly. "Quite so. I am unmasked." She took out her handkerchief and played with it to avoid meeting the serious look in Mr Huntington's eye.

৩৵৩

The next morning when she went downstairs to breakfast with Sylvia, Mr Heaton and Mr Huntington appeared to be waiting for them, coming into the breakfast room within seconds of them entering. Mr Huntington read them snippets of the paper and he pulled faces when Sylvia asked him to read the gossip columns, full of the latest society scandal. He did read them in a very serious voice, which juxtaposed the hilarity of the content. Jemima's face heated as he read out snippets full of innuendo and infidelity. She should confide in him, she thought to herself. This couldn't go on.

Closing the paper, Mr Huntington strode to the window and peered through the curtain. "It is fine out. Do you ladies care for some fresh air? A game of croquet?"

Sylvia grinned at her across the table, her eyes speaking her pleasure in such an excursion.

"Croquet?" Jemima responded. "Are you sure you are able to stand being beaten? Sylvia is a fair player, school champion to be exact."

Mr Heaton's eyes widened as they settled on her friend, a smile playing about his mouth. Not that croquet was particularly athletic, but picturing the elegant Sylvia, who exuded femininity, with a mallet and a determined look in her eye was probably beyond him. As Jemima had been thrashed by her in many a tournament, she was eager to see if Heaton's admiration would wax or wane afterwards.

As they played, Jemima's disappointment in Sylvia grew. She had lost her competitive vigour and spent her time ogling Mr Heaton and flirting with him while she aimed her mallet without any care at all. She thanked Heaton when he helped her hold her mallet, no doubt enjoying the feel of his arms as they surrounded her.

"Are you feeling well?" Mr Huntington asked.

Jemima dragged her gaze from the other couple. "Yes, perfectly."

"You seem out of sorts," he said as he took the hoop they were playing with an impressive swing. She had learned that Mr Heaton and Mr Huntington were firm friends. She had no choice but to be Sylvia's foil in her attempts to thwart chaperonage and keep Mr Huntington occupied, discretely, of course.

"Well, I don't mean to sound malapropos, but you know Sylvia is a very good croquet player and she's letting Heaton win."

"And that upsets you?"

"Certainly, she should be thrashing him as she has done me many a time. Yet..."

Mr Huntington's gaze slid to where the couple were talking quietly, foreheads almost touching. "Perhaps, but they do seem to be enjoying themselves."

Jemima looked the couple over again and then tilted her head to the side. "Yes, I concede they do."

"Perhaps we could give them some privacy? I noticed a nice walk through the park here, with some very old oaks and ash trees. Excellent specimens." He pointed to a gap in the hedge on the other side of the croquet pitch. Should she dare such a thing? Go off with Huntington and leave Sylvia alone? What would Mrs Horton say? Surely it was a bit too daring.

"We won't go far. I promise." He smiled at her, eyes sparkling with just a hint of mischief. It was hard to believe this was her severe, unfeeling guardian.

Jemima looked over her shoulder. Sylvia had given up all pretence at playing and she and Heaton seemed to be heading to a bench in the shade. They talked as they walked, heads inclining toward one another.

She faced her companion and sighed. "Thank you, Mr Huntington. A short stroll might restore my spirits." She happened to glance up and saw his contented expression. He offered his arm and she took it, trying to ignore how the warmth of him enveloped her hand and how she must be out of her mind taking a stroll with her guardian.

They roamed through the park, sheltered by great boughs full of leaves. They looked for squirrels and pondered on the age of the trees. Jemima rested against the wide tree trunk while Mr Huntington threw acorns at a post. He had a good aim, and he was an engaging conversationalist. She found herself relaxing and enjoying their time together. While shaded by the tree, she watched as he gathered more acorns. "Are you keeping score?"

She laughed despite herself. "Yes, you have hit the target eight times."

"Surely not. My aim is much better than that."

The way he moved fascinated her. There was a precision to him and strength too. He really was a handsome man. *Oh dear, she thought. I cannot be thinking like that.*

"We best head back now," he said taking a final shot. "That makes ten from fifteen. I could do better."

"I expect no less than perfection, sir." She laughed when he tossed an acorn at her, which she caught and held.

As they walked back, they caught sight of Sylvia and Heaton walking ahead, and they slowed their step. "Are you sure it isn't too warm for you?" Mr Huntington asked solicitously.

"Er no. It's lovely out."

"You have such fine skin."

Her eyebrows rose. "Really? I mean, thank you."

He smiled at her again and then faced forward. He offered her his elbow and she took it. Such a gentleman, she thought. A beastly gentleman, she told herself. He was horrid to you. How could you forget!

The rest of the day was spent socialising with the remainder of their party, with little opportunity for Sylvia to spend time alone with Heaton. However, the next day and the next, Jemima was called upon to keep Huntington occupied so Sylvia could have time alone with her suitor.

"What are you looking at?" Mr Huntington asked. He was punting her on the lake. Sylvia and Heaton were just ahead.

Jemima was leaning over the side. "Just looking at what is living in there. I thought I saw a brown trout, but I might have been mistaken."

His brow furrowed. "Do you like to fish?"

She sat back. She could not admit that she found natural history interesting. That might jog his memory. "No, just curious about what lives in the lake."

He nodded absently, his brow showing he was deep in thought. "Miss Jemima," he said after a while. "I enjoy spending time with you."

Slightly startled, she replied automatically. "I enjoy my time with you, also." He nodded once and then turned the punt in a slow arc to take them back to shore. The looks he sent her way were deep and thoughtful. Jemima kept her eyes averted, afraid of what she might see in those intense blue eyes of his. Recognition.

Guilt at the game she was playing weighed her down. Why did she not take advantage of these moments to confide in him? she pondered. *Because you like being treated as an equal. You like talking to him and listening to his interesting conversation. You like looking at him period and you do not want your visit to end.*

She tried to picture what the future would be if she got away with this sojourn undiscovered. Perhaps she would meet Mr Huntington in a few years, and he would recognise her then as his ward and as a companion at Primrose Manor and they would laugh about it over tea and sandwiches. She was not stupid enough to imagine such an outcome was possible and began to contemplate avoiding seeing her guardian ever again.

That evening when she came down to dinner, he came forward and kissed the knuckles of her gloved hand. That action did all kinds of things to her insides. Suddenly, her appetite fled as a sudden queasiness settled in the pit of her stomach. He tried talking to her, but Jemima could not summon a thought.

"Are you well?" he asked, his voice pitched low.

"Er...I...perfectly, I thank you."

Sylvia walking up, dangling from Mr Heaton's arm, provided a necessary diversion. Jemima fanned herself vigorously. The room was suddenly too close and warm for her tastes.

Luckily, at dinner she was seated further down the table. Mrs Horton played musical chairs with them, always mixing and matching her guests, except of course Sylvia and Mr Heaton. After the meal, Jemima staged a headache and raced upstairs to her room. The maid brought a note up with the warm water she had asked for. It was from Mr Huntington, enquiring after her health. She stared at the note, admiring the elegant hand, while simultaneously wanting to throw it into the fire in disdain. The situation was impossible.

Thus divided in her emotions she went to bed and had a troubled sleep. She had gone too far to confess, although she replayed imaginary confessions in her sleep over and over again, tormented by the shock and pain in her guardian's visage. And what would Sylvia say, her mother? The shock would be too great for them all.

The next day, she stayed close to Sylvia, worried about all the time she was spending with Mr Huntington. It was Sylvia who was bent on matrimony, not her. She twisted her ankle deliberately, so she could not go on any walks. Sylvia was loath to leave her, and Jemima absolutely refused to let Mr Heaton examine her, so they sat around and read or engaged in idle conversation. Jemima kept quiet, letting out an occasional groan for good effect.

Lady Arbunkle joined them, plonking her ample behind on the sofa and requiring Jemima to move a little closer to Mr Huntington. "Have you seen my new clockwork decanter?" She pointed to the sideboard. "I brought it with me to amaze you all. You wind it up and it pours out wine with no human intervention. Another gift from my husband."

Jemima seizing the opportunity, leaped off the couch to investigate the mechanism. It was a rather ornate contraption, influenced by Indian Raj art and culture and complete with golden elephants and little monkeys in silver.

Lady Arbunkle called from the couch. "A magical device!"

"May I wind it?" Jemima asked.

"Of course, my dear. I brought it down for your enjoyment."

Jemima wound the decanter. "Do you think it runs on magic?" Mr Huntington asked beside her. Jemima glanced at him sideways.

"Of course not. As I turn the key, the energy is stored in the mainspring, which then drives the gears."

"Bravo!"

A blush stole over her features. "I do beg your pardon. You must think me a complete blue stocking."

A light glinted in Mr Huntington's eyes. "Whatever the colour of your stockings, I do not think they are blue."

Jemima's blush grew hotter at the suggestive undertone. A man did not comment on a lady's stockings. By then Sylvia and Heaton had come over. "Jemima what have you been saying? I swear I despair of you."

Mr Huntington came to her rescue before she could defend herself. "Nothing at all to despair of, I assure you. We were admiring Lady Arbunkle's contraption." To Lady Arbunkle he said. "Do you wish to take some wine, my lady?"

"Thank you, young man. I don't mind if I do." Mr Huntington took one of the filled glasses and with a slight bow to her delivered it to the old lady.

Meanwhile Sylvia and Heaton took turns to wind up the mechanism. Wine poured into little glasses. Jemima poured it back into the central bowl where the wine was stored as it was a bit early to drink.

On the seventh night of the house party, Sylvia invited Jemima to join her in her room to dress for dinner much earlier than usual. First, they dallied in Sylvia's room, chatting. Sylvia was full of Mr Heaton. Jemima thought he was a fine young man, a little too impressed with his own intellect. Jemima had to work hard not to correct him when he quoted Latin or espoused an outdated scientific theory such as diseases were spread by miasma. Really, she thought, Heaton must not keep up to date on his medical journal reading. However, he would do very nicely for her friend.

Sylvia chatted away, asking for advice on one gown and the next she laid her hand on.

"Pray, do ask Mr Heaton to give us a detailed account of his most recent autopsy tonight," Jemima asked as they considered what the night's activities would be.

Sylvia made a choking sound, her blond ringlets jiggling. "How horrid! I would not ask him such a dreadful thing. Why I might be sick in his presence. How lucky I am that he never tells me anything about his work that might distress me. He is so considerate."

"Anything is better than being asked to sing. I am trying to avoid it so do not blame me for adopting strategies. I think they will insist tonight, considering I have managed to absent myself from the piano all week."

Sylvia called from her dressing room. "If Miss Blake were here you would not be so bold. You do your best to hide your gruesome tendencies whenever she is around. I saw that issue of the British Medical Journal in your room before we left the school."

Jemima walked to the doorway and put her head in, while Sylvia held up some ribbon to her chosen gown. "I am not gruesome at all. I am interested in facts not fancies. There was a very interesting article on Homeopathy. The medical profession hate practitioners, of course."

Sylvia looked up from her employment, saucy smile gracing her lips. "So you say. I noticed you seem to enjoy Mr Huntington's company. He is handsome but a little old for my taste. He certainly admires you and does little to hide his regard."

"I devote my time to him so that you are free to flirt with his friend. He is likeable, I suppose. Remember, I am doing this for you."

Sylvia called out. "Be careful. You might get caught in your own game."

At the mention of 'game', Jemima considered confessing all to her friend, but her courage failed her. Sylvia would fall into hysterics if she knew who Huntington was. The ramifications for her friend was probably a lot more considering she was complicit in lying to her parents about who Jemima really was. Best not to let on how precarious the situation was.

When Jemima could forget who Mr Huntington was, she found him the most pleasing company but then recollections would intrude, marring her happy thoughts. He was handsome, a second or third cousin, so not a forbidden alliance, but how odious he had been when she was young with tender feelings, full of grief. How shabbily did he treat her all those years ago? She remembered every detail of that moment in the library—his countenance, his words were etched across her heart. How she had hated him. Not once had she been invited home. His home now, not hers.

When Jemima tapped on Sylvia's door later, she was still fussing with her hair and driving her maid to distraction. Jemima decided to go downstairs on her own and venture outside to walk in the garden in the evening sun before everyone gathered for dinner. Draping a shawl around her bare shoulders, for she was wearing a daring low cut gown of purple sarsenet, with a gauze overlay and gold trim. She stepped along the path a short way, breathing deeply of the cooling air. The scent of roses wafted over her. Exhaling, her concerns floated away.

A crunch of gravel heralded the arrival of another. Before she could turn, hand lifted her shawl higher up her shoulders. Turning, she came face to face with her guardian, whose arms circled her in an intimate embrace. She gaped stupidly at him, caught in a moment of surprise. The light scent of his herbal soap spilled over her. The bold brightness of his blue eyes mesmerised her as he leaned his head down. His warm, moist lips touched hers, sending an unexpected thrill through her. The kiss deepened, making her head spin. His left arm held her firmly, as his right hand reached up to caress her neck. She had never experienced anything so potent to her senses. Then she recollected who he was and struggled in his embrace. This cannot be happening, must not let this happen, she thought wildly.

"Uncle!" she blurted out, hand pushing at his chest.

He pulled back, nearly shoving her away in turn. "What the devil did you say?" he said somewhat ruffled. "I am not that much older than you. Why should you call me that?"

Jemima wiped her mouth with the back of her hand, shuddering with a multitude of feelings. Tears pricked her eyes. "You really should pay more attention to your correspondence, sir."

Jemima huddled into the shawl wrapped tightly around her.

"My correspondence?" Her guardian's face was a study in puzzlement. He raked a hand through his hair, disturbing the arrangement of his curls.

"Yes, yours."

"What has my correspondence got to do with you at this moment? Have not your own actions led us to this...Are you so fresh from the schoolroom that you do not know how to...to..."

Jemima let anger touch her voice. "Yes, I am fresh from the school room. The school where you sent me four years ago, uncle."

He backed up to one of the cast iron benches and sat down hard. "Uncle?" He grasped his head in his hands, shaking it from side to side. "No, no. Stop calling me that. I am no one's uncle."

"Let me introduce myself properly." She curtseyed. "My name is Jemima. Lily. Hardcastle. Ward to one Mr Edward Hardcastle Huntington. Recently graduated from Miss Blake's Academy For Young Ladies."

She saw the horrible recognition cross his features. Astonishment turned to anger.

"But you...your name is...Miss Castle...I do not understand..." His forehead rested in his palm, his expression tense.

Her face heated. She was filled with shame. "A slight counterfeit on my behalf. Not done to wound you."

He dropped his hand, his face reddening. "Why you...you hoyden...you...you little flirt."

Jemima sucked in a surprised breath at his insult. "Me? A flirt? But you...it was..."

"You led me on a pretty chase. And you knew who I was from that first moment. Didn't you?"

A guilty flush stole up her neck and stained her cheeks.

He stood up and came forward and she held her ground. "All common decency should have led you to announce yourself straight away. Yet you deliberately concealed it from me. I cannot believe you would try to lure me this way, try to entangle me." He rubbed his forehead, shaking his head.

She swallowed as he ranted at her. "I did nothing of the sort!" Her hands curled into fists at her side.

Jemima's turbulent emotions made it difficult to mount an argument as she was clearly in the wrong.

He glared at her. "No, you meant to wound me. How could you be so irresponsible and so spiteful?"

She blanched at that. "I found myself in a predicament and could not get out of it without causing all kinds of fuss."

"That I do not believe. You excel in making a fuss. Had you spoken to me frankly in those moments when we were alone, we could have worked something out."

Hands on her hips, Jemima's anger settled nicely on her shoulders, replacing the shawl that slipped off. She could forgive him his wounded pride, his surprise and even his anger. However, it was not all her doing. "Do not lay all the blame on me. If you had paid more attention, you would have known who I was."

"Outrageous girl. You used a different name." He smoothed his hair as he paced in front of her. She noted with some guilt that his hand shook. He was rattled, and she was sorry for it. A little calmer, he asked, "What the devil do you do here, anyway? Why are you not at school? And for the record I'm not your uncle, I am a cousin several times removed or something."

Jemima's anger had still not left her. She lifted her chin higher, not to be intimidated by his superior height. "It perhaps escaped your notice that school is finished. Surely Miss Blake sent you notice of my graduation. You cannot keep me prisoner there forever. Besides I wrote to you seeking permission to join my friend Sylvia Horton for a short stay."

He scratched his chin, his gaze distant. "I recollect the letter, but I do not recollect answering it. Moreover, I did not connect the circumstances of this family and you. As a friend of Heaton's I was included in his invitation." He stamped away a few steps, running clawed fingers through his hair. Then he whirled around to face her. "You have behaved most improperly. You should have told me straight up who and what you were to me."

"I behaved improperly? It was you who kissed me."

"I did no such thing."

"What were you doing then? Practising dentistry?"

No longer restraining his anger, she could see any tenderness he may have felt toward her dissolve.

"I see that even Miss Blake did not succeed in curbing your wayward tendencies. You may mock me now, young lady, but you will not be staying here another day."

Jemima sucked in a breath. "But I cannot up and leave. What will people say? Sylvia will be most upset."

"You can and you will. Tomorrow to be precise. I will write a letter to my Aunt Prudence and she will join you presently at Willow Park. I will have my man, Fulton, accompany you and watch out for you until I return. Then we will see what we will do with you."

"Do with me? I am not some baggage to be sent about. I am a person with feelings, a mind and a will."

He took a step closer, his voice low. "As am I. You have outraged them fully."

CHAPTER 2

B oth of them glared at each other. Then as the moments passed, and breaths slowed, the anger began to ebb. Voices sounded in the house, making them both start. People were mingling before dinner.

"We best join the others," Edward said, a blush stealing up his neck.

With a nod, Jemima picked up her shawl, tossing it negligently about her shoulders and preceded him inside. No one appeared to notice that they were both in high colour and entering together. Without a backward glance, Edward went off with the men to converse, leaving her to find a vacant seat on the couch. The only place available was next to Lady Arbunkle. While Jemima tried to order her disarranged thoughts and tangled emotions, she managed to nod as that lady talked about her dress and jewellery. The conversation did not proceed smoothly as Jemima forgot to respond appropriately, leading Lady Arbunkle to stare through her monocle and cough. "Are you listening to me, young lady?"

"Oh? Forgive me, Lady Arbunkle, I have a slight headache. A very delightful brooch, I am sure."

"And did you see my shawl, my dear. One of ten that arrived last month. I've seen none that can compare to them in both style and quality."

"How lovely," Jemima replied, not even glancing at the garment in question. Sylvia chose that moment to arrive. Jemima surged out of her seat and hooked her arm through hers. "What kept you?" Jemima hissed in her friend's ear.

"I was in the library," she said quietly. It was then Jemima noted the bright eyes and the pink cheeks.

"Library?" Jemima blurted then paused. "But you do not read."

Sylvia hid her mouth with a gloved hand. "Charming. Of course, I read...well, when forced." She lowered her hand and whispered. "I happened to meet Mr Heaton there."

"Oh, do tell." Jemima did not have to ask if it was by accident or design. Only Heaton would have lured her friend into the library. In listening to her friend's encounter, she could avoid thinking of her own.

With their heads together, Sylvia regaled her with anecdotes of Mr Heaton's knowledge of anatomy, including his ability to deliver kisses and caresses in the right places and with sufficient fire in them.

At dinner, Sylvia sparkled in the presence of Mr Heaton, who was seated next to her. As Jemima looked on, she realised that she would not be missed at her departure and sulked through the soup, the venison and only rallied when the dessert arrived. There were no more admiring glances from Edward. She cast him angry looks, which he ignored. Yet, even in her anger she saw the evil of what she had done. It was fortuitous he had not denounced her to her hosts. What would he do when he understood the depth of her subterfuge? She would be glad to be absent when he did.

⚜

That night Jemima found sleeping difficult. Full of recriminations, anger, guilt, she punched her pillow so many times she split it and feathers dusted her bed. She lit a candle in order to scoop them up and burn them in the remains of the fire. From the depths of the house, she heard a thump and a muffled cry. Goosebumps erupted on her flesh, and she stood perfectly still. Her heartbeat lurched painfully. With her excited imagination, the dark corners of the room roiled with malevolence. Standing still, she closed her eyes, as she was not interested in seeing any ghost. Not that she believed in them, but one had to have an open mind.

Everyone had been in bed for hours, so it was the early in the morning. She heard another dull thud and the creak of floorboards. Trying to recollect if Sylvia had spoken of any ghosts inhabiting the manor, she shook herself and cursed her own foolishness. After tossing the feathers in the fire, she prodded it with the poker until they caught in the heat of the embers, and then climbed back into bed. Soon the pungent smell of burnt feathers wafted over and she put her head under the blanket.

It was just after dawn when there was a cry and, then after a short pause, a shrill scream. Footsteps thumping upstairs and along corridors echoed within her room and then voices calling out made Jemima lift her nose over the edge of the covers. A few more alarmed cries confirmed that something untoward had occurred in the wee, small hours.

Light footsteps approached her door and the handle turned. Sylvia put her head around the door. "Jemima? Are you awake?"

"Lord, yes. What has happened?"

Wide-eyed, Sylvia entered the room and leaned back on the closed door. Her face pale, she looked ready to faint. Jemima sat up higher, her heart fluttering in her chest.

"Lady Arbunkle...she...she...is dead—" Sylvia's voice choked up and ended in a sob.

"Good heavens. But I sat talking with her most of the evening. She seemed perfectly healthy to me."

Sylvia's head rocked from side to side, tears flowing freely. "No...no, you mistake me...she was...was...murdered."

Jemima threw off the covers and raced across the room to catch her friend before she hit the floor in a dead faint.

Later, after the maid had helped Sylvia back to her room, a note arrived under Jemima's door. She scooped it up before breakfast arrived on a tray. "Mr Horton requests that you stay in your room today, Miss," the maid said.

Jemima nodded and took the tray. "Of course. Do tell me what is happening."

The maid curtseyed and lowered her gaze. "I'm not supposed to say, Miss. But they've called for the local magistrate. I heard from Lady Arbunkle's maid that there was blood on the wall and all over her bed."

Jemima froze. "How ghastly."

The maid nodded. "Yes...and they say she was found naked, Miss...and that there were signs..."

Jemima's brows lowered. "Signs of what?"

The maid lowered her eyes and crossed herself. "Never you mind, Miss. Best an innocent girl like you stays that way." With that, the maid scurried out of the room, leaving Jemima to pour her tea and butter her bread. "What signs?" she said to her food before taking a bite.

Pouring a second cup of tea, she remembered the note. She had already assumed that her hasty departure was not going to be so hasty. Edward's note informed her that she would leave first thing the next morning, due to the most unfortunate circumstances. He requested that she keep to her room, where he considered her quite safe. This was an interesting observation, she thought, considering Lady Arbunkle had been murdered in her room. Then she recollected that her door had remained unlocked the whole night. "Yes," she said to herself, thinking about the potential for danger, "but you do not have rare and expensive jewels in your possession."

Taking her time to dress, she opened up the door and then lifted the breakfast tray to carry it downstairs. She paused on the threshold. Edward was there, pacing in front of her door, muttering to himself. For an instant, she thought he might be disturbed of mind.

In a frosty voice, she said, "Mr Huntington?"

He finished what he was saying with a curving gesture and the slight flick of fingers and then glanced up at her. "Good morning,

Miss...err...Jemima. I will take that tray for you. Please go back to your room and close the door."

"What were you doing?" She was not willing to relinquish the tray, it being a valid excuse for her to extract more gossip from the servants, and perhaps catch a glimpse of the scene of the crime.

"Doing?" he said, feigning innocence. She saw him swallow and the faint flush. "Oh? I...er...lost a button," he said. "Yes, thought it might have rolled over here."

Jemima nodded slowly. "A button..."

"Yes, now the tray, if you please," he said in a no-nonsense tone of voice and went to take the tray from her grasp. She declined to let it go and a short tug of war ensued, making the crockery rattle, the milk to spill and a teaspoon to fall on the floor. A slosh of left over tea made Jemima release her hold. Edward fumbled for the tray and somehow prevented its contents from crashing to the floor.

A severe look overcame his features as he waited for her to close the door. While tempted to slam it, she shut the door quietly and leaned against it. Foiled, she thought. He was wise to every trick. To pass the time, she tried reading a book, but ended up pacing the floor until there was a knock at her door.

Jemima edged the door open. "Sylvia, do come in."

Sylvia made to step forward and then stopped. "I cannot."

"Why?"

Sylvia shrugged. "Not sure. I just don't feel like it for some reason. Perhaps you better step over to my room. I have news."

Grabbing a shawl, Jemima slipped out the door, feeling a slight shiver as she passed the threshold and followed Sylvia to her room. Sylvia climbed up on her bed, leaving a comfortable chair for Jemima. "Well, what you have you heard? The maid said there was blood, lots of blood."

Sylvia tugged a pillow onto her lap and hugged it to her chest, nodding at the same time.

"Jasper came to tell me. Father is so pleased with him because he was able to look at the...at the..."

"The corpse?"

Sylvia nodded, her face pale.

"Do tell."

"Jasper said it was definitely a man who committed the murder."

"Really? How so?"

"Well...you see...she had been undressed and who ever ripped out her throat had his way with her as she died."

Jemima scrunched up her nose, quite surprised Mr Heaton would share such indelicate details with his love. She tried to picture Mr Heaton examining the body and shook her head to clear the image. "That is interesting. She was so old. At least forty I would have thought."

"Oh, I know. Mr Huntington surmised that the intruder came up the wall and through the window and that Lady Arbunkle probably surprised him in the act of stealing her emerald."

"So Mr Huntington is on the investigation, too, is he? And the emerald is missing? Two very interesting occurrences."

"Yes, only the men remain suspects, but the women are free to go. I suppose you will want to go home now. After this..."

"Yes, I forgot to say, I must leave. I do hate to go, but I am happy to leave you in your Mr Heaton's hands."

"Really, Jemima, he has not proposed. He's not my Mr Heaton."

"Yet," Jemima grinned. "I will write a note to your mama, letting her know I will be leaving early tomorrow. Then I best write another note to the magistrate to tell him about the sounds I heard in the night."

Sylvia gasped. "You heard something? You were awake? Oh, how frightful."

Jemima stood up, gave her friend a hug. "I am fine. Best I return to my room and start packing."

Sylvia lay back against her pillows and put the back of her hand to her forehead. "Oh, do send a note to Jasper and tell him I am feeling sadly pulled."

"I will," Jemima said as she slipped out the door and across the landing to her own room. A neat pile of her laundry sat on a small table by the door. Jemima frowned at it, wondering why the maid had not bothered to put it in her room. She swept it up and set about packing. Then when all was in order, she started writing notes, so she could pass them to the maid when her dinner tray was brought up.

☙❧

The next morning, Sylvia fussed over Jemima's departure. "I am so sorry you are leaving. Must you?"

Dressed in a soft, woollen travelling dress in vibrant green, Jemima explained. "My guardian has withdrawn his permission for me to be here and that is an end to it. That occurred before the unfortunate event. I am to be escorted to Willow Park and chaperoned for the foreseeable future."

"Surely it is not as bad as that. Perhaps, you can get me an invitation to spend time with you. I must admit it is painfully boring right now the party has broken up."

Jemima brightened at the thought, until she saw her guardian had joined them, coming up behind Sylvia. "That would be good," she said loud enough for him to hear.

Edward shook his head. Jemima realised that Sylvia would soon be engaged, if what she suspected continued to its natural end. Jemima was glad her own *tete-a-tete* had not progressed that far. What if she had found herself in love with Edward or worse engaged? What a horrible life that would be, following his every dictate. It was bad enough that he had control of her now. As a husband he would be ten times more demanding. What was she thinking? After what she had done, any chance of amicable relations had been destroyed. She had fooled him, lied to him, embarrassed him and hurt his feelings. There was no going back from that. No apology she could make, even if she wanted to.

Sylvia looked behind her, saw Edward standing there and then whispered to her. "You see, he does like you very much. He is attending you at your departure."

"How gentlemanly of Mr Huntington," Jemima said with sarcasm. "Best you go inside now, Sylvie and have your breakfast. I saw Mr Heaton at the door just now. He gave all the appearance of looking for you." She did not see her friend's suitor at all, although her assertion was sufficient to detach Sylvia and send her scurrying to the breakfast room.

Edward had hired a carriage and driving it was his man, Fulton. Bald, rather stocky, the man walked with a limp. He was perhaps only an inch taller than herself. She thought she heard a faint hiss when he moved but shook her head, dismissing it. Fulton did not smile at her or greet her when Edward handed her into the carriage.

Checking that they were without observers, Edward walked over to Fulton. "Take her straight home, if you can. Aunt Prudence will arrive shortly. Keep her safe from harm."

Edward turned to her and patted her gloved hand gently. "Do as Fulton instructs. I will follow shortly. I still have some business here. Then we will discuss your future."

There was no warmth in his gaze, no softness in his voice. However, he did not appear angry, which lightened Jemima's mood. Although being contrary, she decided to say nothing to him and waved to her friend in the distance. The carriage jerked as the brake was let off and the horse sped up, heading for the gates.

CHAPTER 3

The sound of the carriage wheels crunching gravel and the fading clop of horses's hooves echoed behind Edward as he strode away. He dared not look back. He might see that crushed, hurt look on her face or he might see her anger, which likely resembled his own.

As Jemima's carriage swept through the gates, Edward thought better of returning to the house and stalked through the back gardens. Thank heaven, she was safe. Who would have thought murder at Primrose Manor? Poor Lady Arbunkle. That harmless lady did not deserve such a fate. The murder scene sprang to mind, reeking of magic and spent blood. He could not speak to others of what was clear to him, what he could feel in his skin and taste on his tongue—the bitter taste of magic, black magic.

Best to get Jemima far away from whatever had touched this place and hope that she was free from its taint. Best to hope that the emerald was all that the murderer wanted and he would now leave them in peace. The significance of the theft of the jewel was not lost on him.

His brisk stride brought him quickly around to the rear of house, and he chose then to reverse his track. No one from the house was about in the grounds at this hour so he did another circuit, varying his

route at the last minute to take in for one last time the edge of the
rose garden where he had made that fatal mistake—where he had
kissed Jemima. A ripple of anxiety unsettled him at the memory—guilt
and shame for his own behaviour. He had reproached her and was
sorry for it.

Approaching the garden from the woods, his thoughts were
turbulent and his gaze unfocussed. Walking in a straight line, he
berated himself as he traversed the smooth, cool lawn. The sound of
pebbles crunching brought him up short. He was not alone as he had
thought. Slightly confused to find himself observed at such an early
hour, his gaze raked the scene before him. All looked tranquil and
deserted, yet he was certain someone had intruded on his uneasy
contemplation.

Taking another step and another, his gaze travelled slowly along
the hedge line. Behind him, the breaking day sent cascades of pale
light over the lawn. Edward kept moving forward, eyes and ears keen
to see what had disturbed him, be it animal or human. The light
touched the hedge, revealing vibrant dark green leaves and dark
hollows. In a low gap in the hedge, he saw a man crouched, peering
through to the other side and into the house. The silent observer
changed position as if suddenly catching sight of a thing of particular
interest. Edward saw long blond hair, pale hands and a lanky frame,
beneath an outlandish black cloak. The man was not a servant and
obviously bent on nefarious activities. Could it be that man he had
sent packing with a little tweak of power last week? Edward
approached but the sound of his tread alerted the man to his
presence.

A face full of surprise and chagrin faced him. A wave of magic
surged forward. Edward ducked, his hands on the damp grass steadying
him and he deflected the spell. A familiar taste of dark magic tingled
on his tongue. Compiling the words to strike with a counter spell, his
gaze met dark eyes round with fear. The man burst out of his hiding
place and ran for the corner of the house, cloak billowing out behind
him. Surprised by the man's sudden flight, it was too late to throw the
spell. By the time he reached the edge of the house, the man had
disappeared from view, leaving a faint odour of dark in his wake.

"What the devil is going on? A dark magician here?" he exclaimed to himself.

Edward made his way back to the house, deeply engaged with his thoughts. Black magic, ritual murder and Jemima all wound round and round, making his head ache. He worried the stranger signified that Lady Arbunkle's murder was not the end of it, that the killer wanted more, something or someone else. Edward shuddered. Thank goodness he had sent Jemima away.

He spoke to no one as he ascended the stairs to his room, which was convenient because his thoughts were still consumed by his troubles. He had nearly molested his ward, calling into question his honour and duty as guardian. Calm reason showed him soon enough that Jemima had not deliberately set out to wound him as he had only accepted the invitation at the last minute. It had offered an excellent opportunity to consult with Heaton. Unfortunately, Jasper had been instantly smitten with young Sylvia Horton and was not able to discuss anything else. The girl's disposition was amiable and her expectation ample to their needs. Nothing impeded the young lovers.

He entered his room and pressed his back against the door, taking in the crimson velvet curtains, and the heavy oak bed, not yet made up from when he had left it some hours before. He was glad to leave the oppressive room for it reminded him of where his mind and heart had travelled this last week. One minute he had been a man with no romantic notions; the next, one with a serious burning passion. Drawing forth his trunk, he opened the drawers where his clothes had been placed and took them out. After an initial flurry of activity, he took more care with his packing, using it as a means to order his thoughts. He repacked most of his linen and placed his trousers, vest and jackets as his father's valet had once taught him.

When he thought the hour respectable, he knocked quietly on Heaton's door and was admitted entrance. Heaton was finishing off shaving and sent his servant away. "My, you are up early, Huntington," he said, looking at him over from head to toe. "What is the matter?"

Edward threw himself into the wing-back chair opposite his friend, and then ran a hand through his hair. "Something has come up. I must away to London. Hate to leave you in the lurch."

Heaton wiped the last bit of soap from his chin. "That will be awkward. Have you spoken to the magistrate?"

"No, but I will. I saw a stranger in the grounds just now. Didn't like the look of him."

"Really? Do you think it was the murderer?"

Edward shrugged. "I cannot say. It does not seem logical for the murderer to hang around unless he is after something or someone else?"

"This will not do. I will have to get Sylvia away from here—her parents too."

"Then you have proposed already?"

Heaton shook his head. "Not exactly. With all this business, the timing has not been right. But now with the danger still present, I should do it anyway. No delicate way around it. I say, can you stay one more day? If I propose now, I will need you to vouch for me."

"Very well, but I must away tomorrow. I have much to organise and arrange without the first thought how to do it."

Heaton rushed forward and shook his hand. "Thank you, thank you. Now tell me what is driving you away. I thought that little piece, Jemima, had caught your fancy in a very real way."

Edward hung his head, clenching and unclenching his hands. After a pause, he answered, "She did. I have packed her off to Willow Park."

Heaton gaped at him and then said, "Willow Park? My, that is fast work. When am I to wish you joy?" Heaton's manner was light, which belied the concern etched on his brow. He dried off his face and did up his shirt.

A loud sigh escaped Edward. "You do not get to wish me anything. The circumstances are much more complicated than that."

"Come on now, why all the mystery? What in devil is going on?"

Edward stood up from the chair, restlessly moving his feet, not quite sure what do to with himself. "That cunning minx was my...ahh. I should not blame her in all fairness, yet I cannot stop myself." Edward turned away and paced along the short rug, then quite suddenly he turned back and blurted. "She is my ward, Heaton. I am responsible for her, and I nearly molested her. She has put me in a position where I behaved abominably."

Heaton's eyes were very wide. "She is your ward. But you did not know her?"

Edward lifted his hands to his face in shame, shaking his head and then dropping them quickly, letting his friend see his wretchedness. "No, I did not know her and the fault of that is all my own. You see, I sent her away to school quite a few years ago and have not seen her since. As she pointed out to me, I have neglected her shamefully. Now I am to suffer for it."

Heaton sat forward in his chair as if to alight from it. "Suffer? What do you mean? You did not propose to her, did you?"

Edward walked to the window and looked out across the front lawn bathed now in golden light. "No, I did not. I can only thank providence that it did not come to such as I was quite out of mind with desire for her. You see how distasteful that is? How odious that makes me?"

Heaton walked up to him, grabbed him by the upper arm. "I can see it is a difficult situation, one that can be set to rights."

Edward's hope rose. "Do you think so?"

Heaton shrugged and released him.

"I see you mean to make me feel better. Anyway, that is the story. For God's sake do not mention the connection between Jemima and me."

Heaton pulled on his coat. "Certainly, you can rely on my discretion."

⚜

The proposal was managed in very good order. Edward did his best to create diversions for the mother and other guests. Before luncheon, Sylvia emerged from the shrubbery flushed and with very bright eyes. Soon after Heaton met him in the billiard room and gave him confirmation.

While clasping hands, Heaton said, "How I wish you had a share in my joy, Huntington. Too long have you held off in finding a mate. Why it is not natural to be so...well so goddamn pure. Let us hope that you can resolve your moral dilemma with Jemima."

Edward nodded, his friend's word only bringing Jemima to mind again. Whether it was her sparkling green eyes that captivated him first or the light red tint in her thick blonde hair he did not know. Her figure was pleasing, showed best when walking. The pretty manner in which she gesticulated while talking, as did the dainty way she poured tea, had a certain allure. Perhaps it was the turn of her mind, her instant understanding of the wider world, of science. He recalled how she had let slip her knowledge of the mechanics of clockwork. Once, he might have thought such knowledge in a female disgusting but in Jemima it was something that intrigued him no end. It brought him to the conclusion that he could respect and admire a woman, a wife as an equal. That was an astounding realisation.

Felicitations erupted at dinner when the engagement was announced, overshadowing for a time the gruesome murder of the Hortons' house guest. While he sipped champagne, he saw the engaged couple in animated conversation. Edward smiled as he looked on. His job was done. There would be little to occupy his time now the lovers were acknowledged. He could set off to London, deal with his business and return to Willow Park and Jemima.

Edward hoped that the mysterious stranger did not make another appearance. Perhaps, knowing there was a magician in residence, the intruder had been warned off. While he was quite adept at hiding his own nature and powers, he was not sure he could conceal another's, particularly when they were hell bent on advertising themselves. Before he retired for the evening, he walked the perimeter around the house, laying down a ward of protection. He hoped it would be enough.

CHAPTER 4

E xhaustion overcame Jemima. She had no recollection of arriving
at Willow Park or of being put to bed. True to his instructions,
Fulton did not stop, except to change the horses and allow her to make
herself comfortable. She was not allowed to step into an inn, secure a
private room and eat in luxury. Fulton handed her sandwiches and then
kept going. How he kept on without rest she did not know.

The next morning, she felt ill and weak and could not get out of
bed. Her heart beat erratically. She wondered whether that was
because she was thinking of Edward and that terrible moment when
the truth exploded. Despite her illness, the maid opened the curtains
and brought her a cup of hot chocolate and a warm, sweet bun.
Nestled in her pillows, sipping her hot drink, she noticed she was in
her old room and that it had not been altered since her childhood. The
sight brought tears to her eyes. For a moment it was like she had never
left, so strong was her sense of being home. Mrs Eddington 'Eddy'
must have kept it for her. Mr Huntington would not have been so
thoughtful.

"Heavens. I must be tired to feel so sentimental." Finishing her
drink and the last of her bun, she drifted back off to sleep. Memories
of her last summer running wild at Willow Park dominated her

dreams. Images of David Longhurst helping her to cross the stream and capturing tadpoles and frogs. How much she had admired his athletic ability. He could climb trees and leap long distances. Her dreams shifted, leaving her past behind. More recent events replayed, some she struggled to break free from. A summer storm woke her in the late afternoon. Her last dream had been a turbulent affair, featuring Edward as a lover, a tormentor and as the holder of her future. She stayed abed for another night.

The following day, there appeared a letter on the tray by her bed. The maid must have brought it while she slept. Picking it up, she soon saw that it was from Sylvia, written and dispatched the day after she had departed. The news within did not surprise her. Mr Jasper Heaton had proposed and was accepted by Sylvia and her parents. Sylvia filled the remaining pages with raptures of her love's virtues and ideas for her wedding trousseau. There was no room for a mention of Edward. She had better not refer to him as her uncle as it implied a sense of indecency, considering what had transpired between them. From now on, she would call him 'her guardian' or 'Mr Huntington' or 'Edward'.

By mid morning, Jemima was somewhat improved and decided to get out of bed. She bathed and dressed and went downstairs in time for luncheon. Fulton was there eating at the table. That brought her up short. Servants eating at table. He stood up when she came in. "Excuse me, miss. I was not sure you would be down today. Meant nothing by it, eating my breakfast here. I often eat with Mr Huntington."

"You do?" Jemima helped herself to a serving of fresh ham and some coffee, before sitting down. She surreptitiously studied Fulton, hoping to guess his origins and relationship with her guardian. He wore white gloves and had a tattoo on his left forearm, a sliver of which showed beneath the cuff of his white shirt. She thought the image was of an anchor, so that meant a career at sea. Royal navy or merchant seaman? He had good table manners, so she considered navy, perhaps a midshipman. That meant he could have even progressed to officer, hence him not thinking it against good manners to eat at table. However, she thought the relationship with her guardian was not that of equals. Fulton must be in his employ in some capacity. At first, she thought valet, but then she dismissed that idea. Fulton's own dress sense was appalling, opting as he did for baggy trousers and ill-fitting brown coat, rather than more tailored attire.

"It is good to see that you have recovered from your journey. What will you do today to amuse yourself, miss?" Fulton asked, after swallowing a mouthful of coffee. His accent was reasonable. There were some rough edges to it, perhaps garnered from being in the navy.

Jemima arched her eyebrow at the question, and then softened the gesture by inclining her head. "Go for a walk, perhaps. Read a book." She sipped her coffee and nibbled on a forkful of ham, taking her time over her meal.

"No needlepoint, sewing or knitting?" he suggested brightly.

Her cup clattered in the saucer as she placed it down. "Lord no, Fulton. I loathe such activity. Why do you ask?" Miss Blake, though excellent in every respect, had failed to teach Jemima to sew.

"No particular reason." He looked away, blushing at her scrutiny. He had been reading the newspaper she saw. He caught her look and ventured to engage her further in conversation. "Do you plan to walk far today?"

"No, not far. To the lake, a ramble around the woods and then take in the pleasure gardens. It will be nice to reacquaint myself with the place."

He nodded, assessing her with light brown eyes, which appeared almost amber at certain angles. "I will walk with you."

About to place some ham in her mouth, she paused mid-lift. "Why? I will not leave the estate. Surely, I am safe enough here at Willow Park. My guardian's orders to protect me do not extend to here, I am sure."

Fulton shook his head. "I am responsible for your safety until your guardian returns." He stood and limped over to the buffet to refill his cup.

Jemima wanted to shout at him, but she knew that was not very ladylike and would earn her nothing but grief, particularly if such a display was to fall into the ears of her guardian. "Very well, if you insist."

Later, she hardly paused by the front door to allow Fulton to grab his cap before she charged out. Then she was less than careful with her parasol, nearly taking out his eye. After he protested, she calmed down a little. "I am very sorry, Fulton. I should not take my anger out on you."

"That would be good, miss. If you could walk a touch more slowly that would be nice, too."

He limped as he walked along with her. The more he walked the louder the hissing sound. Twirling her parasol as it rested on her shoulder, she looked back at him after getting slightly ahead. There in the shadow of some bushes, she saw steam escaping from the material of his trousers.

"What on earth is that?" she blurted out.

He stopped, eyes widening in alarm. "What miss?" He glanced around him, looking for an intruder or wild animal, she surmised.

She pointed at him. "There is steam coming from your leg."

His eyes narrowed, and his cheeks turned pink. "Begging your pardon, miss, but that's no concern of yours."

She stood her ground. "Why ever not? I am part of this household, aren't I? Why should you keep secrets from me? Besides, if I noticed it others will, too."

"Mr Huntington would not like it well known. In any case, it is not good manners to ask after other people's concerns, particularly in regards to any kind of deformity of their person." He limped forward, coming up alongside her.

Keeping in step with him, she glanced at him sideways. "I am not going to tell anyone. I am a virtual prisoner. Is it a contraption of some sort? Have you no leg? Is that it?"

He gaped at her. "Why, yes. How could you—" He sped up, making her increase her pace. The hissing from his leg grew louder. "You really are too observant for my liking."

Jemima hurried along. "But who made it. Edward?" There was no comment. "It was him wasn't it? He's an inventor of some kind, isn't he? Who would have thought it? Just like papa."

"You do not know him well." He continued to walk, and Jemima could now hear the subtle sounds of gears and pistons.

"I know enough. I know that he is a heartless bully."

Fulton stopped and turned toward her, his gloved hands folded in front. "That is not true and it breaks my heart to hear you say such things. I know he sent you away when you were younger, but it was for your own good. He told me how you had been brought up. He was a young man, barely of age. What do you expect that he could do with you other than send you to school? Give him time. When he returns you will get to know him better. You will see then what calibre of gentlemen he is."

Jemima continued her walk, doing her best to ignore the mixed feelings she held in her breast and the lameness of her companion. On her return to the house, she found another letter waiting for her. It had come express. She was expecting a letter from her guardian but it was from Sylvia.

She opened it carefully, letting out a sigh as she expected more exultations of Sylvia's soon to be wedded state. She read the first few lines. "Good heavens!" she cried out loud. Fulton came limping into the room. Jemima re-read the letter to him. "What do you know? Lady Arbunkle's maid was found murdered in the village. She was there to meet the coach to take her mistress's jewellery case to her husband." She read a bit more of the letter. "Apparently, she was killed in the same way as her mistress, but in a private parlour of the coaching house. That is not something you read in the newspaper every day. Sylvia is loath to say so, but there are murmurings at the house about Mr Huntington, because he departed at an early hour that same day without an adequate explanation.

"It appears that Sylvia's betrothed carried out the examination of the maid's body, too. Although, he is adamant that his friend had nothing to do with the murder or the theft and that Edward's departure was entirely due to family issues that required his immediate attention." She looked up at the letter and met Fulton's eye. "That's a nice way of putting it."

"I wish I was there to help Mr Huntington."

"Has there been no letter?" she asked, folding up her missive and placing it on the table.

His brows furrowed. "Not yet, miss. Perhaps tomorrow. I know your...Mr Huntington is innocent."

"Yet, he was interested in the emerald. That would lead others to suspect him, particularly if they did not know him well."

Fulton ventured further in the room. "I do not like to hear you say it, miss. Although he uses some gems in his inventions, he would not have done anything so heinous as to steal one or murder a harmless old lady or her maid."

Jemima nodded. "It does seem very impolite behaviour that my unc...I mean Edward...oh dash it all...Mr Huntington would not indulge in. Besides, he has enough money to buy his own jewels. He sent Miss Blake some pretty presents while I was at school."

Fulton's face became rather bland. "That's right, Miss Hardcastle, he has the money to buy sufficient jewels for his purposes and knows enough about them and their uses, too." She glanced up at him, when he used her surname. He smiled at her, yet she could see the worry creases around his eyes.

Before dinner, Aunt Prudence arrived. "She got here rather quick," Jemima commented to Fulton as she peered through the lace curtain to see a carriage come down the drive. "I thought we were doing rather nicely without her."

The clop of horses's hoofs, carriage wheels and the coachman calling out, heralded the arrival of the aunt at the door. Cobb hurried to the front door. "Your guardian rents a cottage for her in Kingsfold, a village out of Horsham. Not far away..." He peered out the curtain. "Ah...I see she has brought Millicent with her."

"Millicent? Is that good or bad?" She studied Fulton's face while he peered through the curtain also.

Standing back from the window, his face took on a bland composure. "It would be impertinent for me to say, miss. She is a cousin of Mr Huntington. On his mother's side. Prudence is his mother's older sister. Mr Huntington does his best to help support them."

Momentarily unguarded, Jemima could see a few conflicting emotions pass over Fulton's expression. "I see, and no blood relation to me."

He glanced sideways at her, with a small smile. "Distant and through marriage. I will leave you to greet them. I have to speak to the housekeeper." Fulton turned and limped away.

Jemima had the urge to call him a coward without any real reason to say such a thing. Although, his departure should have served as a warning. She stepped out to greet the aunt and cousin as they alighted from the carriage. The aunt was rather tall and plump, wearing a white dress with an excess of ruffles and plumage. Her hat barely fit through the door of the carriage. The cousin was small, dark and timid-seeming, with a plain grey walking dress and an unadorned bonnet. Millicent looked excessively tired and worn, earning her Jemima's immediate sympathy.

The aunt drew herself up when she turned around. "You must be Jemima, that troublesome girl that my poor nephew has been landed with. How do you do?"

Jemima blinked at the comment. "How do you do, ma'am. Welcome to Willow Park."

"And who are you to welcome me? This is my nephew's house, and I am closer in blood than you are. He has put me in charge so let us get a few things straight. This is my niece, Millicent Smythe-Jones. You may call her Milly."

Jemima curtseyed. "Pleased to meet you," Milly said with a faint smile.

Aunt Prudence stepped closer. "Milly will take precedence over you in this house. You will do as you are told and behave properly, or I will report to your guardian very swiftly indeed. He told me of that awful day when he met you all those years ago—dressed like a child escaped from a workhouse—rude, covered in mud and no manners to speak of. Absolutely no manners, he said."

Jemima sucked in a breath, grit her teeth and then clenched her hands as the woman went through her strictures. "I am very sorry to report, ma'am, that my manners have not quite reached your own standards or that of your nephew's, despite Miss Blake's school's best efforts. Please do step inside. There is time to refresh yourself before dinner is served."

Aunt Prudence hobbled up the steps after her. "Listen here, young lady. I am in charge now. The meal will be served when I say so and not before or after. Send the housekeeper to my room. She will receive my instructions personally."

"Right away, ma'am." Jemima turned on her heel and left them to order the footmen about, directing them to hoist trunks and carry other hand luggage in the house. The butler, Cobb, nodded to her as she passed him in the hall. Although his face was bland as white bread, she detected a gleam in his satirical eye and could not help but smile.

Jemima delivered Aunt Prudence's fateful demand to Mrs Eddington, who took it in her stride. "Who does that upstart woman think she is?"

"The one in charge, Eddy."

Mrs Eddington pushed hair that had escaped her bun behind her ears and adjusted her white mob cap. "Quite right. Very well, but tell the cook for me will you, and do it gently."

"Certainly." Jemima stood aside as Eddy sped past her and then, whistling, waltzed into the kitchen to advise the cook of the changed arrangements for dinner. The cook, a Frenchman called Henri, took exception to her news and exploded in a torrent of French curses, that Jemima had not the right to understand, but did.

After consoling the cook and pouring him a sherry or two, Jemima went upstairs to dress for dinner, not quite sure when it would be served. She mused that Fulton knew what was in store and had taken himself off to avoid it, leaving her to cope. While she was surprised at the aunt's behaviour, she could endure it well enough. There had been many upstart, holier-than-thou females at her school. She was good at ignoring or tormenting them, depending on her mood.

Dinner was served an hour later than usual, with Aunt Prudence taking the head of the table. She fussed over her charge, Milly, enough to make Jemima's teeth grind. "You should be grateful my nephew has offered you the protection of his household and the food off his table."

Looking up from her soup, Jemima smiled. "I am truly grateful, as you say, for his hospitality. The cost of my food you will find is covered by the interest on my endowment fund."

Aunt Prudence sucked in a breath, turning quite red. "You would mock his charity?" she finally expostulated, spilling soup from her spoon, which quivered in her earnest grip.

Jemima sipped her soup carefully and lowered the spoon with slow deliberateness. Facing the aunt, she said, "I do not mock his charity at all. I merely state the facts of the case. My expenses are all covered with my own money. He inadvertently, as I understand it, consented to be my guardian all those years ago and has the responsibility for me. The blame for that action cannot be accorded to me."

The aunt rocked back in her chair, as if she had been shot. "Is this to be the tenet of your conversation? If so, I would rather you do not speak at all."

Jemima let a little sigh escape. "I would be happy to oblige you, ma'am." Jemima put her head down and took a serving of the fish and potatoes. There had been a liberal application of sauce to disguise the overcooking of the fish. Not the cook's fault. It was lucky they had any dinner at all, considering how disgruntled he had been over the delay to serve dinner. The sherry had not helped after all, she thought, as she tasted the potatoes, which had been over salted. During the remainder of the meal, Aunt Prudence and Milly talked quietly to themselves, discussing muslin, embroidery and their current craft projects. Jemima ground her teeth. She would much rather talk about the latest invention or scientific theory. She suspected that the aunt and the cousin would not have heard of Charles Darwin.

After dinner, Aunt Prudence spoke again when Jemima reached for a book in the drawing room. She had settled her niece and herself at the work table, instructing the footman to place candles just so. "You will bring your work over here, Miss Jemima, and join us. Industry is better for the soul than dissipation. A book will gain you nothing."

"I beg your pardon?" Jemima worried that the woman followed puritan values and would have her scrubbing floors and milking the cows before the week was out.

The aunt fixed her with a no-nonsense stare. "You will bring your sewing to the table and work with us until supper is served."

Avoiding the look from the aunt, she tried her luck again. "I am sorry to be disobliging, but I had much rather read a book." She did not mean to be difficult but did not want to own to deficiencies with needle and thread, even though she did consider a night spent sewing a boring way to spend an evening. Even Miss Blake had let her off in the last year of school, given her lack of ability.

"A book will fill a girl's head with useless facts or idle romantic notions. You will put off your reading until after supper. Please do as you are told, young lady."

Fulton, who had been standing in a corner overseeing the footman's placement of candles, left the room. Jemima frowned. She closed the book and stood up from the sofa on which she intended to lounge. She was about to announce that she had no work basket—not one worth looking at, that she hated all handicrafts and that Aunt Prudence could stuff her bonnet down her evil throat. She drew in a breath as Fulton entered the room with a basket. Distracted, she gaped at him and he approached her.

"Your work basket, miss," he said as he handed it to her. He winked at her before returning to his place by the door.

"Show us what you are working on," demanded the aunt, holding out a hand to receive it.

Puzzled, as well as keen to see what Fulton had handed her, she went to the table. "Nothing much at all, I assure you, aunt." She sat down and opened the basket. It was not her work basket, which was a tangle of thread and some awful samplers with botched attempts at embroidery on them. It was relief, because she was sure she would never hear the end of the strictures from the aunt if she knew how poor her skill actually was.

"No false modesty, girl. Show me." She put out her hand and without looking at the basket's contents, Jemima pulled out the folded material sitting on top and handed it to her. It was a linen table runner, exquisitely worked along the edges with an almost complete set of embroidered Narcissus flowers in each corner. While Jemima could not create such beauty, she could admire it. "My that is lovely work, my dear. That school my nephew sent you to has done very well by you, I must say. Yet you display remarkable skill, which comes from within. See Milly. Such even stitches."

Milly smiled at her. "It is very beautiful work."

Her reply of thank you stuck in her throat. She had to work hard to delay the inevitable. She asked to see each piece the other women were working on and then asked them to describe their projects in great detail while feigning rapt interest.

"Let's begin, shall we? All this talking will not get our projects done with it," the aunt said, putting an end to Jemima's delaying tactics.

Nervously, Jemima fished out a needle and thread. She tried several times to thread it and failed. Fulton came over to shift a candle for her. She turned toward him, her back to the others and he quickly threaded the needle for her. She mouthed at him. "What do I do?"

"Sew," he mouthed back and grinned.

Hoping she could not ruin the work, she made a couple of loose stitches, expecting that Fulton could undo them later. It was lovely work, and she would hate to destroy it with her ineptitude. She supposed it was his needlework and not someone else's. The maids would only do plain work, not such beautiful embroidery. Then, again, she did not know for certain and that made her nervous all over again.

Supper arrived in the nick of time. Jemima folded the work into the basket and quickly handed it to Fulton. The butler sat the large tea tray in front of them. Not particularly hungry, Jemima was glad of the interruption. Aunt Prudence asked her to pour the tea and hand around the scones. This she could do creditably. Another half an hour was spent on the tea and on consuming the accoutrements. Jemima thought her time of danger had passed.

The aunt handed over her empty cup. "Now, before I release you to your reading, young lady. I would like to see how much work you have accomplished tonight."

Jemima looked down, pretending to be busy arranging the dirty dishes on the tray. "Oh, I really did not do much at all."

"No false modesty. You have shown yourself very capable. I shall be giving my nephew a good report, better than I was expecting to." She put out her hand. "Come along."

Jemima went to the chair she had been sitting in and could not find the basket. "I seemed to have misplaced it, ma'am. One moment."

Fulton came quickly through the door and surreptitiously handed her the basket. "We need to talk, you and me," she said as he turned away.

Jemima took the basket over to the aunt and gently lifted the table runner out. The horrible stitches she had sewn had been taken out and replaced with a small section of beautiful work. "You did not do a lot my dear, but what you did do is so exquisite I can see why you took your time."

Jemima let out a sigh and then went to the sofa to read. Day one was almost done, and she had survived. How much more preferable was her guardian to this. She was actually looking forward to seeing him again.

CHAPTER 5

Next morning, she caught Fulton as he was leaving the breakfast room. "Not eating at table today I see," she said by way of greeting.

"No, miss. I would rather not antagonise Aunt Prudence. However, she is not up yet so we can talk if you like."

"Any word from my guardian?"

"Not yet, miss." He held the door open for her as she passed through.

While she sipped her tea and ate a warm flat bread, a muffin smothered in jam, Jemima said. "I am in your debt, Fulton. I had no idea you could sew so well."

Fulton looked abashed and then shrugged his robust shoulders. "I spent a long time convalescing once. It was a useful occupation to pass the time and the fine work helped improve my dexterity."

Nodding, Jemima refilled her cup. "There is a problem though. Now that we have started this subterfuge we must continue it or she will be very angry." She took a sip of tea and replaced the cup on the saucer.

"What do you suggest?"

Jemima stared at the ceiling while she thought it through. "I think from now on you will have to keep me apprised of what projects we are working on and also instruct me on what I should do to pass myself off without damaging your beautiful work."

"I will do my best, miss. I can teach you if you like. It really is a science you know. Precision and design." There was a cheeky grin on his face.

"A science you say. I never thought of it like that. You are not funning me, are you?"

"Why no, miss."

"I will think about it. I would like to play billiards for that is much more interesting, the angles, the physics. Can you play?"

"A little, miss, but I do not think Aunt Prudence would approve of you playing at billiards and I do not see how we can play without her noticing for the games room is next to the morning room. The sound of the balls hitting one another can be heard from the hall."

Jemima tried to hide her disappointment. "I suppose you are right. Now, do you think we could go for a walk before the others come down and start dictating what I am to do with my time today?"

"If you have finished your breakfast, miss." He grabbed two muffins off the buffet on the way out, biting into one on his way to fetch his cloth cap. He had finished the second before they made to door.

It was partly cloudy and there had been a rain shower earlier, so they stuck to the paths. "Let us go down to the Italian gardens," Jemima suggested. It had walls and ample pathways that would afford some privacy as well as exercise.

"If it pleases you, miss." He touched his cap at her in mock salute and bowed so that she could walk ahead of him down the path.

The sun broke from behind a cloud as they found a bench to sit on. Digging out a large handkerchief, Fulton polished the seat to remove the last of the moisture, for there had been a light sprinkling since the gardener had dried off the rain earlier in the morning. They sat quietly for a few minutes, each lost in thought as they watched Red Admiral butterflies hover over privet blossoms and the robins dive from their nests seeking tender worms in the lawn. Jemima cast her gaze around her, finally settling on her companion.

Fulton was flexing his leg, lifting it up slowly then lowering it. A soft sigh of steam issued from his knee when he placed his foot back on the ground. A slight flinching in his cheek betrayed that he was in pain. He started when he realised that she was looking at him and not the garden.

"Fulton. Will you show me your leg?"

Fulton sat bolt upright, making himself rigid. "No, miss. It is not a sight for a young lady's eyes."

Jemima rested a hand on his forearm and spoke with a gentle voice. "Please. I will not swoon or take fright. I would so like to see my guardian's handiwork. Did he work with his friend Heaton on you?"

Fulton was uneasy. She thought he would bolt, if not for her hand. Her touch calmed him, reassured him of her integrity. He looked sideways at her and licked his lips. "In this case, Mr Heaton did assist. My leg was a terrible mess. Together they saved my life."

She squeezed his forearm. "Please."

Fulton had taken to blushing. "I do not think..."

Jemima met his gaze and held it. "I want to see it, Fulton. It will not distress me. I am no shrinking violet. Try me. I take all the responsibility on myself."

Seeing that she would not give in, he harrumphed. "Very well then, miss. I did warn you."

Fulton looked around, making sure the walled garden was free of workers. He leaned over and rolled up his trousers. Jemima gasped as she saw the construction of his leg. Fitted above the knee wires pierced the thigh muscle, the puckered skin still red and showing signs of healing. Metal framing braced the thigh, including a metal knee construction with rods that continued down to join his boot. Within the calf space was a cylinder and an array of small copper pipes. At present no steam escaped.

"It is amazing. How does it work? I mean, does he have to service it, top up the water. How does it heat the water to make steam?"

Seeing that she was not fazed by the sight of his artificial leg, he relaxed somewhat. "There is a condenser here on the side that collects the steam and then when it cools it returns it to the steamer unit. Only when I over exert myself does steam emit from the knee casement."

Jemima followed where he pointed as he explained the internal workings. "But the power source? I can see he uses your own body heat but that is not sufficient to heat water is it?"

Fulton gaped at her. "You are a surprise, miss. Yes, it does use my body heat and within the knee cavity is polished amber, which has been treated by Mr Huntington, filled with electricity to a certain point, which then slowly gives it back as heat to create the steam." He rolled down his trouser leg and rearranged the cuff. The reason for his choice of wardrobe was now apparent.

Jemima sat back and smiled. Her anger at her guardian lessened when she thought of his genius, skill and partiality for scientific endeavour. "Thank you for showing me. I did not know such fine work existed outside the science journals. Has my guardian published the results of his work?"

"No, miss, not as far as I know. I am one of a kind. There are many who would like to steal his work. He tries to keep it secret, particularly how he charges the gems with electricity."

Jemima heard her name called. "Looks like the aunt is up. We should continue our walk until I am found."

Fulton stood up and held out his hand to her. "Quite right, miss."

After alighting from the garden bench, they continued on, circumnavigating the garden, past the copies of Roman statues and picturesque fountains. Soon after the maid, who had been calling after her, arrived, cheeks pink with exertion. "Excuse me, Miss Jemima. Mrs Wainwright sent me to fetch you to her."

"Tell Aunt Prudence I will join her shortly."

The maid paled and shook her head. "I'm sorry, miss. I am to bring you to her right away."

Jemima cast Fulton a look. "Thank you for your company, Mr Fulton. I am wanted elsewhere."

He took off his cap and bowed to her. Jemima hoped her look conveyed all the angst she felt toward her guardian. Life was proving more difficult than she could imagine.

Letters arrived from Edward that evening. One addressed to Aunt Prudence Wainwright and one to Fulton. While no one mentioned the letters, Jemima had seen them on the tray in the hallway, while they were awaiting delivery. She knew his handwriting quite well, had studied it, too. The aunt kept her close that evening, so Jemima had hardly a chance to talk to Fulton and find out what intelligence Edward's letter conveyed. She began to suspect that Aunt Prudence was trying to keep her apart from Fulton. The aunt probably did not approve of his ambiguous status. She could not treat him like a servant or as an equal.

At dinner the aunt announced. "I have received a letter from my nephew informing me that he will return here in two days. He sends his regards to all."

"Is that all he said?" Jemima asked. "Did he mention the happenings at the Primrose Manor?"

"It is none of your business, young lady, to enquire to the substance of the letter other than receive with good grace that which I have conveyed to you."

Jemima smiled. "Of course, Aunt Prudence. Forgive my impudence."

Aunt Prudence attacked her dessert of preserved cherries and crème anglaise with gusto. Jemima's gaze travelled to Milly, who sat chasing a cherry around her plate. She wore the same dress as the prior evening and the same grey dress during the day. Jemima decided to feel charitable toward the girl. To be poor must be an awful affliction. Being parentless and under Aunt Prudence's constant care, totally wearing. No wonder Milly displayed no spirit at all. Jemima had with her two frocks that no longer fit. Not much worn at all. She contemplated how to offer them without offending the poor girl.

Miss Blake had excellent taste and had ensured Jemima was always well supplied with the latest fashion. When she had departed the school for the Horton's, Miss Blake had ordered two ball gowns, several evening dresses and a new supply of day clothes and other accessories: parasols, lace gloves, corsets and petticoats, so Jemima did not want in this regard.

After dinner in the drawing room, she tried to engage Milly in conversation. "Do you like to read at all?"

"Not much, no. Do you play the instrument perchance?" Milly returned.

"I had lessons at school." This was all she would admit to. She was not going to expose all her faults to Mr Huntington's relatives. He probably knew them all, being very closely acquainted with Miss Blake.

A small smiled changed Milly's rather dull expression to one of mischievousness. "I see. Will you play for us?"

"Heavens, no! And do be quiet in case your aunt hears you." Jemima whispered the last. "So what do you do to pass the time?" she continued in a normal voice.

Milly's gaze grew distant. "This and that. The time seems to fly."

Jemima was starting to become frustrated. Milly's conversation was decidedly boring. "Do you like to walk? The gardens are lovely here."

"What are you asking, Milly?" came the enquiry from the aunt.

Jemima threw out a brilliant smile. "I was trying to invite her on a walk tomorrow."

"Do not be ridiculous, child. Milly is much too brown to be out of doors. The last thing she needs is a tan," said the aunt from the sofa.

Jemima's smile fell. Rubbing her chin, Jemima considered her reply. Sitting up straight, she patted Milly's hand companionably and replied, "Not that brown and if we go early in the morning, there will be no sun at all. What say you?"

Milly nodded, her eyes brightening.

The aunt accepted the suggestion. "If you are to get up early you should retire early. Off you go then."

"Straight away, Aunt," Jemima said, springing to her feet. Then to Milly she whispered, "Come to my room, I have something I want to consult with you about."

Together they exited the drawing room, nodding to Fulton on their way out. "Good night, ladies," he said with a smile. Jemima turned back to glance at him and finally understood something. Fulton liked Milly. It was hard to tell what the girl's feelings were, as she was so quiet and shy. No money, too, she supposed, which would make marrying anyone, particularly an ex-naval man on half-pay, which is what she suspected Fulton of being, difficult.

Inside her room, she invited Milly to sit. "Thank you so much for joining me. I am glad to have escaped the drawing room, even for a short time."

"Aunt Prudence is not that bad you know. You will get used to her ways. She does mean well."

Jemima repressed a shudder at the thought. "Well...yes...I suppose you are right. Now, I hope you will not think me too forward. I have a couple of gowns here that I have hardly touched but grew out of. They cannot be altered to make them bigger, and I would hate to throw them away. I was hoping that you could help me out. Might you not try them on to see if they fit?"

Milly blushed to the roots of her hair. "I...err...I do not know what to say." She looked down at her dress, pressed out some imaginary creases on her lap.

"Do not make up your mind yet. You may think them in very poor taste and, in that case, I will give them to the maid." Jemima drew out a lovely rose-pink gown out of her chest and followed it up with a pale blue coloured one. Depending on the circumstances, they could be excellent town dresses or suitable for the evening if there was little company. A few trimmings and they could be dressed up nicely.

"What do you think? I fear these colours may not be to your liking."

Milly stood up from the chair and took a couple of careful steps over to the bed where the gowns were draped. She fingered the sleeves, her cheeks pink and eyes sparkling. Jemima thought she liked them very well.

"Are you certain you do not want them?" Milly asked hesitantly.

"Quite certain. Why I have grown a good two inches at least and, with all the rice puddings at the school, I am afraid I have grown in other places too." Jemima had a very nice bust, too big for the dresses, but they were probably the right fit for Milly.

"Would you like to try them on? I can help you."

Milly nodded. "Oh yes, please."

Both dresses fitted beautifully. Susy, the maid, who had looked after

Jemima since her arrival would be required to fix the hem on one and adjust the bodice of the other. The maid was summoned and given the task, taking exact measurements for the hem.

"I do not know what to say, Jemima. I thank you, though, from the bottom of my heart." Milly ventured to give her a quick hug, which Jemima returned.

The smile on her face when she showed Milly out of her bedroom was very broad indeed. "Good night. See you bright and early for breakfast and a walk."

Milly left to retire to her own room. Jemima changed out of her clothes and prepared for bed, deep in thought. When Milly had been trying on the dresses, Jemima could not help noticing that her petticoats and under things were very shabby and much mended. There was no way Jemima could give these things to her without giving her the hint that she knew she was poor. However, the girl was quite capable of making them herself, if given the materials.

Checking her purse, she found she had ample cash on her as well as a letter informing her that her quarterly allowance was now available to draw down. First thing in the morning, she would send a note to the village draper via Eddy, ordering a supply of fine linen and silk fabric, thread and patterns. Then Jemima would find some reasonable explanation for them and how they were to be used by Milly. She went off to sleep, dreaming up various scenarios to account for the material and it being of no use to her or the household. Must add some ribbons, trimming lace and fine lawn to the order, too, she thought as she drifted off to sleep.

❦

In the breakfast room next morning, she found Fulton waiting for her. "Good morning, Fulton. So, what did he say?"

Fulton not being stupid, knew exactly to what she was referring. "Will you take some tea first?" he suggested.

She waved him off. "Do not waste time with that. Milly is going to join us so let us talk now before she comes."

Fulton went quite pale. "Miss Milly will walk with you?"

"Us. You have to come along."

"But I...er..."

"The letter?" Jemima sighed and helped herself to coffee and sat down to drink it.

Fulton folded up his newspaper and clasped his gloved hands on the table before him. "Mr Huntington said that it was odious what had occurred after his departure. He said he was in London by the time the news reached him and, also, that there was talk about him leaving so suddenly. He says he gave a good account of himself to the magistrate, having an alibi in the servants who brought him his shaving water and the coachman who was driving him. He has some business to attend to in town and then he will be here tomorrow. He asked after you. He sent you a message, too. He said he and Miss Blake were impressed by your handwriting."

Jemima nearly choked on her coffee. "He went to see Miss Blake?" she asked, putting her cup down carefully. Her cheeks radiated warmth. Fulton appeared puzzled by Mr Huntington's comment, but Jemima was no fool and did not elaborate on it.

"Yes, they have been friends for a long time and considering the circumstances I am not surprised he went to your school to enquire after your circumstances."

She noted a certain emphasis on the word 'friends'. "Friends? Do you mean she was his mistress? I did wonder with all the correspondence he sent her." Jemima thought it was a relationship that was now over as her guardian had not been near the school as far as she knew in all the years she had been there.

Fulton's face grew dark red. "That is not something a young lady should know about or comment on. Why if Mr Huntington—"

"His morals or lack of them do not interest me. He must have started young if she was his mistress when he sent me there. He was only twenty-one then." Jemima raked the jam over her toast and tried to keep calm, despite feeling very put out, she managed to keep the bread intact.

"I believe their acquaintance is of long standing. They are only friends as far as I know. You cannot assume that he—"

"Has mistresses?" She bit down on her toast and picked up her cup of coffee, ready to wash it down.

"Miss Jemima!" Fulton gaped at her, as if she had turned into medusa and sprouted snakes from her scalp and he had turned to stone.

She swallowed the mouthful of toast and jam and sipped her coffee. She eased the cup onto its saucer and met Fulton's incredulous gaze. "Well, you know, he probably has dozens of them dotted all over London and thereabouts." Miss Blake was a lovely woman, she had thought, yet images of her in certain configurations with Edward turned those recollections grey.

"Dozens of what?" Milly asked from the doorway. Both Fulton and she started, Jemima nearly toppled her cup, making it tinkle in its saucer when she turned around so suddenly. Milly wore the pink dress and had curled her hair, transforming her from plain to pretty in one day.

"Err..." Jemima could think of nothing and cast a look at Fulton. He stood there mouth slightly agape, shine in his eye. He definitely had a thing for Milly. She did look well, too.

"Acquaintances. We were discussing Mr Huntington and the number of friends and acquaintances he must have to keep him from home so long. Will not you eat?" Jemima thought her babbling was a marvellous save. Fulton did not appear to be able to get a word out when Milly was near.

Milly helped herself to a small bowl of porridge and a little glass of warm milk. She took ages to eat it, stopping regularly to look at Fulton. Jemima decided a second helping of toast and jam was in order, otherwise she would sit there sighing, thinking about Edward and his clandestine relationships. The thought of mistresses did colour her view of their romantic encounter. *What if he had turned me into a fallen woman?* She shuddered at the thought.

With Milly joining them, the conversation stalled. She could get neither of them to talk about anything interesting. She was annoyed at herself for inviting the girl, having done herself out of an opportunity to discuss Fulton's leg, her guardian's letter and any other number of things that came to mind.

After walking slowly around the gardens for half an hour, she decided to sneak off and hide in the maze. Perhaps those two could sort themselves out without her around. "Miss! Miss!" Fulton shouted high and low, when he realised she had disappeared.

"Jemima? Jemima?" Milly chimed. "Oh dear, why did she leave us? Am I too dull company?"

"Oh no, miss. You are very charming."

"How sweet of you to say so. Where do you think she went?" Milly asked. "It is growing quite warm. My aunt will be terribly cross if I am out of doors when the sun is full out."

Peeking through a gap in the maze, Jemima saw Fulton check the sky. "I will escort you back to the house, with your permission. I will return for Miss Jemima."

"That is most kind of you, sir."

Jemima saw Milly baldly slide her hand into the crook of Fulton's elbow. He started like a newly-broken filly and then settled with her on his arm. She saw them talking to each other as they made their way back, his head inclined to listen to Milly's every word. That was all the matchmaking she was prepared to do for now. It was rather tedious in the maze after all. What was one to do but linger between two rather tall stands of yew trees?

⚜

"You are the most impudent girl I have ever met," Fulton said when he found her lounging on a bench in the Italian gardens, gazing at the rear of a replica of a statue of David. She liked the shape of the rounded buttocks herself but could not bring herself to say so to Fulton. That was too daring even for her.

Jemima was unfazed by his anger and barely spared him a glance. "Did you enjoy your *tete-a-tete* with Milly?"

Fulton puffed out his chest, squaring his shoulders. "That is none of your concern. A woman like that would not be interested in someone like me and it is just mischievous of you to...to...to..."

"Give you the opportunity to find out if what you believe is true?" She edged past him, looking over her shoulder at his stunned expression. "She likes you. I can see it. If you ask me the only obstacle is her lack of fortune."

He stopped still, eyes wide. "But I am ugly and a cripple. How could a beautiful, sweet girl like that even tolerate my presence?"

"Let me see, because she is gentle and loving." She did not add that he was probably the only man she had ever had the opportunity of meeting, being a virtual prisoner of the aunt.

"Ah, that she is. But her aunt wants her to marry Mr Huntington."

"Oh? That explains at lot." Jemima stopped to tug on the edge of her glove and checked the lace of her boot.

"What do you mean?" Fulton asked, stepping up beside her.

"Oh, why she is so odious to me, of course."

Fulton shook his head. "No, I think not. She is like that to everyone. Come along then. She is asking for you already. By chance, did you order a lot of drapery from the village? A large assortment has arrived."

"Excellent." Jemima sped up, eager to see to the disposition of her purchases.

"Not quite. Aunt Prudence has expressed the view that you should have consulted her before placing such an excessive order."

"Oh. I had not thought of that complication." Groaning, she turned from him and walked off in a huff.

Fulton laughed at her as she entered through the front door.

CHAPTER 6

J emima arrived in the morning room with a triumphant smile on her face only to find the old lady pacing along the Persian rug, her cap slightly askew and her cheeks wobbly and red. She rounded on Jemima as soon as she walked in. "What could you be thinking to order all that drapery from the village? Surely you have sense enough to consult me before making such purchases. I am surprised Mrs Eddington did not seek my approval before carrying out your instructions."

Jemima wanted to say she could do what she liked with her own money but had sense enough to know that was not the issue. Besides, she wanted Milly to have it and not have it returned to the shop, so she bore being castigated as best she could.

"I beg your pardon. I was impulsive."

"And you gave gowns to Milly. Of course, she looks very well in them, but as a courtesy you should have checked with me first. I have the care of her."

"I did not think. Again, an impulse of the moment. I meant no insult."

"That is not all. What did you mean leaving Milly alone with that man? How negligent of you. You are bent on making mischief. I will keep my eye on you. Mark my words."

Jemima gazed up at the ceiling and tapped her foot lightly.

"I cannot believe you over ordered drapery from the village. Why it is absurd. Do you not know that the warehouses in town are so much cheaper?"

"How silly of me, perhaps Milly could...

"No, Milly shall not have it for plain work. I will decide how the excess is to be used. Susy tells me you are in no short supply of anything at all. I cannot comprehend your behaviour. You might be well off, young lady, but such extravagance is a sin."

Jemima pressed her fingernails into her palm. It would not do to over set the apple cart by yelling back. Her smile was rather tight. "Of course, aunt, I will take heed of your recommendations."

"And so, you should. Just think of it. The cost. The waste. What a terrible wife you will make, incapable as you are of making judicious housekeeping decisions."

Eddy came in then with a tea tray, skirting around Jemima, who stood near the door hands folded in front like a naughty child. Jemima considered making a swift retreat to her room, but thought better of it and, instead, decided to sit down and let the tea soothe her nerves. Although the aunt twitched a bit in her presence, letting out comments like little barbs, Jemima nodded and accepted them as her due. Milly came in, looking very pretty, but subdued, and accepted a macaroon and some tea. Jemima blushed, thinking how the aunt's tirade must have carried throughout the house. She took another cup of tea and talked about the weather. She had rather a knack for describing clouds.

A brief respite from the aunt's strictures was had before dinner, as Jemima feigned a headache and secretly read a novel in her room. It all began again over dinner, where Aunt Prudence had an audience. "I do think she is slightly addled," she said to Milly. "She has no need of any clothes at all."

"Perhaps she means to sew for charity, aunt," Milly added, lifting her gaze to Jemima.

"Yes, well that is true, I suppose. But good quality linen and silk?

Absurd. And why buy so much from the village drapery? I only use them in an emergency, a little thing here and there. Best to buy from town, particularly when the order is so large, and I know the best warehouses."

"I am sincerely sorry, Aunt Prudence," Jemima said for the fiftieth time that day. "Please let us have an end to discussing it. I am so distressed I can barely eat my dessert."

The aunt sniffed and bent her head to her food. Milly sent her a little smile, before she, too, lowered her gaze and finished her meal.

After dinner, it was straight to sewing. At least this time, Fulton had sent her a note beforehand, describing their current project and what she could do. That night she was to do a small hem. He was certain she could manage that. Also, in the basket was some knitting. Did Fulton never stop? His predilection for handicraft amazed her and made her reassess the exploits of sailors on long voyages. Her mind jumped from repairing nets to tatting lace in an instant.

When the work was all set out, Jemima was pleased to see that Milly had cut out a chemise with the new fabric and was beginning to stitch up the seams. Despite Aunt Prudence's strictures, she had achieved a small victory. Aunt Prudence stopped often to look at Jemima's work and ask her questions. When Jemima could not answer them, she diverted attention by asking questions of her own or firing off compliments on the work of the others instead. It was Milly's turn to serve the tea, which she did rather prettily. Fulton was in the room, and Jemima noted the frequent looks Milly sent him from under dark lashes.

"Fulton. Will you take some tea with us?" Jemima asked. Aunt Prudence's eyes bugged out of her head as she sucked in a breath. "If that is all right with you, aunt," Jemima added sweetly.

"Certainly. Pour the man some tea, offer him some cake." Yet the look she gave Jemima was very sharp indeed. Milly stood, cup in hand, and walked over to Fulton to serve him his tea. He took the cup in his gloved hands carefully and gave her a shy smile. Milly returned to the tray and retrieved the cake, which she also took over to offer him. Aunt Prudence's cup shook in her hand, tinkling and spilling tea in the saucer as she observed these goings on. Yet she did not reprimand her niece, much to Jemima's relief. Perhaps the aunt was saving it up for later.

⊗⊗⊗

The next morning Milly did not join them for breakfast and a walk, sending down word that she had a headache. Jemima knew better. Aunt Prudence had been in her room arguing with her until late. She suspected it was about Fulton, although she made no mention of it. The knowledge that Milly had suffered for serving him tea would only pain him. Not that it was Milly's fault. It had been Jemima who had been the instigator. Yet, it had been plain in the passing of tea that Milly thought highly of Fulton. There were some things that could not be disguised, the look, the smile, the angle of the head and the slight touching of hands when the cup passed over. Jemima surprised herself, considering how little she had been in company. Perhaps there was some worth in the novels she had read while idling away summers at school.

"I hope she is all right," Fulton said in concerned tones, disturbing her train of thought.

Jemima smiled brightly as she pulled on her gloves. "I am sure she is. When we get back I will go upstairs and check on her. What time do you think my guardian will arrive today?"

Fulton glanced at her, his face once more assuming his normal bland expression. "He would usually leave quite early so before dinner I expect."

"Oh good. Some new conversation." She rubbed her hands together in anticipation. "I am looking forward to it. Do you think he will send Aunt Prudence packing when he gets home?" she added, turning to Fulton, her eyes wide with expectation.

Fulton raised an eyebrow. "Why would he do that, miss? It would leave you without a chaperone and that would be beyond all decency, wouldn't it?"

Jemima passed through the door and preceded him down the path, frowning. "Quite true," she said and walked a little further until another idea popped into her head. "He will not pack me off to live with her, will he?" The thought of spending her life with Milly and the aunt in some dull, obscure village promised to sour her mood considerably. At least Miss Blake's had been in London.

"I know not. I recommend you be on your best behaviour."

As they walked in the garden, he asked, "You had a bad day with the aunt yesterday. Did you order that drapery for Milly?"

She cast him a quick, guilty look. "What makes you think that?"

Fulton rounded on her, stopping her forward movement. His gaze travelled over her face, a slight smile evident. "You had such a pleased expression on your face when you saw the aunt had let her have some of it."

Jemima was unable to meet that direct gaze. "I cannot have you thinking good things about me can I, Fulton?" She tried to step around him, but he edged sideways, blocking her path. She lifted her chin and avoided meeting him eye to eye, opening her parasol to distract him. "I must have made a mistake as to the quantity I ordered."

He let her pass in front of him and fell in beside her, careful to avoid the tines of her parasol as they walked.

"The dresses, too?" There was a twinkle in Fulton's eye. One she had not seen previously.

Jemima relaxed, realising that he was not trying to make her feel awkward. "They do look well on her, do not they?"

Fulton's smile slid away. "She deserves more than I can give her."

Jemima leaned in close and whispered. "You would keep her safe and happy. You would look after her and that is more important than pretty dresses. If you ask me she knows how to manage on a small income. Perhaps Mr Huntington can do something to help her out. He has no children or family to support."

Fulton pulled back, a look of horror on his face. "Oh no. Do not start on him, he will not take it well you organising his life for him. He manages quite well on his own and has his own charitable concerns. I warn you now, do take care. I can see only conflict and grief for both parties if you do not."

Jemima walked on, waving a dismissive hand in Fulton's direction. "He cannot possibly do more than he has done already. There cannot be another school he can ship me off to."

Fulton caught up with her, touching her forearm to slow her down. She faced his solemn expression. "Actually, there is a finishing school in Switzerland I have heard him mention and another two in France that he said were quite reputable. Any one of those should suit his purposes and keep you out of trouble for a few more years, perhaps until you come of age and are no longer his responsibility."

Jemima's mouth hung open. She shut it abruptly, trying to organise her thoughts and control her outrage. How dare her guardian seek to organise her life further without even discussing the matter with her? "You cannot be serious. Why I would rather run off and marry the stable boy than go to another school."

Fulton's face again transformed with shock. "The things you say, miss. You would do no such thing. You are much too clever to behave in such an odd way."

Somewhat mollified, she continued to walk, letting out a breath. "You think so?"

Fulton nodded. "Yes, miss, and brave too. You looked at my leg and took no fright at the sight of it. Believe me, I could not look upon it for months, much to the disappointment of Mr Huntington. You have given me hope that I can bestir myself and once again mix with good society. I had not thought such a thing possible. I am forever in your debt."

They walked on further, Fulton's words causing her mind to turn over thoughts very quickly. She was pleased to have helped him feel valued in society. "I have been meaning to ask you. Why the leg? How is it better than a wooden one? You limp still, so I wonder as to the purpose or the benefit to you."

He unconsciously touched his thigh, his fingertips brushing the top of the metal frame in which his stump sat. "I am still healing. That is why I limp, and there are adjustments to the structure to be made when I am all better. What the leg will do eventually is allow me to run—run very fast and jump also, because the knee articulates you see. The structure is very strong, much stronger than a real leg. No wooden leg could offer me that.

"Also, the original wound had never healed properly and more and more of the flesh had to be cut off. Mr Huntington and Mr Heaton put their heads together when they designed the contraption. You remember the wires?" Jemima nodded, fascinated by his account. "They deliver some current to the flesh and keep it from rotting. The work they did saved my life."

She walked along, twirling her parasol. "How remarkable. I wonder how they conjectured that the electricity would stimulate your flesh and address the putrefaction issues."

Futon's eyes widened and then he shook his head. "You have had a terrible education, Miss Jemima."

She paused before they turned to head back to the house. "Why on earth would you say that? I am very well educated, particularly for a woman. I have a mind to sketch it."

Fulton took off his cap and ran his hand over his scalp. "It is unnatural. The gruesome things that you have exposed yourself to. I will not allow you to draw my leg. The very thought of it."

"No matter. I can do it from memory."

Fulton shook his head and muttered to himself as they commenced the return walk, stepping lightly on the freshly cut lawn. "No gentle lady would let on that she understood scientific concerns or be interested in the inner workings of the Human body."

Jemima laughed softly. "What a wonderful compliment you pay me. Thank you."

Fulton looked at her sideways. "I meant no compliment."

She smiled at him. "I know and that makes it all the nicer."

CHAPTER 7

U pon leaving Kent, Edward Huntington arrived in town and hired a Hansom cab to drop him at his lodgings. His landlady took his order for dinner, and he sat down to do some correspondence. He sent a note off to Stradbroke, requesting an appointment first thing in the morning. This missive he entrusted to the kitchen boy, who ran around to Stradbroke's home to deliver it. He wrote another note to Miss Blake, requesting an interview the following day and this he was able to consign to the penny post. Once his immediate concerns were dealt with, he sifted through his accumulated letters finding one that raised an eyebrow—an invitation—one he planned to accept. All this activity and the fatigue of the journey kept him from dwelling on Jemima and the events at Primrose Manor.

The next morning, he paced in Stradbroke's entrance hall until he was ushered into the solicitor's study.

The solicitor rose from his desk, hand outstretched. "Mr Huntington. How pleasant to see you. I saw from your letter that the matter was quite urgent. Nothing serious I hope. All is well at Willow Park Estate?"

They shook hands and Stradbroke indicated a chair, which Edward chose not to sit in at that moment. "Yes, yes, the estate is fine. It's about Jemima that I want to see you." He paced around the room.

"Miss Hardcastle? Is there a problem?" he asked, returning to his desk.

With a loud sigh, Edward took a seat and rubbed his chin. "Not a problem as such. I want to get out of the guardianship of her, if I can."

"Is there a particular reason?"

"I'd rather not discuss it. I feel she can do better than me. I have neglected her shamefully all these years."

Mr Stradbroke sat back, his hand going to stroke his moustache only finding it not there, for he had had it trimmed. Instead, he tugged on his ear. "I fail to see how you have neglected her. You have followed your mother's philanthropic ways, assisted many a young lady less fortunate than yourself."

"I know, but true charity should be shown to one close to me in blood, and that I have not done. Why I have not even thought of her all these years."

Mr Stradbroke leaned over his desk and wrote some notes. "I will see what can be done. At present, you let me manage her finances. Do you wish that to continue?"

"Yes, of course. Surely there is some other relative..."

"I will look into it for you."

Edward stood up and reached out to shake Stradbroke's hand. "Thank you. I will be returning to Willow Park tomorrow. Jemima is there at the moment with my aunt."

Mr Stradbroke nodded. "I will write to you when I have made some enquiries."

***

After leaving the solicitor, Edward made his way to his club, down the noisy, dirty street, where his low spirits could have company. As he walked along, he felt a slight tremor in the air behind him. It niggled so much that he ducked around the corner and leaned against a building to hide himself. Then after a minute, he peeked around the corner and checked the street. There were a few people walking along:

a nurse pushing a perambulator, an old lady with wafting feathers in her hat, a street hawker selling spoons, a few officers in uniform. Nothing which seemed out of the ordinary, but he was sure he was being watched. Coming on top of the incident in Kent, he grew concerned. How could the death of Lady Arbunkle have anything to do with him? The theft of the jewel gave him more concern though. Jewels, he understood, and knew that emerald had been special.

After a good dinner and more than enough port to elevate his sprits, a waiter arrived with a letter on a silver salver. Picking it up, he saw it was from Heaton. He thanked the waiter and tore it open. When he read the contents, he fell back into the high wings of his chair. Heaton wrote that the old lady's maid was also killed in the village the very morning of his departure. Indeed, they were booked on the same coach. While he had been waiting to board, the maid had been brutally murdered, and the remaining jewels stolen.

He wiped his brow and ran his hand through his hair. This was indeed serious. Before he left Primrose Manor he had left a ward around the house. Theoretically, those inside should have been safe from intruders. However, the maid had been killed in the village. Although his wards were strong, nothing could have protected the village as well. He thought back to the sensation of being watched, one which was growing stronger as if this person who dogged his steps was growing bolder. Could this business involve him and his work in some way?

With the assistance of a hot toddy from the landlady, Edward slept well, waking in time to make the appointment with Miss Blake. Miss Blake welcomed him to her establishment with much grace. He had had the privilege of assisting her in the past and had helped her set up the school and was part of the management board which supported it. She was his first charitable project, one that had been most successful.

After tea and sandwiches, he had been able to allude to his letter and his chance meeting with Jemima. Together they examined the letter Miss Blake had received. While he was aghast at Jemima's audacity, he was more amazed at her skill in copying his hand. He himself was hard pressed to distinguish where his words ended, and her addendum begun. Even her phrasing was so like his own.

"So you did not give your consent?" Miss Blake grew pale and put her hand to her breast. "Mr Huntington, I am mortified. When I think of what could have happened. Indeed, the Horton family are very respectable. I would not have allowed Jemima to seek your permission otherwise and would have vetoed the visit at the outset."

"Please rest easy. Jemima was very safe."

"But I read in the paper that there was a murder."

Edward sighed. "Yes, there was. However, I was there and sent Jemima home with ample protection. My good friend Heaton has proposed to the Horton girl."

Miss Blake nodded and offered him more tea. "I assure you, sir, that Jemima has not left the premises previously. I am sure this letter is her first counterfeit. Normally, she is very honest and forthright."

"Tell me about her."

They then discussed Jemima, the kind of girl she was, her talents, her desire to belong, to even be loved and the circumstances that hindered these desires. He learned that she had little aptitude for needlework, though her reading, comprehension and languages were excellent. Her artistic endeavours were more scientific than artistic, often taking pleasure in scaring the other girls with drawings of spiders and other creatures in minute and accurate detail. Miss Blake had allowed her to keep her microscope despite the uproar her use of it caused. Mostly because it was something her father had given her before his death.

The rest of their discussion covered what a genuinely bright, intelligent and kind young woman she was. This news served to cause further pain to Edward, because it confirmed to him what he himself had conjectured about her through his own observations and discourse. The more he thought on her excellent character, the more he despised his own behaviour. He had thought himself a good and just man, but his actions brought into focus by the incident with Jemima proved to him otherwise. None of the reasoning that had seemed so right and adequate at the time, justified his continued neglect of her.

Nothing could clear him of the crime of putting her away and forgetting about her.

"Thank you for being so frank with me, Miss Blake. I must return to Willow Park and try to right the wrongs that I have done. Even if it means putting up with my aunt."

"You are too severe upon yourself."

He thanked her for her words, smiling until he recollected his cousin, Milly, realising that she was another victim of his charity and thus neglect.

"Do you depart for Willow Park today, Mr Huntington?" Miss Blake asked as he was leaving.

Securing his hat, he replied, "I have one more issue to deal with. One young lady, who I hope will choose the helping hand I am offering."

Miss Blake blushed a little at his words. He felt shamed for reminding them of their own bargain. "If she is smart, she will do so," she said with a smile. "I have no regrets."

Edward nodded with a smile. "Adieu, Miss Blake. Do keep up your excellent work. You have achieved much good with your life."

He took a Hansom cab to the address in the letter of invitation. Still his mind was full of thoughts of Jemima and what he must do next. So engaged was his mind that he had arrived in the vicinity of Edgware Road before he knew.

He walked up the steps and knocked at the roughly painted door. An elderly woman greeted him and led him to the kitchen. A measly fire glowed in the grate of a grimy stove. The old woman moved stiffly and slowly around the room, and opened a cupboard and reached for a mug on a shelf. Muttering to herself, she thumped it down and then placed a decanter of wine on the table. "She will be along in a minute."

Edward stared at the decanter, a finely wrought crystal so at odds with its surroundings. He ventured to sniff the contents and found the bouquet rather promising.

Soon after, the young woman entered the room, dressed demurely in a grey twill skirt and high-necked blouse, with her brown hair in a bun and her face bare of makeup. Her brown eyes were small and bright. Edward was pleased with her attempt at gentility.

"Would you care for a small cup of wine, Mr Huntington?"

Edward agreed. It was a good to accept her hospitality. He commenced the interview by reiterating his proposal. "As I was saying in my letter to you, my foundation can pay the rent on the house and assist you while you establish yourself as a seamstress. You are talented and skilled, and soon you could have others working for you, without the need to overburden yourself with labouring all day long. Surely that is appealing to you."

Her expression changed from one of pleasant listener to one of scorn. She sat back and put her untouched mug of wine on the table. "In what way is it appealing, sir? I would not be able to join good society. I would still be outcast, with my current occupation forever hanging over my head."

Edward had not expected this opposition, considering it was the woman who approached him for assistance in leaving her current line of work. He took a sip of the wine and then another to give himself time to consider what to say next. His proposal was to give her the means to remove herself from constant exploitation by men who treated women as objects and found in them no value other than vessels in which to derive their own gratification.

"Forgive me. I misunderstood. I was of the opinion from your letter that you would welcome my assistance. I have no right to enforce my morals or remedies on you."

The woman started, her shapely eyebrows arching. "Oh, not at all, sir. I meant no disrespect as I had heard of your good and benevolent services to people like myself and so approached you." She stood up, took up the poker and stoked the paltry fire in the grill, doing more to extinguish it than enliven it. She turned toward him, poker still in her hand. "It is difficult. If I am hesitant to embrace a new way of life, it is because the uncertainty makes me afraid."

Edward was nonplussed. Was the woman now contradicting herself? In his current mood, he found it difficult to deal with. He took another hasty sip of wine. "Well, I must go. If you think better of my offer, then please send me another letter. I will get my solicitor to make the arrangements."

Dropping the poker with a loud clang, she surged forward,

exclaiming, "Oh, do not leave. You have yet to finish your wine...such a shame to waste it."

Edward stood up quickly, reacting to her sudden movements. His head spun and dizziness washed over him. It was then he suspected something untoward was happening. The woman had not taken one sip of her wine. Surely, he had not imbibed so much as to affect him. He stared at her, not quite able to form a question. He noticed her gaze shifted focus to a spot behind him. It was then that the sack captured his upper body and a blow to the head robbed him of consciousness.

CHAPTER 8

M r Edward Huntington did not arrive at Willow Park in time
for dinner. By midnight, all had given up hope of him arriving
at all that night and yawning went off to bed. The next morning
brought no letter or excuse or the man either. At the end of the week,
they were quite frantic.

Jemima sought Fulton out and found him in the library. "Have you
written enquiries? Have you heard anything? Is he in custody?"

Fulton looked up from the newspaper he was reading. "Yes, of
course I have written. There has been no word. His letter came from
his London lodgings. I have sent letters to his club and his friends.
There is nothing in the paper about any arrests or any mention of Mr
Huntington."

"Friends? Lovers you mean. Goodness the man is profligate in his
tastes. How abominable!"

Fulton made an angry sound. "Do not leap to conclusions. I have
told you before you should not even discuss such things—a young,
unmarried woman like yourself."

Jemima shut the door firmly, angry at Mr Huntington's continued
absence. He was probably this moment cavorting with some bit of

muslin in some fancy salon, without the least bit of conscience as to the worry he had caused his dependents.

"You suggest I should be stupid and dull and not know when a man has evil and immoral tendencies? The more I know the happier I will be in the long run."

Fulton stood up and walked to the window. "No, you will not. You look for perfection in a man without any real understanding of what his needs and wants might be. You know nothing of life, your experience being derived from novels."

"What choices did I have? Sent away to school. Cloistered. Surrounded. Suffocated."

Fulton sighed loudly, rubbing his hand over his bald head. She saw that there were bristles there and that he must shave his head for some reason. "There is little point in this argument. All I ask is that you not judge him without knowing him better."

Pulling out a chair, she plonked herself down. After a moment, she sighed loudly, while waiting for Fulton to get over their little tiff. She had to own to his greater knowledge of Mr Huntington and factor that into her consideration of their situation. When he returned to the table, finally, his face once again bland, she said, "So what do we do now?"

He picked up his paper again and made to peruse it. She waited a little longer, putting her elbow on the table and her chin in her hand while she stared at him. Another sigh escaped her. She thought she saw his eyebrow twitch. Bored with trying to annoy him, she sat back suddenly. "We cannot stay here waiting. We must go in search of him. If what you say is true, then no letter means trouble. It would not be his way to leave us all in the lurch, particularly if we were expecting him."

Fulton lifted his head and regarded her, then with a shake of his head, folded his paper away. "I agree. I cannot leave you though to go in search of him. I am torn in my duty."

Jemima sat back startled. "Why ever would you think I suggest that you leave us? I intend that we will go with you."

"What all of us?"

"Why certainly. How much money do you have?"

"Miss Jemima, I do declare you are the most impertinent woman I have ever met. How Huntington was ever taken with you is beyond all reason."

"I am not being impertinent but serious. I am sure my guardian has left some cash with you. Is there enough for us to go to town, pay accommodation and so forth?"

Fulton's expression changed from one of quiet outrage to serious thought. "Well, I do have some emergency money laid aside. Mr Huntington said I should keep it for such things. I am not sure it is enough."

"I can draw down my quarterly allowance. It is at the bank. I have hardly spent my previous one. So I probably have about four hundred pounds scattered about me."

Fulton's eyes lit up. "That is a goodly sum. How do we manage it? Aunt Prudence, I mean."

Jemima once again placed her chin in her hand and concentrated. It did not take her long to come up with a solution. "Do you have a sample of Edward's letters?"

"Yes. Why?"

Jemima stood up and paced the room, somewhat reluctant to advertise her underhand tendencies, which bordered on the criminal if seen in a certain light.

Fulton turned in his chair following her passage. She paused in front of him. "I am good at copying his hand. I will write to Aunt Prudence, inviting her to town with Milly to shop for clothes. He wants to thank her for coming to his aid to mind his wayward charge and to make up for his neglect of Milly."

Fulton's bland expression dissolved instantly. She hoped it had been transformed by awe and not horror. "You would counterfeit a letter? Ahh that makes sense of his comment. Is that how you managed to get to the Hortons'?"

"Not precisely. In that instance, he was referring to the addition of a couple of lines to an existing letter to Miss Blake, containing some boring information about school maintenance."

"How did you manage that?"

He seemed genuinely interested so she pulled out a chair next to him to explain. "Well, I saw his letter on the tray waiting for Miss Blake. I opened it, checked that he had forgotten to give his permission and added in the lines and resealed the letter."

Fulton's complexion grew pale. "Why do I get the sense that you have done this before? What other liberties have you granted yourself? I am not even sure what you have done is quite legal."

"I care not to reveal the details of past deeds. I prefer to let you and my guardian wonder."

"I cannot permit it." Fulton slapped his hand on the table.

"To save his life, I would fake a letter to Aunt Prudence."

"You cannot know that he is in danger. You suspected him of dalliance at our expense."

"I know I said that, but it was anger speaking and not reason. You are very worried as well. I can tell as you have not shaved your scalp as you usually do."

His eyebrows jumped up. "Why you..." he spluttered, while trying to think of terrible insults to apply to her. "You!"

She reached over and patted his hand, distracting him. "It is not normal for him to have no correspondence with us, therefore, I do assume that something untoward has happened. I am not saying it will not be an adventure also."

She blinked a few times. He frowned at her and stood up to pace the room. At least he was considering it, she could tell by deep crease in his forehead and the way his lips moved as if he was talking to himself. He stopped suddenly and turned to face her. "I cannot agree to it. Mr Huntington would be very disappointed in me if I permitted such a thing."

"Worry not. I will employ you if Mr Huntington lets you go."

Fulton paused mid-step, nearly faltering and turned toward her, his almost amber eyes rather round with astonishment. "You would? My word, your audacity amazes me."

Jemima stood up and faced him. "Never mind that. I feel there is danger. Obviously, something has occurred to prevent him from writing to us. There were two murders in Kent you know. He was on his way here and has not arrived. We must retrace his steps in London to determine where he is."

Fulton shrugged nonchalantly. "That I can do through written enquiries."

"Perhaps. But what if action is required?" Jemima now paced the room, tapping her finger against her temple as she did so, looking for more arguments to throw at Fulton. She did not like having her very good ideas discounted. When another came, she swung round, her skirts spinning around her. "You mentioned that people were after his research. What if there is a connection? Now, I assume as he is of a scientific bent, he took over father's laboratory. In fact, I know he did because he tossed me out of there years ago.

"Do you have access? Perhaps having a look around will provide us with some clue as to what he is working on, which in turn may point us in the direction of his trouble."

Fulton shook his head, his expression defeated. "I do not think he would like it if I showed you his work."

Jemima smiled, sensing that she was winning the argument. "What choice do you have? We cannot leave here blind. There may be some clue."

Fulton nodded, she could see the resignation in his hangdog expression. "Very well. I will show you but after the others have gone to bed. I will meet you in the basement around one in the morning. All the servants will be abed by then. I pray to God that he comes home before then."

"Very well. Pass me some of Mr Huntington's letterhead will you, and his latest letter. I best start on that all important correspondence. Better put on the kettle, too. I'll need to gently steam his seal and transfer the stamp."

⚜

The house was cool and quiet when Jemima stepped out of her room draped in a dressing gown. Underneath, she had men's riding breeches, short boots and a shirt and vest. It had taken her a while to decide what to wear. She could have gone in her night clothes but thought that would not be proper, particularly if she was caught. Although Fulton was above reproach and her appointed protector, being found in the basement in the middle of the night in one's bedclothes would stretch even her sense of polite behaviour. She could have worn a dress, but the wide skirts would have impeded her inspection of her guardian's laboratory. She was loath to accidentally knock something over. Why, that would be unforgivable. As she stole down the steps, pausing when the risers creaked under her weight, she reminded herself to sneak the fake letter in the day's mail, early in the morning. Fulton agreed to distract the butler for her.

On the ground floor, she paused further, listening for the sounds of the servants. All was quiet. Guarding her candle, she opened the door to the basement, seeing Fulton's distorted shadow on the wall.

While she trod down the staircase, cringing every time it groaned under her weight, she could see Fulton's worried face peering up at her. He was clothed in his day clothes, which was a relief. She did not think seeing him in his night attire was something she could cope with, or explain, if discovered either.

Fulton brandished a large key and inserted it into the lock. Jemima held her breath, but the lock proved to be well oiled and opened with a quiet snick. Pushing the door open, Fulton stepped in first and went to light the gas lamps. Jemima was impressed. The laboratory was better equipped than the rest of the house. Memories flooded into her then. So much of her childhood had been spent there with her father, playing at pretend experiments while he worked away, often sent on errands to fetch some plant from the garden. In his day, the tables were full of flora and fauna both local and imported. She had studied, too, gazing into microscopes at minute creatures captured in the pond or strange African beetles. They were such happy times, full of freedom and, if not laughter, contentment.

Edward had converted the place into a modern laboratory with racks of metal parts, cylinders, pistons and gaskets. Wires hung from walls in various lengths and copper piping hung in niches. She walked along the long benches, seeing his notebooks in a neat pile and a half-constructed piece of machinery. She turned the corner and continued her inspection, hitting her toe on a box on the floor. It had been haphazardly placed, the contents spilled. She knelt down to inspect it, picking up the gems and placing the whole on the bench. Inside were an array of small crystals, a couple of emeralds and rubies. "What were these doing on the ground? Everything else is so neat. My word, these are real jewels."

"Begging your pardon, miss. What do you mean?"

"This box here was on the ground with its contents all askew, very special contents. I thought it odd that my guardian would leave it so, considering their worth."

Fulton picked up a small gem and used a gloved finger to push it along his other palm. He bit his lip. "It does appear odd."

"Do the servants come down here?"

"No, miss, Mr Huntington would not allow that unless he was here to supervise any cleaning. I have the key, and I have let none in here."

Jemima hunted around and saw a journal further under the bench with loose pages hanging out of it. "Look at this." She picked it up and slapped it down on the table.

Fulton came over and exclaimed at the sight before him. "Good God! Pages have been torn out. Impossible. Huntington would not have defaced one of his journals so."

Jemima considered the possibilities, either Mr Huntington had left in a hurry and created this disturbance to his otherwise neat possessions or someone had broken in. "I take it Mr Huntington has a key himself."

"Of course, I have the other key. As far as I know there are no copies."

"Then consider this. He could have returned without us knowing, entered here and departed with some gems and tore out the pages of notes. Maybe he was in a hurry."

Fulton shook his head. "No, that he would not do. He would have left me a note, I am certain and, as I said, I could not imagine him doing this to his things. He is so particular about them."

"Yes, that I can see, just like my papa. What if he was in trouble and could not let us know because it would put us in danger?"

Fulton nodded, his hand on the top of the journal. "To save us all, he would. The other alternative is much more dire."

"What is that?" Jemima's gaze was already tracking around the laboratory, looking for signs of forced entry. Small windows dotted the upper wall on one side. She tried to picture where that would be in relation to the house. The rear, partially obscured by bushes. Someone could have broken in during full day light without being noticed. The noise obscured by the normal daytime sounds of pots clanging and maids chatting. When she stepped closer to the windows, glass crunched under her boot.

"Look here, broken glass."

Fulton raced over, his face sunk in despair. Examining the windows, he observed. "But none are broken. Perhaps some accident, some test tube smashed."

Jemima noticed that all the windows were whole. Someone had come prepared. "In the morning, you should check the rear of the house. Perhaps there will be some clue."

Fulton sucked in a breath, finally conceding to her way of thinking. "Someone has him, then. That is the only explanation that comes to mind. He would not willingly give over the location of his laboratory or his key."

"For this they did not need the key, simply the knowledge of what he was working on and where. Can you bring me some more candles? I need light to study his journal. We might find some hint."

"Very well, miss. I have to trust to your silence at what you read. Mr Huntington is very particular about his scientific experiments."

With a sideways glance at him, she nodded. "If he is in trouble and we are able to assist him free of it, I do not think he will complain. If he does, he would be very ungrateful."

The notebook was on the topic of machinery, particularly the theory of the perpetual engine. Mr Huntington's own theory was that this was not possible. However, he did theorise that the larger, hardier crystals could be treated to take up an electric charge. Then, depending on how the crystal was tapped to ration the amount of energy discharged, the engine could keep going as the motion of the engine would continually recharge it. He was looking to build and test a rather large engine and it was there that the pages had been ripped out. Had he succeeded? Was this why his research was plundered? A reputable scientist would not steal his work surely. In that case, some other nefarious organisation was involved. Jemima shut the notebook and ended that train of thought.

Before the cock crowed, Jemima snuck back upstairs, yawning all the way. She hoped she could pass herself off as being ill, as she was very tired and in need of sleep. She had charged Fulton with slipping the letter in with the rest of the post as she could not stay awake any longer. He assured her he could function quite well with little rest and manage the task.

It was hard to get to sleep. The contents of her guardian's notebook swirled around her head. There had been talk of crystals and electricity in the newspapers, although not much had come of it. It could be supposed that Mr Huntington had had a breakthrough where others had failed. He had extended the idea, using the power of his crystal to fuel many gadgets for long periods. There were fantastic drawings, too, of body parts built with metal and copper wires, of moving machines and idle drawings of things she could not put a name to. If anything, she thought her guardian was quite the artist. He had a wonderful imagination and a certain amount of genius.

Fulton had examined the contents of the box and compared it to an inventory he found in one of the drawers. From that he could tell that a number of sizeable and, hence, valuable, jewels had been removed. Apparently, Mr Huntington had a mine or two in India himself, from whence he acquired the precious gems he needed.

❦

The maid was sent up before luncheon, passing on the intelligence that she was wanted in the morning room, post haste. There had been news from her guardian. Jemima took her time with her toilet and dress. She decided a lavender-coloured dress would ill suit her complexion, thus adding to her image of frailty. This she hoped would spare her some of the aunt's exuberance and allow her a vacation from the worktable after dinner. With luck, there would be ample activity with the journey preparations to keep even the diligent aunt busy.

On entering the morning room, she found Fulton and Aunt Prudence in deep discussion.

"We should take the train from Three Bridges. It will be faster than taking a carriage. We can send the bulk of the luggage with Mr Coachman."

"Yes, Mrs Wainwright. Excellent idea. I will send one of the footman to procure our tickets." Fulton was enjoying the opportunity to be valued in the household. Her guardian's letter had requested the aunt to consult with Fulton and nominated him the keeper of funds. This had decidedly lifted Fulton in Aunt Prudence's esteem. Jemima was sure that the funds allocated to her and Milly's shopping expedition had nothing at all to do with it.

Aunt Prudence noticed her standing by the door. "There you are, my dear. I am sorry you are feeling poorly. However, you really must pull yourself together. We depart for London tomorrow and there is so much to do to prepare."

"Thank you for your concern, aunt. I am sure if I take it slowly today I will be fine for travel tomorrow."

"Is that all the excitement you can muster? We are going to London."

Jemima acknowledged Fulton with a slight inclination of her head and returned her attention to the aunt. "I do apologise. I am looking forward to it immensely. If you will excuse me I will make sure all my things are laundered and packed for the journey."

"Very well then. Make sure you pack your workbasket. We will have a lot of time in the evenings to keep to our industry. I think Milly could use some extra ribbons, if you can spare them."

Jemima paused by the door and looked back. "Of course, ma'am. Milly is welcome to any ribbons she fancies. I will tell her before I retire upstairs. Where may I find her?"

"She is in the library, I believe," Fulton replied. "Sewing."

"Thank you. I am sorry I cannot be much help in organising things." She turned to leave but not before she saw the aunt's expression. Jemima grinned to herself. Her aunt would not appreciate a word from her on any of the arrangements and would possibly have apoplexy if she knew what Jemima had already arranged.

Milly had her head down, sewing away on her chemise. It was coming along very nicely with sweet flowers embroidered on the neck line in soft, pale pink silk thread. "My that is very pretty, Milly. Do you think you will finish it before we leave?"

"Yes, I think so. Such lovely cloth. I am very grateful to you for sharing with me."

"Not at all. Now your aunt has said you should choose some ribbons. How about I leave the parcel on your bed and you can choose as you wish." Jemima yawned heartily. "Forgive me. I am still so very tired."

"Thank you. I will select some and return the rest to you later."

After dinner, Jemima went in search of Fulton and found him in the library. "So what did you find?"

Fulton frowned at her. "You were right, miss. Someone had broken in and replaced the glass. The putty was still soft and footprints led away."

"I thought they must have brought the glass and putty. They must have had previous knowledge of the size of the pane, which means they are familiar with the house."

"How did you know? I did not know a young lady would even know about glass and putty and windows."

"At school I broke a few windows in my time. The last few times I was required to assist the glazier as part of my punishment."

Fulton gaped at her. "Did you break them in a rage?"

"Oh no, why would you think that? I did it playing cricket."

"You play cricket?" Fulton's eyes were very round.

Jemima grinned at him. "Sometimes, when I am really, really bored. You mentioned footprints. How big was the foot?"

He frowned at her. "How would I know?"

Jemima let out a deflated sigh. "Well, were the prints well formed? Could you tell if it was a woman's footprint or a man's. Was it a boot, a shoe or barefoot?"

Fulton creased his forehead. "There were two distinct prints in the soil. They looked to be medium sized and boots. There was a strange indentation on the sole of the boots and it left an imprint in the soil."

"Imprint? Show me what it looked like, please."

Fulton took out some notepaper from the writing box and drew a design like a crucifix except it appeared to be winged.

Jemima turned the paper and studied it. "Have you seen this symbol before? Is it military? Or the mark of a particular cobbler?"

Fulton studied the paper again. "Not military as far as I know. However, designs such as these are not something I take an interest in."

Jemima took the paper and folded it, sliding it carefully into her purse. She had decided to make her own notebook to jot down facts. It may be that some light could be shed on occurrences which now escaped understanding.

"We know that Edward is missing and that someone broke in here and stole some of his research. Once we are in London we will have to work hard to find him."

"How do we do that and keep Mrs Wainwright in the dark? Think of all the shopping that must be done."

"I can manage the shopping. It is whether you can bend your scruples enough to leave us to it and do some investigating on your own."

Fulton lowered his voice and leaned close. "That may prove difficult. What if you are in danger or Milly? What if you were to be held in ransom for some patent of Mr Huntington's?"

Jemima leaned back and regarded him. "My, you have been thinking a lot lately." She was concerned that she was a bad influence on him.

"I foresee other issues, as well. Aunt Prudence is bound to write to him as soon as we arrive."

Jemima nodded. "I think she will last a week before she makes a hue and cry about not hearing from Mr Huntington. We might be able to stretch that with another letter."

Fulton, who had been arranging his neck cloth, dropped his hands dramatically. "Jemima is there no end to your schemes?"

"Apparently not!"

CHAPTER 9

Consciousness came slowly to Edward and along with it, confusion. Remnants of a sour drug coated his tongue. Grimacing, he took in the room, glad the rough sacking had been removed from his face. He was in a laundry, a basement room full of sacks. His hands and feet were bound, and his bladder was uncomfortably full.

Outrage and anger swelled in his breast, but he quieted them. To extricate himself, he needed to be calm and to concentrate. He mumbled and twitched his numb fingers, working his bindings loose with a small spell. A bucket had been placed in the corner, so he used it, rolling his shoulders to relieve the stiffness from where he had landed heavily.

He had no idea why he had been taken, perhaps footpads looking for a ransom. It was likely that the girl he was trying to help had ulterior motives for contacting him and unsavoury connections into the bargain. He had no time to waste dealing with thugs. Feeling ready to make good his escape, he turned his attention to the simple lock. At his command, it opened readily. Putting his head to the door, he listened for any indication his captors were on the other side before opening it. Silence greeted him. He listened a while longer, the distant sound of street traffic gently penetrating to the basement room.

The door opened to a dingy hall, thick balls of dust rolling along blown by a draft entering somewhere. No sign of anyone. No footsteps, voices, sounds of chairs scraping or pots banging. Yet he did not trust that he was alone.

A lone staircase presented itself. As it was the only way out, he had no choice but to use it being below street level. Absently, he checked his pockets and found his wallet intact. Frowning, he considered that he had been abducted by strange thieves, indeed, if they failed to relieve him of a substantial sum. A loud growl emanating from his stomach reminded him that he had not eaten for some time. He was quite thirsty too. Could he have been unconscious for a whole day?

No point in delaying, he thought. The quicker he moved, the quicker he could get away. Taking the stairs slowly and placing his foot close to the railing to minimise creaks, he paused every step, listening for signs of the occupants. Near the top stair, he paused on hearing a clink—the sound of a cup or tankard being placed on a table. Then a footstep and the groan of floor boards in the room beyond. He dived for the cover in the shadows near the door, as it swung inward. Shutting his eyes, he willed his breath to slow. Someone stood on the threshold, not leaning through the doorway, but listening, waiting. His skin prickled, with a familiar sensation, making him frown as he tried to remember where he had felt something similar. Edward tried to calm himself and to make ready to pounce at the same time. If only his gaoler would step through, he could act.

The door closed slowly, an audible squeak in the growing darkness. After it shut, Edward could tell that someone stood on the other side waiting. He had been detected but knew not how. Edward had to move; to linger was madness. He grabbed the handle of the door and flung it open, hoping to crash into the person standing behind. The door met with no resistance. A swirl of black cape startled him as the man was revealed. "You!"

There was a laugh and a ball of invisible power shot at Edward. Diving out of the way, he drew the words of his counter strike and hurled them at the tall man's head. Again, the taint of black magic clogged in the air. This time it thickened his lungs like coal smoke and made his head spin.

His spell landed on the dark magician but fell in tatters. "Not bad for a country bumpkin like you," his assailant said. "I like to keep my skills sharp. You never know when there is sport to be had." He flung another bolt, this one with a tail of pain in the spell. It was all Edward could do to deflect the blow and divert the power out the window, ripping off one of the shutters in the process and hurling it to the street below.

The taller man assessed him. "You have some skill. No match for me, I'm afraid."

Heavy footfalls came down the hall and the other door to the room flew open. Three burly men stood there. "Take the salted leather straps from that sack. Be ready to bind him as I instruct."

Edward's gaze shifted from the man to his accomplices. "What do you want with me?" He eyed the salted straps. They would contain his magic, make it harder to escape.

The blond eyebrow rose. "Your talents, Mr Huntington. Only your talents." Then he made a fist, spoke a word and Edward's chin jerked back. After a flash of light, he felt himself falling.

Aware, but not able to move, he could not resist when they tied his hands and feet with the salted leather. The cloaked man leaned over him, sealing the bindings with a spell. Edward could not access his power. A cup pressed against to his lips and drugged wine slid down his throat.

CHAPTER 10

Fulton secured them lodgings within walking distance of her guardian's rooms in Curzon Street. After unpacking, Jemima declared herself in immediate need of a walk. "Fresh air, fresh London air will set me to rights. Milly, could I prevail upon you to accompany me?" If Milly detected the satirical air in which she said this, she gave little sign.

Aunt Prudence was too worn out to complain, already half-dozing in the sitting room. "Make sure you take Susy with you. Fulton is not a sufficient chaperone in town. Do not take too long. I think I shall order us an early dinner."

Milly went to collect her bonnet from her room and tell Susy to make ready, allowing Jemima to whisper hurriedly to Fulton. "Take us past his lodgings. We shall dally in the street while you go inside. Is there a park nearby, where we can pass our time in a less conspicuous manner?"

"No, miss, but there is a bakery. Perhaps you could gaze through the window and admire the display. I will be but a minute."

"Good idea. Otherwise we would have to sneak out at night."

His eyes widened. "Best not you do that, miss. I will do my upmost to make sure that is not necessary." He shook his head.

"What's the matter?" she asked with a grin.

"Only that I worry for Mr Huntington with you on his hands. You are bad for a man's nerves."

Jemima waved a dismissive hand. "Oh fiddlesticks. I can look after myself."

Fulton wiped his sweaty brow with a large handkerchief. "Go on believing so, if that makes you happy. Ah, here is Miss Millicent." Jemima noticed the softening of his expression.

Milly gave them an odd look as if finding them with their heads together whispering was a bit suspicious. Jemima wondered if the girl was suddenly jealous. That could be a good thing, particularly if Fulton played his cards well. He seemed oblivious to the sharp look Milly sent their way.

He opened the door for them and ushered them out. Susy hurried out after them, keeping a discreet distance behind. Jemima tried to place herself apart from Fulton so that Milly could walk next to him. However, Milly was determined to be difficult and stuck to her side, making Fulton walk slightly ahead of them. As he knew the direction they should take that was ideal, except Jemima did not like missing an opportunity to throw them together. For once though, she was out of ideas. She cast a glance at Susy and realised that the aunt had upped the stakes, putting further obstacles in the way of the burgeoning romance.

Fulton kept a steady pace and soon Jemima had to request that he slow down. While she was normally energetic, she found that her strength failed her more frequently of late. Fulton probably kept ahead of them to avoid the sound of his artificial leg reaching them. Jemima noted it was slightly noisier than usual.

Fulton slowed his step and then turned the corner where he stopped. Jemima drew equal to him and smelled the aroma of baking bread. "My, I am suddenly famished. Do you think we could look in the bakery, Milly? Would a sweet bun spoil our dinner do you think?"

Milly looked between Fulton and her. "I am not hungry, but do not let that stop you Jemima, or you, Mr Fulton."

Fulton flushed a little as he spoke. "If you can spare me for a moment, I have an acquaintance hereabouts that I would like to call on. If you were both to go to the bakery and await me there I would be most grateful. I do feel terrible asking you to wait."

Milly smiled, her face and mood suddenly transformed. "We do not mind do we, Jemima? Let us see if there is something to tempt us while we wait for Mr Fulton."

"That would be nice." Jemima linked arms with her and headed down the road.

After checking that the maid was still with them, she dared not look behind at what Fulton was doing, lest she encourage Milly to do the same.

"Mr Fulton is a nice, gentle kind of man, do not you think?" Milly commented casually.

Jemima opened her mouth and shut it again, swallowing her surprise before speaking. "Yes, he should make some woman a good husband."

"You say that as if he does not suit your taste," Milly said, with a serious expression.

Jemima shrugged. "He is quiet and attentive. I, myself, would prefer a much livelier man, a bit younger, taller and with more hair."

"Oh?"

"I am sorry. Have I said the wrong thing? I know he likes you."

"Really, Jemima, you are most impertinent at times. You could not possibly know such a thing, and it would be most improper to discuss my feelings or his with either of us."

"If I must be impertinent I should do so in a good cause. I am not a simpleton. He could not keep his eyes off you when you wore that pink dress the other day. We must make sure to find more excellent gowns while we are in town so that you may drive him to distraction."

Milly giggled. "You are quite ridiculous really. I cannot imagine Mr Fulton fazed by anything. He is always so calm and assured as if he knows exactly what to do in all circumstances."

Jemima was diverted by such praise, ready to giggle, too, because she herself had made a good job of driving Fulton to distraction on more than one occasion. Although, Fulton had proved himself quite reliable and capable, too.

By then they were standing in front of the bakery. They stood there in the noon sun sheltered by their parasols, looking at the various tarts and sweet buns. "What do you think? Anything take your fancy?" Jemima ventured, daring not to cast her gaze up the street.

"Well, yes. We must consider the household and buy a few items and take them home for supper. Aunt Prudence would be most upset if we tried to eat them ourselves and in public."

Jemima poked around in her purse for some coins. "Very well then, I shall buy us up a supply for tonight's supper."

Inside they went to make their purchases, taking their time picking and unpicking which of the tarts and buns to buy. By the time they had completed their purchase, Fulton was waiting for them on the street. His countenance gave nothing away, which made Jemima grit her teeth. She would have to wait to speak to him and, situated in lodgings as they were, opportunities to meet and discuss things in private would be denied them. As they walked along, Milly tried to get the conversation going. "So, was your acquaintance in good health, Mr Fulton?" She blushed and kept her gaze to the ground.

Fulton's eyes widened. "Reasonably, thank you, Miss Millicent."

"Milly. I asked you to call me Milly."

Fulton coughed, his own cheeks reddening. "Yes, Miss Milly."

Back at the lodgings, Aunt Prudence was perched on a sofa in the room they had designated the drawing room, the room in which they would receive any callers. "I am glad you have returned. It is very odd, but there is no note from my nephew to welcome us here. How strange to invite us here and not meet us or send word."

Jemima ventured to offer an excuse. "Perhaps he is otherwise occupied. Did he not leave sufficient funds for our various shopping expeditions? I am sure he would hate to take us around to the various businesses while we transact. I am convinced a young gentleman, such as he, would find the occupation most tedious. We could, perhaps, write to him when we have finished and are ready to show the results of our hard work."

"That may be. However, good manners would dictate that he respond to my note, which he has not done. I will send another tomorrow."

"That sounds like an excellent plan, aunt." Fulton and she shared a look. Jemima was running out of ideas. The aunt had already sent a note. *Bother!*

Milly informed her aunt of their purchases before they retired to their rooms to prepare for dinner. Jemima changed her dress when a soft knock on the door alerted her to a note sliding under it. She bent down to pick it up and turned it over. It was from Fulton, saying the landlady had not seen Mr Huntington for three days. His luggage was still in his rooms. Fulton planned to visit a good friend of Edward's that evening and should have news for her after dinner.

Jemima paced, thinking hard about their next step. She hoped that Fulton had extracted Edward's post so that they could see if there were any assignations planned. She sat down at her desk and constructed a short note from her guardian to Aunt Prudence. In this she said that he was indisposed with a summer cold and was unwilling to infect them and expressed the wish that they enjoyed their shopping expeditions and he would see them in a few days when his health improved. Pleased with the text, she folded the letter and placed it in her purse in readiness to pass to Fulton at the first opportunity.

For three solid days, Aunt Prudence, Milly and Jemima courted the boutiques, the various drapery warehouses, milliners and jewellers. Jemima had no idea the money she had handed over for this adventure could procure so much. Milly was so well set up with dresses and bonnets and shoes that she had very little to complain about. True to her earlier boastings at Willow Park, Aunt Prudence did know where to get the best bargains in London. Jemima bought hardly anything at all, except a new ball gown. Not that she had occasion to wear the ones she already possessed. She liked the pale green of the smooth silk and the cut of the gown she had procured. It enhanced her figure. If only they had a ball to go to.

They were finalising the purchases at one such establishment when she suddenly felt in need of fresh air. Horses's hooves clopped, carriages wheeled by, and people talked. Piles of horse dung and other muck attracted flies and exuded smells. Wrinkling her nose, she lingered on the street, waiting for Aunt Prudence to complete her directions to the merchant. All items purchased from the premises were to be delivered and Aunt Prudence furnished the details of their address in a loud voice.

The street traffic had her back out of the way as people tried to edge around her.

"Jem?" a male voice spoke behind her.

Jemima had her back to a lane and swung around.

Standing there was a tall thin man, with white blond hair kept unfashionably long. He had dark, almost black eyes, which were round with surprise. Slowly, did his features reveal themselves to be familiar.

"David? David Longhurst. How long it has been?"

He rushed forward to greet her, grabbing her up in an embrace, hugging the breath out of her and planting a kiss on her forehead before mumbling a few words she could not discern. Jemima froze with surprise, and David released her. "Forgive me. I forgot myself. It has been so long since I have seen you and you have grown so much, grown so beautiful."

He spoke it all in one breath. Jemima could not keep her gaze from him, tracing the lines of his aquiline nose and the trim mouth that had once kissed her. Strangely, she felt no attraction to him now. But years ago, she had idolised him. Perhaps it was because his dress was strange, not that of the fashionable world, or because he had deserted her, and she could not expunge the hurt. "You stopped writing to me."

He looked down at his feet, then glancing back up, replied, "I know, I am sorry. Forgive me?"

Those dark eyes of his looked sorrowful. "Of course," she said, "but will you not tell me why? What prevented you from writing to me? I was in want of a friend at that time."

He looked to the side, distracted by a set of young men who were talking animatedly as they walked along. With his head turned, she caught the glint of a medallion around his neck, silver against the white of his shirt. Her eyes were drawn to it, eager to see its full design. He spoke again, distracting her and the jewellery was once again disguised by the folds of his neck cloth. "I am sorry. I went abroad for a while. Your letters would not have reached me. Not where I have been dwelling."

This answer did not ring true, but she quickly lost interest in the conversation. Obviously, they had nothing in common now and only politeness made her ask, "I see. What do you do with yourself these days? Have you a profession? Do you live in London?"

People edged around her, so she was forced further into the lane to avoid being an obstacle to the other pedestrians. With his hand on her elbow, he gently guided her down the gutter and further into the small, dark lane.

He smiled at her, though the merriment did not quite reach his eyes. "I sometimes live in London. As to profession I have various occupations."

Jemima smiled broadly and laughed lightly. "You do sound mysterious. Did you become a magician then?"

David started, his eyes growing rounder at her words. "How could you..."

Jemima narrowed her gaze. "Do not you remember? That last day. I told you I wished to be a scientist...you said—"

"Yes, I recall it very well." He extended his hand, the tip of his finger tracing the contours of her lips. Jemima blushed deeply, his touch reminding her of their infantile but passionate embraces. It occurred to her then that he was a couple of years older and how lucky she was that her conduct had not let her down a very immoral path. The timing of her guardian's intervention had been entirely appropriate after all. However, she was not going to admit that. Not yet. She stepped back and he dropped his hand.

"Jemima!" An excited screech reached her ears, making her cringe as she turned around.

Aunt Prudence hastened forward. Jemima realised that she was quite within the secluded laneway and was guilty enough to blush. "Aunt Prudence, may I introduce to you to..."

She turned back, and David was gone. She blinked. "Where did he go?"

"What were you doing fraternising with a common street boy in a dirty little lane? Where are your senses girl? A lady does not speak with strangers in the street, and she certainly does not let herself be lured into a dark alley with a man of dubious origins." She turned haughtily to Fulton, who stood with a stunned expression on his face. "Fulton, you must keep a closer eye on this wayward girl."

Fulton's eyebrows clenched over his glowering eyes. It pained Jemima to see her conduct had disconcerted him. Putting that aside, she focussed her attention on the aunt. "But he was not a stranger. It was David Longhurst from Willow Park village. We were childhood friends."

Aunt Prudence lifted her chin, the ties to her bonnet and the rapid movement of her head jiggling the fat just underneath. Jemima did her best not to be distracted by it. "If that is the case, why did he run off when I appeared? His conduct leaves much to be desired." Aunt Prudence lifted a gloved finger and wagged it in Jemima's face. "Guilty is as guilty does, I always say. Come along then. I am feeling excessively tired. We must away now so I can rest before dinner."

❧

Fulton was not able to be alone with her, given the hustle and bustle of them arriving home with the bulk of their packages already delivered and the excitement that ensued as each one was opened, checked and admired. Futon gave her a hard look, appearing grumpy for some reason. No doubt he took Aunt Prudence's side with regard to her talking to Longhurst in the street.

Jemima spent considerable time in consternation that evening and barely spoke a word at dinner. While she had not seen her childhood friend for some time there was something familiar about him, like she had seen him before that day and had not known him. For the life of her she could not pinpoint when or where.

Before seeking her bed, she was able to mouth to Fulton, when no one was looking, that they should meet in her room later. Given the circumstances, she could think of no better option. It was not that she did not trust Fulton but entertaining the opposite sex in one's room invited trouble, particularly if Aunt Prudence was to hear of it. Jemima was sure she would have them married off under special license before breakfast. That was a particularly odious scenario. Besides, Fulton was in love with Milly. Jemima recalled an adage that Miss Blake often repeated with regard to assignations with men, 'make not trouble in one's own bed, or your sleep will be disturbed forever.' The way Miss Blake said this made Jemima think she was speaking from experience. That only led Jemima to think of Edward again. How could he? Miss Blake was so much older than him. Why she must be thirty or more. Thoughts of him kissing and embracing Miss Blake caused her to feel very tense. She found that she had ground her teeth and made an indent on her tooth brush.

Jemima did not dress for bed, considering Fulton was due to visit. However, she washed her face and let down her hair, in readiness for sleep. She was gazing at herself in the mirror, twirling her hair and bemoaning the ginger tinge, when she noticed the curtains billowing behind her and a faint mist along the floor. She did not recollect leaving the window open. The maid must have done it when they were at dinner. Alarm prickled her skin. She stood up, kept her gaze on the curtains, heart thumping a tattoo. The feeling that someone was watching her was very strong. A knock on her door, and she jumped. Before she could open it, a note appeared underneath.

Bending to pick it up, she saw it was from Fulton. She read the note twice and then ripped the paper up. He would not see her that night and though he gave a reasonable excuse, she was sure he was angry with her. Turning back to her window, she strode over and threw open the curtains, quickly sticking her head out of the window. Nothing, but an empty, greasy lane below. The mews it was as she looked along it, seeing the stables and horses' droppings. She shut the window and threw the latch, before closing the curtains. She went to comb out her hair and found her hairbrush was gone. Jemima rummaged around her things for a spare and thought to ask the maid what had become of it. After climbing under the covers, she shivered at the remembered sensation of being watched—the sensation of a cool hand sliding down the back of her neck.

❦

The next afternoon, they sat drinking tea in Piccadilly. With a view out to the street, sandwiches and pastries filled their plates as they drank blended tea in fine china. Milly's eyes sparkled as she gazed around the room, looking at every dress and bonnet. "I never thought to have high tea in a place like this."

Aunt Prudence sat up straight in her chair, her eyes only straying to older persons. She poured more tea into Milly's cup. "Your expectations are always so modest. They do you credit. Do drink your tea, dear."

"I wish Fulton had been able to join us," Jemima commented before she took a bite of custard tart. "It seems so rude to leave him outside in the street, while we sit here."

The old aunt sighed heavily. "Young lady, when will you learn that you cannot have everything your own way? I do not feel that it is proper for him to sit with us in such a place as this, in society. What would people say?"

Jemima took her cup and drank more tea. She could accept the wisdom in the aunt's words but did not like them. Her gaze kept going to Fulton, who stood outside. He nodded to people occasionally, touching his cap to them. Did he know them? she wondered.

The aunt leaned over and scribbled a note. "Jemima as you have finished your tea, do take this order to the clerk. Make sure he follows this blend. A pound should do and request delivery."

Jemima was happy to oblige, leaving her gloves on the table, took the order. She waved at Fulton through the shopfront as she walked along. His brow furrowed as he acknowledged her. The clerk scooped the different teas onto the scale, mixing them with the scoop before packaging it all up. After dictating the address for delivery, she turned on her heel, only to be confronted by David Longhurst, standing with his back to a pillar.

Genuinely surprised, she gasped. "Good afternoon." She thought it rather curious to encounter him twice in as many days. He smiled down at her, drawing her forth with his outstretched hand. Before she knew what he was about he had touched the skin on both her arms. She wanted to step back and upbraid him for his boldness but felt strangely calm and complacent.

"You look very well today, Jem."

Her heart pounded. She felt confused. It was hard to form words to speak. Minutes went by before she could talk. With a hand to her forehead, she rubbed at a sudden ache. "Do forgive me...I...er...meant to say that you went away yesterday before I could introduce you to my party. Pray let me do so now."

He shook his head and let her step back from him. "As you can see I am not dressed for polite company. I only wished to see you once again. We were such good friends once."

"Yes, we were." A door opened, and a cool breeze brushed by her and cleared her head. Indeed, she noted, he was dressed most oddly.

"Jemima?" Fulton strode toward her, his expression quite outraged.

She stepped forward to meet him, putting her hand on his to draw him forward for an introduction. A loud crash of breaking plates startled them both. They swung around to look behind them. On turning back, David Longhurst was gone.

Jemima frowned as her gaze swept the room. There was no sign of David. "But...he..."

Fulton leaned in close. "Do go back to the table. I will talk to you later."

Rather offended at his tone she replied hotly, "Good. I want to talk to you, if you will get over whatever sulk you are in. We have to make more plans." With that she stepped around him and headed back to the table. The aunt was ready to depart. Milly's gaze narrowed. She had seen the exchange with Fulton. "Sorry to have kept you. The clerk could not blend the tea properly."

Fulton handed Aunt Prudence and Milly into the hired carriage. Before he assisted Jemima, he spoke quickly. "What are you about encouraging that man's advances?"

She gaped at him. "I did no such thing. How could I?"

"Yet, he was there this afternoon, knew that you were there. I saw him."

Jemima gripped his hand rather firmly as he assisted her. "It must be a coincidence. I have had no opportunity to contact him. I neither know where he lives nor care."

Fulton climbed up after her. They sat in opposing seats, glaring at each other unrelentingly for the whole journey. If Milly and the aunt noticed the mood of their companions, they did not comment.

CHAPTER 11

Fulton escorted them out again the next morning. Aunt Prudence deemed it necessary for them to take a walk in Hyde Park and be seen. "We may meet some acquaintances and that can only be beneficial."

Jemima smiled at the thought of a walk. Despite being out most days on shopping excursions, she had not had a chance to lengthen her stride or talk with Fulton. She was hoping that the aunt would fetch up on a bench in the shade, keep Milly by her side and let her go to feed ducks. As it transpired, it almost happened like that.

Fulton's eyebrows were like ripe thunderclouds for most of the outing. He appeared disinclined to leave Milly's side. "Do you mind awfully, Fulton. I would like to go to that pond and feed the ducks. Could I prevail upon you to lend me your arm?" she asked him sweetly.

Fulton's gaze flew to her hers, his eyelids partially closed as he assessed her and kept his mouth pursed tight. For a moment, Jemima realised he would not budge so she increased the stakes by applying to Aunt Prudence. "Aunt do you mind if I borrow Fulton for five minutes?"

The aunt waved her away. "If you must, Jemima, but only for a short time and within view if you please. I will not have you conversing with anymore strangers."

Fulton glared at her and then bowed to the aunt. "As you wish, ma'am." Then he charged off in the direction of the duck pond, leaving her to hurry after him.

When they were out of earshot, she said, "Really, Fulton. Do you have to be so damn prickly?"

"I do not like to hear you speak in such a manner," he said without a hitch in his stride.

"So sorry. But we really must talk and plan. Have you any news?"

Fulton kept walking, his gaze ahead. "No."

"Oh bother. Will you talk to me like a person and not like I was a silly child."

He stopped suddenly, and she heard the hiss of steam escaping from his leg. "If you would cease behaving like a child. Your conduct has been reprehensible."

"Really? To which conduct do you refer? Forgery? False pretences?" As the pond was close by, she put her hand in her purse and pulled out some breadcrumbs.

She bent to feed a bold white duck who waddled up in search of a free meal.

"I refer to you meeting this Longhurst chap clandestinely."

Standing up, she slapped the crumbs from her hands. "Well, it can hardly be clandestine if you know about the assignation, and I met the man in full view of you and the aunt, now can it?"

He turned to her, fists tight. "You...you are trying to weasel now."

"Not at all. I did meet him."

Fulton threw out his hands. "See!"

"But not by design. I swear." She riveted him with her steadfast gaze.

Fulton looked down, unable to meet her frank look. Shaking his head, he said, "Very well, I will accept that, but the situation is very vexing to be sure."

She reached out and clasped his forearm. "Thank you." He smiled at her, and she felt at ease once again. After casting a light wave to Aunt Prudence and Milly on the bench, she felt a moment's alarm. Her eyes widened, and she sucked in a breath. There was a bad feeling crawling up her spine.

"What is it?"

"I cannot describe what it is I feel." She turned full circle, casting her gaze over the bull rushes and the ducks and then over to the other side of the park. She thought she saw someone pull back behind a tree —a flash of blond hair and dark eyes.

"Well?" Fulton was also on the lookout.

She opened her eyes and narrowed them, not quite believing what she had seen. "I thought...I mean..." She touched the tip of her bonnet and played with the ribbons while she waited for signs of movement again.

"What?" Fulton said.

It took a moment to believe what she was feeling and witnessed. "I saw someone, perhaps David Longhurst, behind that tree over there." She turned her body away so that she was looking in another direction and discreetly pointed to the tree. He nodded, getting her meaning.

"It is best if I escort you back now." His face clouded for an instant then settled back into a bland expression.

"Yes, of course, but please meet me after dinner in my room."

"Very well," he replied without a sideways glance. "I will try."

Fulton accompanied her back to the others, and they sat there while Fulton went for a walk ostensibly to nod to a few acquaintances he had seen. Of David Longhurst there was no other sign. It began to worry her—these frequent meetings. Too uncanny by half.

Later, back at their lodgings dinner passed off smoothly. The aunt complained of no answer to her second letter. Milly did her best to assure her aunt that they were sure to hear again soon. Jemima gave a start, realising that she had not had the opportunity to pass the letter she had prepared to Fulton. So that she did not forget, she would slip it under his door so he could place it with the household mail. Letting out a sigh, she was glad he appeared to be over his pout and willing to move their plans on. When she was finally free of the after-dinner activities, Jemima went to her room, retrieved the letter and slid it under his door. Returning, she eagerly awaited Fulton's arrival. She missed their easy banter—a pity lodgings did not afford the same freedom as a country house.

As she let down her hair, she found her thoughts consumed by David Longhurst. Why did he keep appearing everywhere she went? Certainly, he was following her. Why do that after all this time? She pulled the brush through her hair, admiring the sheen of it in the mirror, frowning when she realised the candlelight enhanced the red hue. David, she thought, lifting the brush again, had seemed happy to see her and was even a little boisterous in his welcome. Tugging a section of hair over her shoulder, she aimed her brush yet again and drew down. Yet, why did he turn up again and again? She frowned at her reflection, growing tired of grooming her hair.

In the mirror, the curtains billowed and a mist roiled out from under their hem. Putting down her brush, she mumbled to herself about the maid leaving the window open again and went to close it. "I specifically told her not to leave it open."

Venturing close to the window, the curtain billowed in her face. Slapping it aside, she was about to draw it apart, when a hand grabbed her wrist. Before she could scream, she was swung around and another hand covered her mouth.

"Forgive me," David Longhurst whispered in her ear. "Please do not scream when I take my hand away. Nod, if you understand me."

She complied, there being nothing wrong with her hearing. The hand dropped away, though she was not let go.

"I am sorry for the intrusion, but it has been virtually impossible to meet with you. You are so well guarded."

She puzzled over this, as he had clearly reached her a number of times and behaved most peculiarly. "This is most irregular." She tried to extract her hand from his grasp and while unsuccessful, retained a modicum of outward calm. "We have not been close in years."

Drawing her close, his dark eyes bored into hers. "But we were once. I thought our friendship meant something to you. Are you now such a lady that our bond is meaningless?"

Jemima tried to step back, his fervour frightening her. "It has been a long time and, well, circumstances are rather complicated right now." She managed to put a space between them. "If you had allowed me to introduce you in the street the other day, you could have, perhaps, had leave to call on us."

"No, that would not be allowed."

"Why? I don't understand."

David smiled at her, a flash of white pearls. His eyes though were hard dark glints. Before she could blink, she found herself unceremoniously shoved up against the wall, her mouth once again covered by his hand.

"Huntington's a fool for not proposing to you at the Horton's," he hissed into her ear, his warm breath moistening the skin of her neck. Danger prickled up her spine. He did not appear to be stable. Keeping her body flaccid, she did not fight him, even though his comments about Edward confused her. She had to try to calm him, to get him to leave her alone.

"Now you are unprotected. Now you are at my mercy."

Taking his hand away, his forefinger traced her lips and then the tip of her nose. Her heart beat leaped as he touched her. Fear excited her breathing, making her chest heave. Why did he think Edward would have proposed? How did he know she was at the Horton's?

David pressed his body close to hers. Jemima knew that it was most improper behaviour and tried to worm away. "David," she whispered. "Let me go. Please, I don't understand what you are doing here."

He let her move to the side and then pulled her back again, one hand on her waist the other stroking her neck and then lower, to the curve of her breast. "Stop—"

David's mouth smothered hers, his hand now holding the back of her neck while his vile tongue probed her mouth. She struggled against him, but he pressed his body hard against her. He stopped to draw breath and then grabbing a handful of her hair, he ravaged her mouth once again. Jemima panicked, fighting to free herself, clawing at his hair, his face.

He released her, but still clenched her hair in his hand and controlled her attack with his other. "Speak quietly. Why did you leave Willow Park so suddenly? Why London?"

"Shopping." Jemima could not hide her surprise at his question, at such a time.

"Liar. I saw you send Fulton to Huntington's lodgings. What are you looking for?"

Jemima gasped. "Nothing. He invited us here. We are to meet him."

He grabbed her again, squeezing her chin painfully. "Why do you lie to me?"

"I am not. I have no reason to lie," she gasped out through her near immobilised jaw.

When he released her, he slapped her face softly, half-toying, half-menacing. "Really? I remember how it was between us. You were ready to give yourself to me that last day at Willow Park. One kiss and you would have done anything I asked." His face drew very close to hers. "A little more time, a day maybe, and I would have taken you, too, if not for him."

"Heavens! I was barely fourteen, just a girl. I did not know what I was doing. You cannot think I care for you like that now."

Jemima turned her face away, tried to edge sideways. David grabbed the edge of her bodice to tug her back, his fingernail gouging the flesh there. "You were ready to give yourself to me. I saw how you watched me, wanted me. You would have been mine."

A burst of rage, gave her strength. "How dare you? How dare you talk to me in such terms." She broke free and struck him with her hand. Retaliating, he overbalanced her and pushed her down on the bed and threw himself on top of her.

Jemima sucked in a breath to call out. A small cry escaped before David covered her mouth. A floor board groaned. Someone was outside the door.

"Miss?" It was Fulton's voice. She bit down hard on the suffocating hand.

David lifted off her. "Slut!" he said, holding his injured hand. "You have invited Huntington's creation into your bed."

Jemima sat up, a retort on her lips, when David belted her across the face. The world went black for a moment as she was thrown against the mattress. Sluggishly, she struggled up on her elbows only to see David vanish before her eyes. Gaping stupidly, she tried to think through what she saw. David had taken two steps toward the window and then disappeared. She shook her head, bewildered and scared. Her heart thumped. Her face stung. Tears pricked her eyes as the enormity of what had occurred sunk in.

The knocking grew more insistent. "Miss Jemima?" The door edged open slowly, as Fulton poked his head in. "Miss?" he whispered. When he caught sight of her, he rushed over.

Jemima sat on the bed sucking in breath after breath, fighting to calm herself and brushing away tears.

"Miss," Fulton sat on the bed next to her. "Are you all right? I heard a disturbance."

For a full minute, she could do nothing but gape as the terror in possession of her body ebbed. David had come to harm her. It was the only explanation. Such mortifying intentions. She could not deny it.

Fulton reached out and smoothed the hair away from her face. "Jemima?"

His voice broke the spell, she fell onto his shoulder and sobbed. Fulton patted her on the back, making crooning noises as if she was a child. "Tell me...please."

Pulling out of his embrace, she stared at his chest, not quite able to meet his eye. "David...the man I met...the one from...childhood... the one I thought I saw today...he...he...came in here...he tried to...to..."

Fulton eased her down to lie on the bed and went to the window. He shut it and checked around the curtain. Jemima pulled herself together and tried to fix her gown and tidy her hair. Her hands shook.

"It's a long way up. He must have scaled the pipe. Did you give him this address?"

Jemima's room backed onto a lane, the mews used to take horses to stable. She shook her head, trying to arrange her thoughts. "I did not tell him where we live. I did not even say I was staying in London. I did not get the chance."

"So how did he find us?" Fulton regarded her under a furrowed brow.

Jemima wrung her hands and chewed on a nail broken in her struggle. She watched Fulton as he paced her room. "I do not know, but it is not good, Fulton. David knew things."

Fulton came forward, lifted her chin. "What things?"

Ashamed of the hot tears that fell down her cheeks, she wiped at them. "He mentioned the Hortons and Mr Huntington. Something about him proposing to me and not doing so and said I was unprotected now. Then he said he saw you going to Mr Huntington's lodgings."

Fulton's eyebrows rose. "Really? How odd? He was not a guest at the Horton's place so how could he know these things."

"Could he be involved in this dreadful business?"

Fulton walked back to the window, stared at it for a moment. "Longhurst? Damn the man. He is not one of Mr Huntington's regular acquaintances. And Mr Huntington consorts with all sorts."

"When I was a girl, he was the son of the local vicar."

That made Fulton fall back a step. "The son of the vicar?" His eyebrows were on the rise. "What did he want? If he was not half crazed, why did he attack you?" Fulton came closer and kneeled by her as she sat on the edge of the bed. He reached out to smooth her hair from her face.

Jemima wanted to weep rather than admit what she had done in the woods at Willow Park that day. "He appears to have formed some very strange notions about me." She was about to tell about the kiss, the pledge of teenage love when the door swung open.

"Jemima?" Milly stood by the open door. Both Fulton and Jemima turned toward her, both of them flushing guiltily. Milly's gaze switched between them, her eyelids narrowing.

"This is not what it seems," Jemima said hurriedly as she leaped from the bed and took a step toward the girl, her torn bodice gaping open. Too late Milly turned and ran from the room.

Jemima followed and said over her shoulder. "You best follow along, Fulton."

She was able to get through Milly's door before she had bolted it. "Sorry to burst in on you, Milly, but what you saw just now requires some explanation."

"Lies you mean." Milly almost hissed at her before burying her face in a handkerchief.

Fulton slipped in behind her.

"No, the truth. All of it." Jemima said, feeling tears burn her eyes. She would not weep, not now.

Fulton touched her on the shoulder. "But Jemima, he would not like it known."

Jemima shook her head. "In this case, we must trust as well as explain. Milly could easily misconstrue what she has witnessed and unlike you she did not see the full of it."

Milly's eyes were bright, and there was an expression of pain in her eyes as she looked at both of them in turn.

"There can be no other explanation. You had Fulton in your room. Look at you. It is obvious what has transpired between you. I heard...heard it all, which is I why I came to investigate."

Jemima went over to a chair and sat down, feeling that her legs would not hold her up. "Yet there is another entirely plausible and truthful explanation. If you would allow me to speak it, painful as it is. You were right that Fulton was in my room. I invited him there to discuss some urgent matters. Mr Huntington has disappeared. We are in London to find him."

"But..." Milly gasped, pressing her handkerchief to her chest and sat down on the edge of her bed with a somewhat dumbfounded expression.

Jemima held up a hand. "Please allow me to finish. The other day, I met an old acquaintance, a young man I once knew in Willow Park, before Mr Huntington inherited the estate. He said some odd things to me in the street, before he disappeared, before I was able to introduce him to you. Lucky, in a way, that I did not introduce him to you. God forbid that he had become a regular acquaintance, one with free admission to this house. As far as I can determine, he has been following us...me. He has proven to be a most disagreeable man. Tonight, he broke in here, into my room and attacked me. If not for the intervention of Fulton, who disturbed the attack, I think that I would not be standing before you now. Not whole as I am."

Milly let out a horrified shriek and then covered her mouth.

"I beg that you keep what I have said in the strictest of confidences."

Milly's eyes widened, and her gaze had shifted from Jemima to Fulton with great rapidity. "Then you...did not..."

"No. He saved me, Milly. That is all. We did not wish it to be widely known that our benefactor has gone missing. We have been working quietly behind the scenes to find word of him. You must promise to keep what you know to yourself."

Milly nodded but her gaze was stuck on Fulton. "Then you are not...in love...with—?"

Fulton took a step forward, his expression softening as his amber-tinged eyes glowed. "No. Not with Jemima."

Milly came forward and placed her hands in his, lifting her face to gaze up at him. The expression in her eyes revealed a tender heart.

With a sigh, Jemima saw that she was no longer needed and slipped out of the chair. So much for her condition, the fright she had received, the comfort she was due. No! All paled into insignificance when love was revealed. As she opened the door and tiptoed out she saw Fulton, mesmerised by Milly's countenance, lower his lips to hers and proceeded to crush her in a passionate embrace. By rights, she should not have left them alone, but who was she to interfere. Fulton was an honourable man and would not behave too inappropriately.

Not long after there was a tap at the door. Fulton entered bearing a tray with a glass of port on it. "I thought you could do with something to calm your nerves." His face bore a very wide grin and his eyes were lit with sparkles.

"Thank you. I see you have proposed and been accepted."

Fulton paused in placing the tray. "You leap to conclusions, as usual. I would not engage her affections, without the proper authority. I will venture to say that we understand each other better."

Jemima grinned, not quite ready to laugh again. "Excellent. Though I do think you should propose to her straight away."

"You really like to interfere in other people's lives, don't you?"

Her grin widened.

He inclined his head. "In the case of my own life, my own heart, I do beg you to leave me to my own direction. Now that I have begun, I can manage quite well."

She took the proffered glass and took a sip. "Will you approach the aunt for permission?"

"No. I will speak to Mr Huntington when the time is right. For now, we will keep our mutual affection quiet, just between the three of us."

Jemima glanced toward the window and shivered. "What if he should return? I am not afraid to confess that he frightened me. There was something very sinister in his way. If you had not intervened when you did...he would have...I am sorry I cannot say it. I do not understand—"

Fulton drew himself up, thrusting out his chest. "There is no need to, Miss. I fully comprehend your danger. From what I know of you, you have little inkling as to your attractions."

"My attractions? I have little enough of those. A penchant for trouble lacks allure in the romance stakes. And I have way too much red in my hair."

"You are an attractive and intelligent woman. I heard Mr Huntington say so myself."

Jemima stared and then burst out. "Hah! He is a womaniser with a trail of mistresses. I would not believe anything he said. He did not know who I was. I was probably his next victim."

Fulton frowned at her and then bent to tidy the port decanter on the tray. "Your identity was unknown to him, but to the best of my knowledge he was not idly flirting with you at the Horton's house. I prefer it that you do not speak of him on such terms. You do not know how wrong you are."

Jemima sat very still, feeling herself blush. Although Fulton had not accused her, she felt she needed to explain her behaviour. "I did not mean to encourage Edward. I was not deliberately flirting, truth be known, I was trying to avoid him."

Fulton left off playing with the tray and stood up, a smile once again in his eye. "With good reason as we now know. However, I had not seen him so smitten before. He was truly shaken to learn your identity. Angry, too, but that will soon be got over."

"Do you mean that he could forgive me for deceiving him? That is hard to believe. I would not be surprised to be cast off."

"Mr Huntington is a good and generous man."

"So you keep saying but that does not accord with his actions."

Fulton lifted a quizzical brow. "Actions? I am afraid I do not understand you."

Jemima sighed loudly. "Mistresses. He keeps mistresses."

Fulton chuckled at her and stroked his head with his hand.

Jemima squirmed. "Get out of here. I will not have you laughing at my ignorance."

"I am not laughing at your ignorance only your ignorant assumptions. Take that man, Longhurst. He would take you to bed without thought, without conscience. He would probably marry you to gain your inheritance and then care little for you, except as a thing. Mr Huntington is a different breed of man altogether."

"I do not want to think of him, of Longhurst, but we have to consider that he may be involved with Mr Huntington's disappearance. He knew things..."

Fulton picked up the tray, took the empty glass from her hand. "If that is so, then we know more than we did earlier today. It is a lead, one that we can follow. Best you try to sleep now. I will stay below and guard your window tonight. Tomorrow, we will seek more information. I think Bess is the first place we should try. I will also send out enquires about Longhurst. Something may come to light."

Jemima went to open the door for him. "Bess?"

"A new acquaintance. I have not met her, but there was a note from her at Mr Huntington's lodgings."

Jemima insides twisted, with anger and with jealousy. How could she care for a man who kept mistresses? It went against all her principles. She refused to be like Lady Arbunkle, adorned in trinkets and keeping up a facade of marriage while her husband did what he chose with any number of women. Without betraying her thoughts, she asked, "Can I come with you?"

"I think not. Mr Huntington would not approve of you mixing with such low company."

Jemima lowered her voice. "That is hilarious. He does more than mix with low company if my guess is right. There must be some way.

Can you not arrange to meet her in Hyde Park, for example? I could be walking with Milly."

Fulton's expression darkened. "You would expose Milly to such a person?"

Jemima shook her head. "No, not really. But I would like to get a look at her. There was something about David, something I cannot place. Something sinister. When we were young he said he wanted to be a magician. Perhaps that is what he has become. Did you not see how he disappeared twice today?"

"Mere trickery. Not magic."

Jemima nodded. "I would not have thought so myself. Magic has always been balderdash in my opinion. But I am beginning to see that not everything can be easily or logically explained."

Fulton scoffed. "He is but a man, a flesh and blood man. We will catch him. Mark my words."

"I hope so, Fulton. For to entertain the other idea scares me to my very soul."

CHAPTER 12

M illy was in very high spirits the next morning. Her aunt remarked upon it, and Milly could give no good reason. She blushed and stammered. Jemima came to the rescue. "It is the shops, ma'am, and the new clothes."

Giving the appearance of being in a good mood, Aunt Prudence replied. "Nothing so common-place as that, my dear. Did you not see that we had an invitation to a ball tomorrow night? Lucky for you I met Mrs Parson-White yesterday in the park. Very good notion of mine to parade ourselves there. It is she who secured us the invitation to the Viscountess's ball, those genteel ladies being the best of friends."

"How exciting. Do you mind if Milly and I go to the park before luncheon? Milly has a new walking dress to show off. I am sure Fulton will not mind escorting us."

Aunt Prudence's expression revealed that she knew she was being bamboozled but could not pinpoint in what way. "You may take a walk for a short while, with Susy for company. I want you back here in good time. I am expecting Mrs Parsons-White to visit, and I do want her to meet you, for she will have some investment in you carrying yourselves off creditably. Not that I fear for Milly."

Jemima ignored the jibe. "Oh, I long to meet her. Do you not,

Milly?" Jemima leaned over and patted Milly's hand with exaggerated exuberance. "We can thank her for her kindness in person."

Milly added her own shy smile, lowering her lashes when she caught sight of Fulton standing in the corner. "Yes, a very kind invitation."

※

At Hyde Park, Milly and Jemima strode arm in arm, taking in the surrounds of Stanhope Gate, while Fulton loitered under the designated lamp post. Susy sat in the shade, keeping them company from a distance. Jemima had alluded to secret discussions between her and Milly and the maid had acquiesced, quite happy to rest her feet.

About half an hour after the appointed time, a woman entered the park, stopping every now and then to look about her. She had blonde hair, rather too blonde to be natural, yet her sense of dress was modish. Jemima could only admire the grey-striped skirt with matching narrow-waisted jacket. Jemima walked Milly in the newcomer's direction, catching sight of glittering rings on the woman's fingers as they passed her on the path. When the woman turned her head, her gaze searching the park, Jemima noted her face was made up, but not too overtly. A touch of rouge to the cheek and lips and little Kohl around the eyes. She was not too tall but had a buxom figure and a very narrow waist. Jemima frowned, not impressed with Mr Huntington's taste in 'bits of muslin'. Surely, he could do better than that.

The woman went up to Fulton, who took off his cloth cap and bowed. Maintaining some distance between them, they began to converse, edging around each other in a slow circuit.

Milly clutched her arm tightly. "Oh dear, is she really a fallen woman?"

Patting her friend's hand, she replied. "It is all right, Milly. I do not think her condition is catching."

Milly leaned closer to whisper. "Please do not be so absurd. I know that. Look, the woman seems to be shaking with fear."

Jemima studied Bess, nodding when she saw the trembling hands and the worried frown as the woman engaged in conversation with Fulton.

"Nothing bad can happen to us in the park." Jemima hoped this to be true.

"But you were attacked in your own room, in our lodgings. If you cannot be safe there, where are you to be safe?"

Jemima nodded, feeling suddenly faint at the recollection of her unexpected and violent visitor. "I take your point." Jemima expanded her gaze, sending it all around them, seeking lurkers behind bushes and lampposts. Now deep in conversation with Fulton, Bess edged a little closer, tightening the circle before standing still and shaking her head.

Milly was right. There was something odd about the woman. Although outwardly confident, she did appear afraid, as Jemima had noticed, frequently checking over her shoulder, as if expecting someone to accuse her of something.

As they walked along, her gaze kept slipping back to Fulton and the woman. How she longed to speak to Bess herself. However, she had sincerely promised Fulton to stay away from them and leave all the questions to him. As such, Jemima turned them around and headed away from the conversing duo.

All of a sudden, their voices rose and both Jemima and Milly stopped in their tracks and glanced over their shoulders in time to see the woman slap Fulton across the face. Milly gasped, gloved hand covering her mouth.

Bess swung around and glared at them, before gathering up her skirts and running off back the way she came, as fast as her dainty shoes allowed her. She looked back once as she passed through the gate, large, dark eyes wide with fear.

Once the woman was out of sight, Milly let go of Jemima's arm and raced over to Fulton, throwing herself at him as if he had just been saved from being run down by a runaway carriage. Fulton rubbed his cheek and otherwise appeared unharmed when Jemima joined them. Milly proceeded to cover his face in kisses, in a surprisingly forward display of affection.

Jemima gaped and then smirked. Luckily, Susy had dozed off and caught nothing of the display and there was no one around to notice such goings on. Just think of what Aunt Prudence would say. Jemima shrugged. It was likely she would get the blame. Yet she did wonder at such a quiet girl, hiding all that passion. Fulton looked bemused and pleased at the same time, talking in quiet tones to Milly so, that by the time the maid roused herself, it was as if nothing out of the ordinary had transpired.

Together they headed back to their lodgings. "So what did you learn from her, Fulton?"

"At first she denied knowing Mr Huntington at all. When I said I had seen her note to him, she became flustered and admitted knowing him through correspondence. Then she said he had not kept the appointment and declared she knew nothing of what became of him."

"How did she explain the note? Surely, she does not write to a man, inviting him to her for…well you know without actually having met him."

Jemima felt awkward discussing such matters in front of Milly, yet the young woman seemed unfazed. Either she was totally ignorant or chose to ignore the implications of Mr Huntington's conduct.

"My thought exactly. Also, Mr Huntington would not have answered such an invitation without some degree of acquaintance. When I told her so, she grew angry and slapped me."

"She was frightened of something," Milly commented.

Jemima raised an eyebrow surprised Milly would put her point of view across. Obviously, she was at ease with Fulton more and more.

Jemima was of the same mind. "I was certain she sensed she was being watched. Well, she was by us, of course, but that does not count. She kept looking around as if she expected someone to jump on her. We must talk to her again. Perhaps in her own apartments where she will feel relaxed. You do have her direction?"

"No," Fulton glared at her. "You will not attempt to meet her. I will not permit it."

Jemima lifted up her chin. "You are charged with my safety, not my moral dignity. I assure you I can stand to converse with a fallen woman, if you cannot."

Milly lifted her chin, casting off her meek temperament. "If

Jemima can, I can also. You would not have her go alone. I would not like you to go there in any case without me."

Fulton looked exasperated and flushed, his gloved hands clenching. "No, and if you discuss it further, I will tell all to your aunt about Mr Huntington's disappearance and you will find yourselves straightway at Willow Park, and I will be forced to put the matter to the police. In fact, I am now tempted to involve them in any case. I fear he is in terrible danger."

That outburst kept both of them sufficiently quiet. Later, while serving afternoon tea, Jemima managed to convey gratitude to Mrs Parsons-White for her bounty in gaining them an invitation to their first ball. For years Miss Blake had schooled her students in dancing and in deportment and appropriate dress. Jemima had mixed feeling, considering their situation. She had taken Fulton's prognosis to heart. Milly, though, was thrilled to be wearing her first ball gown and was genuinely excited, which pleased both her aunt and her old crony.

۞

Staring at her reflection, Jemima considered herself to look elegant in her pale green ball gown, complete with a peridot necklace and matching earrings. Her fingers slid along the soft, smooth fabric as she gazed at herself in the looking glass. She had to admit she looked very fine, her bust was shown to great advantage and still not too risqué with the décolletage. Her waist, not quite as narrow as it should be, showed nicely the curve of her hips. The dressmaker had done a wonderful job fitting it to her. The maid had done a better job lacing her into her corset.

It was a short carriage ride to the night's entertainment. Milly exuded excitement. It was pleasing to Jemima to participate in the other girl's delight. Stepping out of the carriage, Jemima managed to keep her shoes adorned with silk flowers clean as she stepped through the street dirt to enter the viscountess's apartments.

Milly's dress was a soft shade of pink, with bold crimson flowers embellishing the skirt in an ever-widening trail from the narrow waist to a large trail along the hem. Her hair had been curled and decorated with flowers. She looked beautiful and garnered a few admiring glances on entry.

Eighty or so people crammed into the rooms. Voices competing with the music made Jemima's ears hurt as they made their way through the throng. Fulton remained standing by the door, as if making ready his escape. He could not be convinced to dance with either of them and made himself useful in bringing refreshments to the aunt, while the girls mingled. He nodded to a few acquaintances as they passed him through the door, but Jemima was too diverted by all that was going on around her to notice if he engaged in conversation with any of them. How good was his acquaintance with those people?

About midway through the evening, Jemima saw him standing there with a slight smile about his lips and a sparkle in his eye. He was gazing intently at Milly while she danced a quadrille. After walking up to him, she stood close and leaned sideways and said, "I see your smile. Are you not jealous of her admirers?"

Fulton turned his gaze on her. "Why should I be? It pleases me to see her so happy. This ball is beyond anything she has ever expected to experience. If she ever chose to marry me, I will be happy to know that she regrets nothing. I cannot thank you enough for making this possible for her."

Jemima considered his position, his notion that he was not worthy of Milly due to his disabilities, and her esteem for him increased. "It was nothing, I assure you. A complete coincidence to our being here. But tell me why would it be beyond her dreams to be at a ball? Surely Mr Huntington could be prevailed upon to present the girl in society."

Fulton's eyes darkened as they focussed on her. "Ah no, miss. The actions of the aunt put a stop to what might have been in that regard. Straight away when Milly first came to live with her, there was more intimacy between Willow Park and her household. However, the aunt harangued Mr Huntington, trying to get him to marry his cousin. She was very bald about it. In detailing Milly's attributes and bestowing on Mr Huntington more duty than a cousin should rightly bear, she achieved the opposite aim. He barely sees them and fulfils his duty by sending them money to assist with their expenses. Milly is a lovely girl, but too quiet and dove-like for him. He has done his best to distance himself without disadvantaging them, not wanting gossipy women in his life or Aunt Prudence trying to take over his domestic affairs. Or so he said.

"He provides for them in a pecuniary sense but does not understand the social isolation they both suffer. He is quite happy to work for months by himself with no society at all. A young woman has different needs. I have seen Milly resigned to her fate only to have it fill me with sadness. Now to see her blossom and embrace life, even for a few short weeks, it is everything to me."

Jemima felt deflated, seeing the larger picture for once. "Oh dear, I did not know all that. How angry he must have been with me having to invite the aunt back again to Willow Park and to send me there also. What a disarray to his domestic affairs. I do not blame him for staying away."

Fulton's expression softened with the memory. "Yes, he was angry, miss, but I have never seen him angry for long. He has a logical mind and he will work it out eventually."

"Really—"

"Jemima, what do you do here?" a familiar voice said. Turning she came face to face with Constance Furley, an acquaintance from Miss Blake's.

"How do you do? I am in town for a few weeks." Jemima kissed her on her cheek in greeting.

Constance grabbed her hand and shook it. "Oh do come along and meet my brother. He is dying to meet you."

Jemima nodded to Fulton, who resumed his position by the door.

Constance was with a group of friends from school, who in turn introduced her to their brothers. Jemima had a full dance card within half an hour. It was then she was glad of the dance lessons forced on her by Miss Blake. She did not like to dance that much but she remembered all the steps as geometric shapes and passed herself off creditably. She even enjoyed herself, accepting compliments about her person, her smile, her wit, her hair, her dress. There seemed no end to how a man could compliment a woman. She recalled what Fulton had said to her about Mr Huntington, which left her confused.

When they left, Jemima managed a few words with Fulton while the aunt was in the throes of saying goodbye to her their hosts, with Milly beside her. "Can we visit Bess tonight?"

"No, miss. I have another lead to pursue first. Tomorrow, we will go to a factory."

"Factory?"

Milly turned around. Fulton went to fetch Milly's cloak from the footman. After Milly was cloaked and had walked to the carriage with her aunt, Fulton hung back and whispered hurriedly to her. "Mr Huntington had a newspaper article on his sideboard. The article discusses machinery that is of interest to him and the factory where it is made. Tomorrow, I intend that we visit this place. If that leads us nowhere then I will call on Bess myself."

"I see, that sounds excellent." Jemima blurted without caution.

Aunt Prudence paused and turned toward her. "What are you talking about, Jemima?"

Jemima tied the cord of her cloak under her chin. "Fulton has offered to take Milly and me to see a factory tomorrow."

Aunt Prudence glared at him. Fulton stiffened and then bowed his head.

"Why on Earth would a young girl want to visit a dirty factory? Heavens, you will have a number of callers tomorrow if the admiration shown here tonight is any indication. I doubt you will have time to go on any outings. With luck we can have you married and settled before my nephew recovers from his cold."

Jemima frowned and then hid it quickly. "Aunt, it was a ball. Everyone was dancing. It does not mean admiration. Besides marriage takes more than a few days to organise, consider the license, the posting of the banns, the ceremony, the purchasing of a trousseau."

"Mark my words young lady. There will be posies and cards and callers tomorrow."

Jemima sighed. "How annoying." Yet, she was glad that the aunt did not suspect that the letter she had received from her nephew explaining he was laid up with a cold was counterfeit.

Fulton smirked at her. Obviously, he agreed with the aunt about the attentions she should expect. It was very late when they arrived back at their lodgings. She went straight to sleep despite the excitement of the evening, though found herself seeing David appearing in her dreams, which was odd. She hated to admit that the scenes involving him were disturbing—dark dungeons, endless corridors, naked shoulders, chains around her wrists and ankles, the sinister sound of chanting and the golden light of guttering candles. So close he seemed that she thought she could feel his warm breath on her exposed flesh, his firm caresses invading, his mouth demanding. She did not want to be thinking of him at all. If anything, she would prefer to dream of Edward. When that thought intruded, she sat bolt upright in bed.

The curtain billowed, reminding her of Longhurst's attack. Calming her excited breathing, she went to the window and looked down to the lane. In the greasy shadows of the moon Fulton's familiar bulk stood. He was guarding her through the night. Shaking her head, she wondered at the necessity and how Fulton would function throughout the day without a decent sleep. Jemima's own sleep patterns required her to sleep the requisite nine or ten hours or she was hopeless and listless until she found she had caught up. Being like this herself, she found it hard to imagine something different in another.

When Jemima came down to breakfast, she was surprised to find that an abundance of posies and cards had been delivered for both her and Milly. The aunt glorified over them while they ate breakfast. For some reason, the aunt was up early, perhaps in expectation of the deliveries. "You see, I told you girls how it would be. I expect both you girls to be in residence for visitors this afternoon."

"Oh we will, won't we Milly. We can visit the factory with Fulton this morning and be back here to meet our new admirers this afternoon."

Aunt Prudence put down the card she was reading and leaned forward, her large bosoms nearly knocking over her tea cup. "Do not get ahead of yourself, girl. I do not like this plan, visiting a dirty factory. It is not appropriate for ladies."

Jemima sat back, with exaggerated surprise. "But it is part of this modern age. One has to understand the great changes taking place in society. Even last night, Mr Curry asked me if I knew what a vacuum cleaner was, a very recent invention he told me. Now, I will be able to regale him with firsthand knowledge of a piston or a steam condenser or some such. Milly does not think it will be a bore, do you?"

Milly blushed. "Ah no, aunt. You see there are steam-powered looms, which make cloth and spin thread. I would find it most interesting. We would not stay out for long, if you could spare us."

Aunt Prudence pursed her lips, her gaze flitting from Milly to Jemima and then to Fulton. Fulton stood by the door in his usual fashion and pretended to be ignorant of the conversation like a well-trained butler.

"Very well, you will return here by Two O'clock. No later or there will be no more outings unless I accompany you."

⚜

A hackney carriage pulled over to the curb with a squeak of brake. Fulton had ordered it earlier. The horse snorted, its breath misting in the cool of the morning. Jemima shivered in her cloak as she took her seat. Milly squeezed in next to her. Casting her gaze out the window, she saw grey clouds littered the sky, competing with coal smoke billowing from chimneys.

It did not take long to reach the industrial area.

"I suggest we sneak in, pretend we are meant to be there when challenged."

Fulton frowned at her. "I will seek a tour of the place."

"And if they refuse?" she asked.

"We will do it your way." He turned to Milly. "Please wait for me here."

Fulton stalked off through the iron gates. "We will wait here, shall we?" she said to Milly, who laughed softly, her eyes following Fulton until he disappeared into a doorway.

All around were tall, dun coloured buildings. Milly remarked upon the smell, a sooty, sewer-cloaked stench. Jemima's attention was caught by the children in rags, who exited the nearby factories and squatted in the street, looking tired and hungry. The narrow street had a stream of dirty water and rubbish in it, oozing along. The children had to work to support their families. Jemima thought she had suffered at the hands of Mr Huntington, and she realised with a certain amount of shame that she knew nothing of suffering and hardship at all.

Fulton returned with the foreman. "Mr Blackheath here has consented to take us on a tour of the factory."

Covered in grime and smelling of soot and sweat, the foreman took his cap off and bowed to them. "How very kind," Jemima said, and then smiled to cover her discomfiture as the man looked to be an older version of the children. He had the same dull expression and similar sag to his posture. Milly screwed up her nose.

Fulton lifted an eyebrow at her, as if to say I told you so, as he put Milly's hand through his elbow and walked after their guide. Once inside, Jemima could barely breathe. Fumes spilled out of large coffers full of boiling liquids. Steam hissed out of pumping valves. So many workers, all dressed in grey rags, tugged on levers, hauled coal, cleaned floors and otherwise attended the various machines. The place was cramped and the spaces between the rows of machinery and workers were very narrow. Jemima despaired of her dress, seeing straight away the streaks of grime on her skirts and the layer of muck beginning to cling to her hem. She vowed she would throw the gown out when she returned home, convinced the fabric could not be saved.

Following Milly's example, she carefully extracted a handkerchief and held it to her nose as they followed the foreman around the large factory floor.

A huge machine with visible parts that twisted and spat, dominated the tall building. She could not imagine what function it served. The vibrations of its workings travelled along the floor, trilling the bottom of her feet. Huge wheels turned. Cogs ground against gears. Long pistons groaned as the foot of a press stamped down against thin sheets of metal, cutting them with a high-pitched shriek.

The foreman spread his arms wide, pleased with their looks of awe. Both Milly and Fulton were similarly entranced with the contraption. It looked to be more than twenty-foot high seeming to surpass the ceiling, with the very tip of it obscured by shadow and soft puffs of smoke.

"This is the machine that makes parts for other machines, which we usually assemble and sell. Depending on the settings, we make parts that can then be assembled into more machines. See here is the press for cutting out gaskets. Then we will reset it to make another part. Over there near the kiln is the pipe maker."

"Fascinating, sir," Jemima commented. "And what is the machine you are making at present?"

"We are not making a machine exactly. Not as far as I know. It were an order for parts. Once they're produced, we're to send them. I imagine they be making their own machine."

"Really? And where are you to send it?" Jemima asked with feigned innocence. She batted her eyelids, hoping it made her look insipid and slightly stupid.

The foreman screwed up his dirty brow, bringing the grime into three distinct lines. He turned to Fulton. "She is an inquisitive girl, sir. I mean no offence to her, but I am afraid I cannot answer."

Fulton bowed his head in acknowledgement. "Yes, she does not know when to keep quiet, I'm afraid. Do you know, sir, what kind of machine you are manufacturing here?"

The foreman moved them on, indicating they head back to the entry. Jemima kept her eyes downcast, acting like she had been duly chastised for her outburst. Milly walked closely behind her as the aisle was not wide enough for them to walk together. "Why no, even our own inventors have not been able to figure it out, and they have gone over the specifications more than once."

Fulton asked, "You have your own research laboratories here then?"

"Of course, we do. It is the only way to stay ahead of the competition. And before you ask, no, you cannot see them."

"Oh, that is a shame," Fulton said. "I so wished to see your basements."

"Our basements? How did you..." He smiled and tipped up the peak of his cap. "I will show you out now. I think you've seen enough."

❦

Out in the grimy little lane, Fulton ventured up the main street to hire them a carriage to return home. Jemima and Milly could not afford to stand still as little urchins swarmed around them, so they followed along behind. When they were in view of Fulton the children ran off, not without leaving paw prints on their skirts. "Let's walk on," Fulton said.

"I feel an urgent need to bathe," Milly commented as she looked behind her at the group of children still lingering in the streets.

"The industrial revolution is not as impressive as I expected," Jemima said, hurrying to keep with Fulton.

"Oh dear," Milly said. "There isn't a hackney carriage to be seen."

Fulton nodded and hunched his shoulders. "Best we keep walking. Once we are out of the dockland area, we'll find something."

Before Fulton could hire a conveyance, it rained. Dirty, wet and depressed they climbed into the carriage when they finally found one.

"I think that factory holds a clue," Fulton said, leaning back into the seat and offering his handkerchief to Milly to wipe the rain from her face and hands.

"Definitely," Jemima agreed as she patted the excess moisture from her face with her gloves and tried to shake some rain from her ruined skirts.

"I would love to look at the basements. Perhaps that is where Mr Huntington is being held," Fulton said, his voice low.

Jemima considered his words while she tucked her soaking gloves into her reticule. "I think it is the intended recipients of that mysterious machine that is more likely our quarry."

"Why do you say that?" Fulton glowered at her, accepting the handkerchief back from Milly, which immediately softened his expression.

Jemima shrugged. "I have a strong feeling. If I was working in secret I would commission others to make the things for me, without letting on what I was doing. That appears to be the case here."

"I don't agree."

They pulled up outside their lodgings. "Are you going to break in there and search the basement?"

Fulton assisted Milly out. "Are you?" the girl said softly.

Jemima stepped down, hand resting in Fulton's. "Well?"

"Never mind both of you." He bowed and indicated that they should precede him into the house.

Aunt Prudence stood in the sitting room, hands wringing. "You are an hour late!" she cried when they walked in. Then she looked them up and down. "What a state you are in. Quick upstairs and get changed this instant." She waved them on the way. "Susy! Susy!" When the maid come in, Aunt Prudence, waved her on as well. "Attend these girls and mop up that puddle they made on the floor."

Milly and Jemima disappeared into their respective rooms, the aunt following behind berating them. "What shocking behaviour. I cannot believe you were seen in the street looking like that. And for goodness sake, what is that stench?"

Jemima swung round. "Exactly so. We have behaved abominably."

"Don't stand there blathering, girl. Make haste. Change your gown."

While they had been out at the factory, several visitors had been and gone they learned from Susy, who delivered warm water for them to wash in. More visitors were expected, the maid said. And she kept delivering messages from the aunt for them to hurry up on what seemed like a minute by minute basis.

Frustration brooded in Jemima's breast. It was another day that Mr Huntington was missing, another day with him in who knows what danger. She was certain the girl, Bess, knew something. Somehow, she was going to find out. Now if she could find her address. Let Fulton be distracted by the factory. She would pursue her own hunches.

Fulton was listening to more of Aunt Prudence's complaints about the factory excursion. Jemima could hear the tirade from the hallway. While pretending to be still at her toilet, Jemima slipped into Fulton's room across the landing. Carefully, so as not to disturb his neat and tidy possessions, she searched for Bess's address. She was about to give up, certain that he was to retire to his room before she succeeded, when she saw Mr Huntington's post tied together with string. Quickly, she extracted the letter from Bess and memorised the address. Then placing Huntington's correspondence back carefully, she eased the door open a smidgen and peeked out. The hallway was clear. Dashing to her room, she eased the door shut. Checking the time, she realised that she had little time to right her person and fix her dress. Better to be fashionably late, she said to herself, as she searched through her clothes for something appropriate to wear. Her dirty dress she consigned to the maid to do with what she will.

"I never want to see it again, Susy. Throw it out or keep it, I care not."

Susy held the gown and stared at it. "But it were new miss, you said you bought just last month."

Jemima waved a dismissive hand. "It is ruined now. What do I want it for? Take it and keep it."

The maid left, leaving Jemima considering her person in the mirror. There was nothing to do about the taint lingering in her hair. There was no time to wash it. She sprayed it with scent, hoping to disguise the smell it had acquired from the factory and its filthy neighbourhood.

Finally, she felt ready to face the day's visitors. Once installed in the sitting room, she found the goings were something to behold. Several of her school friends visited with their brothers in tow. These, while amusing on the dance floor, proved to be boring indeed one on one. Mr Holesworthy never spoke a word, and instead gazed at her non-stop. Mr Pilger talked endlessly about his horses, the ones he owned and the ones he wanted to own. Mr Henkel and his sister talked to each other, ignoring everyone else. Milly had better luck with her suitors, though she did often look in Fulton's direction, as if expecting censure at every moment.

Aunt Prudence presided over the afternoon, adding her inane comments to the general conversation. Jemima thought the afternoon would never end and nearly choked on laughter as Aunt Prudence suggested all of the gentlemen in turn as suitable husbands for her in the intervals between one of them departing and a new one arriving. She was truly bent on saving her nephew the trouble of her. Her mirth soon grew to quiet anger when as the afternoon wore on, the aunt alluded to the guests the generous inheritance that came with her. Jemima did her best to not smack the old lady's lace cap off her head. Surely, a potential husband would be more discreet in his enquiries than expect it to be heard in the woman's sitting room.

One time, Milly had interjected, saving Jemima some embarrassment. She did not want to be sought after because of her wealth, any more than Milly wanted to be overlooked for her poverty. They were the opposite sides to the same coin.

ᏬᎧᏺ

That evening at dinner, Fulton sat down with them. Jemima said nothing, but it appeared that Milly had insisted. "Aunt Prudence. Thank you so much for hosting this afternoon," Jemima began. "However, as a favour to me, I would wish that you did not speak of my...my financial circumstances in such common terms."

Aunt Prudence's eyes bugged out and as she was chewing some beef could not speak. Jemima seized the opportunity to finish her point. "If I find a suitable person to marry, I expect that he could make his own enquiries about my circumstances and that my wealth or otherwise would be secondary to his choice of wife."

"Upon my word, you dare to reprimand me?" Aunt Prudence's knife slipped from her hand. She reached for her wine and downed a very unladylike gulp.

"I do not mean to. And I do beg your pardon, but I was rather embarrassed by your revelations about my circumstances to our guests this afternoon."

"Yes, aunt," Milly added. "It was a trifle embarrassing. It brings into relief my own circumstances, my own lack of fortune."

Aunt Prudence gaped at Milly, her cheeks colouring. "You have nothing to be ashamed of Milly. Why this impertinent young girl deserves no consideration at all. After everything I have done to help her along to be castigated at the dinner table in front of... " Her gaze passed over Fulton, who was studiously studying his fork. Once again, she waved her finger in Jemima's direction. "Why you could be engaged within the week if you would put your mind to it. Yet you abuse me to my face about my efforts."

Jemima stood up. "Let me get one thing clear. I do not wish to be engaged within the week and in such a fashion. It may be news to you, aunt, if I marry, and there is nothing compelling me to do so, I would do it because I chose to, because my partner in life would be someone

I can respect and love and who returns the same feelings. I am fortunate in this regard because I can afford to be choosy."

Quite out of patience, she left the table and escaped to her room. There had to be a way out of this situation. The only one coming to mind was the restoration of her guardian and him allowing her to go on her way.

While she was contemplating at what time and in what apparel she should escape out the window to visit Bess, a knock at the door startled her from her thoughts. Milly entered. "I am so sorry to disturb you, Jemima. A Mr Stradbroke has called to talk to you and he is waiting downstairs."

"Mr Stradbroke, the solicitor?" As she was still dressed, she stood up and stroked the creases from her skirts.

"Yes, I believe that is what he said. Shall I tell him you will come down? Supper will be served soon, and you must be hungry. You missed most of dinner."

Jemima grimaced. "Is your aunt still downstairs?"

Milly shook her head and gave a shy smile. "No, I am afraid she was taken quite ill after dinner and took herself to bed."

"Have you been alone with Fulton all this time?"

Milly blushed and nodded.

Jemima refrained from comment. The old lady must have been sadly put out to neglect Milly's chaperonage. "I see. I will come right down."

Milly shut the door behind her and within a few minutes, Jemima followed.

Mr Stradbroke stood and came forward to shake her hand when she entered the room. As a child, she had thought him rather tall, now he was a head shorter than her. His ridiculous moustache was now a rather brush-like affair adorning his upper lip.

He indicated a chair. "Please sit. I have some news for you. Your friends may listen if that is all right with you, Miss Hardcastle."

Jemima sat down, glancing from Fulton to Milly and then to Stradbroke. "Do you have news of my guardian?"

Mr Stradbroke stroked his abbreviated moustache unconsciously and then sat back. "Why yes. My visit does concern him. He came to see me a few days ago in a high state of agitation."

"What day was that?" she asked, before Fulton could.

"I think it was Monday...or maybe Tuesday, quite early in the morning."

Jemima clutched the arm of her chair, sitting forward. "Is he in some trouble? Do you know where he is? What happened?"

Mr Stradbroke lifted an eyebrow at her excited barrage of questions. "I have not seen him since. I have no idea what has transpired to have you so agitated. I take it he has not informed you of the instructions he gave me."

"No, I have not seen him since I was at the Horton's place."

Mr Stradbroke again touched his moustache. "Ah, I see. Mr Huntington instructed me to draw up some papers regarding you. He wished to relinquish his guardianship of you."

Jemima sucked in a breath. "What do you mean? Can he do that?"

"It is possible, though as yet we have not found anyone suitable among your relations to take his place. He is your closest kin."

She clenched her hands and did her best not to weep. Her instinctive response was feelings of rejection. "Why did he want to do that? Oh dear I have really upset him. I am sorry."

"Miss Hardcastle?" Stradbroke asked.

"It is my own doing." Jemima found her breathing quite agitated. She got up and paced, realised what she was doing and sat down again. All eyes in the room on her.

Mr Stradbroke smiled. "There, there. Nothing so dreadful I am sure. Mr Huntington did not describe to me all his reasons behind his request. Rather he owned to me that he was now in a position where being your guardian was untenable to him. He wished to be free of the responsibility and the stewardship of your affairs. He has desired me to continue to administer your trust fund and ensure that you receive your quarterly allowance. You see, nothing to overset you." He frowned and rubbed his chin. "However, I have been unable to contact Mr Huntington since our last meeting. After making inquiries, I found that you were in London yourself and chose to make known to you all that has transpired. Mr Huntington is still your guardian until he signs the documents I have prepared."

His explanation did nothing to ease her disquiet. Her breathing grew agitated. Jemima stood suddenly, too disturbed to sit still. Then as if a blanket had been thrown over her, her vision went black and she could not stop herself falling into a swoon. Next thing she knew, Milly was chaffing her wrists and Fulton was holding one of Aunt Prudence's vinaigrettes under her nose. She waved them away. "Please let me up. I must speak to Mr Stradbroke."

Milly and Fulton ceased their ministrations and sat back on either side of her.

The solicitor was on his feet, leaning over her. "Miss Hardcastle, are you quite well?"

Jemima sat up, holding onto the back of the sofa. "Yes, quite well. I do not know what made me faint. Perhaps standing up so quickly." She placed a hand on her chest, detecting her uneven heartbeat. "I beg you, Mr Stradbroke, if you hear from Mr Huntington, ask him to talk to me first before he makes a decision. Please pass onto him my most sincere regrets for my behaviour and tell him...tell him...I feel truly sorry for what happened."

Fulton blinked and sat back in surprise. Milly smiled at her, while stroking her shoulder. Mr Stradbroke nodded as he listened. "I will do my best to convey your sentiments, Miss Hardcastle. So I take it you do not know his whereabouts?"

"No, unfortunately we do not." Jemima said, and the others added their agreement

The solicitor sighed and then nodded his head slowly as if deep in thought. "Very well, it is late. I will take my leave of you. Do write to me if you have need on any further funds."

"I will, thank you, sir."

Fulton stood to show Mr Stradbroke to the door and Jemima took the opportunity to eat some bread and jam and gulp down some tea. Milly had been right, she was hungry.

"Are you sure you are feeling well?" Milly asked touching her hand briefly.

"Much better now that I have eaten."

Fulton returned to the room, brow disturbed by a frown. "Jemima, can we discuss—"

"No. I do not wish to discuss Mr Huntington at this moment."

Her voice was rather shaky, and Fulton, nodding, sat down next to Milly. They chatted quietly, while Jemima poured herself a second cup of tea. Her gaze travelled around the room, looking at anything that would stop her dwelling on Mr Stradbroke's news.

"I will turn in now," she said to them, standing up and straightening her gown.

Milly stood, too, Fulton holding her hand to assist her to stand. "I should retire for the night, also."

Fulton banked the fire, checked the doors and followed them upstairs carrying candles.

Before she could return to her room, Fulton stopped her on the landing. "You will promise me, miss, not to venture out tonight on your own."

"I will do as you ask." She turned, feeling very downcast as she opened her door. Her mood and her health appeared depressed this evening.

Fulton stopped her with a touch on her forearm. "You will find this news is not as bad as it seems."

Catching herself, she threw up a smile. "Do not mind me. I am feeling poorly, that is all." Then stepping into her room, she went to shut the door only to find Fulton blocking the way.

"I thought you wanted to be free of your guardian." Fulton wore a bland expression.

"Of course, I am very pleased to be free of my guardian," Jemima replied, shutting the door quickly so that Fulton had to step back.

CHAPTER 13

Jemima stripped off her clothes, hiccupping as she held back her
tears. Without seeing her reflection, she brushed her hair at her
dressing table. She wanted to be free. Yet she did not wish to be
cast off by Mr Huntington. It did not feel like freedom; it felt like
abandonment.

After drawing down her sheets, she climbed into bed, knowing that
while she ached to direct her own future, she found being with Milly,
Fulton and even Aunt Prudence gave some structure to her life, made
her feel valued. What would she do on her own? What would she do if
no one cared about her? Turning on her side, she shrugged the covers
higher and thought about setting up lodgings and hiring a companion.
The question arose: what would her life be? Although she had wanted
to be a scientist and many new inventions and discoveries still held her
interest, it was not the life for her.

Her sense of hurt at Mr Huntington throwing her off was
overwhelming, even though she did understand his reasons. She had
behaved abominably. He probably did not want to see her ever again.
The tears flowed freely then. She could not stop remembering that
happy week at the Horton's, the conversation, the embrace, the kiss.

Sitting up, she lit the candle. On her bedside table, a decanter of wine stood with a small glass beside it. She had not ordered it placed there and did not usually drink wine before bed. However, after the night's events she was in need. After pouring a generous portion, she drank it in three swallows. Languor came upon her quickly. She blew out the candle and covered herself with the blanket, falling asleep in moments.

The dream pounced on her in the dark of night. It grabbed hold of her and would not be shaken free. More potent than the previous dreams, with detail more exact, she found herself bound to an altar. Cold stone pressed against the naked skin of her back. Her ankles were tied down in such a fashion as to spread her thighs apart. The remains of a shredded white gown covered parts of her body. Cool damp air teased her skin. Her wrists were above her head, one each side, anchored also to the stone table. All around her was a heady chant of words that sounded like butchered Latin.

Incense smoke curled upwards from six huge censers, infiltrating her nostrils. Torches spluttered in their holders attached to the bare stone walls. The scent of perfume on the air barely disguised the dank musty spell of the place. Then before her standing at the base of the altar, stood a figure cloaked in black. She screamed when she saw him, trembling with cold and fear.

Face in shadow, she did not recognise him, except for the medallion around his neck, partially obscured. He pushed the hood of his black cloak back, revealing his blond hair unbound. His eyes glittered as they travelled over her barely clothed form. He wet his lips with his tongue, like some figure from a horrible gothic tale.

Terror made her forget her near nakedness and the shame it should have made her feel to be thus exposed. He ran a hand across her belly, stroking down. She cried out in fright. "Fear not, my lovely." His voice sounded far away and was heavy like syrup. "It is not time yet to take what is mine. What you offer me is very tempting, but I need something more."

He brought forth a jewel-encrusted goblet, not dissimilar to a chalice used in the sacrament, and brought it close to her face. "You see I need your virgin blood."

Jemima screamed as he leaned in close, mouth open to bite her neck, teeth elongating. She sat up, feeling a burning sensation on her cheek. Heaving in huge breaths, candlelight dazzled her. Fulton stood there holding a light. "Jemima?"

When she could talk, she gasped out. "Oh, thank god, Fulton. You saved me from an awful place."

"Place? But you were here in your bed. It was but a dream."

Jemima stared at him, mouth slightly agape. Again, she took in a deep breath, steadying her nerves. "I know it was a dream, yet it was more than a dream. Nothing could be that real. It was like I was held in a magic spell. Longhurst wanted my blood. He nearly sucked it out of me like a vampire."

Fulton reached out to pat her shoulder. "There, there, Miss. It was only a nightmare, brought on by anxiety."

Jemima shook her head. "No, it was more than that I tell you. It was black magic. A ritual like I have read about. David told me he wanted to be a magician. I fear he has become something worse, a sorcerer, a worker of dark arts."

"Now, now miss, it is all just fancy."

"Is it? I do not like to entertain the idea myself. I do not like things I cannot explain because it opens up this world to questions, to things that cannot be controlled." She grabbed hold of Fulton's hand and squeezed it. "That is much more frightening, believe me."

"Now calm yourself. You are overwrought."

"Am I? My hairbrush went missing and next you know he broke in and attacked me. He scratched my skin, taking my flesh away under his fingernail. Tonight, he wanted my blood. Does that not sound like something sinister to you? Something that could be black magic?"

"But it was a dream. I heard you call out and came straight away."

Jemima released his hand. "Fulton, it is not the first time he has reached into my dreams, but this was the most real, the strongest pull on me. How I wish we could find Mr Huntington and return to Willow Park. I do not like it here. I am afraid."

Fulton stroked her hair with his free hand. "There is some wine here. Will you not take some? It will calm your nerves."

"Yes, I will, thank you. Although, I took some before the dream came upon me. Come to think of it, I became very tired after I drank. I do not know who put it there for I did not order it."

Fulton removed his hand from hers and poured out a glass. Before handing it to her, he swirled the glass and inhaled. "What is it?"

Returning the glass to the tray, he said, "Something is not right with this wine. Corked perhaps. Let me go downstairs and bring you up some port wine. It is sweet and will soothe you."

He took the tray away with him. Soon after, he returned with a single glass of port. He watched over her while she drank it off. He waited a few more moments, then went to the window, looked out before closing it and locking it tight. Had the other wine been drugged? Was there a scientific explanation for her dream and David's presence in it?

"Good night, Jemima," he said softly as he closed the door.

This time Jemima fell asleep and no dreams assailed her.

In the morning, Jemima did not want to get out of bed. She had been abandoned by her guardian for her behaviour, and she had to apologise to the impossible aunt. She truly felt alone in the world. Would Fulton even guard her now that his benefactor had freed himself of responsibility for her?

Milly knocked on her door. "Please come down. Fulton says we must go on another excursion."

She poked her head in the gap in the door, seeing Jemima sitting at her dressing table still undressed for the day. "Can I help you dress?"

Milly was dressed very prettily in a white dress with soft pink embroidered roses along the bodice. The handiwork reminded Jemima of Fulton's work. Surely, he had not sewn on her clothes. Jemima shook her head. No that would be most inappropriate. "I will be down soon. Please let Aunt Prudence know that I am very sorry for my outburst and am ready to apologise."

Milly smiled. "I will, though I did think she deserved it. I wish I had the same audacity as you sometimes."

Milly's companionable comment lifted Jemima's spirits and allowed her to dress with some care as to what she was wearing. Aunt Prudence was less welcoming.

"I accept your apology with reluctance. Seeing that my nephew is soon to wash his hands of you, I will exert myself no longer in trying to put you in the way of a good husband." So Aunt Prudence had heard the news.

"I appreciate it, aunt," Jemima managed to say, although the words were difficult to get out, over the hurt she felt. She did not wish to be reminded that Mr Huntington, she dared not think of him as Edward, was desirous to be rid of her.

Try as she might, she had not been able to see how the situation could have worked any other way. At least, with her deception she had gotten to know him as a stranger might. Had she introduced herself as she should have done, he would have packed her off immediately, and they would have never known each other on the same intimate terms. While she was miserable in his rejection of her, she did not regret that they had spent a week together at the Horton's and that he had kissed her. This was a rather tremendous realisation that caused her to sit down and request a cup of tea.

❦

"Where are we going?" Jemima asked Fulton as he led her and Milly down the front steps.

"We are going somewhere you know quite well. We are going to take tea this afternoon with Miss Blake."

Jemima gaped at him, until she made the connection. "Of course, Mr Huntington went to see her. She may know something. Why did I not think of her? I am sure she will have gotten over her disappointment about the letter by now."

Fulton grinned at her. "She did not mention it to me when we corresponded."

Jemima slipped her arm through Milly's. "That is wonderful news. I am looking forward to seeing her." Her own comment surprised her. She was going to meet Mr Huntington's former mistress. Yet, she had such a close acquaintance with Miss Blake and had adjusted herself to the circumstances that she had got over her jealously enough to continue their former friendship.

The school was as she remembered it, though no students paced in the small grounds. The window boxes were full of begonias and the window casements had all been newly painted white. They had been rather scruffy a month or so earlier. She remembered that Mr Huntington's correspondence gave approval for some maintenance to the school. She had been rather focussed at the time in making her forgery so had not paid it much mind. Now, she realised that Mr Huntington was perhaps Miss Blake's or the school's benefactor.

Gray, the old manservant, opened the door to them and ushered them into Miss Blake's small sitting room. Her former school mistress stood up from the sofa as they entered and rushed over to embrace Jemima, who entered before the others.

Holding her at arm's length, she gazed earnestly into Jemima's face, a slight frown marring her near perfect brow. "I am so pleased to see you, dearest girl." Releasing her, she led her former student to sit by her on the sofa. "What brings you to London? I understood from Mr Huntington that you were at Willow Park."

Jemima did her best not to blush but did not succeed, her cheeks burning despite her best efforts. "That is a long story. First, let me introduce to you to my friends, Miss Millicent Smythe-Jones and Mr Fulton." Both Milly and Fulton had entered the room and had stood quietly by while Miss Blake reacquainted herself with Jemima. Milly curtseyed. Fulton held his cap in his hand and bowed his head.

"Pray do sit down," Miss Blake said in a most welcoming manner. "Any friends of Mr Huntington are welcome here."

After the introductions, Miss Blake welcomed a tea tray from Gray and time was taken up as she poured them all a cup and served them some very moist lemon cake. Conversation was restricted to the weather and in complimenting the cake, until everyone had relaxed somewhat. "So, Jemima, did you enjoy your time at the Horton's?"

Jemima gazed down at her hands, not daring to look the older woman in the face. "I did, although it did not work out as I expected."

Jemima snuck a look at her former school mistress. Miss Blake raised that eyebrow of hers, an expression with which Jemima was familiar. To avert a scolding, even a gentle one, she changed the subject. "You have heard, of course, that Sylvia Horton is to be married."

Putting down her tea cup on the side table, Miss Blake delicately wiped her mouth with a serviette before replying. "Yes, she wrote to me. I understand that the nuptials will take place in two weeks. The family are wasting no time, are they?"

"I suppose you are right. I forgot to let Sylvia know my change of address. I must write to her straight away. I would not like to miss out on my invitation to the wedding."

Miss Blake leaned over and patted her hand. "Why are you in London? I am surprised Mr Huntington let you out of his sight, considering the circumstances."

Jemima did blush again, feeling very uncomfortable. She looked away, unable to make eye contact. "You allude, of course, to that dreadful letter."

Miss Blake nodded. "Yes, the letter."

Jemima shifted so she was facing Miss Blake and looked her in the eye, the way Miss Blake had taught her to. "Do forgive me, Miss Blake, for deceiving you."

Miss Blake smiled sweetly and then her expression turned serious. "I have already and so has Mr Huntington, after we discussed your behaviour at length. I do believe he considers himself at fault for not taking the time to pay closer attention to your upbringing. Being a bachelor, he is quite ignorant of the needs of a young lady, particularly in the social sense."

Jemima's mouth fell open, which she proceeded to shut and then did not know where to look.

Fulton coughed, into his elegantly gloved hands, reminding them that he and Milly were present and there for a reason.

"Speaking of Mr Huntington, have you heard from him, Miss Blake, since you saw him last?" Fulton asked as he placed his cup on the tea tray. Jemima noted his genteel tones and was puzzled by it.

Miss Blake looked at them one by one, as if trying to solve a riddle. "No, I have not. Why is there something amiss?"

Fulton avoided answering. "Did he say anything about what his plans were?"

Miss Blake frowned and turned to Jemima, her gaze searching. "Why to Willow Park. He said he was off there as soon as may be. Wait, he did mention that he had one appointment, some charity case that he was working on and then he was to leave."

"When was that? Can you recall?"

Miss Blake focussed her attention on Fulton. "It would have been Tuesday last. I am sure. Do tell me, has there been an accident? Is he hurt?"

"We do not know?" Jemima whispered.

"What?" Miss Blake blurted in distressed tones. She then took out a handkerchief and wiped her eyes. "Forgive my reaction. We have been acquainted for some time. I owe him so much. To think that something might have happened to him. Well, it is too distressing to consider."

"We do not know what has befallen him," Fulton said. "He did not return to Willow Park as he planned. We have come to London to find some trace of him and render him assistance if needs be."

"Oh, dear me. That is dreadful." She sat there thinking for a few moments. "Yes, I can add nothing more. He had one appointment."

"I knew it!" Jemima blurted.

Fulton turned to her. "Now do not jump to conclusions, Miss Jemima."

Fulton focussed his attention on Miss Blake. "We thank you for meeting with us and for the delectable tea. Your own blend of black tea is it not, with just a hint of lemon zest?"

Miss Blake blushed. "Why yes. What a discerning palate you have Mr Fulton. And pray do not thank me as it was nothing. The pleasure was all mine. I only wished your tidings were gladder. You will keep me informed of your progress, won't you?"

Fulton stood and bowed low to her. "You have been most helpful. Our thanks to you. If we have any news we will let you know as soon as we can."

After bidding each other adieu, Miss Blake showed them to the door herself. Before Jemima left, Miss Blake grasped her hand and squeezed it. "I do wish you and Mr Huntington all the best for the future."

Jemima blinked. "Thank you, Miss Blake. I am sure we will find him, and all will be well." Miss Blake waved to them from the door until they reached the pavement.

Out on the street, the carriage Fulton had hired waited, although it was only a short walk to their accommodation. "Now Fulton, you must agree that we should speak with that woman again."

"Leave it to me, miss. I will get the information out of her."

On the way home, they stopped the carriage at a strange house on a dingy lane off Edgware Road, which proved to be Bess's home. Milly and Jemima watched as Fulton knocked on the door. It opened a fraction and there was an exchange of words. Fulton headed back, shoulders hunched after obviously being refused admission. While they sat in the carriage waiting for him, Jemima did her best to assess the establishment. Plans set themselves up in her head. She would get in, either through the front door or otherwise. She carefully noted an open window and the sturdiness of the cast iron downpipes, a good escape route, if necessary, and a way in if her first option did not work. Not only did Bess have good taste in clothes but her rented home had robust plumbing with ornate hopper heads, which would be very useful for grabbing hold of during a climb.

Jemima said nothing to Fulton when he rejoined them. He held his shoulders tight and his mouth in a grim line as he eased himself into his seat. He was not happy. She did not blame him for being so. Jemima kept her gaze on the building until it was out of sight and, then returning her attention to her companions, she noticed that Milly glanced between them both with an air of expectation.

When no one ventured to speak, Milly said baldly. "I am sure all will be fine. Jemima and I could call on her tomorrow, before lunch."

Jemima nodded but Fulton cut her off with a savage swipe of his hand. Milly jumped in her seat surprised by the sudden movement. "That is out of the question. Ladies do not visit bawdy houses at any time of the day."

The carriage jerked as the driver released the brake, and they went directly home. Fulton appeared to expect an argument and sat there slightly dumbfounded when neither of them ventured a further word. Milly because she did not wish to anger him, and Jemima because she refused to give out information or make him suspicious of her plans. In fact, she turned on him the most innocent of her expressions.

That afternoon a selection of their admirers called again. Jemima was too excited to sit still and entertain them. Her distraction may have wounded the pride of one or two of them. That was neither here or there, as Jemima had schemes brewing and could not be fussed with paying attention to youths who professed their love so easily. For once she was thankful for Aunt Prudence's presence, even though she turned a blind eye, actually shifted her body so she could not see Mr Henkel, who had come alone, try to embrace her. Outraged, she shoved him away. He sat there gaping at her, surprised by her strength.

Dinner was a slow affair. Aunt Prudence professed to being tired and did not speak hardly a word. Jemima thought this was more likely a result of her guardian's disavowal of her and sulked as a result. Only Milly and Fulton were animated at the table. Milly talking about an item she intended to knit and the yarn she desired to purchase to complete it. Fulton listened keenly, asking her what stitches she would employ. Jemima wanted to kick him under the table but could not reach. He would give the game away if he kept on. As a man he should have no knowledge of needle work or knitting. Milly was no simpleton and would figure out that Fulton could sew and knit with the best of them. It was not a long leap from there to figuring out Jemima's ignorance in such matters.

Fulton grew quiet, finally catching a look from Jemima. Aunt Prudence pulled out her work after the dinner things were cleared away, requesting Milly to join her. Jemima was not invited. She stood there glancing awkwardly between Fulton and the two women at table.

To cover the awkwardness of the situation, Jemima ventured to say, "Forgive me for not joining you, ma'am. I have a slight headache and will take myself off to bed directly. If that is all right with you."

Aunt Prudence looked up from her work. "Very well dear. I do hope you feel better in the morning." The delivery of this comment could not hide the insincerity behind it.

"Good night, Jemima," Milly added, a bright smile as she drew out some green thread and eagerly threaded her needle.

Jemima did put herself to bed early, with every intention of getting up again when the house grew quiet. She napped and ignored the tap on her door some time later. She suspected it was Fulton but did not wish to speak to him. Better she not lie to him. Better she say nothing at all and give him the impression that she had gone to sleep. He knocked again and then went away. Jemima dozed for a while, waking up every now and again to check the time.

Approaching midnight, she lit her candle and gathered her clothes together. She put on some breeches, a shirt, vest and neck cloth. Then she slid her arms into a jacket and piled her hair under a cap. With the jacket buttoned up, she could disguise her figure, although she would need a cloak to keep the mist off her. This she tied around her waist because if she wore it while she climbed out the window and down the guttering, the folds of the material would get in the way.

Carefully she peered out the window. There was no sign of Fulton below, which was a good thing, although she did wonder at it. Normally, he would be keeping watch, protecting her from attackers. Perhaps now Mr Huntington no longer cared for her, he had relaxed his guard. Nevertheless, she opened the window, stuck her head out and assessed the piping and the dark nooks in the brick work, which would make good footholds. Turning around, she lowered her body out of the window and moved her foot around to find a niche to put her toes.

She found purchase, and made a slow, careful descent. Her foot slipped once or twice. Luckily, she did not fall, despite her sweaty hands and quivering limbs. She was seriously out of practice, as she had not climbed a tree or scurried over a dry-stone wall since she was banished from Willow Park. The guttering provided some leverage to ease her down to street level, the roof of a shed giving her a break fall if she needed it. The roof was a bit dilapidated and barely held her weight when she placed her foot on a roof tile. Yet, it made the descent easier than she had hoped. Looking about her, she was still alone. She prayed that Fulton would not choose that moment to take up his place of vigilance.

Jumping the last few feet from the window sill of the shed, she rolled to absorb the impact, hoping not to land in muck. Fortunately, the lane was quite dry, with only a few traces from the horses. These she avoided. Untying the cloak from her waist, she swung it across her shoulders and secured it before setting off.

From the ground, she looked up at her window and wondered how she would get up again. She would worry about it later. The thought did occur to her that Longhurst must have some supernatural powers to leap from the window and disappear without a trace. Shaking her head, she slipped into the shadows, in case Fulton had arrived on the scene. Then when there was no sign of him, she ran to the end of the lane to the intersection. Shivering, she gathered her cloak around her and set off down the road.

Despite the firmness of her plans, this was the first time she had ever ventured out at night on her own. Courage in action was a lot harder than in mind. A dog barked as she passed a gate, making her squeak in fright. The sound of a tomcat screeching startled her and nearly made her cry out. Shivering, she huddled further into her cloak, hoping to avoid meeting anyone on the street. What kind of rescuer was she to be quaking in fear? She had to have greater courage than that if she was going to rescue Mr Huntington.

She reached Bess's home and found a position in the shadows to watch the house. The door opened about ten minutes after she settled herself. A man drew on his cloak and the door shut behind him. A client, she thought. To her amazement, the reality that Bess really was a prostitute struck her hard. Her mind was caught up in the how, and the what, that could possibly transpire within those doors between Bess and her clients.

Did Bess offer them tea first or did she invite them to ravage her as soon as the door shut? Did she engage in conversation? She imagined that Miss Blake would have when she was occupied with similar activities as she was so educated and refined. Shaking her head, she thought the better of it because that led her to think of Mr Huntington kissing and touching the attractive Miss Blake, the older woman. All kinds of jealous feelings overcame Jemima. Did this mean that she herself was attracted to her guardian? She thought back to their week at the Horton's. Yes, it was obvious that was the case so there was no use in denying it to herself. Luckily, the attraction had been mutual. Had being the operative word, for that was all to be forgotten, with Mr Huntington now ready to throw her off. Jemima had well and truly wiped that slate clean. Mr Huntington had nothing but anger and disdain for her now.

Still gazing up at the attic window, she wondered if she should climb up there or be brazen and knock at the door and seek admittance. Perhaps she should try her luck, pass herself off as a man. If that did not work, she would fall back on the other plan—the one to climb to that window. The prevaricating client slunk away and was soon lost in the shadows.

With heart thumping hard in her chest, she walked up to the door and knocked. Soon after, an old woman opened the door, peering at her through heavy lidded eyes. "Yes?"

Jemima sucked in a breath and consciously lowered her voice. "Mr Brown to see Miss Harrington."

The old woman's gaze roved about as if she could not quite focus on her. "Do you have an appointment?"

"Ah...no...I...er...was hoping...my first time and all that."

The old woman considered, breathing quietly while her odd gaze roamed over Jemima's form.

"Wait here," the old woman said at last and then shut the door in her face. Jemima had not tried to talk in a deep voice before. She came out sounding rather adolescent. She hoped that fit the look of her. The porch was not well lit, and the cloak hid her shape. The old woman appeared nearly blind, so Jemima stood there, hope rising in her heart.

About five minutes later the door opened again. The old woman poked her head out the door.

"Miss Harrington will see you for two pounds." Jemima did not react the cost, not knowing if it was reasonable or not for the type of services Bess provided.

Jemima fished around for some coins and plonked them in the old lady's hand.

"Follow me," she said after securing the coins in her apron. The door swung wider. Jemima stepped inside, waited while the old woman bolted the door behind them. Jemima noted that a locked door would slow her escape.

Inside was a kitchen, with a small fire and simple furniture. A rocking chair, a bag of knitting and a kettle gently steaming in the fire place indicated that this was where the old woman passed her time. "This way, upstairs," the old woman said. Her gait was rather lopsided as she dragged herself up the stairs, one riser at a time. Jemima followed behind, half-expecting to catch the woman when she finally over-balanced.

The third landing was achieved, and the old woman's breathing laboured with effort. Jemima grew increasingly out of breath with the exertion but felt more relaxed than she did walking the streets alone. Something about the old woman's presence calmed her, made her feel at home. She wondered whether all the men who came there to see Bess experienced the same thing. If so, the woman was well worth the expense. Unless, of course, she was a relation and then the situation would be scandalous. Imagine a mother or an aunt, profiting from their young female relations as she plied her trade, sold her body to men for money.

As they travelled up the stairs, Jemima thought they were headed to the room with the small window, the attic. She swelled with pride that she had picked their destination and had already worked out how to escape from it, if needed.

The old woman knocked on the rather small door and on hearing the word 'enter,' opened it. Standing on the threshold, she moved to the side so Jemima could enter. The room was poorly lit, so Jemima had to squint to see something of the room. Once inside, the old woman drew the door shut, and her clumping steps could be heard descending the stairs. In the room, shadows loomed and dark curtains covered the walls, giving it a strange air. Also, with so many curtains, Jemima could not see the small window she had seen from the outside. Jemima took a few more steps into the centre of the space. She turned slightly, taking in the day bed on which reclined Bess, dressed in a fine silk night gown of pale pink that showed more than it hid. The cloth of her gown fell to the ground in graceful folds. It was a pretty picture, alluring, daring and she supposed suggestive.

"Bess," Jemima said in her young man's voice.

"Come in, sit down by me." Bess beckoned with her hand, waving Jemima closer.

When Jemima drew near, extending her own hand to shake, Bess tugged her forward by her fingers tips, drawing her down beside her. Her rear had only touched the chaise, when Bess's lips drew close to kiss her.

Jemima sucked in a breath as Bess, reached into her mouth with her tongue, her hands aggressively touching her. Jemima reacted, standing up suddenly. She had not even taken off her cloak.

Bess gazed at her, her eyes travelling from the top of her head to the tips of her boots. "Definitely your first time. I will make it easy for you."

Bess rose to her feet elegantly, then slipped the straps of her gown down over her shoulders, letting one well-formed breast fall out, followed by the other. Her skin was white and creamy. Jemima was fascinated, not seeing another's body before but her own. Her nipples were large and brown, pulled into tight knots. Her skin was like milk, her delicate navel a dark hollow in the firm flesh of her stomach. "It will be over quickly, Mr Brown, if you relax now and lie back on the chaise, you will not even need to take off your clothes. I can do that for you."

Jemima dumbly did as she was told, not quite sure when she should speak up. Something about this moment fascinated her. How did a woman seduce a man? Would it be useful information or just morbid curiosity? She was about to find out. Bess stood in front of her, sliding the gown over her hips, and stepped free of the pooling cloth at her feet. Jemima was spell bound. Bess looked beautiful, like some Greek statue gracing the edge of a pool. The woman was so calm, her skin so smooth and she really was at ease being naked in front of a man. Jemima shook her head. She herself could not imagine herself being so bold, so at ease in her own skin.

Bess leaned down to kiss her again, placing her hands either side of Jemima's arms. The kiss was deep, penetrating and oddly arousing. Bess closed her eyes, running her hands over Jemima's head, accidentally dislodging the cap that held Jemima's hair and then continued the caress along down to her hips. The hand groped about the junction of her breeches. Bess suddenly pulled back. "What the hell!"

Jemima sat up, her hair falling down to her waist. "Oh dear." Hands on her hot cheeks failed to cool their heat.

'A woman? Here?"

Jemima nervously ran her fingers through her hair, her gaze looking everywhere except at the naked woman. "I do beg your pardon. I had to speak to you and this seemed the best way."

Bess gaped at her. Then her countenance changing to severe, she placed her hands on her generous hips. "Speak to me?"

"Yes. Just talk, but I was uncertain how to begin and you er...started to..."

Jemima glanced at her, eyes travelling up and down, taking in the flawless skin. Had Mr Huntington enjoyed touching those breasts? Had he found ecstasy between those long legs? Before her thoughts run away with her, Bess let out an expletive and turned to grab a Chinese robe, to cover her nakedness.

"You want to have sex with a woman?" Bess was at first outraged at the thought, then calmed, her eyes assessing Jemima in a most forthright way. "I have not been so lucky in a while. I will oblige you. I like the look of you."

Jemima's eyes widened. "Heavens forbid, no such thing." Throwing out a placating arm, she reiterated. "No, no. I wanted to talk to you, truly."

Bess stood taller, hand still resting on her hips, the part in her gown opening wider. "Talk to me. About what? What could you have to talk to be me about at this time of night, dressed like that?" Bess frowned at her. "You are not someone's wife are you, come to attack her husband's mistress? I have protection you know. I will not stand for a scene right now. I am a busy woman."

Jemima stood up. "No, I am not a jealous wife...I want to talk to you about my guardian."

Bess sat down on an adjacent armchair, tucking her robe about her to hide her nudity.

"Guardian. That is a new one."

Jemima met her gaze. "You have met him. Mr Edward Huntington."

Bess sucked in a breath at the mention of the name. "It was you in the park, you walking close by when I met that Fulton chap? I told your friend, and I will tell you I never met the man."

Jemima frowned and shook her head. "So you say...but you know what happened to him. You must know what happened to him. As far as we can tell you were the last person he saw before he disappeared."

Her eyes widened. "You cannot possibly know that."

"All the evidence leads to you. We have been down every other trail."

Bess stood up and paced the room, pausing at the window. She shifted the curtain and looked out. "It is dangerous for you here. Best you leave now while you still can."

Jemima stood up, trying to push her hair back under the cap. Her gaze went to the candle, caught by the shine of some object on the table beneath it. There she saw the medallion. The full design was before her—a stylised cross with wings on it. Pieces of the puzzle fell into place. That design matched the imprint from the intruder's footprint from Willow Park. She kept looking and mentally matched the edges to the medallion David Longhurst had worn. It matched the one she saw in her dream.

Her gaze flicked up to fix on Bess. "Are you an acquaintance of David Longhurst?"

Bess swung around. "You dare speak his name. What kind of little fool are you? Get out now while you still can."

"I will leave. Before I do tell me one thing, does he have Edward?"

Bess laughed. "Edward? Ahh Huntington...do you know he tried to reform me? Offered me a house and help to set me up as a seamstress. It appears his mother was a great philanthropist and he follows her example. He had no idea of what I was into and how deep. It was impossible for me to break free even if I wanted to. He could not help me. Neither can you."

"What do you mean?" Edward, a philanthropist, trying to reform Bess?

"I cannot change anything about my life."

"It is your life, you make the choices. If he tried to help you why did you not take up his offer?"

Bess came close to her, pointing to her own chest. "Help me? Hah! I love what I do—what I am. I don't want to change nothin'."

Jemima stunned said, "Truly?"

Bess laughed. "You have no idea."

Jemima nodded, seeing now in the woman some madness, some obsession. "No idea, thankfully. I think I would like more control over myself and my actions."

"So you say now. Virgin. Innocent. Wait until you have a real man."

"You are quite correct. I should wait for some empirical evidence before I make judgement."

Bess glowered at her. "You think you are so clever using big words, but you really do not understand." She pointed at her chest proudly. "I was the bait, the lure. It was all set up to capture him. I was never in want of changing my ways."

"So Mr Huntington came here? Where is he? Please tell me?" Jemima was ready, ready to run to wherever he was.

There was a sound by the window. Bess flinched as if someone had snapped a whip over her head. Then heavy footsteps echoed in the room. A curtain billowed and parted. Mist rolled along the floor as if a fog had rolled in from the river and entered of its own accord.

"You have said enough," David's disembodied voice said.

Bess let out a terrified squeak, body poised and still as stone. From the direction of the window Longhurst strode further into the room and into the light, his cape whirling around his long legs.

As if suddenly released, Bess cringed away from him, turning her face away, covering it with a folded arm. "Forgive me," she said, meek and cowed by David's presence alone.

At the same time, Jemima gasped, the full recollection of his intrusion into in her dreams, making the blood thump in her veins. She could hardly breathe as trepidation constricted her chest. Where did this man get this power to influence those around him? It was not scientifically possible. Although frightened, her gaze darted around the room looking for some mechanism, some means that would explain how he had arrived so calm, his cloak billowing, complete with roiling mist.

She stepped away from the chaise, knees feeling weak. "David."

He grinned, his eyes glittering as his gaze travelled over her, assessing, intimidating, intruding and seeing deeper than they aught. "Yes, me. Did you think you could clumsily seek out your uncle without me knowing about it? I watched as you and that fool Fulton bumbled about, travelling to factories and your old school, seeking your little clues, little puzzles that you could not decipher. Yet now, you have come too close, little one. I knew you would come, of course, and I have permitted it because you have something I want."

Jemima thought of the dream and prayed that it was not true, that the words he had said then were the dark conjuring of her mind. "What do you want?"

He stepped toward her in a swirl of cloak. "But you know that already." He pointed to Bess and whipped his hand in Jemima's direction. "Prepare her."

Bess leaped forward and grabbed Jemima's wrist, twisting it so that Jemima fell back on the chaise. Was David's movement just a gesture or was there unnatural force in the movement? Was David indeed a magician? Bess's grip was strong Jemima found when she could not free herself. Surely such a slight a woman could not be so muscular on her own without some augmentation.

Once she was subdued, David rushed forward, pulling out some rope to bind her legs, while Bess held her down. Frightened now, Jemima kicked and writhed, knocking Bess in the face. The pause where Bess registered the hit, gave Jemima the chance to break free. The woman shook herself, aiming a stunning slap across Jemima's face and then she sat on Jemima's stomach, winding her. Bess grabbed her by the hair, forcing her head back. David tied her legs down and then rushing to the head of the sofa, he poured liquid down her throat, holding her nose and mouth shut until she had no choice but to swallow. Soon after the potion went down, the room swirled around her head, making her feel dizzy. Jemima felt them pull her right arm out straight and roll up her sleeve. It was if she had no strength in her limbs or even the will to move them.

"No, no, no," Jemima said, not being able to mutter more than denial.

"Bring the chalice," David said over his shoulder to Bess.

Backing away, Bess nodded and went to a cupboard, which had previously been disguised by the drapery. Taking out a large golden chalice, remarkably like the one in Jemima's dream, Bess returned to the chaise.

As she walked toward Jemima, a visual distortion made her body appear to undulate like a snake. The drug was playing havoc with Jemima's senses. Feelings of nausea and euphoria changed places with rapidity.

Bess held the chalice as David kissed a knife he brandished in front of Jemima's face. He began a chant, words achingly familiar from her dream. She watched as he drew the knife across her skin, slicing her vein, as would a doctor in order to release the humours from the body.

Jemima's vision swam as the blood flowed in two streams either side of her elbow into the chalice. At first it bled quickly and then lessened. The chalice held the dark crimson liquid, her essential essence. After a nod from David, Bess took some cloth and bound her wound.

Bess knelt beside the chaise, gazing longingly into David's face. "What will you do with her? Take her with you?"

David nodded and removed the chalice, waving it under his nose and inhaling it like one would a good vintage.

Bess stood back and opened her robe. Her look was full of worship.

"Before I leave, my eager trollop, I will give you your reward." He placed the chalice on the table as he stood.

Bess's eyes widened, and she backed away from him, face full of rapture and anticipation. David advanced on Bess, and she tore her robe from her shoulders when her back slammed against the wall. David surged forward with unnatural speed, aiming his mouth at the side of her neck and then biting down when his lips met her flesh. Bess moaned as he bit her, her knees bending.

He released her neck, blood snaking in a small trail over her collar bone and down her front. Their bodies joined.

Jemima realised what they were doing, what she was witnessing and tried to turn her head away but found she could not. Bess moaned louder, her voice rising higher. Finally, she cried out. When he stepped away from her, she fell to her knees and kissed his feet.

Then abruptly he pushed her away. "Enough for you. You will drain me. I have better things to do." He whirled around, sending his cloak flying about him like dark wings.

He approached Jemima on the couch. "Getting an education, are we? You missed your chance to escape. I have other uses for you. Fear not though. The ultimate end is for you to be my slave. I will own you body and soul."

He took the chalice from the table and sipped the warm blood. "Tasty," he said, licking his lips. "I need this to complete my incantation and when that is done I can do what I want with you."

A loud thumping sounded from below causing him to startle. Shouts and a scream pierced the night. "The law?" Bess said, eyes wide. "It is the law."

David stood up, listening. "Police or some other unwelcome intruder. Time to go."

Bess threw herself at him, wrapping her arms around his knees. "Take me with you. Oh please take me with you. I can bear the separation no longer. I am yours. Take me."

David shook his head and kicked free of her. Tucking the chalice close to his chest, he strode to the window. "Find your own way out." Then he was gone.

David was there one minute and gone the next. Bess wailed and writhed on the ground, without the wit to cover herself or even to run away. Shadowed man shapes invaded the room and Jemima heard her name called as her awareness winked out.

The next time she saw candle light, she had come awake in her own bed with a savage headache. Milly stroked her brow from her perch on the edge of her bed. Jemima had no recollection of being rescued by Fulton, of seeing him there, though she was certain it was him.

"You are safe now," she whispered, kissing Jemima softly on the forehead. Jemima's arm ached. She lifted it to see the bandage. The incident did happen. That awful scene did occur. On first waking, she thought perhaps she had dreamed the whole. But the encounter had happened. The blood taking, and the hints that Longhurst held Mr Huntington.

Milly rose from the bed to fetch something from the side table and came back again. Leaning over she held a glass. "Here drink this. It is warm water. Nothing more. It will help flush that drug from your system."

"Bess?"

"I am sorry. I cannot say, and I do not know all the details. Ambrose said I should wait before telling you anything at all."

Jemima took a sip of the water. It tasted sour on her tongue. "Who is Ambrose?"

Milly blushed. "Ambrose is Fulton. Who else could it be?"

Jemima nodded, still feeling very vague. "Oh...I see."

"But did she reveal where Edward is? I mean Mr Huntington?"

Milly shook her head then turned to the door when it opened. Fulton entered the room, clasped Milly's hand and then ushered her out, whispering to her as they passed close to each other. Milly left the door ajar.

Jemima struggled to sit up. "Fulton, I am so sorry. You were so right. Do I have you to thank for saving me?"

Fulton stepped up to her bed and clung to Jemima's hand, squeezing it hard. "There is no need to thank me. We can talk more when you are feeling better."

She noted a bruise under his chin and the scrape of a fingernail on his cheek "What happened to Bess? Did she reveal all she knew?"

Fulton frowned and looked at her hand, playing with her finger tips. He sighed once or twice before he spoke. "Bess ranted some strange words, screamed curses at us before she threw herself to the ground from the attic window. She will speak no more."

Jemima sat up, her head spinning. "She did what?" Dead? Bess dead? Jemima found it hard to believe.

Fulton looked her in the eye. "She killed herself rather than be caught. The old woman who worked with her will not speak either. She is overcome with grief. The police think that she is Bess's mother, or close kin."

The reality of what had occurred hit Jemima. "She killed herself rather than speak? I had not thought...I did not...Heavens. I did not think that David had the power of life or death over her, but he must. She worshiped and feared him."

"Longhurst was there? While you were under the influence of that drug you talked about that Longhurst fellow. Did he molest you?"

"Yes, he did this," she indicated her arm. "He has other plans for me. If you had not saved me, he would have borne me away. Maybe to where he has Mr Huntington."

"It is confirmed then, this blackguard Longhurst is involved? So very sinister after all."

Jemima nodded and whispered. "What have we fallen into?"

Fulton pushed her back down to her pillow and raised the bedclothes higher. "Some very serious trouble, miss. Now you must rest. I believe Mr Huntington to be still alive, otherwise his body would have shown up by now."

Putting her hand to her head, she quietly and brokenly related to Fulton what she recollected of the conversation with Longhurst, the blood taking, the hints and threats. She had the presence of mind to tell of the neck biting. "Do you think he has him and that he is alive?"

Fulton paced the room, rubbing his hand over his freshly shaven head. "Why would they court trouble otherwise? He must be of some use to them."

Fulton passed the water to her again, and Jemima sipped it. The headache was improving, but she still felt fatigued. "David mentioned he needed my blood for an incantation. I thought, Mr Huntington was a scientific man. He did not dabble in the dark arts did he, Fulton?"

"Not to my knowledge, miss. He associated with scientific and medical types. I think it must be his inventions they are after, or his scientific knowledge. He has a powerful knack when it comes to machines. Then there is that power source he invented."

Jemima sat back thinking. The gemstones. There had been some experimentation recently. She could not recall who had written the article she had read. She had seen the glowing jewel in Fulton's leg so knew that it worked. The prosthesis was a melding of flesh and machine. Could the same be achieved with magic? Magic and machines. Could such a hybrid be created? It was very hard to think clearly as her head was murky as a sewer and equally polluted. For what purpose would such a device be put?

Fulton stood there watching her, seeing the play of her thoughts on her face. Gazing up at him, she smiled weakly. "I am glad you think him still alive." Elbowing her way further up the pillows, she remembered something important. "Another thing you should know, David seemed to know all our movements, all our steps as if he could see all that we do and say. He is laughing at us. Have any of the enquiries you sent out concerning him returned anything useful?"

Again, Fulton paced the length of the room. His shoulders hunched, and his fists clenched. She assumed he did not like that David knew so much and they knew so little. Jemima did not like it herself, being outsmarted, feeling stupid. She had taken risks and they had not gained much at all, only an inkling that her guardian still lived and that Longhurst possibly held him somewhere, most likely in London.

"Not much," he began, pausing in his rapid pacing. "After leaving Willow Park, he went to London with his family. A year or so later, there was a terrible house fire and most of the family were killed, I understand. There it appears there is a gap in his history, like he disappeared from society. Except about six months ago, there is mention of one David Longhurst returning to this country, bringing with him a large shipment of relics from Moldavia."

Jemima wrinkled her brow, trying to recall some detail from her studies. "Moldavia? Is that not in Eastern Europe?"

"Yes, I believe so."

"What on Earth was he doing there? Is that not where vampires dwell?"

Fulton lifted an eyebrow with an expression of humour. "I do not know, miss. I do not read novels."

Jemima gave him a sour look. "I did not read it in a novel but in the newspaper. Very sickening reports, of the dead walking, of creatures who drank the blood of their kin. I wonder. David bites necks. Do you think he could be a vampire? He did take a sip of my blood, but that was from the chalice."

Unseen, Milly had slipped back into the room. "He drank your blood?" she gasped, her face pale.

Fulton stood up, went over to Milly and clasped her hands in his. "I am sure Jemima is exaggerating. Why not go downstairs now and do some sewing? It will calm your nerves. I will be down shortly. I think Miss Jemima needs to spend the day in bed. Please make the appropriate excuses to your aunt on her behalf. I am afraid we have much to explain when Jemima is well enough."

Milly nodded and, after casting a look at them, closed the door.

"I wish you would not alarm her," Fulton said with feeling.

Jemima looked at the ceiling. "It is all right for me to be alarmed then?"

"That is different, miss. You are an unnatural creature, and I am not in love with you."

Jemima frowned at him. "Oh dear. He walks in the daylight, so he cannot be a vampire, can he?"

"I have no idea. There is no such thing as the walking dead."

"But even in England, suicides are buried at the crossroads and are staked through the heart to prevent their restless souls walking."

Fulton gaped at her. "How would you know a thing like that?"

Jemima grinned. "Polite conversation, Fulton. We live in a civilised society."

With an arched eyebrow, he replied. "Quite so, but it is an old custom, mere superstition. There are no vampires."

"If you say so, but perhaps you should do some reading on the subject in case we encounter any."

Fulton sighed, his eyes rolling up toward the ceiling. "I will leave you to rest now. Sweet dreams."

The pillow Jemima tossed at him met the closed door. That man could move fast, and she swore he did not limp any more.

CHAPTER 14

E dward Huntington sat in the dank, dark room with plenty of time to consider what had transpired to bring him to this moment. Worry harried him, more for those he had left behind than for his own health. Surviving the current situation did not seem likely. What his captors wanted him to do was unspeakable.

Longhurst had taken him to see the machine he was assembling and the remains he had brought with him from the far reaches of Eastern Europe. There, with a zeal worthy of a missionary converting heathens in darkest Africa, he elaborated on his appalling vision. Longhurst thought his machinations led to power and eternal life. Yet, Edward thought they led to death and damnation. There was no road to compromise. Unable to gain his voluntary support, Longhurst kept Edward a prisoner. Bindings of salt and leather around his wrists inhibited his magical ability. He could neither free himself nor summon aid.

A rattle near the door alerted him to someone opening the small hatch. A pale sliver of light penetrated the darkness. A hand shoved a tray through the opening. Edward sat there on the floor, looking at the food until hunger overrode his caution. His captors had drugged him more than once, usually by concealing it in his food and drink. Often they moved him in the dead of night, so that now he had no idea where he was. Although he had lost track of time with the frequent drugged hazes, he thought he had been in this particular location for a few days.

He crawled over to inspect the tray, wincing as his bound feet banged against the floor. So tight were the bindings his feet had gone numb and tingly. Breathing through the pain, he saw that the meal consisted of cold meat, stale bread and a tankard of ale. How he wished for a nice warm meal, even a broth would be good for the room was cool and he had developed a slight fever. His surroundings and lack of activity were not good for his health. No sun, no fresh air, and no liberty were wearing on his spirits. He took a chunk of meat, which tasted like mutton, and chewed slowly. It was necessary to eat and keep up his strength even though hope of rescue was slim.

Wilbur Hardcastle had said in his journals that he knew only defensive magic and that is all that Edward had learned. That and what his own talent had led him to develop. The three ancient tomes came with a warning, which he had heeded. They contained dangerous magic and, if used, would be enough to bring the attention of unsavoury entities. Wilbur had urged absolute secrecy and bade Edward to conceal them. Now, with some regret, he looked back on the last four years and wondered how his encounter with the sorcerer would have gone if he had been able to attack, if he had studied those texts and learned deeper and more powerful magic. He had not been tempted to delve into their secrets as the wonders Wilbur had led him to had been sufficient to keep him amazed and challenged in the learning. He thought he knew a lot and now he had learned that he knew but little of magic.

Later, he dozed against the wall, images and conversations darting across his consciousness. The door opened a crack, allowing light to spill in, which brought pain to his eyes. Lifting his bound hands to shelter his gaze, he tried to make out the form standing before him.

"We meet again, Mr Huntington. I will give you one more opportunity to assist us."

A lanky, caped form stepped through the door. He recognised Longhurst's familiar raiment and general stature. Edward lifted his chin, his only show of defiance. "I told your associates as I told you that I will not assemble the machine, and I will not assist you to power or operate it. I demand you release me this instant."

Longhurst's cloaked figure nodded. His voice calm, even. "You speak as if you have rights here. Believe me you have none and exist through my mercy alone. I am afraid time has run out. Without your aid, I cannot justify your continued...incarceration."

"Then let me go."

Longhurst shook his head. "You know too much."

With his bounds arms held to his chest, Edward said, "Then do what you must. I will not traffic with you."

The calm voice spoke again. "What misplaced bravado. You care not for your person, for your life, but what of those who are close to you, those you care about. What of their safety, their lives?"

"Lucky for me there are none such. I have no close relations or friends. I spend my time alone, shunning company."

The man laughed, his silhouette showing an aquiline nose and high brow. "You think me ignorant? You think I have not studied your ways, your intimate concerns? You think I was not there at the Horton's, or at Willow Park or at Miss Blake's school."

Edward could not stop his sharp intake of breath. "No. It is not possible."

"You were carefully selected, Mr Huntington. So let us speak truth. Care you not for your half-creation, Fulton? Your aunt, your cousin?"

Edward remained silent, refusing to be baited.

"No? No protests? No begging for their lives? Impressive. What of another?"

"There is no other."

"What about young Miss Jemima Hardcastle?"

Edward's heart leaped. Surely, they could not know of her, of his duty toward her. He stayed silent, hoping to put the man off. In his heart he despaired. Longhurst had been there observing them, even at that fateful moment when he had taken Jemima and kissed her.

Edward fought for silence, even though a scream of denial ached to tear out his throat.

Longhurst waited a few moments before speaking again. "You do not wish to know of her? I saw her only last night. She is rather a sweet girl, attractive, smart...luscious."

Edward clenched his fists. "You lie. She is safe at Willow Park and well protected."

The man laughed eerily. When his mirth had died off, he spoke again, calm, certain, predatory. "You are mistaken. She is currently in London with the aunt, the cousin and the bumbling fool, Fulton. They are on a mission, you see, to rescue you."

"I do not believe you." Edward was ready to explode. If his feet were not bound, he would have leaped on the man. He tried to crawl forward.

"Save your strength." He lifted his hand and without touching him, Edward was thrown back against the wall. It was as if the wind had lifted him, yet there was none. The salt and the leather meant he could not respond in kind. "You see, you have no choice. Not only have I met Jemima, I have tasted her, I have taken her virgin blood. I know her every step. I know that even now she recovers in her room in her rented accommodation soon to be cast out by your aunt, deserted by your cousin and abandoned by your man, Fulton. The last will be my doing. I will remove him, destroy him and then dismantle him. I would know the secret of him.

"Then sweet, smart Jemima will have no one to turn to but me. You see she knows me as a childhood friend. We were once playmates at Willow Park before you came and sent her away. I could have corrupted her then, was about to until you intervened, and packed her off to school. If you value her, you will aid me."

Edward struggled with what he had heard. Could it be true? Could this man be so close to Jemima as to expose her to danger? He wanted to rant and scream.

With a sudden movement, his captor struck a light to a lantern he had brought with him. The illumination hurt Edward's eyes. The man was still a foggy outline, barely discernible through his squinting gaze.

"Agree to help us," he said, voice rising in pitch. "Write to Jemima telling her to meet you at this address, and I will make sure she is taken to safety."

Edward blinked, his gaze sharpening. His captor pushed paper, pen and ink toward him and a scrap of paper containing the words he was to copy out. Edward looked up, saw the fair hair, the pale skin. "Let me go to her and see her to safety, then I will help you, let me remove her from harm's way."

The man's head shook. "That is not possible. She is leverage and once she is abandoned by those protecting her she will be alone, helpless. Let us see which one of us she chooses."

"No!"

"Let me fetch her to you in that case. Let me show you how well I care for her."

"You do not care for her and only wish to use her."

The pale eyebrow arched, as he pushed the paper closer to Edward and unstoppered the ink.

"Having custody of her will force you to help us. If you do not, her life will be forfeit. However, she has some use. I find her most alluring, stirring my passion. She will amuse me for a short time."

The smile on Longhurst's face when he leaned forward to gaze into Edward's, forced a growl of frustration out. His words curled around his gut. Edward clenched the muscles of his jaw and knew Longhurst enjoyed the struggle within.

"My colleagues find themselves similarly aroused by her. You can guess the rest, knowing who we serve. Her innocent flesh will be a sacrifice to our dark lord and his host. All will ravage her, and her screams will serve to waken those who now lie dormant."

"No!" Edward sucked in a breath. "You cannot."

"I can. I will. I won't leave you to imagine what will happen to her as I will ensure that you are there, watching, participating in her utter annihilation as we deliver up her life's blood." Nose to nose, he hissed. "You could save her this if only you would act." Longhurst tapped the paper.

Leaning back, Edward rested his head on the cool stone wall, his heart and mind tormented by the man's words and plans. He did not doubt them. "What proof do I have that you will keep your word, that you will not expose her to your depravations if I cooperate?"

Longhurst shrugged. "I could have killed her last night, when she foolishly entered the premises of one Bess Harrington, her investigations in search of you having led her there. Dressed as a man she gained entry. I am afraid I had to drug her to take her blood. She would not give it willingly. I allowed her to live, to go free. I did this in charity. Yet, I can easily lay my hands on her, having already entered her bedroom and ravished those tender lips."

Edward realised then that the man spoke true. If Jemima had come to London in search of him and he had no doubt with her skills she could do it, Fulton would not have abandoned him and would not have deserted his post. That fit with what was possible. The letter from Bess would have been with his other mail and it would have led them to Bess and Miss Blake, too. He shook his head, amazed at Jemima's audacity.

Fear made him tremble and bile rose in his stomach for he felt suddenly very ill. "I will write your letter. Please send her to safety, I beg you. Just bring me word, proof that she is in safe hands and I will start work on the machine."

"You will have your proof tomorrow at the earliest."

Edward took his time with the letter, drawing designs in the margins, little daisies and ornate swirls and seemingly random shapes. He prayed that he was not being deceived and that the letter would reach Jemima and guide her to safety.

CHAPTER 15

After spending the previous day being indisposed and vomiting for the most part, Jemima came downstairs the next morning. While she did manage some sleep during the night, her dreams were vivid streaks of horror that she would do well to forget.

Dizziness still assailed her as she navigated around trunks arrayed in the corridor. Raised voices greeted her outside the sitting room door. She paused there, knowing that it was because of her that this situation had now come to a head. Fulton had been gracious, not letting his anger out on her, not even reprimanding her with a look. Milly was certainly a lucky woman if the manner in which Fulton contained his feelings of betrayal and anger was an example of his normal behaviour.

After sucking in a breath and garnering up her courage, Jemima pushed open the door. Aunt Prudence appeared to be in fine form, her screech at Fulton cut off at her entrance.

"You dare to show your face in here?" Demanded the aunt, rounding on her. "After your shameful act?"

Jemima quite calmly entered the room and sat down on the sofa. She had no choice really because of a sudden onset of queasiness. She leaned over and held her head in her hands. "Which particular shameful act do you mean, aunt, for there are many?" She looked up again at the aunt and felt the room spin around her.

Aunt Prudence sat down on the nearest chair with a thump. Milly had been crying and was already seated, her hands twisting the life out of a wet-looking handkerchief. Fulton stood very straight, a slight tinge of red high on his cheeks, betraying his heightened feelings. A reaction could be got out of him, she thought. She had begun to think he was a machine.

"Jemima," Fulton said, turning toward her, a welcoming smile not quite making it to his eyes. "You do not need to..."

Jemima spared him a glance. "Yes, I do. You have not told me how you found me or how I was rescued and returned to the safety of my aunt's protection. I imagine she is not ignorant of it, is that not so?" She focussed her attention on the aunt.

Aunt Prudence turned away her face. However, as they sat in silent expectation for some minutes, she turned her body slightly and seeing that all present had their attention fixed on her, she began to speak. "I was woken in the middle of the morning by Fulton banging on the front door. In his arms was you looking as pale as death. He had with him at least two uniformed policemen. Without any word of explanation, he took you up to your room, woke Milly and begged her to change you out of those...those men's clothes.

"In his high-handed way, he escorted me out of your bedroom and did not answer any of my questions. Yet, I am not stupid. I could see what you were about, dressed as a man, intoxicated to unconsciousness."

Suddenly Aunt Prudence bolted out of her seat. "Outrageous! Absolutely dreadful behaviour."

"Yes, ma'am. I agree." Jemima was not quite able to hold the other woman's gaze.

The aunt turned away and walked to the table, where she foraged in her work basket for some yarn. "I cannot even imagine what you were about." She unravelled the ball of wool, tearing at it heedlessly. "Moreover, I cannot have you in this household any longer." Realising what she was doing, she began to wind the wool back on the ball with rather vigorous movements. "My nephew was preparing to throw you off." She jerked the wool. "I will follow his lead." The yarn once again in its basket, she walked back to her seat. Sitting herself down calmly, she said, "You cannot be allowed to influence Milly more than you already have."

"But aunt," Milly interrupted. "Jemima has been nothing but kind to me."

The aunt cut her off with a slash of her hand. "Who knows to what abominations you have been exposed."

Jemima sat up straight. "Why none from me, I assure you."

The aunt heaved in a breath. "You are a changeling set among angels."

"Oh dear, aunt. Do not say such things," Milly said, scrunching her handkerchief into a ball.

Surveying her audience, she nodded her head, before speaking again. "My trust in you, Jemima, has been...been...well entirely misplaced."

Jemima looked down at her hands, feeling a wave of shame burn her face. "I see...I do apologise to you and to Milly." She lifted her gaze and regarded them in turn. "My behaviour has been very bad indeed. I will reform my ways immediately."

Aunt Prudence spluttered before continuing. "It is a bit late for that now young woman. You think that I can forget all that you have done?"

Jemima sat thoughtfully for a moment, the full weight of guilt on her shoulders. "I do not expect that much, but I would ask that you at least listen to some of my reasoning. My actions may be bad, but my motivations were good...well mostly."

Aunt Prudence, quite active in her chair, reeled back. "Really? You expect me to listen to your hastily constructed excuses?"

"Not so hastily constructed, I assure you."

Leaning forward and wagging a finger at Jemima, she continued, "That is not all that I am dark on you for. Do you think me ignorant of your other machinations? You have encouraged my darling Milly to form an attachment with that man." She gestured abruptly at Fulton, who graciously ignored the insult.

Jemima looked from Milly to Fulton. Milly lowered her head and began weeping again. Fulton showed no reaction at all, used to as he was of hiding his feelings. "Do you mean Fulton?" she turned her body to face him. "Then you finally proposed? Excellent!" Fulton did not get a chance to reply for the aunt interrupted him.

"There will be no such arrangement. Milly is destined for her cousin, and she will not marry someone so far beneath her."

Jemima blinked. "Beneath her? Fulton is a very worthy gentleman. He is not rich, but he has more funds than Milly. It is a good match for her and more importantly she loves him."

"Fiddlesticks and nonsense. She knows nothing of love." Aunt Prudence's nose went in the air.

Jemima had nothing to lose and spoke her mind. "I fear the opposite is true. It is you who knows nothing of love. Milly is a wonderful, caring woman, who deserves more than to expend her life being your companion."

Aunt Prudence gasped as if slapped. "How dare you? I mean to help her find a husband. Did not my work this last week prove this?"

"No, not entirely, because before you is her chosen match and you refuse to acknowledge it. You pretend to pursue Mr Huntington on her behalf, yet you know he is not interested. If Mr Huntington wanted her for a wife, I think he would have accomplished it by now. You know this yourself and you do not want to be alone, so you keep her by you, deny her a life of her own by placing before her a goal that is entirely unrealistic and unattainable."

An aghast-sounding hiss escaped from Milly. "Jemima, you should not say such things. They are not true."

Jemima faced her young friend. "I am sorry to offend your sensibilities, Milly, but I do speak true and Aunt Prudence knows it."

"I know no such thing." Smiling maliciously, she added, "This does not change your outrageous conduct."

Jemima looked to the aunt and then lowered her gaze. "You speak truly. There is no end to my mischief. If Fulton has not told you then I will. Mr Huntington went missing more than a week ago. You recall, I expect, that he did not arrive at Willow Park as planned. In short, I conspired with Fulton to bring us to London, so we could go in search of him. It was all my idea so do not blame him. He was duty bound to stay with us but extremely concerned for the welfare of Mr Huntington and coming here together was the only way we could manage it. I offered him a solution, while underhand, it was effective. Since being in London, we have followed many traces of Mr Huntington but had not found him. I stole from the house last night to meet with the person who last saw him. It was there that I met with mischief.

"You remember that man who spoke to me while we were shopping, my childhood friend?"

Aunt Prudence nodded, her colour draining away. She hoped Milly was on the watch for Jemima thought the old woman would faint. She could almost hear the cogs turning in the woman's brain as she put the facts together. Jemima and Fulton had done a pretty good job of bamboozling her.

"Well, he, it turns out, is the villain in the case. I am not sure why Mr Huntington is his prey. All I know is that this David Longhurst is part of some dark cult, who do blood rituals and say they perform black magic."

"God save me," Aunt Prudence exclaimed and managed to make her complexion even paler. Jemima looked to Fulton, who had stood up behind the old lady in case she was overcome. Milly's eyes were round and wide.

"He also employs drugs as well as other trickery. The woman I met with confirmed that Mr Huntington was in his power. Longhurst showed up you see." She held out her arm with the bandage. "He held me down and forced some evil concoction down my throat. While my senses were addled, he lanced my arm, so he could steal my blood for use in some dreadful incantation."

"Upon my soul. I never thought to hear such a tale." The aunt looked Jemima up and down, appearing to decide whether Jemima was an accomplished liar or possessed by demons. "You say this person has my nephew captive?"

"Oh yes, and I fear for his safety. I, also, fear for my own. David Longhurst will return for me, I am sure. He knows things about us, about me."

Jemima managed to tell the remainder of the story, including the details of the letters, the financial transactions, which raised the old lady's eyebrows somewhat, realising it was Jemima to whom she was indebted for her new wardrobe and Milly's. Fulton relaxed a little and added to her tale, filling in the details of their investigation and the results or lack of to be precise. Although Aunt Prudence was duly scared out of her wits by the facts related to her, she managed to sit still and hear it all without further interruption.

When the story was all told, and the aunt sat there speechless, Jemima leaned forward, her hands beseeching. "I have no right to ask for your assistance or even your friendship. I leave the matter entirely in your hands, Aunt Prudence. I would not blame you for throwing me off and leaving me on my own."

After sucking in huge lungfuls of air, the aunt drew herself up in her chair, squaring her shoulders and eyeing them all haughtily. Her face was pale and her lips quite grey. Jemima was conscious that she had served the old woman a severe blow to her peace of mind and possibly her constitution.

"I will retire to my room to think on matters."

Her gaze travelled over them and with much dignity, she eased herself out of her chair and ambled out of the room. From her vantage point, Jemima could see her trembling hands. It made her feel terribly guilty for being the cause of it. If it was not for Jemima, the old lady would be in her cottage in the little village of Kingsfold, whiling the way her time with Milly, pouring her cups of tea and embroidering cushions.

To balance such morose feelings, she considered that Milly had probably enjoyed the adventure to some degree and had gained the love and affection of a very worthy man. Jemima only hoped that no ill would come to Milly as a result of the exposure to her and her outrageous adventures. The thought did occur to her that without Mr Huntington both Milly and Aunt Prudence would be in very poor circumstances indeed. She understood from Fulton that almost the entirety of their income derived from an annuity he provided them. He also owned the cottage in which they resided. She had no idea who would be his next heir as the Willow Park estate was bound in an entail to male heirs. He had money of his own, too, but she knew nothing about the disposition of those funds on his death.

Jemima turned to Fulton. "Oh dear, have I done the right thing in telling all? I did not wish to overset her or drive her out of her wits."

Fulton patted her on the shoulder, an unfamiliar gesture from him. "You did what you had to do. We can only wait for her decision. At least now, she has all the facts as her earlier decision to depart this place and abandon you was made without them. Perhaps with repose she can set aside the conjecture of your awful deeds and re-order them with the facts of—"

"My awful deeds." Jemima finished for him, managing a light laugh.

Milly wiped her eyes and came up to Jemima and knelt by her knee. "You are truly brave, Jemima. I could not have spoken to her or anyone the way that you did. I, for one, am grateful for all that you have done. I wish that you could be rewarded with my cousin walking through that door right now."

They all looked to the door and then jumped at a knock.

However, it was a caller who they had to direct the servant to turn away due to Aunt Prudence being indisposed. Jemima worried about turning away Mrs Parsons-White but she herself was in no mood to entertain. A collective sigh escaped them. The wish that Milly expressed had excited a deep disappointment within her breast. How different circumstances would be if Mr Huntington had been at the door.

The knock on the door brought home the state of their appearances and disposition. Milly showed much evidence of her distress, her face streaked in red and her eyes blood shot. Jemima's head felt light as if it might float away, still suffering from the after effects of the drugs, assault and resulting sickness. Fulton, who had many sleepless nights either guarding or rescuing her, looked no worse for wear.

"Perhaps you should both take a rest until Mrs Wainwright delivers her decision."

"Good suggestion, Fulton. But first what of the police? Am I to be questioned? Were they able to add anything to what we know?"

"The police have confined their questions to me. I believe they will not trouble you."

"I cannot believe Bess killed herself. You say she jumped?"

Fulton's gaze slid to Milly, signalling that he did not wish to discuss the event. Jemima caught his eye and nodded, lifting herself up from her seat on the sofa, she shambled to the staircase.

On the landing, Milly spoke from behind her, disturbing her from her thoughts.

Jemima swing round, "Oh?"

"Rest well, dearest," Milly said, patting her hand.

Turning to Fulton she said, "I will see you soon." He had followed them upstairs. Perhaps he would take some rest, too, like a normal human being.

Jemima pushed open the bedroom door and seeing the curtain billowing gave a start. Recovering, she raced forward to shut the window, heart thudding in her chest as she rested her face on the window frame, grateful that she did not have to fend off an unwelcome visitor. The maid had opened it to let in some fresh air. Indeed, the bed had been newly made up and the jug of water refreshed. As the effect of the drugs were still with her, Jemima poured a glass of water and drank it down before sinking into the softness of her bed. Laying back, a feeling of weakness spread to her limbs and soon she was deep in sleep.

When she next woke, the afternoon sun filtered through the curtains into the room. For the first time in what seemed like days, she felt hungry. The house was quiet. She hoped that did not bode ill for Aunt Prudence's big decision. Surely the woman had not quit the premises already. Jemima surveyed her room, dresses hung on hooks, petticoats half out of draws and strewn from trunks. How odious it would be to have to pack. She was in no mood to confront a life alone in the world. She did not know where to begin or how such a thing was to be accomplished.

When she went downstairs she found Milly at the table sewing. She looked up from her work and smiled. "Will you take tea? I have ordered some with cake from the landlady."

Jemima nodded and sat back on the sofa listlessly. "Aunt Prudence?"

Milly shook her head and put away her sewing when the landlady came in with the large tea tray. The landlady gave them both a long lingering look and Jemima looked away, her face burning. The landlady had obviously been disturbed by the police, too, and quite predictably had overheard their earlier discussion as their voices had been raised at times. Perhaps they had no choice but to remove themselves to new accommodation after all.

Fulton joined them not long after. His casual glance around the room spoke volumes. The aunt was still absent. This was not a good thing. After they had finished tea and eaten the light fruit cake supplied by the landlady, Susy came down to bring them word that Aunt Prudence was feeling poorly and would not be joining them for dinner.

Milly stood up. "I will go up and check on her. I will first see to the ordering of our dinner and supper. Aunt Prudence usually sees to that."

Jemima looked up at her, clasping her hand and shaking it. "Thank you, Milly. Do send her our regards and tell her we hope she feels improved soon."

Milly smiled at her sweetly, giving her hand a slight squeeze before pulling away. She turned her face to Fulton and then left after a nod from him. After Milly left the room, Jemima stood up and paced, feeling fretful and anxious.

From a chair in the corner, Fulton observed her silently, his eyes peeping over the top of his newspaper. She stopped her pacing and confronted him. "Maybe it would be better for me to go. Then Aunt Prudence would not have to make such an appalling choice."

Fulton raised an eyebrow at her. "Where would you go?" He folded the newspaper into his lap and his face resumed its usual bland expression. "You belong here with us."

Jemima glanced at him and smiled thinly, turning away to resume her pacing. "I thank you for your sentiments so well expressed, but the aunt has the right of it. Mr Huntington was about to throw me off and, considering what has occurred, he had great foresight."

Fulton folded the newspaper into neat sections and placed it on the table beside him and leaned forward in his chair. "You forget the terms in which he spoke of you to Miss Blake. I did not get the impression from her that he was ready to be rid of you. If anything, quite the opposite. Why would he waste his time discussing your school career, your talents and your preferences if he did not care to have a further association with you? Of course, Mr Stradbroke's news is disturbing but we do not know the full meaning behind it or what he intended by it."

Jemima put her hand on her hips as she swung around to face him. "He did not want to be my guardian any longer. Could it be any plainer?"

Fulton shook his head and picked up the newspaper, shaking out the creases. "I thought you were an educated and intelligent young lady and now I find that in matters of emotion that you are quite irrational. As irrational as any other young lady your age."

"Fulton! Take care in what you say. I am entirely logical. It is you who refuses to see reason."

"No, I am waiting for more facts before coming to a determination. I advise you to do the same."

CHAPTER 16

Milly came back down the stairs in quite a rush. She looked hot and bothered as if her sensibilities had been quite overturned.

"Milly?" Fulton said with feeling, rising from his seat to go to her. Jemima's heart palpitated painfully, expecting that David Longhurst had broken in again as was at that very moment lurking upstairs.

"I will be fine in a moment," she said before collapsing in a chair, and throwing her face into her hands. Fulton and Jemima shared a look before Jemima went over to console her.

"Good God what is it? Aunt Prudence hasn't had apoplexy has she? Or a stroke? Oh Lord, she has not been struck down with suffering due to my wicked ways?"

A muffled sound emitted from between the hands covering Milly's face. "Oh please, Milly, do say something." Jemima stroked her back, trying to administer comfort but feeling like shaking the girl to get some intelligence from her. She had almost resolved to run upstairs herself when Milly lifted her face.

Fulton started when he took in her countenance. Jemima stepped back to behold a conflicting set of emotions. There were a number of tears stealing down Milly's cheek and yet she smiled before collapsing once again into a paroxysm of laughter.

Jemima shot Fulton a sharp look before giving up her station beside Milly to him. After some soothing and a sip of wine administered by Fulton, Milly at last calmed enough to speak.

"Pray forgive me. I find the situation so unprecedented and out of the ordinary that I am quite overcome. Aunt Prudence is intoxicated, quite out of her head on wine. It is so absurd because she is always so careful and rarely partakes. Her ways are so puritan at times. So to see her so well into her cups, I could not contain my feelings, which I assure you passed many stages from incomprehension, to shock, to horror and then the upmost mirth. Susy told me that she had ordered a decanter and then a refill in rapid succession. I doubt we will see her before noon tomorrow and even then not in good spirits."

Jemima did not find the situation funny at all, though Fulton let out a chuckle. She suspected that was relief that his dear one was not overcome by some horrible circumstance and that the old lady, who often plagued him, had her own weaknesses exposed to all.

"Will she be all right?" Fulton asked. "Should we send for a doctor, perhaps he may do something for her present condition?"

Milly shook her head. "No, in this case she is resting, and Susy has agreed to stay with her during the night. We have already set up a trundle bed for her in my aunt's room."

Jemima stood up and paced the room. "This is frightful and all because of me. And now I must go another night not knowing what is to be my fate. I cannot bear it."

The landlady knocked on the door. Fulton stepped up and began conversing with the woman. After Milly hastily packed away her work, he then opened the door so that places could be laid at the table. Soon after a few dishes were brought in, bringing a casserole of beef cooked in ale, pureed potatoes and a serving of French beans in butter. Simple enough fare and very filling. After the food was laid out, the landlady informed them that dessert would be sent up, a delightful chocolate mousse.

Milly retired to bed soon after the meal. Jemima was also tired but contrived to corner Fulton in sharing his information on all that occurred with Bess Harrington. "Time to tell all now. How on Earth did you follow me there? I did not see you below."

"That is because these last few nights I have been set upon while guarding you from below."

"Really? But you did not say. Who was it that attacked you?" Jemima studied Fulton's face closely. There were dark circles under his eyes and some further bruising had come out on his chin. His hands were gloved so she could not see if there were any grazes or cuts. Good to know that he could be hurt, after all. Not that she wished him ill, but she was quite out of countenance when she heard that he had been repeatedly attacked with no visible signs of it.

"Not your friend, Longhurst, but ordinary thugs. They were not trying to enter but to put me out of the picture."

"You do not appear to be seriously injured. How did you manage to hold them off?"

Fulton studied her face, tilting his head. She thought he was choosing what to say to her. "I am quite resourceful. They on the other hand are rather worse for wear."

"You box, I suppose."

"Something of a kind. Anyway, I was busy dealing with the latest set of thugs as you descended from your window. From time to time, as circumstances permitted, I observed your very precarious and unladylike descent from your window. You did give me palpitations once or twice when your foot did not appear to make an adequate purchase."

"I had no idea. I heard nothing. I suppose my heart was beating rather rapidly at the time, which prevented my hearing anything else."

"I dealt with the scum rather quickly and was not that far behind you."

"Oh, I do apologise to you for trying to trick you. If I had known you were so close behind me, I would have felt less fear perhaps. Then, again, I would probably have worried that you would try to stop me or interfere." Jemima replied, adjusting her position in the chair. She was feeling quite agitated.

Fulton nodded gravely. "Longhurst seems to know the most intimate details of our lives and that weighs heavily on my mind. Is there a spy among us? If so who could it be? It seems likely that he, or some agent for him, has been following either Mr Huntington or you for some time."

Jemima clenched her hands in her lap and lifted her head in surprise. "But if that is true and he was there at the Horton's, then it is more likely to be him who stole the emerald and assaulted and killed Lady Arbunkle. Why he has no hesitation in committing very low acts himself that I would think killing a helpless old lady and availing himself of her jewels and virtue is not beyond him."

"What do you mean?" Fulton's hazel eyes narrowed. "What did you witness at Miss Harrington's before we arrived?"

The tone of his voice gave Jemima a moment of fright. "Pray do not get angry or think less of me, but I did witness some things that I ought not to have. Besides nearly being seduced by Bess, I saw...er...well. Oh dear, I cannot think of a polite way to say this. David had relations with Bess before you and the police arrived. I saw them, though my gaze was influenced by the drug he forced into me."

Fulton's brows drew down over very dark and brooding eyes. "In front of you?" His face grew red, in anger or embarrassment, he palmed his forehead and shook his head. "I should have stopped you, should have acted sooner."

Jemima wary at how upset he was patted his forearm. "Now, Fulton do not go off on a fit of remorse. Longhurst had assaulted me in my bedroom and said things to me that were equally disturbing. He also appears to have the power to reach into my dreams and fill them with dark and evil deeds. You could not protect me from that. No one can."

Fulton rubbed his hand over his face and smiled at her wearily. "I suppose you are right. You are such a young, innocent thing. I hate the thought of any corruption touching you."

Jemima thought she had let him down. "Ahh well, I feel unchanged, though life holds less mystery for me. But we have digressed. As the police were in attendance, I surmise you had an opportunity to inform them."

"Just that morning, I had informed them of Mr Huntington's disappearance and what I suspected of Bess's involvement. They were willing to put Bess's premises under surveillance. Once you entered, I found the three policemen, one senior constable who I had spoken to before. I told them you had entered the house to try to obtain information. It was then we decided to break down the door, considering the danger too great for you. Once the door was off its hinges, the old lady screamed at us like the devil himself had invaded her home.

"We pounded up the steps and again put our shoulders to the door. When it opened, you were there on the couch, quite out of your senses, your clothes dishevelled, legs bound, face as pale as death. I told the police I would attend to you for I had heard you moan and cry out something insensible.

"Bess stood there gaping at us and then backed up slowly, shaking her head."

"Did she say anything?"

"Well, she did, but it did not make sense at the time. She repeated "No. No. I will not tell. My life for his. No. No. I will not tell. My life for his. That is the law." The three policemen had surrounded her, walking forward slowly, talking to her calmly. Then she screamed once, turned on her heel and dived for the window. The police had no hope of stopping her. The window was open and the curtains slightly parted. A wind had picked up the curtains sending them out like two ribbons. Her perfectly aimed body went straight through, like she had taken flight. Indeed, for a minute I thought she had. We jostled to get a look out the window and at last saw her inert form on the pavement below, her blonde head surrounded by a halo of blood, being pulverised by the fall. The police then took up the investigation. I picked you up and brought you home."

"How terrible for you, Fulton." She was slightly appalled at Fulton's graphic account.

"No, it was nothing to me. I have seen worse in my life time, believe me. All that mattered was your safety. Now we know Mr Huntington met foulness and betrayal at the hands of this lady and her vile lover. There must be some strange coincidence at play here though. I do not understand this connection between you and Longhurst and Mr Huntington."

Jemima stroked her chin. "Longhurst is into something dark. Dare I say even supernatural. It may be coincidence that he knows me, some fortuitous circumstance that he could bend his way. Could it be that it is Mr Huntington that he is interested in solely? That would tie together some loose ends, such as the gems, if you agree he is the culprit with the theft of the Arbunkle emerald, and Mr Huntington's research."

"It may have been so, but he is actively seeking you now. Somehow you have become integral to his plans. He took your blood and, if not for our intervention, he would have taken you as well. Our attempts at locating Mr Huntington appear to be annoying your dark, magical friend. You say he calls me bungling, yet we must be getting close. He is behind the attempts to be rid of me I am sure. With me gone, he has free access to you as there would be no more protection."

"Yes, that certainly seems like a plausible explanation." Jemima shivered, realising that Longhurst was not going to leave her alone very soon at all and they were no closer to finding Mr Huntington.

"How badly hurt were you in that last attack by the way? How is that leg of yours? Should not it be needing some attention?"

"I appear to be quite resilient. Though my leg is overdue for maintenance."

"Then let me help you, for you know I am curious and not repulsed at all."

Fulton nodded. "I have the equipment with me and would be most obliged if you would assist me."

They worked into the late of night. Fulton had with him Mr Huntington's tool kit and was able to guide Jemima's hand. The wires seemed to all be in place, though there was some bruising. Fulton explained that it was due to the thugs who had set upon him and not the original injury and prosthesis itself causing it. The flesh was better healed than previously, which probably explained why he no longer limped.

Jemima filled the water cistern from a small hand pump made for the purpose and cleaned the various joints with an oiled cloth that was in the kit. She had been careful to use distilled water, deciding that it was less likely to cause issue with the delicate machinery. "Every time Mr Huntington examines my knee, he tightens those knobs there." Fulton pointed.

Jemima did as he instructed, the screws allowing her to do three revolutions. These appeared to control the powerful springs she could see that aligned with the knee and the ankles.

"How does that feel?"

Fulton stood up and walked around, bending his knees and jumping. "Excellent work. I swear your hand is as good as Mr Huntington's."

Fulton packed away the little kit. Jemima yawned as she watched him and stood up to stretch her arms wide. "I say for all my protestations of not being able to sleep tonight due to anxiety, I am exhausted. I will take myself off to Bedfordshire."

Fulton smiled, bending his knees, testing out the efficacy of their manipulations. "Good that you are tired. I will check your room first and keep guard."

Jemima followed him up the stairs. "I do not know how you do it, Fulton. Stay awake to all hours."

Fulton checked her room, while she waited on the threshold. "It is my secret, miss." He drew her inside and left the room. "All clear. Good night."

❦

The next afternoon, they were seated in the sitting room awaiting the imminent arrival of Aunt Prudence, who had sent word that she was coming down to discuss matters of concern with them. Jemima's tea had gone cold while she waited, wringing her hands and sighing, which occasioned looks from both Fulton and Milly, who otherwise sat conversing in quiet tones. Jemima thought she heard some words of poetry but shook her head, wondering at her own flights of fancy. Milly and Fulton, well Ambrose, did not seem the type to quote poetry.

The door burst open and Aunt Prudence lumbered in. Her skin was pale and slack within the confines of her over-embroidered widow's cap, which looked like it had been filched from the ample supply of doilies in their accommodation. Her dress was gaudy and rumpled, indicating to all that she had not recovered from her overindulgence the previous day. Straight away Milly poured her some tea and handed her a cup. With a screwed-up face, Aunt Prudence took a sip and then handed the cup back, rattling in its saucer.

"Too cold, too strong," she said by way of explanation as she looked about the room, inspecting each of them with her bloodshot gaze. "Good. All here. I have been a long time deliberating on what do to and how to proceed. My nephew's action regarding you, Jemima, weighed heavily with me. He was going to throw you off with good reason."

Fulton coughed into his hand to gain attention. Aunt Prudence paused and turned her head toward him. "He also requested of you, ma'am, to come to Willow Park and care for Miss Hardcastle."

Aunt Prudence sniffed and sat back a little further in her chair. "That is true and in my mind I cannot determine which action took precedence. Did he at first mean to keep her cared for and then change his mind?"

"Perhaps the reasons for Mr Huntington wishing to relinquish his guardianship require further explanation, which as you know cannot take place in his absence. It is not entirely certain that he wished to cast her off."

Aunt Prudence made a face like a prune and continued to speak as if Fulton had not said anything at all. "Through Jemima's machinations, we find ourselves in London and we cannot in all good conscience remain here. The matter of Mr Huntington's disappearance must be put in the hands of the proper authorities. Milly and I cannot remain here, spending the money of Miss Hardcastle and my nephew."

Jemima watched Aunt Prudence from under her lashes. "It is my money and I have used it most willingly to our advantage. We are close to finding him. I am sure he is alive."

Aunt Prudence lifted her head and fixed Jemima with a fulminating stare. "You, young lady, would do well to hold your tongue. Too long has your head been in a novel, mind left to wander in imagination, not on industry. May I recommend to you a daily visit to the chapel for prayer and meditation. It will do much to quiet the fever of your brain."

Jemima was puzzled. "Thank you for the recommendation, ma'am.

I have not yet understood your decision regarding me. Are you abandoning me or not?"

Aunt Prudence drew herself up, wavering slightly as she did so and put her hand on the table to keep steady. "I have determined without much effort that you have a deleterious effect on this household, on Milly particularly. I would, therefore, think it prudent—"

A sharp knock on the door interrupted the aunt's speech. With a nod, Aunt Prudence sent Milly to answer the door. The landlady entered bearing a platter with letter on top. Fulton stood to take the letter and shut the door behind the landlady. He took the letter and stared at it, turning it over once and then back again. "It is in Mr Huntington's hand."

Milly and Aunt Prudence's accusing gaze went directly to Jemima. "I did not write it."

Fulton walked over to her, proffering the letter. "Indeed, she did not for it is addressed to her. What point would there be in such a counterfeit?"

Jemima's eyes snapped open. "For me?"

Aunt Prudence closed her mouth, moving her tongue around while thinking of something to say. "I would not put it past you, young lady. You would do anything to get your way," the old lady said at last, while trying to peer at the letter.

Jemima took the letter, taking time to examine it as Fulton had done. The script did look like Mr Huntington's hand. The letter had been hand delivered as it bore no postage stamp.

"Come on then. Or do you wish me to open it?" Fulton said, standing at her knee, hand reaching forward to relieve her of her correspondence.

Moving the letter out of his reach, Jemima turned her body and said over her shoulder. "No. I can do it. His hand looks shaky. See."

"What does it say?" This was from Aunt Prudence, who it appeared was ready to finally accept that it was a communication from her nephew.

Opening the letter and unfolding it, she found there was not much written there, except a few words and an address. "Come to me at 10

Leather Lane, by 4.00 pm today." Fulton snatched the letter from her, reading it twice over.

"It is a trap. He cannot be there." Fulton let the letter fall from his hand, shock and speculation crinkling his brow.

Jemima stood up and walked over to the window, looking down on the street below. "For certain it is a trap. He warns me away."

Fulton faced her. "What do you mean? Quite plainly does he ask you to go there."

A design in the margin of the letter disguised the word. It looked like Mr Huntington had doodled it to pass the time. Yet quite clearly was the Greek word for danger. She pointed this out to them.

"Upon my word. How did he know that you can read Greek?"

Milly gaped at her. "Greek?"

Jemima had no time to take pride in her achievements, for she had a very dangerous path to tread. "My father taught me Ancient Greek and Latin before he died. I think that is the main reason Mr Huntington sent me to school. My father had given me a young man's classical education, at least the beginning of one. He was appalled when he met me to hear of it. Packed me up to Miss Blake's to learn to be a lady."

"How extraordinary," Aunt Prudence said, holding out her hand for the letter. Fulton passed it to her and she studied it. "What does this mean? I do not know what to do. I cannot read Greek."

Jemima sat down again, barely able to think. Mr Huntington was alive and in need. His captors wanted her, too, that much was evident. Would the instigator of this latest scheme be David Longhurst? Yet why would having her in their power assist them in their dealings with Mr Huntington? Jemima shivered. If it was Longhurst then she was in trouble. She feared she would not escape their next meeting unscathed. They had come too far for that.

Jemima finally came to a decision. "Aunt, is it possible for you to delay your decision until tomorrow? By then we may have more news of Mr Huntington."

Aunt Prudence grew even paler. "You mean to go there, do not you?" She sagged into a chair.

"Why of course. Why ever not?"

Fulton let out a yelp of surprise and Milly gasped. "My, you are quite extraordinary," Aunt Prudence commented, looking around the room at the stunned faces of the others. "I do not know if you are brave or addled."

Jemima laughed and gave a little shrug. "Oh, both I expect. But I will go nonetheless."

"Jemima," Fulton and Milly exclaimed unison.

She turned toward them. "What? If you mean to tell me it is a trap, I am not stupid, I understand that much. Yet, I am interested in finding some clue. This letter was written today or perhaps yesterday. It gives me hope that we are not too late. He is alive, then there is hope to spring him from this trap."

"But you said he warns you off?" Fulton declared.

"Yes, he does. What has that got to do with anything? Surely you do not expect me to do nothing."

Fulton shrugged and looked to the others for inspiration. Milly sat there pale and limp. Aunt Prudence looked in need of some brandy.

"Now tell me, Fulton. How badly were you hurt when assailed by those thugs last night? Is it possible to pretend that you are out of action? Although that odious man does seem to know everything that is going on here, perhaps we can use it to our advantage."

Fulton blushed at a gasp from Milly. "No, miss. I was not attacked." Jemima realised he did not wish to alarm Milly.

"How tiresome, I wonder if I could write to this address and put off my visit until tomorrow, so you could be attacked tonight and, therefore, be out of action for my visit." She thought about it for a few minutes while the others stared at her as if she was some creature with two heads, five arms and a tail. "No, I suppose I could not. Now, Fulton and Milly, I have an idea."

CHAPTER 17

M iss Jemima Lily Hardcastle left the house at three fifteen in
the afternoon. She wore a demure gown of pale blue and a
short, navy-coloured jacket that buttoned at her waist. Stout white
boots and a little straw hat completed her ensemble.

A lot of commotion had ensued after the letter's arrival and
Jemima's avowal to walk into a trap to save her guardian. A doctor had
been sent for, with as much fuss as could be mustered by those
present. Milly had cried and wailed loudly and even Aunt Prudence
was observed telling the landlady of the terrible misfortune that had
struck down their trusty protector, Fulton. The poor man was at
death's door. Apparently, he had succumbed to an untended injury
obtained through being viciously assaulted in the lane. Rumours of a
fainting aunt, a hysterical Milly were judiciously repeated by the
landlady to all the staff, the milk maid, the butcher's boy, the baker's
apprentice and any other tradesman who ventured to the house and its
environs during the day.

Jemima smiled at the thought as she got into a Hansom cab and
gave the driver the address that Mr Huntington had shakily written in
his letter. The driver gaped at her stupidly before asking, "Are you sure
you want to go there, Miss? 'S not a savoury place."

"Quite sure. Drive on if you please." She lifted her chin and put on a determined expression. Inside, she was at once excited and full of trepidation, and these feelings appeared to assail her in waves. The result of which was that she could hardly sit still or stop herself from wiping her brow with a handkerchief as the cab bustled along, jolting her quite discommodiously. The owner of the cab needed to do some work on the carriage's undersprings as soon as may be, she thought. Such attention to minutiae allowed her to stop thinking of Longhurst and the terrible fear of him that had grown inside of her. Before she mentally tallied the vehicle's defects, she arrived at her destination.

After paying the driver, Jemima stood in front of the house. It looked shut up, unoccupied. When she entered through the gate, she saw there was no knocker on the door. As she trod closer to the house, she saw boarded-up windows and the front door ajar. She paused to look behind and around her. No one was near. The windows of the houses opposite stared blankly at her, not inhabited by a nosey Parker or a peeping Tom. No one walked along the lonely street. That gave her a shudder. No one to hear her scream.

As she expected, the door opened at a touch with an accompanying creak reminiscent of a Regency-period gothic novel. Stepping across the threshold, she trod down a bare hall, her heels thudding on the floorboards and entered the first room on the right. A thick layer of dust greeted her. All the ground floor rooms were in a similar state, except in one she saw evidence that a squatter had spent a night or two in the back room. The remains of a fire in the hearth and some screwed up newspapers all the evidence required to confirm her suspicions.

The house was quiet. Standing once again in the hall, she looked upwards, waiting and listening. There was no sound, no hint of movement, yet she decided each room must be checked. She prayed that it was not some awful game where instead of falling into a trap as she supposed, she would stumble upon the corpse of her guardian. That random thought made her shiver. Sweat gathered on her lower back. It was very unladylike to perspire so much. Miss Blake would not approve.

Again, she trespassed, checking in all the upper rooms. Here, there were scattered items of furniture, beds, wardrobes, dressers and a few upholstered chairs. She lifted the dust covers and looked underneath, slightly unnerved by the looming shapes in the dark rooms, which were illuminated solely by the patches of afternoon sun making their way around the edges of the window boards. The absence of signs of life made her doubt her first conjectures. Could this be a terrible hoax? No, she argued with herself. Only Mr Huntington would recollect that she had been taught Greek and Latin. While it was rusty, for she had not opened her readers for some time, she saw quite plainly his silent plea. One that she chose to ignore. Well, what did he expect from her?

She walked back down the stairs, each riser protesting and advertising her presence with loud creaks and groans. As she descended, she realised that the only other place she had not searched was the basement rooms. How she had wished she tackled them first, as the hour was growing late, and she doubted the late afternoon sun could penetrate so deeply, as the house was shadowed by close neighbours. She stood there staring at the door to the basement, hesitating. One part of her mind was telling her to turn and run out the door and the other part urged her forward, urged down below to spring the trap. For surely that was where it would be. She dared not contemplate mortal danger.

With a shiver, she rubbed her arms, touching the bandage covering the wound that Longhurst had inflicted. Was there worse in store? With a final garnering of courage, she tore open the door, rapidly descended the steps and plunged herself into total darkness. She paused before reaching the final stair. The blackness surrounding her was cloying and oppressive. The sound of loud creaking reached her. Her breathing increased; her chest heaved with alarm until she reminded herself that it was only the normal noises of the house.

Perched as she was on the staircase, she found herself disoriented, not quite sure how much deeper the stairs went. Looking back at the door, which was still open at the head of the stairs, she saw the straight lines of the risers ascending and the railing in the dim light. Then while she watched the door swung shut, groaning on its hinges. "Oh!" was all she could get out. Her feet refused to move, refused to run back up the stairs.

Now, she was suspended there in total darkness. After she calmed down, her ears listened for a clue. Taking careful steps, she eased her way down, feeling with her toe whether it was a step and then finally her boot met the hardness of a stone floor. There were sounds around her—something that could be vermin scurrying past or the sound of fabric rustling.

She thought she heard breathing and tried not to conjure thoughts of ghost, when suddenly a light went on, like a bright lantern uncovered. It blinded her for a moment. Hands grabbed for her. She let out a scream. A rough sack was thrown over her head and as she struggled, she was lifted and thrown over someone's shoulder. Some light filtered through the sacking. A door opened, and she was bundled outside then dropped onto a carriage floor. Grunts gave her little clue as to the origins or the character of her captors, except for the smell of pipe tobacco, a rich aromatic blend, stale ale and unwashed bodies. Ruffians and vagabonds to the one.

The carriage rocked forward and turned, backing up and then someone else entered. "Get the chloroform."

Jemima thought perhaps it was time to call out, yet as soon as she opened her mouth she smelt a sweet odour. She cried out, only to find the sack and a hand almost smothering her. Her heart beat erratically. Instinctively, she struggled until the last of her consciousness evaporated.

🕸️

Jemima woke with a dry mouth and a dull headache. She put her hand to her head, realising she was free of the sack. Other things intruded on her notice. She was once again in the dark, yet this was not the basement of the house at Leather Lane. There were other scents and sounds within this room. Objects too. She put out her hand and touched a piece of wood, which was smooth and polished like the side railings of a bed. Keeping quiet, she looked around. Not completely dark, as she could see shapes but could not distinguish what they were. A smell, too, dank, musty—urine and more in a bucket, like a chamber pot neglected. She heard breathing.

"Hello?" she said in a soft voice.

No reply to her query. "Is anybody there?" she ventured in a voice that trembled. Still there was no answer but there was a harsh intake of breath. She was not alone. Carefully, she groped along the wall, identifying obstacles and working around them. She found the corner and continued along, her questing hands moving up as she searched for a window but found none. The walls were rough cool stone, slightly damp. An older house she thought. Her fingers crawled along the floor until they touched skin—a hand. She let out a shriek.

Panting, she crouched there until calm enough to reach out again. The breathing told her whoever it was was alive. Yet no response made her worry. She reached again in the same spot. Touched the hand, which did not move. Her hands travelled up the arm, feeling warm skin beneath a shirt. She could smell the body's scent, unwashed for many days. Tentatively, her fingers lightly followed the contours of a shoulder and a neck. Still no word, no movement. Her breathing grew hoarse in her throat. The silence deepened her fear. Nevertheless, she continued tracing her fingers higher, feeling a chin deep in bristles, a full mouth, lips that she gently caressed with the tip of her fingers, even though there was no movement, no twitch of response. Why would this person ignore her, pretend that she was not there?

"Is that you Mr Huntington?" she whispered, half in hope, half in despair.

The stranger's hand reached for hers, removed it from the vicinity of his mouth. "Yes, you little fool. Now matters are worse."

He sounded careworn. And while his words were peremptory, they were spoken gently, resignedly. Jemima oriented herself, touching his shoulder so that he would know where she was. She did not want to spoil this moment by taking his eye out. She embraced him, placing her face in the crook of his neck, wanting so much more from the embrace than she dared to ask for. The skin of his neck felt warm, too warm. He was running a fever.

She pulled back but could see nothing of his countenance. She embraced him again. With her face pressed to his chest, said, "We have all been so worried. But I fear you are unwell. How is it you came to be here? Why did you not reply when I first spoke to you?"

He leaned his head back against the wall and let out a sigh, not returning her embrace at all. "I cannot believe all Longhurst told me was true. You were in London and you brought the others with you. There is no end to your interference."

She pulled back and glared at him. Well, she faced the direction of where his head should have been. "Interference? But you went missing. What were we to do? Fulton was beside himself with worry. You had charged him with my care; he could not leave me. It was a brilliant idea for us to go to town, as that way he could do both."

Edward moved his arm, she thought to run his fingers through his hair but could not see. He let out a frustrated 'ahh' before speaking again. "Yet, for what purpose did you come here? You are now his prisoner, as well. I will be powerless to stop him from harming you. Now he may use threats against you to force me to assemble his infernal machine."

Jemima chewed her lip as she considered his words. "I do see your point. However, I have to tell you Longhurst has had ready access to me already. He broke into my room at our lodgings one night and assaulted me and another time he drugged me and cut my vein to take my blood when I went to see Bess Harrington to find out where you had gone. I cannot be safe from him wherever I go. He always seems to know where I am and when I am vulnerable."

He stiffened. "What the devil! That blighter took blood from you, cut you? I thought it all lies."

"Yes. He said he needed it for some incantation. Well, that is what I recollect. I was a bit senseless at the time. The potion he gave me made me quite ill afterwards. I had to stay in bed for a day or two."

He became restless. "Oh heaven above, this is not good, not good at all. He is deep into the supernatural—blood, ritual and sacrifice as well as perversion of the mind and body." He grabbed her hand and kissed it before placing it back into her lap. "I hope, in time, these appalling events will fade from your mind."

"They will, now that I know you are alive."

"Jemima. I hate to torment you but me staying so is by no means certain. What Longhurst intends will be bad for all Britain. I thought I had convinced him that I would not—could not help him. Now he has

possession of you, threatens you—well I'm in a dashed bad position."
He threw his head back and rocked it from side to side. "How does he
know?"

"Know what?"

"Things I wish he did not."

Jemima shrugged. "David seems to know everything about me. He
must have observed us at the Horton's, because he mentioned seeing
us together. Perhaps it was he who killed Lady Arbunkle and stole her
emerald. Since we have been in London, he seems to know where
Fulton and I have been and who we have visited. It is uncanny. If I
could suspect a spy in our midst, I would, but that does not seem
possible."

"He does have some extraordinary abilities. Jemima..." He lowered
his voice. "I have to say...I know I have behaved badly toward you. I
am sorry my neglect has brought you to this."

In an effort to make herself comfortable, she undid her jacket and
sat on the floor with her legs to one side. "What have you got to be
sorry for? I am a grown woman and know right from wrong. I am
responsible for my actions."

"No, you would not be here but for me. You fell into a trap."

Jemima smiled, though he could not see it. "Do you think me
stupid? I knew it was a trap. I can still read Greek."

He drew in a loud breath. "You knew but you came anyway? How is
that logical? I had not thought you daft."

Jemima tut-tutted and shook her head. "I suspect you and Fulton
pass the time most enjoyably, discussing logic and a woman's
application of it. It was perfectly logical to spring the trap. I am here
with you. I know that you live. Now we can work on a way to escape."

He groaned, letting his misery escape. She found his hand in the
dark and squeezed. "There, there, do not fret. I have a plan."

"What the devil. A plan you say? But you are a prisoner in a
basement who knows where."

"Yes, I quite comprehend that. Before we go any further I must get
something off my mind, something that has been plaguing me."

Edward said nothing, but he sat very still, his breathing shallow.
"Edward, please forgive my terrible behaviour to you in adding those

sentences to your letter and not making my relationship to you clear at the Horton's. I had not expected...well I could not anticipate...oh bother it! I did not think that we would like each other's company so well..."

"You called me Edward," he said in a soft voice.

"Yes, I did. Was that too bold?"

His chest vibrated and then she heard his chuckle. "Not too bold. Better than uncle, I am sure."

A grin spread over her face. "Now, let's remove the binding from your hands."

He moved. "Yes, yes, my feet too. Can you manage in this light? If you do my hands first, I should be able to help you."

Jemima grabbed the leather ties and tugged around the knot. It was a strange binding, she thought as there was enough give in the leather to allow him to use his hands. She wondered why he had not managed to undo the bindings to his legs himself, or why he sat there so helpless. The knot was difficult to undo, and it took quite a lot of effort to untie him. Mr Huntington managed to hold onto his patience and when he finally shook the leather free, chanted a few words and shook out his hands. Then he bent to the task of freeing his tightly bound feet. Jemima wondered why he was still wearing his boots. Surely, he could have freed himself easily, by slipping his feet out. Once his boots were free of their ties, he cried out in some pain for his circulation had been impeded and now that the blood run freely he had to adjust.

He was a dark shape in the gloom. She heard Mr Huntington massaging his limbs and trying to stand. Using the wall for support, he crouched and stamped his feet, trying to wake them. Jemima decided it was time to attack the locked door. For this task, she had brought some metal tools, which Fulton had assured her were good for picking locks.

"What are you doing?" Mr Huntington asked after Jemima had reached into her bodice and felt around for her implements.

For a moment, she paused, thinking he could see what she was doing clearly and then realised he could not. "Fetching these little tools," she said drawing them out. "Fulton made a present of them to pick the lock."

"Let me feel them." She passed them over, the dim light allowing her to see his outline.

"Very clever of Fulton," he said. "Now that my hands are free we will not need them. I could only wish it was he that was here and not you. That I could bear better."

A bit crestfallen at not having her heroism appreciated, Jemima bit back a retort. In the dim light, she saw him slide her lock picks into his coat pocket. "Well then, let us look at this door."

Jemima could make out the movement of his hands as he traced the shape of the door and muttered to himself as he did so. "Come, Jemima. I think we can leave now. There does not appear to be a guard."

The light outside the room stung her eyes. She blinked a few times until she could see without pain. Edward, she saw, was also dazzled. Once outside, they crept up the corridor, pausing at the intersection to listen for the presence of others. Mr Huntington quickly found a stairwell and grabbing her by the hand, led the way upstairs. Here, there was more light as they were no longer below ground and even the grubby windows could not block the sun. His face thus illuminated, she could see the week's growth of beard and the crushed and stained appearance of his shirt and trousers.

Without pausing, he continued down a corridor, checking doors, which were invariably locked. "What are you doing?" she whispered, checking nervously over her shoulder.

"Looking for a way to get you out."

Jemima pulled on his hand. "I am not leaving without you. Why not find a place to hide? Help will come along soon."

"Help?" he said, stopping to look back down the corridor. "What help?"

"You will see. I am not entirely a nincompoop." Moving away from him, she tried one of the doors herself and found it unlocked. Carefully, she opened it and stole a look inside. Tea chests reaching head high lined the far wall. Elsewhere some were open, no longer containing tea but had other packages inside, half spilled onto the floor. "In here," she hissed over her shoulder.

Straightaway, Mr Huntington was there. Again, he muttered under his breath as he checked the room. She was beginning to wonder whether the ordeal he had been through was too much for him and that he was now suffering from some form of nervous complaint. A few days rest would put him to rights. She hoped so, for her sake and for his.

Luckily, there was a lock and this Mr Huntington engaged, before leaning his head on the door and sighing audibly.

"Here we may be at ease for a time. There does not appear to be any pursuit as yet." His gaze scanned the room. "No windows, what bad luck. I thought perhaps I could hand you out to the street."

Jemima tilted her head and smiled at him shyly. A weight of worry had lifted from her shoulders. Mr Huntington was before her, whole and hardy despite his ordeals. Now they had some time, she felt awkward being alone with him. He had forgiven her, but he did not know all that she had done. On second thoughts, she was not sure it was good policy to confess all.

Mr Huntington paced the room, peering into the tea chests and appearing to be engrossed in that. Jemima got the impression that he was as shy as she was. Pulling out a tea chest, she perched on it and regarded him. A need to hold him close to her settled in her belly, but she could not conceive of how to bring it about. If he repulsed her she would be utterly sunk.

Pushing another tea chest close to her, he sat down and reached over to clasp her hand. She looked down at it, unable to lift her gaze. Warmth radiated from her cheeks. In all this time she was looking for him, worrying about him, she did not imagine she would feel so uncertain when the time came to be together.

"I would hold you close to me, Jemima, but I fear that I am wretchedly unkempt and am loath to soil you or even let you linger close to me for I am sure I exude a most foul odour."

Jemima lifted her gaze to his and tried to hold it. "You have not said explicitly if you forgive me. I am afraid there are more things that I have done which you will not like either. So you must let me list them for you so that you know it all. Here goes: I wrote some more letters, pretending to be you, to Aunt Prudence in order to remove us from Willow Park to London. I am afraid I spent a rather a lot of money. All of my allowance, actually so I may need a loan when we get out of here. I used the money taking Milly and Aunt Prudence shopping. Poor Milly was in need of a wardrobe and some social activity, so I do not feel as guilty as I should. I also commandeered the emergency funds you had left for Fulton."

"Emergency funds?" Mr Huntington had a surprised look, which made her reconsider Fulton even further.

"Yes, Fulton owned that you had left some for such purposes, though I suppose you did not think we would use them in such a fashion to come in search of you."

"Fulton is extremely reliable." There was a sparkle in Mr Huntington's eyes.

"Yes, he is a wonderful fellow."

The smile that lit his face, reached his remarkable blue eyes. "You are entirely dangerous," he said with a warmth that severely interrupted the beat of her heart. Jemima had to lower her gaze, unable to bear the intensity of his. He patted her hand. "I am glad you were good to Milly. Trapped here I have had time to think about the past and my behaviour. So selfish I have been. I should have done more to help her. It warms my heart that you have shown her kindness. Miss Blake said you were tender-hearted and generous."

For a moment or two, Jemima wished they were still in the dark room below, for then her blushes would be more easily disguised. She had not anticipated talking to him would be so difficult.

"That was very kind of her to speak well of me, considering what I had done. I had deceived her. I am very pleased you did not admonish her for my own bad deeds."

"Dreadful girl," he said with feeling. Her head snapped up to see that smile again and the warm glow to his eyes. "Yet, I had driven you to a desperate act."

Jemima could not help but smile when he teased her. "Well, yes," she replied. "But I chose to act in a way I knew to be wrong. That is not your fault."

"It lightens my heart to hear you say it." Mr Huntington stood and put a finger to his lips, urging her to be quiet. He prowled around the edges of the room and paused by the door to listen. He glanced back at her and shook his head. "No one has noticed us missing yet, which is a surprise."

He came and sat down beside her and lifted her hands into his lap. It felt nice to sit there like that. Before a few moments had passed, Jemima's busy mind prompted her to speak again. "Before I forget, I must tell you...well provided you give your blessing, I think Fulton will have the worry of Milly now. Although, you may need to give him better wages so he can support a wife. Then again, I am not certain because I have no idea what you pay him."

Mr Huntington's eyebrows lifted and he turned an incredulous face toward her. "Fulton is not in my employ. He is my friend."

"Your friend?" Jemima gaped, then covered mouth with her hand. After a moment of stunned silence, she added, "Oh dear, but Aunt Prudence treats him like a servant. You called him 'your man' when you packed me off to Willow Park with him. I assumed an unequal relationship of some kind. Oh no! Will he ever forgive my impertinence?"

Mr Huntington shrugged indifferently. "At the time, I was rather angry with you and thought that an appropriate introduction. I trust Fulton with my life and, therefore, yours. I had not expected to leave him with the responsibility of you for so long. He must have his reasons for letting you all continue to treat him that way. He is a very respectable gentleman."

Jemima was surprised and pleased by the news about Fulton and began to reassess her previous conclusions about him. Then, before she indulged in too much speculation about Fulton, she thought she should get to the point. "Are you still angry with me? Can you not find it in your heart to forgive me? Mr Stradbroke visited and said you wanted to be rid of my guardianship."

"I do. You have put me in an awful position. I have shamed myself. I have abrogated my responsibility as your guardian, breached the faith between guardian and ward. I behaved most inappropriately."

Jemima frowned, not quite understanding. He had not exactly

answered her question. "Do you mean inappropriate because you kissed me?"

Edward snorted. "That and more. For afterwards, when my anger was got over, I thought things through from your perspective and I saw Miss Blake and I realised how badly I had behaved."

"No, no. I will have none of that. I cannot regret the life you have provided for me. Yes, I missed Willow Park when you sent me away, but Fulton was right. You were a young man. What could you have done with me then? You were not in a position to offer me a home."

"Then you do not hate me?" There was something akin to awe in his voice. She found his soft tones caressing.

Jemima squeezed his hand. "I did hate you, as a child hates with ignorance. I also have learned much in these last couple of weeks. I have seen lives much worse than my own and realised my own good fortune. I know you find it hard to forgive me for what transpired at the Horton's. I can only say to you that I do not regret it."

"What did you say?" There was a stillness to him, an earnest look in his eyes.

Carefully, she lifted her face and held his gaze. "I do not regret that week or the kiss."

The eyes widened. "That cannot be possible."

"Oh, it is entirely possible and true."

A sparkle filled his gaze and a smile lifted the corner of his mouth. "Jemima," he whispered her name.

Unable to hold his gaze, she looked away. "If only you did not have such profligate tastes."

"What?" He went still again, tight like a spring.

She could not quite meet his eye, yet she blundered on, for it was something she felt strongly about. "Profligate, a penchant for loose women wearing nothing, but petticoats. Mistresses and the like."

He sat forward, eyes now dark, brows drawn low. "You believe this about my character? That I keep low company? That I am some kind of libertine?" His voice had a hard, sharp tone.

"Heavens, you want me to repeat myself? Next, you will be lecturing me, like Fulton, on what a lady should and should not know."

His gaze held hers, searching and then he relaxed against the tea chest. "Most probably I should do so. I take it you think I keep mistresses and habitually visit houses of ill repute."

She nodded.

"But, you do not regret kissing me or spending time with me at the Horton's?"

Again, she nodded. He lifted a finger and tilted her chin, his gaze once again searching. "You are extraordinary," he said, his voice caressing.

"So Aunt Prudence tells me. However, if I marry I must have equality and honesty. I could not abide a man who does not love his wife and visits other women to...to...well you know..."

"I do know. Jemima—"

A sound of boots running down the hall disturbed them. Edward tensed and dashed to the door. He shook his head and drew his finger to his lips, then placed his head against the door to listen. Jemima stood up and edged into a corner, hoping they would pass them by. Edward backed away. With a loud bang, the door flung open, casting him backwards. Through the pall of acrid smoke, David Longhurst strode.

"Enjoy your reunion?" Longhurst wore a happy smile. Then other men came into the room. "Time to separate you. Bring her below and confine her. Take him and clean him up."

"No, do not harm her," Edward said with a raised and excited voice as he struggled against the brutes who held him.

Two burly men pounced on her and dragged her out. While putting up a fight, screaming as well, she managed to slip free only to have her hair gripped and pulled, successfully immobilising her. Pausing at the threshold, the men held her while David caressed her neck. She was positioned in such a way that Edward could see everything, "So ripe, so succulent. Do you not envy me, Mr Huntington? She will be mine for the taking if you do not agree to do as I ask. But first, we will meet again after we prepare her. I have a little spectacle in which your little ward is to feature. Then, we can elicit the promise from you."

"Keep your hands from her, Longhurst, or I will strangle the life out of you with my own hands." Edward broke free but was felled by a punch from behind. Her last sight was of him sprawled senseless on the floor.

As they dragged her along, Jemima was not averse to screaming and let loose a full-throated screech they could hear in the Tower of London. Her misery and fear were not feigned. She was horribly afraid. How was she ever to escape from David? He knew exactly where they had hidden. It was as if he had been toying with them, allowing them to think that they were home free. If only help would come soon.

Her immediate fear that they meant to harm Edward was quite dispelled. He had a use. It was her that was in danger, for her life, and, perhaps, her soul, for she had no use. One comfort in all this turmoil was that Edward harboured some tender feelings toward her—feelings more intimate than those of guardian to ward.

The way David Longhurst played up in front of him confirmed her suspicions. Although Longhurst had acted lasciviously toward her on more than one occasion, she felt there was more in the last transaction for Edward rather than herself. He meant to excite jealously and generate protective feelings. Not that she counted her danger less than it was. The threat to her was quite real. Longhurst had proved himself a murderer and a blackguard.

Down the dark stairs she was dragged, her hair in the brute's eager hold. At the base, they tried to lift her, but she kicked one hard in some soft portion of his person. The other man, who held her by the hair, yanked hard so that she could not struggle at all. They then succeeded in carrying down the corridor and throwing her bodily into another room. For a moment, she was stunned by the impact of her landing and, while gathering her senses, noticed that the brutes were gone, and the door left ajar. She crawled forward, as best as her skirts allowed, only to be brought up short by the entry of David Longhurst. He flung the door shut, leaving them alone. Dressed in trousers, shirt and jacket, he was much more ordinary looking without his black cloak.

"So we meet again. Though this time in circumstances which I control completely. No police to interfere. No Fulton to stumble upon us. I knew you were impetuous and that you would answer your uncle's summons."

"Actually, he is a cousin a couple of times removed."

Longhurst laughed. "Play your role well and you may yet live. Uncle, cousin, lover, it matters not. He will sacrifice his life and principles for you. That is all the control I need and you, little sweet thing, are the lever."

Using the wall for support, Jemima climbed to her feet and did her best to smooth her hair, which had been most shabbily treated. One could not hope that her bun could have survived. Longhurst watched her, while she arranged her tresses. "Why do I find that hard to believe that you will let me live? You left Bess to die, and she was your lover. If that is all the care you have for those who are dear to you, then I expect even less, for I know for a fact that you care nothing for me."

Longhurst lowered his head and ran a finger down his aquiline nose, while he formed an answer. Looking up again, he said, in a serious voice. "I had no control over Bess's choices, nor did I love and desire her. She had no particular affection for me, only my position and a certain physical attribute I possess."

Jemima, sickened at the sound of his words, edged around the room to maintain her distance. "You have a very high opinion of yourself. I despise you more than anything in this world. I pitied Bess and her adoration of you. You did not deserve such loyalty."

He stepped closer and she backed up, hitting against some large sacks.

"You offer nothing. That is entirely right because taking, hearing you scream, will be more than satisfying because unwillingness is more pleasurable than that which is freely given. Believe me, I could ravish you right now, in this room. No one would come to your aid."

He reached out and seized her chin, gripping it hard and forcing her face up. With his tongue, he traced her lips, while she struggled. "You will be a willing servant for the dark lord. He will command your blood."

Fear speared through Jemima, making her knees bend and she covered her mouth with her hand to stifle her cry of fright. He had taken her blood. Was he going to offer it to this dark lord of his?

"Good, I like your fear. Love the feel of it in the air right now as you tremble before me. Yet it is not time for my pleasure. You are here for another purpose."

Jemima locked her knees together, gathering together her shredded courage. "I would rather die than be subjected to your evil practices. Do you think I am ignorant of what dark arts you have dabbled in?"

An eyebrow lifted, and a lopsided smile greeted her words. "Dying can be arranged but rather premature at this stage. I was not going to insist on it, having already sufficient blood for my needs, but it does excite my followers somewhat seeing the blood flow and the flesh rendered. It sends them into frenzy. If you have any inkling of what I am truly involved in I will hold myself duly surprised."

He drew away from her, though his hand was still upon her, sliding to the back of her neck, which he squeezed and shook lightly. "In the corner there you will find a robe. Take off all your clothes—all of them, every piece of undergarment. Put it on or I will have my followers dress you and they will be none too gentle. We will return for you shortly. Meanwhile, I will have some refreshments brought in. You must be hungry. We cannot have you fainting at an important moment."

He turned and left the room abruptly. The light was dim, a pale gold. There was a window, but it seemed there was a lantern on the other side providing the illumination. She was sure it was night and that it was an internal window rather than letting in sunlight from the street.

In the corner, she found a sack and pulled out the white gown. It was plain, with copious material. With a start she realised it was the same one from her dream, the one where she was tied to an altar and Longhurst had done unspeakable things to her. Deciding it was better to dress herself than have her clothes forcibly removed, she unbuttoned her blouse and then after undoing it stepped out of her skirt. She hesitated with her under things. The corset was not easy to undo. It took a bit of manipulation to get the busk to unclip. After some struggle, she was free of it and the rest of her underclothes came off easily. Kicking free of her draws, she slipped the white gown over her head. The neckline was rather loose, and she could see no way to tighten it.

A noise at the door made her heart leap. She crouched low to the floor, resembling some animal about to leap. The door had a small hatch, which opened, and a tray of food was pushed through it. Jemima went over to it and bent down to inspect it. Bread, cold pie and some ale. While she was thirsty, she hated the taste of ale and took some of the bread to gnaw on. Not long after a hand reached in to remove the tray.

She sat on one of the sacks, pondering her situation. So far everything was going to plan—almost to plan. She was in far more danger than she could ever have imagined, and help was rather longer in coming than she had hoped. Being separated from Edward after their reunion was not part of the plan either. She had imagined them being together to the end.

With a loud thud, the door burst open. She stood up, holding the neck of the gown close to her throat and gaped at the men standing there. It was the two men who had dragged her down the stairs.

"If you would come this way, miss," the man whom she had kicked said. She thought it particularly bad luck that he had suffered no permanent harm.

Jemima, preferring to walk rather than being dragged, held the neck of her gown with one hand and looped the voluminous train with the other so she could move freely.

They marched down the corridor and paused before a set of large, rusty doors. The man who had dragged her by the hair leered at her before pounding on the metal surface, engendering a loud boom. The doors opened ponderously, with Jemima keen to see what was on the other side. Her eyes took in the cavernous room, gaslights burning yellow and blue along the walls and casting ripples of shadows in all directions.

With a gasp, she noticed the table in the centre as it had appeared in her dream. Beside it two large urns flamed and smoked. At the head of the table was a winged cross, such as the one depicted on the medallion Longhurst had worn, though this version was larger and more intricately carved. Turning her head, she saw that the air was filled with smoke, and laden with heavy incense and other herbs she did not recognise. Dark cloaked figures gathered around the walls of the room, hoods drawn over their shadowed faces. They chanted their quasi Latin song monotonously.

Panic assailed her, and she readied herself to bolt. However, she was seized by the arms and drawn inexorably to the altar. Her heart beat erratically and painfully. She found it hard to draw breath and these physical symptoms of fear only added to her distress and compounded it.

As if he had stepped from the slanting shadow, David walked to the foot of the table, cloak billowing around him and mist rising from where he stepped. After bowing to the winged cross, he turned toward them, his face void of feeling. "Place her on the table."

Before she could protest, she was lifted, and her struggling body placed on the cool marble. Details she had not remembered from her dream leaped out at her. The table had a lip around it, to catch blood perhaps. Jemima shivered and closed her eyes, lest she scream at the anticipated horror. The figures, who had been chanting along the walls, moved forward to form a circle around her. Lowering himself to his knees, Longhurst began a chant in the harsh tones of a language she did not recognise. Acolytes brought a large chalice and finely tooled bronze pitchers, which he used to mix the various liquids. He lifted the chalice as would a priest seeking a blessing of the Eucharist and again she was struck with the similarity with her dream. David approached her, bearing the chalice. One of the men lifted her head.

"Drink," he instructed her.

Jemima was transfixed by the chalice David held. Her heart thumped in her chest and her breathing was now quite ragged. She wondered if he had drugged her with the bread, but then she drew in a breath, feeling the effects worsening on her. There was something in the smoke, some type of mind-altering substance. The edge of the cool chalice touched her lips. Jemima swallowed a mouthful and it was taken away. Longhurst raised the chalice to the winged cross and spoke again. His acolytes repeated his words and the chalice was placed against her lips once again. Again, she took a sip, likening the flavour to a cough syrup, even discerning a faint liquorice taste on her tongue. He repeated his ritual until she had tasted six sips of the potion.

Already her feet were tingling, her lips numb, her head a swirl of thoughts and her vision distorted. Her body flaccid and her limbs unresisting, she could do nothing when they tied her wrists to the corner of the table above her head. Her feet were likewise tied. David drew down the neck of her gown and placed a kiss on her chest. Jemima could not react, could not pull away. All sensation centred on that touch of his lips on her pure white flesh. A guttural moan escaped from her as she undulated. He drew away and the world stopped still. She was a perceiver of action, no longer being able to shape what was going on around her.

"Bring him," David said while he still bent over her, inhaling the scent of her and caressing her skin. Smirking at her, his pale eyebrows lifted archly, daring her to protest. While he waited for Edward to be brought in, he ran his hands down her limbs, then drew up the hem of the gown, arranging it so that one of her legs was exposed almost to her hip. Removing himself to the foot of the altar, he ran his hands down the centre of her starting between the breasts and ending at the juncture of her thighs.

The touch made Jemima shiver, even though he had touched her through the fabric of the gown. Her mind was centred on David, as he spoke to her, as if whispering a chant in her ear, staring at her with those deep, dark eyes of his. Mesmerising her. When she realised that he was trying to hypnotise her, she tried to fight against the tide of drugs in her mind. Unfortunately, the seeds had already been planted in the preceding dreams. Edward. She had to focus on him instead.

Again, David caressed her skin and all the blood followed his touch so that she arched her back and cried out. It was then he began to talk to Edward.

Jemima wanted to cry out. She wanted to deny the situation, beg Edward to look away from her shame. Her volition had been paralysed, like a butterfly pinned to a board.

"You see how totally in my power she is? Do you abandon her to her fate? Will you watch while I sacrifice her, use her blood in the ritual or will you assemble the machine, power it with your invention and raise him, raise my lord and his host?"

Jemima's head swam. She saw Edward sitting there on a chair, cleanly shaven, dressed, his hands once again in the strange leather bindings. Two men held him in the chair, their hands pushing down on his shoulders.

"Edward?" she called out, finally able to speak. "Forgive me."

"Jemima!" Edward's voice rang out. She could see his skin was flushed and angry as he fought to stand up and come to her.

"Well?" David asked, walking toward him. "What say you? She looks rather delightful do not you think? You could have her now, take my place, if you could bear to be our performance. Privacy is not a luxury we can afford. I am afraid my followers would not be satisfied."

Jemima threw her body to the left and to her surprise it moved. Her gaze fell again on Edward, who looked so handsome sitting there, gazing at her with his penetrating blue eyes, fists clenched tight. Did what he see disgust him? Did her helplessness appall him? Was she now like one of the fallen women he knew?

Still Edward gave no answer to Longhurst, his gaze riveted to her. He rose from his seat only to be shoved back down again by the men who restrained him.

"Very well. Watch as I begin the ritual."

David once again loomed over her. He kissed the ornate knife he held in his hand and ran the blunt edge over the top of her breasts. "No," she called out, conscious that Edward was watching, seeing her helplessness, her reactions.

David murmured words as he cut into the flesh of the top of her left breast. She cried out and the noise she made sounded more like pleasure than pain.

There was pain, but Jemima did not react as she should. It was dull. She felt the cut and tug but not sharp pain.

"Oh God, no! Leave her. I will do as you ask." Edward's yell reached them, full of anguish.

David finished his cutting. One of the acolytes came forward, poured something hot on the wound from a small jug. Jemima screamed as it scalded her.

David smiled at her, reached down and kissed her. He locked gazes with Edward. "How do I know that you will do as I ask? What oath could you give me?"

Edward did not speak at first. His eyes were fixed on her, but he shook with the force of his frustration. He was held to the chair, when all the straining of his muscles she saw he wanted to come to her, to free her. When he did not answer immediately, David returned to her side.

David's hand once again caressed her, his hand sliding up her exposed thigh. Her heart now was beating very erratically. A powerful faint was on her. She felt herself sinking, sinking as a black bank of fog in her peripheral vision threatened to close in.

Edward yelled so loudly that it pierced into Jemima's drug-filled mind. "No," she screamed out with all her might, that last vestige of conscious thought. "Do not promise them, Edward. Leave me."

Edward managed to shrug off the men who restrained him and bolted toward her. David retreated, a smile playing along the edges of his mouth. Edward's eyes glittered with unshed tears as he reached out to stroke her hair and adjusted the robe to hide her exposed flesh.

"Oh God forgive me! I cannot bear your suffering." He lifted a gaze, full of hate to David Longhurst. "What kind of beast are you to use an innocent this way."

"Tut! Tut! She's not so innocent."

"No," Jemima cried. "Edward do not listen. Do not give in." She was not sure her words formed correctly as her mouth was not moving as it ought.

Longhurst lifted his arms, sending his dark cloak billowing. The chanting grew louder. Jemima had trouble staying focussed on Edward, on what was important. She fought hard against the tendrils of magic that lured her away.

"Make up your mind. I grow impatient. Or do you leave her with me for a sacrifice. Leave her flesh for us to do with as we please."

"No!" Edward's jaw clenched as he fought against Longhurst's threats.

Jemima chanted repeatedly—*leave me, leave me*—in a monotonous tone or moan. She could not be sure.

Edward clutched at her hand. His eyes swelling with tears. "God forgive but I cannot...No...I must not...but I..." He let out a growl of rage, then facing Longhurst, his cheeks florid, Edward grounded out.

"I swear on the life that I hold dear..." He swallowed, cast one more look at her and said in a defeated tone. "I will do as you ask."

Edward sagged, his chest heaving in huge breaths. The oath had cost him. Her vulnerable state cost him.

Longhurst smiled, an evil smile. "How do I know you will keep your word?"

Edward raised his face to regard Longhurst. There was a calmness in his features now that he had a pact. "Free her. I will work to the best of my ability until the task is complete. You have my word as a gentleman."

Longhurst assessed him with a slow gaze and nodded. "That means a lot to you, I suppose. The word of a gentleman. Hah! I will make sure you keep it."

Edward continued to stroke her forehead, gently brushing the hair from her brow, his eyes brimming with unshed tears. "Forgive me. I will do my best to spare you more hurt."

"Oh, Edward. Help is coming. Hang on."

Longhurst signalled his men. "Enough. Take him to the factory floor." The two men, who had restrained him previously, moved forward and grabbed him.

"Do not harm her...set her free."

"Free her? We will see. Harm her? I think we have different interpretations of harm."

"Do not mince words with me for I know you have a perfect understanding of what I mean. If you harm her, then my vengeance you will perfectly comprehend."

"Take him," David ordered the two men. When he had been taken from the room, David turned to his acolytes and commanded them. "Untie her and place her in the cell. I will go to the factory floor and observe Huntington. Keep her safe: do not molest her. I will not jeopardise this agreement by having her harmed or interfered with."

Jemima throbbed with the potion she had been fed.

They carried her to the room, where they had kept Edward, and locked the door behind them. The latrine bucket had been emptied. One small mercy given her. Rather unsteady on her feet, she used it and waited. They did not bother to bring her clothes. A tankard of water was pushed through the hatch door. Her heart beat was still erratic and as she felt faint by turns she lay herself down. Lying there, she slept, her dreams filled with strange images and colours.

She awoke to the sound of heavy pounding. Each concussion caused agony. Her head felt like a pin cushion, with stabs of pain shooting down her neck. Her injury throbbed, and she touched it gently, pulling her hand away when it smarted.

The door flung open and light flooded in. "Jemima?" It was Fulton's voice. He grabbed her to him, hugged her fiercely. "Thank God, you are all right."

Her eyes would barely open, headache and the light making her squint at him. "Fulton? Edward?"

"The police continue the search. The place was empty, except for you. Evidence of occupation is here, but they have run before us. Somehow, they knew we were coming. Damn Longhurst and his preternatural ability." He endeavoured to cover her with the white gown, holding it in place as he comforted her.

"No, no, no," Jemima cried in frustration. "He is gone. Oh my God, no."

Fulton held her to him until she calmed, wiping her tears away. "I am sorry." He caught sight of the wound on her chest and shook his head. "You have sold yourself cheap for little reward." He hoisted her up. "Come on little one. Let's get you home and let the police do the rest."

Jemima squeezed one of Fulton's shoulders. "But he was here, Fulton. I spoke to him, touched him." She fought against the weakness plaguing her. "They have...have taken him to some factory... to build Longhurst's machine." She paused and tried to get the last of her thoughts out. "They had to torture me to make him agree. Edward says the machine is for some terrible purpose. He fears what it can do, fears for all of Britain."

A paroxysm of weakness swallowed her consciousness. When next she woke, Fulton was stroking her hair and she was sitting in a chair.

"You have been sadly used, Jemima." He reached for a blanket, which he placed around her shoulders. "Quiet now. I will get you home first and get the doctor to look at you."

Jemima suffered herself be carried out and placed in a police carriage. Sobbing uncontrollably, she refused to be comforted. Fulton spoke to the policeman standing by the vehicle and then climbed inside. Soon it was moving. Fulton held her carefully and keeping the blanket wrapped around her to hide her state of undress. "There, there, miss. We will find him."

"Fulton. Find out where that machine is being built. I am sure it is the one that factory was making."

"Leave it to me now." Fulton comforted her as best he could. Tears soaked her face and hair by the time they arrived at their accommodation. Fulton did not ask permission before he lifted her to carry her into the house and up the stairs. The landlady let out a shocked noise, while Fulton spoke calmly to her, telling her nothing except for her to send for a doctor.

At the door, Milly was there exclaiming and together they took her up to her bedroom. Fulton left her in Milly's hands. Warm water was brought and Aunt Prudence herself brought in a cup of tea. The gown was cut off her. It was stained with blood. Milly gently swabbed at her wound.

"Show me," Jemima asked, and Milly brought her a hand mirror.

Jemima fell back onto the pillows. David Longhurst had cut the winged cross medallion shape into the top of her left breast. Already it had a scab. The hot liquid his followers had poured on it, ensuring that the shape was indelibly etched onto her flesh.

CHAPTER 18

A knock at the door and Milly went to answer it, stepping back to allow a barrel-chested man through the door. The man's cheeks and nose were a deep crimson and adorned with a fulsome moustache and beard. A shock of white hair set off his sombre black coat.

"It is the doctor come to see to you."

The doctor turned, handed Milly his hat. "Take that downstairs for me, missy. I will send for you if I need you."

"Yes, doctor," Milly replied, a worried glance in her direction. Jemima knew it was bad, how bad she did not know. She had never been as ill as this before. She tried to smile and failed. "Hello, doctor."

"I am Doctor Simpson, Miss Hardcastle. Let's have a little chat while I look at you."

The doctor counted her pulse, pulled down her lower eyelids, listened to her heart, checked her wound and chatted quietly. While he poked and prodded, he extracted all the information he could from Jemima, not only the account of various noxious potions forcibly administered by a strange sorcerous man in recent days but even the details of childhood illnesses and the circumstances of her birth.

Jemima found it hard to keep her eyes open, the doctor stayed so long. He ummed and ahhed many a time, before straightening himself up and scribbling in his note pad. "Now, then may I listen to your heart once again, Miss Jemima?"

He put the cone stethoscope to her chest and placed his head close for some time. He was quiet and while he listened to her heart. Jemima could smell a light hint of snuff on the doctor. Under the pressure of the stethoscope, she detected a lurch in her heartbeat. "There it is," Doctor Simpson said, sitting back up.

"There is what?" Jemima asked, her voice faint. She could not rally her strength. Her legs, her arms, all her muscles felt weak.

"That sign again. The cardiac dysrhythmia."

Jemima blinked at him. "That does not sound good at all. I think that is the condition that killed my mother."

He sat down on the edge of the bed, picked up her hand and held it. "That could explain it. You may have inherited the tendency."

"What tendency?"

"The weakness of the heart. In your mother's case, it was probably the pregnancy and the birth that taxed her, shortened her life by a few years. She was destined to die young, I fear. For you, the dubious potions, the excitement, the fear response have all taken their toll. The potions, in particular, have interfered with the natural rhythm of the heart."

Emotion roiled, choking her. A sob escaped.

"There, there, now keep yourself calm."

Jemima squeezed his hand, wiping at a stray tear. "Are you...are you telling me I am dying?"

He nodded. "Normally, I would not say something to the patient. In this case, you do not have long and may wish to put your affairs in order." He left her bed and packed up his things. She lay there silently too shocked for speech. "There is no point in keeping the truth from you, as your condition would be obvious the moment you tried to leave this bed."

Jemima stared at him unbelievingly. "I will not leave this bed? I die today or tomorrow?"

The doctor looked down at her hand, unable to look her in the eye. "I cannot be precise in the matter, but yes. I cannot see you living beyond a week. The defect is very pronounced. Rising from this bed could bring about the final crisis. You would not survive that, I think."

He hoisted his medical bag and went to the door and paused. "Who below should I speak to?"

Jemima did not want to talk to anyone. She did not want the aunt or Milly fussing over her. "Fulton."

"Very well, miss. The landlady knows how to contact me if you need me."

The door shut, and Jemima let her misery flow. The life she had set out for herself was to be cut short. If she had allowed herself to she could have imagined herself in love, married to Edward and with a family of their own. Fond memories of Willow Park swamped her, laughter with her father, tears when he cried out in the night, calling for her long-dead mother, running free through the woods, playing with David. Silent tears fled down her cheeks, dampening her pillow. All future joy was to be denied her. David, her bosom childhood friend, had killed her as surely as if he had driven a stake through her heart.

Jemima lay alone in her bed for quite a while before Fulton came upstairs bearing a tray. "I thought you would like some broth."

He placed the tray down on the table, avoiding looking at her. "Fulton."

"Yes, miss." Still he kept his head turned away, busy arranging a spoon.

"I know...the doctor told me. You do not have to pretend with me. I have already succumbed to despair more than once this afternoon."

Fulton kept his back to her and she saw his shoulders shaking. It touched her heart that he wept for her. She had wept so much in the last hour or so that she needed the bedclothes changed and new nightclothes.

"The broth is beef...will keep up your strength." Fulton still did not turn around.

"That is good...I am hungry."

Fulton put a seat beside her bed and brought over the bowl and spoon. "You mean to feed me?"

"Yes, miss."

His eyes were red from weeping and his cheeks were high in colour too. "You can call me, Jemima, and stop the act. Edward told me you were his friend, not an employee."

"He did?" His grew redder.

"Yes," she reached up and stroked his cheek. "Thank you for everything."

He hoisted the spoon. "I have been thinking about how to set things to rights. Assumptions were made and that makes things awkward for me, does it not?"

She swallowed a spoonful of the warm liquid. "Most certainly, you will find your actions hard to explain. Though I suppose your real identity as a gentleman will cause delight in more than one quarter. How could Edward make me think you were his man?"

A small smile lifted the corner of Fulton's mouth. "He was a portion overwrought, if I recall correctly. I value his friendship more than I can name. He had done me a great service, and I had great pleasure in being of service to him."

He spooned a few more spoonfuls into her mouth. She lifted her hand to stop the next instalment. "Longhurst will come for me. You must take Milly and Aunt Prudence away immediately."

Fulton's eyes lowered, and his hand shook as he placed the spoon in the bowl. "I thought he might. Milly and Aunt Prudence are packing at this very moment."

With her hand on his, she said, "You cannot take them to Willow Park or Kingsfold village. He knows these places."

Fulton nodded and dipped the spoon into the broth once more. "Yes, I have thought of that. I have made arrangements to take them home."

"You have a home?" Jemima asked, before taking a swallow of the broth.

"Yes it is—"

Jemima put a finger to his lips. "Shush. Do not tell me. I think I am the reason David knows everything."

"How?"

Jemima sat back and stared at the ceiling, still arranging her thoughts. "You may not believe me, particularly if you do not believe that Longhurst has some supernatural abilities. I believe he has put spells on me. There has been a pattern to his behaviour, which I have only just now considered could be the moments when he has cast them. The first one was when we met in the lane. He kissed my forehead and muttered some words. I thought nothing of it then, only that he was rather forward. It is that one I believe that connects us, connects our thoughts. From that time, I have experienced vivid dreams, yet they were more visions than dreams. It must have been him that sent those images to me. How did he know to abandon that warehouse where he kept Edward? He knew to evacuate. That knowledge must have come from me."

"Come now, you take a fancy to an idea."

"No, not fancy. There have been other instances. How did he know I was with Bess that night? Also, when Edward and I escaped, for we did for a short while, he came straight to us. No searching other rooms. He knew exactly where I was."

Fulton packed up the broth and put it on the tray. "Very well, I suppose I must own that your ideas are not that strange to me. Huntington's method is not all science, this much I know."

Sudden amazement made her heartbeat flutter. "Not all science. Please, explain."

Fulton turned back to her, the tray neatly packed up. "No, I think not. It is a feeling I have but that is not my story to tell. As for Longhurst, he does seem to know more than he ought. For this reason, I will keep where I live a secret from you."

Jemima had to be satisfied with that, although she ached to know more. She reached out. He stepped forward, placing his left hand in hers, squeezing gently. Her gaze travelled over his face, his expression open. "I take it you can provide for Milly and give her a home."

Fulton blushed and lowered his gaze. "Yes, amply. It touches my heart that Milly would take me poor as she supposed and deformed into the bargain. She is an amazing woman."

"Yes, she is very sweet. Take them to your home, Fulton, and then look for the factory. Find the address. Use the police if you have to. Save Edward. Please. Tell him...I..."

She dropped her hand, suddenly faint. "I will Jemima," he said, stroking her forehead tenderly. "I will go presently and send Milly and Aunt Prudence to say goodbye. We must make the 4.20 train." He leaned over and kissed her both her cheeks. "Goodbye, Jemima. God be with you and keep you from harm."

With the tray in hand, Fulton left the room, not looking back. She closed her eyes, exhausted from the interview. Milly's light touch on her fingers roused her from her doze. Milly could not disguise the fact that she had been weeping, although she put on her best sick room face and bustled about the room.

"Tell me what can I do to make you more comfortable?" she asked, her eyes encircled with dark smudges.

Jemima tugged at her nightgown. "I could do with a change of clothes and bedding, if that is not too much trouble."

Milly nodded. "I must fetch Aunt Prudence. It will take two of us, I think. You must not exert yourself."

Jemima nodded, unable to utter a word of protest. She did not wish to expire at that moment and listened to her body telling her to stay as still as she could.

Milly exited the room, returning very quickly with the aunt.

"How do you do?" the aunt asked, in a voice as soft as she could make it.

"I am well, thank you," was Jemima's absurd reply. One does not admit to be dying in polite conversation. With this piece of etiquette, she was in complete accord. She was growing up, finally, caring for the feelings of others and worrying about scandalising them with her thoughts so quick to her tongue.

"We will have you feeling comfortable in no time at all." The aunt went to the door to receive a jug of hot water. Together, she and Milly efficiently bathed her, put on her prettiest nightgown and robe and remade her bed with clean sheets. They did not talk much, other than to say lift this, move that and put your arm through here. It was all so normal that Jemima found their presence comforting.

Aunt Prudence arranged all the dirty bedclothes and handed them to the maid, Susy. "I hope to see you soon, dearest. Fulton it appears has been rather a dark horse. He is taking us to his home in...well, the country. He says you may join us there when you are well enough to travel."

Jemima patted the aunt's hand softly. "I would love to see you there, aunt. Thank you for caring for me so well."

The aunt's expression changed, the smile fell and there were tears in the corner of her eyes. She turned to go, pausing by the door, looking back once before letting herself out.

"I told you she was not that bad if you gave her a chance." Milly grinned at her, with an 'I told you so expression', though her eyes were watery as well.

Jemima laughed softly. "You did. Be happy, Milly. Fulton...I mean, Ambrose, is a wonderful man. You are very lucky."

Milly trailed her fingers across Jemima's brow. "I know I am lucky, far luckier than I deserve. If only..."

"If only...."

Milly looked at her watch and then kissed Jemima's forehead. "We are leaving now. Ambrose will return for you."

"I know he will. Take care."

And then Milly was gone, and Jemima was left alone. After staring at the closed door for a while she slept. How easy it was to sink into a doze and then feel herself float away. At times, she woke because her heart made a painful, irregular lurch and then it would take time to settle, easing back into its regular though weak rhythm.

"Come and get me, David," she said to the air. "Take what is left of me."

The curtains billowed but Longhurst did not step from their folds. Jemima fell asleep only to be ensnared in a dream. The chanting filled her ears and fear made her heart thump in her chest. The dark lord was coming, and he brought his host with him. Fear flowed along her veins when she saw the vision. Head bowed, arms outstretched, stood the undead remains of he who had terrorised many. Geneck who had taken the blood of all his kin, making them as he was. It was the figure portrayed by the medallion, the symbol of the dark lord they worshipped. In Moldavia, his family had haunted the woods and the neighbouring villages, attacking the weak, the old, the children and the

frightened villagers who had not the wit to flee before the tide of blood
and death. Then came those who conquered and contained, wielding
wooden stakes, pegging them in their graves. There they remained,
quiescent and silent in their prison until David Longhurst came, drawn
by legend, drawn by power, drawn by need and he liberated them.

The sound of his footsteps helped her crawl free from the vision.
Turning her head and opening her weary eyes, she saw him there, black
cloak billowing. Lifting her eyes to his, she saw that he knew. His face
was haggard, no longer triumphant.

"Take me to him. Take me to Edward."

David approached the bed. "You are mine. I will not give you to
him."

Jemima shook her head. "No, David. You belong to another. You
belong to your dark lord, Geneck. I want to be with Edward."

"But the dark lord can save you."

"No, he cannot. He can only condemn me. I do not want that. You
have shortened my life, taken precious moments that might have been
and crushed them in your eager grip. For once that we were friends,
release me. Give me to Edward."

"I am sorry, Jemima. I did not know. I did not want—"

Jemima could feel a coldness climbing up her limbs. It was a
struggle to stay alert. Her heartbeat was irregular and painful. "Hurry."

CHAPTER 19

E dward laboured long hours on the partially assembled machine. The vast array of dynamos and gears that Longhurst had designed and which required completing was more for show than function. Within the cavernous warehouse, Longhurst's contraption held his undead lord, Geneck and his companions—two sons and a daughter, his host as they were called. Workers connected the last of the cables and closed various hatches as the time for the ritual drew close.

Erect at the front of the machine in his dais was Geneck, his shrivelled body encased in a metal array, with nodules connected to wires leading to the generator. He looked to either side, where the two male corpses stood to the right of him and the female to the left. These were emaciated husks, mere mummified remains of the long dead. Each had a gaping hole where they heart should be.

The machine, rising nigh unto the ceiling almost fifty feet above him, had the capacity to sprinkle their skin with electricity. It was not that which would reanimate the undead monsters. When Edward had pointed out the uselessness of some of the apparatus, Longhurst ignored him and ordered him to finish building it as instructed. It was then he realised that for Longhurst the spectacle was as important as the result.

Edward could not have cared less about display. He wanted the machine to fail, and by extension the whole damn procedure, if only those he held dear were not put at risk if the resurrection did not work. What he operated on was far more intricate and was the real linchpin in the revival of Geneck. Building the small device required the upmost concentration. While he was an unwilling participant to this manufacture, he could but not marvel at the workings of it. Based on his stolen designs, with an energy source similar to one used in Fulton's appliances.

The stolen Lady Arbunkle emerald spun in a charger and whirred away as it drew in more energy. The initial spark had come from Edward himself, placed there through his own will and then he was able to draw more power in by spinning the device in his generator. While appearing to be a scientific assembly, it was not. Something from within Edward enabled the charging of crystals. That was why he had not published the papers, could not, as it would cause a scandal and he would never be able to show his face in society. His workings were an amalgam of science and something else—magic. A process he had discovered by accident. First, he had thought it was science until he realised he was putting a part of himself into the gem.

Only in a case of life or death had Edward been brought to use his gift of knowledge and power. For example, to save Fulton's life. Despite all involved swearing secrecy, some inkling of what he had done must have leaked out. How else had Longhurst known or even suspected?

Edward shook his head as he readied the second gem, destined for a machine in one of the dark lord's host. He would not be able to fashion more as there was only the time and the equipment for one extra.

As he looked upon the emerald, he could see the inner glow growing, soon to be perpetual, radiating the life energy to merge machine and flesh. Longhurst's ghastly ritual would revive the terrible soul of Geneck, who he had dug up in Moldavia. It was this device, however, that would replace the heart pierced by a stake, more than a century before.

Edward knew the history, as all unusual tales, particularly Calmet's account from the 18th century, led him to believe there were entities, corporeal and incorporeal that inhabited the Earth, whose existence could not be easily explained. His own talent had taught him that much.

With his custom-made implements, fine screwdrivers, tiny pliers and wire cutters, he adjusted the mechanism, tested it and stood back. He had not seen Jemima since commencing this task. They had not returned him to his previous cell. When taxed, Longhurst admitted that he had returned her to her friends. Edward believed him, because the man did not look happy about it.

Perhaps, Jemima had brought rescue with her as she had claimed. How sorry he was that he had been removed to different premises. He could be with her now, far away from here. He shook his head. Longhurst would not let them rest in peace. There was nowhere they could escape to, of that he was sure. All he would achieve was delaying the inevitable, unless he took his own life. Something he had thought of doing these last weeks while he had been incarcerated.

Just then the door kicked open, slamming against the wall. Edward turned around stunned by the sight of a woman in Longhurst's arms. He recognised the pale skin, hair falling in long golden waves, body as still as death.

"Jemima?" he ran forward and clasped her cool hand.

Longhurst placed her on the cot Edward had been using as a bed, while he pushed off the bed clothes and other paraphernalia laying there, books, pen, cogs and wheels, a few scattered gems, which clattered onto the concrete floor.

"What has happened?" he asked, running his hands down her arms, her inert body, dismayed that she did not appear to know he was there.

Longhurst did not speak as Edward examined her further. He looked into her eyes, checked her pulse, felt her pale, cool skin. A weak pulse, very weak pulse, irregular and fading.

Glaring at Longhurst, he leaped forward, grabbed the edges of the sorcerer's cloak and dragged his face closer. "What have you done to her? Drugs? Potions? Spells?"

Longhurst's gaze was riveted to her form on the cot. "Nothing…it is a sickness within her."

Edward released him and fell back. "Sickness?" He thought otherwise. The sorcerer was complicit in this. He read it in the man's posture, the guilt-stricken expression. Fist clenched, he lifted them, ready to hit the vile brute. "No, there is more, and you aren't telling me. What is it? She is dying. You must have poisoned her."

Longhurst blanched. His gaze resting on Jemima's sleeping face. "Not intentionally…but, yes, the potions I have forced on her and the ordeals I have subjected her to have taxed her, more than they ought. You cannot know how much I regret this. I have toyed with her, used her…but I did care for her in my way. I did not realise there was some hereditary weakness of the heart. Her mother died of it."

Stricken, Edward fell to his knees by the cot. "No, no. This cannot be. She cannot be taken from me, not like this. We had barely begun. She does not know what is in my heart."

Longhurst knelt beside him, hand on his shoulder. "This does not have to be the end. She can be of use to me in the ritual and then the dark lord can remake her. It will be the boon I ask of him in return for resurrecting him. He would not deny such a faithful servant."

Edward lifted his head from Jemima's cot. Incredulously, he stared at the other man. "You trust that monster? You will be lucky to escape this with your own life. No, no. I will not allow you to involve her. You have exposed her to too much already. I have laboured as you ask so that she may go free. You may choose to break your word, perhaps, I expected it from one such as you, but she is so weak she will not live that long in any case. Her time is very short. Give her to me. Let me do what I must to save her."

Longhurst moved away from him, dusting the dirt from his cloak and the knees of his trousers. "For the love for her that I bear, I will do as you ask. I will leave her in your hands."

Edward climbed to his feet, put out a hand to stop the other man from walking away. "No, wait. You mistake my meaning, although I do claim her. I mean for you to give her to me, literally. Release the various holds you have on her."

Longhurst shrugged, attempting to dissemble. "What do you mean?"

"The spells."

"What spells?"

Edward placed his hand on Jemima's forehead. "This one is the all-seeing eye."

Longhurst took a step forward, his head swivelling as he looked between Edward and Jemima. "You can see them? I would not have though it possible. Your skills seem so paltry. You are no sorcerer."

"No, I am not, praise God. Not one such as you, at least, but I have the sight and some talent. At first, I deduced that they were there when Jemima told me you knew so much of their movements. Now that I am close to her and her own life force wanes I can feel them. Remove them and leave her to me."

Longhurst thrust his gaze on Jemima and then knelt beside her, placing her limbs straight and her arms by her side. He spoke the incantations with hands resting on Jemima's forehead. When he removed his hands, the spell was gone.

He put his hand on her chest, over the mark he had cut into her. "She will bear the mark, but the dark lord's power *should* not hold sway over her, I think."

Then he moved his hands to her fingers and toes, chanting low and even.

"Her heart was always yours. Pity, she expires as we speak."

"Edward?" Jemima's eyes opened, her gaze unseeing. "Are you there?"

Edward threw himself down beside her, taking up her hand, kissing the cool fingers. "Yes, I am here."

Jemima looked in his direction. "I am so sorry. I must tell you...the doctor—"

He placed his forefinger against her lips. "Shush, now. It does not matter. Do not worry, do not worry at all. All will be well."

"But I must speak to you." Her eyes fluttered for a moment and then an exhausted sleep took her.

Longhurst loomed over them. "Is all prepared?"

Edward squeezed Jemima's hand and then spoke to Longhurst.

"Yes, the mechanism is inserted and working. All you need now is sunset and your ritual."

Longhurst's gaze rested on Geneck within the contraption. Longhurst was convinced his devotion to the secret order of the Vermilion Crux was sufficient to revive, the leader, Geneck, his dark lord and perhaps his children.

"Were you able to construct the hearts for the hosts?"

"I told you before there was not enough material for them nor time. I had started on one more but I have another use for it now. I could use it to save Jemima."

"Our bargain..."

Edward barely spared him a glance. "Is done. If your dark lord is as powerful as you think, he can raise the others by himself. He needs no assistance from me. You have destroyed my life and the life of the one I could love. What you have already asked of me will kill many; bring terror on all who dwell in this great island. I hope you enjoy this hollow victory, for hollow it will be."

Longhurst growled at him, swirling his black cape so that it spun around his body. "That was not the deal. You had gems a plenty."

Edward came close to striking him, but he could not risk an altercation, not now, not when he had to save Jemima. Instead, he let his breath slide out of him, let his anger drain away. "Do not speak to me of deals and bargains when you have not kept yours. You have harried her, taken from me the years I could have spent with her. There were gems but not machine parts, but more importantly not time."

Longhurst cast his gaze over Jemima, his mouth drawn into a thin line. Edward thought he saw regret there. The man shook off his more tender feelings, drawing close to Edward. Almost nose to nose he said, "Very well. You are on your own. I can do nothing to spare you from Geneck's wrath for those who are present and not one of his worshipers are still within his dominion as prey. I wash my hands of you."

Longhurst strode away towards his great machine. Edward called after him. "I expected as much from you. However, I am prepared for what is to come. Are you?"

Longhurst paused, turned to spare him a glance and then continued. Edward watched him while he went to inspect the glowing metal and gem heart inserted into the gaping hole of the dark lord's shrivelled corpse. Once an aspen stake had been forced through the chest cavity, forcing the unholy life from that evil creature, a vampire of Moldavia. The head was still intact and Longhurst meant to revive him with blood and ritual, with Edward's mechanism serving for that organ for which had ripped from his body. The mechanism glowed faintly green, the colour emitting from the emerald inside it.

On his return to his makeshift work area, Jemima reached out to him, brushed his hand lightly with her fingers. It sent shivers through him. Trembling, he knelt beside her, gazing into that sweet face, stroking an errant lock of hair from her cheek. "Hello there. Awake, are you?"

"Hello," she replied, smiling at him, her eyes glittering with unshed tears. "We meet again."

"Yes, we do." He leaned over to touch his mouth to hers, a light, quick kiss. "Now, I have something to ask you."

"What?" she asked, her gaze bewildered by all that was transpiring around them. Acolytes ran about shouting to one another, while Longhurst yelled instructions, heavy trunks grated as they were dragged along the floor.

"Do you trust me?" he whispered to her, unable to take his gaze from her face.

Her finger traced the outline of his bristled chin. "Yes. Completely."

Grasping hold of her hand, he kissed her knuckles and kept hold of it. "Do you trust me with your life?"

A smile lit her face. "Yes. Are you proposing to me?"

"Not exactly. Do you want me to?" He could not stop the sudden beating of his heart. Could she want him after all that he had done?

Her eyes glittered with happiness. "Yes!" But then other thoughts intruded, clouding her expression and chasing away the joy. "Only...no...there is no point. Edward. I must tell you..."

He put his finger to her mouth to stop her speech, then he kissed her again, deeply, passionately. Then we he lifted his face away, she lay there silent, regarding him with her inquisitive eyes. "I give you my life, such that it is, Mr Edward Hardcastle Huntington."

"Thank you."

He sat beside her, while preparations for a dire ritual took place around him. Her breathing slowed and then stopped. Edward sat a few moments, wiping at the silent tears that had escaped down his cheeks.

CHAPTER 20

"Ice! Bring ice," Edward yelled to a passing workman, one of Longhurst's acolytes. He grabbed the man and thrust him out the door. "Hurry. You must hurry." Next to the warehouse was an ice store, used in the cooling of meat.

Longhurst drawn by the shouting came up to him. He saw Jemima's still, pale form. "What are you doing? She is gone."

"Do what I ask. You lose nothing." Edward had no time for niceties, as he almost spat the words.

Giving him a long look, the sorcerer nodded to his acolyte, who sped off to fetch ice. "You there," he gestured to another. "Help him. Bring as much ice and whatever else he asks for. There is not much time before we begin." To Edward he said. "Whatever you do, do it quickly. The ritual begins in an hour. Then I cannot answer for anything."

"Leave me to do what must be done."

Longhurst looked over to Jemima's still form, her hair lay in golden waves along one side of her face, the rest spilled to the floor. There was great beauty in her death, thought Edward. Longhurst frowned and turned to walk away. "A waste. She died a virgin. I aroused her passions. A pity she did not last to sate the dark lord."

Edward could not stop the hot flow of anger that suffused him. Longhurst had desired her, so had Edward, he thought guiltily. "Care you nothing for her, her intellect, her heart, her love? Do you dwell on nothing but carnal desires?"

Longhurst looked him up and down. "How wrong was she about you. She was convinced you had unmanageable sexual desires, yet I see that it is otherwise. Your prudish values make me sick."

Edward was at once revolted and angered by Longhurst's words. "I have much love in me, much desire. I am more careful how I expend it and with whom. Leave me to my work. I must prepare her."

"Prepare her? But she is dead. I thought you were set only on preserving her body until it could be removed." Speculation glittered in the Longhurst's eyes as he surveyed her corpse. He took a step closer. "You mean to reanimate her?"

Edward positioned himself between Jemima and Longhurst. "Stand aside. You have given up your claims. What I do now is my own concern."

Longhurst inclined his head. "As you wish. My earlier warnings must still be heeded. I can do nothing to assist you against Geneck." He turned in a swirl of black cape and was gone.

Edward once again examined Jemima. The first of the ice arrived and he placed it around her and over her. Then he took from his pile of gems, which Longhurst had pilfered from Willow Park, a pale, flat river stone. This he breathed on, then chaffed between his palms until he could feel it warm. Then he placed it on her forehead, where it cast a soft yellow glow on her features. The stone would aid his work, keep her safe until it was time. He had discovered that it could pause time within a limited range for short periods. At least that is what he thought it could do. He had used it in the past to stop the decay of flesh and the flow of blood when working with live specimens. He had last used it on Fulton.

Then leaning over her, he tore her nightgown down the centre, revealing her soft white breasts. His finger traced the awful wound that Longhurst had cut there. How could that man profess love and then carve her helpless flesh? He was prepared no doubt to offer her to his dark lord for his first meal and sating. Edward had not witnessed such ceremonies, but he had read of them when researching arcane matters. The link between blood and sex was very strong with these creatures and their followers. Only Jemima's mortality had saved her. Had she been healthy, able to withstand the ritual, he doubted Longhurst would have returned her to him.

Edward kissed her breast bone, feeling the cool stillness of her flesh. Sitting back, he reached into his kit and took out a scalpel. Adjusting the lantern, he drew the blade down her sternum, leaving red line of blood in her flesh. He did not have time to assess the best, most discreet place for his device, he had only time to place it close to her heart as quickly as possible.

Using a small cutter, he cut a space in her rib cage, snapping bones to make sufficient space to hold the metal frame in which to sit the device. It was rectangular in shape, two inches in height and about one and a half across the breadth. He used wires to connect the casing to her flesh, to help it adjust and not rot. Within this metal casing, he inserted the tiny machine. Getting up from his labours, he wiped his bloody hands on his trousers and went to the generator where a ruby was currently spinning. It was ready. Deep within the dark red jewel a glow emanated. He took it out reverently, cupping it in his hand as he gazed upon it. "Take my life if you must and give it to her."

A loud detonation startled him, nearly causing him to drop the jewel. The sun had set and Longhurst had pulled the lever on his great machine. Mauve-coloured arcs of electricity snaked up to the iron ceiling, reaching out like clawed hands and splitting the air with loud concussions. The acolytes cheered and then settled into a chant. The power to revive the undead was in the ritual, and the power to maintain that life came from the mechanism that Edward had crafted.

The incantations filled the air with the twisted words of that great old language. Edward hurried over to Jemima's body. He was running out of time. If he did not reanimate her now, she would be gone, her brain destroyed beyond repair, her blood so congealed it would not slip easily through the heart's chambers. The stone was effective for the short term. He did not know if it would keep her whole for a longer period and he would rather have her back whole, than a pale shadow of herself—a shuffling, mindless creature.

With a worried glance behind him, he realised his error. It had taken far longer than intended to complete the operation. He had not wanted to be there once the dark lord arose. Even his sound heart and mind might not withstand such horror. Close to Jemima once again, he mopped the excess blood from her chest and then inserted the jewel into its place within the machine. The machine whirled inside its casing, delivering short bursts of electricity into her heart. Edward rejoiced that his tiny machine worked as planned. He raked his gaze over her, looking for signs of life. Yet she did not wake. It was not working.

The ritual continued behind him. His own heart palpitated with fear, interfering with the cool calculation of his mind. There had to be something more he could do, something left to try. In theory it should have worked. Time was running out. Looking behind him, he saw Longhurst before his machine in front of the platform where Geneck stood. The heart machine spun, sending out intermittent shafts of green light over worshipers who stood with hands aloft in adoration.

Longhurst thrust a jewelled encrusted chalice high, one filled with Jemima's virgin blood, no doubt.

Tearing his gaze away, Edward focussed on Jemima's still form. The machine worked but there had to be some impetus, some initial force to raise her, just as Longhurst was doing with his dark master. He removed his stasis stone. That was not the cause of her not reviving.

Running his hands through his hair, he considered his options. Could he manipulate the heart? Yes, he must. There were no other choices left to him.

"Come on, Jemima." He leaned on her breast, pushing down, massaging the heart.

While he tried to reanimate her, Edward spared a look behind to measure the progress of the ritual.

Crimson blood dripped into the dark lord's mouth from the lip of the chalice. The ritual had begun in earnest. Edward could see the eerie glow of the mechanical heart from his position. Purple-tinged lightning rippled over the gathered host, revealing deep fissures in their blackened dead flesh. Dragging his gaze away, he thumped

Jemima's chest in desperation. "For heaven's sake. Beat damn you. Beat."

Again, he thumped her chest, enough to make her corpse jolt and dislodge ice that fell bouncing and skidding to the floor.

The machine spun, sending its pulses of energy into her body. Still she did not revive. "I need something else. What I have done is not sufficient?" Edward berated himself, time was running out.

Again, he ran through the possibilities. Either he needed a strong electronic shock, or the machine was not near enough to her heart to effectively stimulate it. He picked up another wire and measured it. He attached it to the top of the dynamo feeling an electric charge that numbed his finger. Then carefully as he could, he slipped it in under the flesh to reach near the base of her heart. With a jerk, her body lurched under him. Her mouth sprang open, sucking air. Her eyes wide and staring as her chest heaved again. It had worked. She lived.

"Jemima. Jemima."

She did not recognise him. The opening of the eyes was a reflex only. Yet she breathed. Her heart beat. He lifted her wrist and felt the pulse. Warmth was returning to her body, colour to her cheeks. He had broken faith with death; would that he not suffer for it. He quickly brushed the ice away and draped a blanket over her.

There was a ferocious wail. Edward jerked around, unable to keep his eyes from the terrible transformation taking place. Vibrations from the giant machine made his legs tremble as power erupted and sparks rained on those gathered beneath it. Smoke rose up and joined with the creeping dark of night now perched above their heads within the cavernous building.

He went to his box of gems and stones and found the set of seven he needed. Placing them in a circle, he invoked their magic before returning to Jemima's side. A ruby glow suffused her skin. He tugged the blanket over her.

Again, an unnatural howl erupted from within Geneck's corpse, creepily amplified in the space around them. Edward's skin tingled as the hairs on his arms and neck rose and bile slid surreptitiously into his mouth. He caught a slight movement in the body of the monster. Blood trailed from its twitching gaping mouth. A hand moved stiffly. A fist clenched with the sound of bone grating on bone. Unfortunately the ritual was working.

David Longhurst stood before him in rapture, arms raised in worship. The flesh of the corpse began to bubble as the power of Jemima's blood coursed through the tissue. More electricity flowed over its skin like hundreds of tiny flames. Longhurst called out excitedly, his body held in rapt attention, his gaze following each small movement, each tensing and releasing of muscle.

The beast became aware, its head moving in a slow arc, taking in the acolytes around him. Longhurst shouted now, calling out the beast's name, bringing the attention of his awful dark lord to himself. With glowing red eyes like coals, Geneck searched those around him and then his vision centred on the man who had revived him. Stepping stiffly down from the dais, he still towered over Longhurst, broad of shoulder and hip and thick armed, he stretched like one awakening from slumber. Ever so slowly, he reached out with a claw-like hand and caressed David Longhurst's head, gently touching the man's lips with his bare-boned distal phalanx.

When his hand reached the back of Longhurst's neck, the grip changed dramatically, capturing the jaw with a bony thumb, bending the head back, dragging Longhurst forward. As if waking out of a stupor, Longhurst struggled against the hold. He let out a mighty scream as the dark lord's cavernous mouth lowered, white sharp canines extending. The dark lord ripped the flesh from Longhurst's neck and shoulder with a sound like wild dogs snapping the neck of a faun and tearing into its still warm flesh.

Arterial blood sprayed over the floor and cloaked the monster's body, the hot blood painting his still dark flesh with swathes of red. He bit deeper. This was no sampling of blood by Geneck, but a ravenous feeding. The long tongue lapped, sending tendrils of ripped flesh flying off to the side to plop on the floor. Blood splattered against the machine's facing. In a few minutes, Longurst hung limp and empty. With a flick of his wrist, Geneck flung the corpse to the floor with a sickening thud.

Pausing for a moment, his flesh rippled, swelling in places, fading from black to grey. Geneck was coming back to flesh and blood. The dark lord moved unnaturally swiftly, suddenly he appeared ten feet away, its arm snaking around an acolyte too paralysed by fear to flee. This time the dark lord was gentler, his kiss seeming soft, tender and passionate. The acolyte was a man, Edward thought by the deep tones of his surprised yelp. He moaned at first in terror and then in ecstasy, his hands grasping onto the dark lord's body as the blood drained from him, the strength leaving him soon after. After his drained shell was discarded, more flesh erupted on the foul beast.

Naked, he stood there, red eyes fading to a fathomless black, glittering with the reflected lightning, still snaking out from the top of the machine. He strode through the acolytes, each throwing themselves this way and that. Some drawn. Some repelled.

One acolyte stepped into his path, throwing off her robe, revealing plump, female nakedness. Pausing, the dark lord noticed her and then his arm snaked out to draw her to him. Her screams grew louder, more agonised as he tore into her flesh. Blood bathed her breasts and trailed down her flaccid arms to puddle on the floor. His flesh was now soft and smooth though with a sickly grey tinge, his teeth pearly white within blood stained lips. He hunted for more victims, grabbing the first within a few footsteps.

Edward turned away and his gaze fell upon Jemima. Her skin tone had returned to its normal colour. He leaned in close, stroked the hair away from her face. "Can you hear me? Jemima?"

There was no response to his touch or words. Her wound bled now that her circulation was restored, so he reached for a swab, mopping up the excess blood and wondering how he could cover her nakedness. He had to get her out of there and he needed to attract the least amount of attention.

The robe that covered her nightdress had escaped the worst of the blood and gore from her surgery. It was then he saw the stasis stone lying on the floor. He reached out to it, drew it into his hand and then rubbing it anticlockwise until it no longer glowed, placed it in his pocket. At least in her unconscious state, she had been spared a terrible sight. The noise surrounding them was deafening. The machine ground out, noise, sparks and smoke and the horrible screams of the dying and the terrified pierced the air with regularity.

Her eyes fluttered open. This time they saw the world with intelligence. She frowned and then winced, reaching out with a hand to touch her chest. He caught her hand and brought it to his lips.

"Jemima," he whispered.

Her gaze flew to his, her hand clasping his strongly. "Edward? I feel strange. Something is not right. I remember closing my eyes, feeling myself lost in the darkness." She put her other hand to her head. "Something happened. I was sure I died. My chest hurts."

He stroked her hair, smoothed her brow while he made small comforting noises. This action seemed to calm her. A loud concussion made her start. Her eyes grew wild, trying to make sense of the scene around them.

"Edward? Tell me..." Her hand clung to his, her eyes imploring, their expression lost, confounded.

"You live." Again he stroked her, calmed her. "I was able to intervene in time to save you. I am afraid I have ruined your beautiful body somewhat."

"Intervened?" She glanced down, seeing the blood and a portion of the wound. "How? My heart?"

"I have placed a machine there. It will keep your heart beating for a very long time."

Her fingers sought to free themselves from his grasp. He took her hand and helped her probe the edges of the wound and the rim of the frame wired to her flesh. "It will take some getting used to. It is unsightly. I had no time to hide it within your body or make it pretty with a casing."

A rosy glow suffused her skin. "What is that red light?"

"You have a ruby in you." He tilted his head sideways and gave her a timid smile. "A ruby heart."

Jemima's mouth dropped open and her eyes grew round. It took a while for her to respond.

"Do you mean you have made for me a device like Fulton's leg?" She did not sound appalled, rather she looked and sounded excited.

His brows drew together, wondering at how she knew about his work. "Yes. How could you... You have seen it?"

Jemima rolled her eyes and slapped him on the hand in a friendly

way. "Why, of course I have. I have tended it as well, using the little kit
Fulton had with him."

Edward reeled in surprise. How could she be tending Fulton's leg?
How could Fulton show it to her? He tried to think up a rational
explanation for this occurring and gave up. "Truly?" He found it hard
to keep the amazement out of his voice. "And you were not revolted by
the sight of it? Fulton was sure that any woman, or man for that
matter, would be repulsed. In fact, he was ill himself, violently as I
recall, upon seeing it."

Jemima smiled, though her eyes were inwardly focussed as she
touched her forefinger to her chest. "Not at all. Your creation is a thing
of beauty."

Screams echoed around them, louder, closer. The stacks of crates
disguised the number of acolytes gathered for their dark lord's
awakening. Jemima winced, drawn from her introspection. Her head
swivelled, taking in their surroundings, a puzzled frown wrinkling her
brow. "What is happening?"

A circle of light sprung up around them. Edward stood, instantly
on alert. "What is that?" Jemima asked, not quite able to sit up.

"A dark and dreadful beast. Do not fear. He cannot touch us. I have
created a barrier that even he cannot cross."

The warding stones he had set in place sent up columns of power
to protect them when the dark one approached. Edward considered
his barrier impenetrable, even though it had never been used to hold
off a being of such might and power. However, the old magic had not
failed him before.

There beyond the glare of the light of the warding stones, stood
the dark beast, nearly full-fleshed and unfortunately not sated by the
blood he had already consumed. An outraged inhuman growl sprang
from his throat as he was forced to prowl the perimeter, seeking a way
through to his intended victims. The beast puzzled out the columns,
reaching out to touch them and then recoiling, the flesh of his hand
giving off smoke. The contact hurt, too, if the yowl he emitted was any
indication. Further, he circled them, prowling, eyes never leaving
Edward, the dark orbs tinged with the glow of the inner red coals.

Jemima and Edward clung to each other, not daring to speak. They watched the beast as it circled them, seeking a way through. Then the beast's eyes glowed red.

Jemima stiffened and then jerked upright.

"Jemima?" Edward called.

Getting up from the cot, she hesitated before she took a step, all her resistance crumpled.

Alarmed, Edward put his hand out to hold her still. She flung him off like he was a feather. "No, stop. Jemima."

His gaze slid to Geneck. A horrible grimace graced the beast's awful features. His finger curled and Jemima took another step. His barrier would keep Geneck out, but it would not keep Jemima in. He had to act fast. The blood tie was active. Geneck was revived using Jemima's blood.

"Jemima fight him." He dragged against her shoulders, turning her back. Her face was an empty mask. He saw Geneck beyond the barrier gesturing. Jemima reached out and picked up a scalpel, which she weaved in front of his face. Her hand shook, her jaw clenched.

"Jemima. Fight his hold."

Crouching, she squared off opposite him, thrusting the blade toward him before moving the weapon in a circle, looking for the next opening.

When there was no reaction, he called out. "Jemima. Look at me. I am yours. You don't have to kill me as my life is already yours."

Edward channelled his power, hoping to break the hold. When it hit, the ruby sent out a shaft of crimson light before settling back into its rosy glow.

Shaking her head, Jemima's eyes focussed. She gaped at the scalpel in her hand, glanced at Edward, gave him a fiendish smile and swung. The scalpel flew out through the barrier and struck Geneck in the chest, before falling to the ground with a clink. Jemima stood up, arms crossed to conceal her breasts and the ruby glow.

Geneck growled, a low guttural sound that sent shivers up his spine. Stepping forward to drape the blanket over her shoulders, he buried his face in her hair. "Thank god. I thought I had lost you."

So much for Longhurst's assurance that Jemima would have no connection to the beast.

Jemima kept her gaze on Geneck. The beast swung around and stalked towards the machine, where his dead sons and daughter stood, awaiting resurrection.

Edward remembered the story of the man as he once was, retold many times through the years. Geneck had been a large man, with big hands used to cutting wood and labouring on his farm, before fate intervened. Absent for some ten days in the rugged mountains, he returned to his family no longer the man he had been. Something had taken him in the dead of night, beneath a cold full moon, by stealth or consent no one knows.

When the wood cutter returned to his home, the life force animating his body was not his own. It was a fake, a sham, a mimic. Worse still it was a force hungry for death and destruction. His family welcomed him only to be exploited by the evil seed within their father.

At first, he fed on his eldest son, the strongest one who took so much after the father. Still with that strength, the son died, weakening from blood loss, week after week until death. Then before the first was buried in the hard, unwelcoming ground, he sought his younger son, who was not yet a man. This life he drained in one attack. To the grieving daughter he then turned, removing her clothes of mourning, and sated his unearthly lusts in her innocent flesh before she too fell like chaff from the thresher, her life and blood sucked into his unholy gullet. Then he did call them all from the grave to serve him as his host.

Now, Geneck's rage spilled out around him, when he saw their lifeless and shrivelled corpses arrayed in the niches. They had not been resurrected as he had. The bristling power of the machine had done nothing to animate them, to call forth their restless, hungry spirits.

Geneck touched his mechanical heart, whirring away within his chest, the light from the emerald burnishing his undead flesh a sickly green. His head, now fully clothed with long dark hair, turned to Edward and knew, knew who had created it. Those dark fathomless eyes delved, seeking knowledge but could not penetrate the barrier. With a sneer on his face, he returned to the study of his host. Would he now try to resurrect his children?

In a moment he had disappeared, shot away from his position in front of the machine like a bullet from a gun. Edward looked around him, seeing no one but the still fleeing acolytes, yelling in fright as they crossed one another, more often than not, colliding as they ran to and fro.

Renewed screams alerted him to the reappearance of the beast. Brandishing the fallen chalice, he slashed throats with his claws, filling it with dark rich blood. Acolytes fell together in a pile, bleeding over one another as they lay supine on the floor.

Once he had filled the chalice, he went to each of the desiccated corpses of his children and poured the blood into their mouths stretched into a rictus grin by their hideous deaths. For many heartbeats Edward waited. Nothing happened. Thank heaven, he thought, the beast did not have the power to raise them. Seeing this, the beast let out his rage in a blood curdling roar. Jemima shuddered beside him, and Edward held her closer, feeling with joy her soft sweet breath on the skin of his arm.

Hurling the chalice from him, the beast disappeared again. When he reappeared in front of the machine, he dragged two or three struggling acolytes with him. He drew each close to him using some power of the mind to subdue them. He stripped their cloaks, leaving them kneeling naked before him. Two men, one larger in stature than the other and a woman, who looked too young and innocent to participate in such a ritual. The similarity to the host was not lost on Edward. Yet behind the barrier, he could do nothing to stop what he anticipated would occur. When he considered what he was up against, there was little he could do in any case.

Geneck kissed the acolytes in turn, his embrace passionate. Then grasping the first man by the hair, he twisted until his neck was barred. Again, those teeth extended, tongue and lips sucking and licking the blood that bubbled free of the wound. He drank until he had drained the first man almost to death and then he paused. The man sat back on his heels, skin pale, eyes dark hollow orbs. While standing over him, Geneck invoked some phrase, which Edward could not make out. Then brandishing his wrist, he bit it, until blood drenched his chin and then forcing the man's mouth open he dripped the dark blood of a vampire into his victim's mouth. The two other acolytes looked on as if mesmerised, swaying slightly to the beat of some lullaby. Geneck repeated the ceremony with the second man, who was younger and smaller in stature than the first. The beast was recreating his host. Seeing he could not raise their actual corpses; he was bringing forth their spirit.

Next it was the girl's turn. Dark, curly hair framed her face, her eyes glowing with admiration. She had obviously been ensorcelled by the beast. Geneck's conversion began differently to the others, starting with a tender kiss to the forehead and then the lips. Next he lifted her up so that she stood in front of him. He proceeded to molest her and suck her blood.

"Do not look, Jemima," Edward whispered to her, but found that she had already shut her eyes.

"I have seen enough. I have felt him in my mind. You cannot know...you cannot see."

Edward grabbed her to him, his hand stroking her back. Her body quaked in fear. He hoped the heart mechanism would stand the stress of their current situation. She looked whole, more whole and animated than he had expected.

The bodies of the acolytes appeared dead. On his command, they rose as if lifted by some unnatural force, pivoting they all faced their new master.

"Feed," he commanded them in accented English. "Feed."

His new host sped away faster than humanly possible. One smashed into his barrier, causing a wall of colour to erupt. Finding its way barred, it screeched before running away. Into the cavernous building with supernatural speed, they sought the first of their prey. Edward thought that many of the acolytes had fled. It seemed the rational thing to do when the bloodlust began. Judging from the screams, he realised that many had hidden themselves, thinking the shadows of nooks, crannies and cupboards sufficient to hide them. Screams echoed from the deep reaches of the warehouse and some of the acolytes, now dressed in their normal street clothes, fled back into the vicinity of the great machine, chased out of their hiding places by the newly created host.

As he looked around him, he could see no way to combat the beast, not with a mechanical heart maintaining its unnatural and evil life. A heart that would beat in perpetuity unless he could find a way to stop it. He needed to survive to find a way to right this wrong.

A new sound imposed itself on Edward's ears. Coming from a different direction, shouts and commands and then further surprised screams. A new faction had entered the scene. Hope rose in his heart. They might survive after all.

Darting out from behind a stack of crates, a figure ran past, a familiar figure running faster than a normal man could. Edward peered into the dim light. It was Fulton. Edward caught sight of uniforms. Fulton had brought the police with him.

The large male host accosted Fulton. In a crouch, the male circled his friend, hands held ready to grasp. Fulton tilted his head to the side as if trying to assess his opponent.

"Ware, Fulton," Edward called. "He is a vampire."

Edward did not know if Fulton heard him.

Jemima snapped open her eyes and jerked her head around. "Fulton? He is here?"

"Do not look, Jemima. It is too horrible for your eyes."

Jemima looked pale, the shock of what had gone on around her taking its toll. He thought she had blocked out the sight, but now he wondered. Her visage certainly showed a knowledge of events. He could not be angry with her for defying him. She was far too spirited and brave to spend her time cringing, eyes closed without an inkling of what was going on around her.

Jemima clutched him and eased herself around, so she could see Fulton. "Fulton!" she yelled and gasped. Edward winced at her pain. Her wound was still fresh. She paused for a moment, breathing shallowly until the pain passed. Lifting her head, she called out again. "You need to take its heart or its head. It is the only way."

Fulton did no more than shrug at her words, his attention fully focussed on his opponent.

"How do you know such things?" Edward asked shocked by what she had told Fulton. "I do not believe a gentlewoman would even know such things, let alone scream out such horrid instructions, even in jest."

"I read," she said with a smile into his shocked face. "And I do not think I am a gentlewoman, well, not really, if truth be told. I am an unnatural creature as Fulton has informed me on more than one occasion." She pointed to her ruby heart. "Now unnatural in other ways, too."

He wanted to hold her to him, protect her. Instead, he grabbed her hand and kissed her knuckles. "A remarkable girl."

Edward met her earnest gaze until the commotion caused by the arrival of Fulton and the police caused him to look away. The standoff continued with both assailants assessing the other. The vampire lunged, and Fulton dodged, his mechanical leg making him nimble and quick. The vampire spat, its fangs extending. Its nose twitched as it smelled the pulsing blood in its prey. Again, it dove forward, barely missing Fulton the second time.

For an instant they were close together. Without blinking, Fulton punched the vampire in the chest, smashing through bone and sinew. The vampire looked stunned. With a twist and a crunch, Fulton pulled out its heart, still pumping. The lump of muscle spurt blood over his fingers. The vampire's eyes were wide with shock. It opened its mouth as if to scream, and then its body sagged, falling lifeless to the floor.

Fulton paused to gape at his hand and the gore coating it. Their eyes met. Edward nodded. The arm had always functioned better than the leg. Fulton had better control of it and exercised it daily while recuperating from the surgery, honing his fine motor skills with needlework.

There was the sound of movement and more screams off to the right of the great machine. Fulton dropped the heart and ran into the shadows there.

"My God! How did he do that? It was as if he had a mechanical arm as well as a leg." Jemima's eyes were wide with surprise and her chest heaved with excited breaths.

Edward turned to Jemima, feeling himself blush. "Yes, I made him an arm and a leg. It had been a shocking accident. Fulton was sure to die if nothing was done. Only that would force me to try something so unconventional."

A look of wonder passed over her features, and she put her hand on his and squeezed. "When I saw Fulton's leg, I admired your skill and intellect. Now, with what Fulton accomplished just now, I admire your foresight."

Edward looked back to the crumpled remains of the newly-made vampire. "But I did not know he would need to use it in such a manner. You cannot praise me. That beast, Geneck, is alive and free because of me."

She clung to him then, squeezing him tight around the waist while gazing up at him. "Under duress. You did it to save me, to stop Longhurst from hurting me. No one can blame you for that."

He stroked her cheek, smiling at her lovely eyes. "Yes, I know I was forced, but it does not change the outcome does it? A great evil is now free in our land, and I have no idea how to stop it. The blame is mine alone. It was my invention that gave Longhurst the means to resurrect Geneck."

The guttural roar of the beast filled the air. Jemima shivered, and Edward started. It was so loud and deep, Edward felt it vibrate in his chest cavity. The younger male of the host appeared, drawn by his master's summons. At his feet, he dropped a uniformed policeman whose neck had been ravaged. Naked skin streaked with the blood of his victims, the young male vampire strode forward, stepping over the fresh corpse.

Fulton burst out of the smoky shadows into the light of the machine, veiled with a hail of sparks, anger staining his countenance red. Fulton had up a head of steam and attacked the vampire at a run. The momentum, the strength of his mechanical arm and the surprise of his attack that had worked in his favour before did not work this time. The vampire let out an unholy scream, and flew into the air, perching on a high stack of packing crates before jumping to the floor and running off into the darkness.

Edward worried for his friend. He seemed almost too calm and controlled as he faced this vampire. Fulton stood there panting, his gaze assessing. With a nod to Edward, he turned full circle taking in the towering machine and the obscure places where things could hide. There was no sign of the second vampire.

Around them fresh screams erupted. The young female host was visible through a stack of large wooden packing cases, her mouth engaged in ripping out her victim's throat. Somehow, Geneck had infused the spirits of his children into this new host. From what he had read, Geneck's daughter had been a seductress after she had been turned. No longer the innocent country girl she had been previously, her powers had allowed her to overcome even the most chaste of her prey, sating herself on their flesh, before draining them dry.

Guilt rose within Edward. Although he had been forced to assist in their reanimation, he was responsible for this new blood bath, which was surely the beginning of a plague. He could only calculate the horror that would be unleashed if these vampires were not dispatched immediately. Although Fulton was powerful, he doubted he could achieve it. Not alone. Not without preparation.

The female vampire finished with her victim and sprung forward, her movement blurred by speed. Edward gasped, his attention was once again caught by Fulton, who was using a piece of wood to keep the female vampire at bay.

"I must help him!" Jemima said from behind him.

Edward put his hands on her shoulders to urge her back. "No, you cannot. Do not even look."

"Edward, stop." Edward held her suspended, looking into her eager, pleading eyes. "Help me. I must see. Fulton is in danger. It was I who told him to come here. We must try to help him."

She winced and cried out as her wounds were still fresh and each contraction of muscle, each twist and turn of her torso, caused her pain. It would take a while for the wound to heal and for her body and mind to adjust to the device.

He supported her while she looked on. "Oh my, how did Fulton do that?"

Fulton had jumped over the head of the male host, who had attacked, while the female vampire taunted him, swinging the plank at the same time. The host fell to the side, nearly senseless. However, with its new-found power it was recovering quickly and was soon poised to leap again. Fulton turned, aiming his foot at the chest of his assailant, kicking him backwards and then striding forward to punch down with his arm, once again ripping the heart from the host.

The female vampire screamed then crouched low, hissing at Fulton like a cat to a menacing dog. The death of the second son got Geneck's attention. His roar of outrage shuddered the very fabric of the building.

More police came into the place, boots thumping. Edward swung around and saw weapons raised. Fulton threw himself to the ground, suddenly in the line of fire. Shots spat from the barrel of the guns causing Geneck to flinch. If any found their target, it would be hard to tell. Geneck strode around, eyes on his host, assessing the wastage of his two new creations. His gaze locked with Edward's and then he nodded. Confused, Edward wondered what he meant. Was he going to attack or was there another message that was meant to pass between them? He thought it was more like a sign to him that this was not over. It did not end here.

Fulton turned toward them, quite willing to expend his life to protect him and Jemima, who stood there shakily, hands clenching Edward's shoulder.

The police were reloading their weapons. Once again, the barrels of the guns rose and pointed toward the beast.

Geneck called his host daughter. She swooped toward him, in a blur of movement. When she came back into focus, she clung closer than any vine. The police did not fire, not certain the girl was the villain in the piece.

Slowly Geneck edged back toward the great machine. Then before anyone could act, he turned and reached into the machine, ripping out the guts of the mechanism. Electricity arced out across the ceiling in streaks of violet lightning, creating a distraction. Police and others, who were still standing, gaped at the spectacle. When it had expired, and the last filaments had faded away, Geneck and his host daughter were nowhere to be seen.

The guns lowered, and orders pierced the darkness. Many heavy boots thumped against the concrete floor of the warehouse, as the police sought the beast and uncovered those cringing in hiding places. Cries of horror resounded as bodies were discovered. Blood and gore made a treacherous path and many a policeman was heard to slip and fall. Cries for mercy became sobs of gratitude when wayward acolytes were swept from their hiding places. The law was a welcome relief from the ravages of a savage, bloodthirsty vampire.

"Dear god! I do not believe we have this reprieve," Edward said, checking that the predator had indeed gone from the premises before picking up his guardian stones and ending the warding spell.

"Thank heavens for that. I do not think I could have stood a moment more. So much death and blood." Jemima sat on the edge of the cot, shaking her head in disbelief. She pulled the discarded blanket over her to hide her ruby heart for the torn gown did little to disguise it.

A young policeman approached. "You are Mr Edward Huntington?"

"Yes, I am. This is my ward Jemima Hardcastle."

The officer looked at them in turn. "You right then?"

"Yes, thank you," Edward replied. Jemima nodded, her eyes dark shadows of fear.

"That's good, sir. My superior wants to talk with you. Please wait here." The policeman turned on his heel and disappeared into the smoky shadows.

Fulton loped over. They caught each other up in a hug, the scent of blood hanging over them. Fulton's from the hosts he had vanquished and Edward's from Jemima's operation.

They stood back from each other and then Fulton pulled him close and hugged him again. "I thought we had lost you forever. Only Jemima gave me hope. How is it that she is still with us? I thought...well the doctor said..."

Fulton's gaze fell on Jemima, who had taken a seat on the cot. The blanket she clung to barely disguised the blood-stained clothing hanging from her shoulders.

"Jemima? It was you who called out to me."

Carefully, he picked his way over to her, with Edward following on behind. Kneeling, Fulton edged the blanket aside, touching his finger to the metal frame embedded in her flesh. "Oh my word, I cannot believe it possible."

Jemima put her hand over his, tears streaking her face. "I did not believe it either. I should be dead. Edward is truly a marvel."

He reached up and cupped her chin, squeezing it gently. "Then

Edward saved your life as he did mine. I cannot wait to hear the how of it, perhaps when we are at leisure."

Jemima nodded, finally giving into tears and throwing herself into Fulton's arms. Edward did not know where to look. There had been no time to deal with Jemima's emotions, her shock with all that was going on around them. He looked on as she clung to Fulton, her protector, her friend. How he wished that she clung to him so, but circumstances had made it otherwise.

Edward bent to pick up the choice pieces of his remaining gems and essential equipment and thrust them into his tool box. "Best we not linger here."

He was so distracted by collecting his things that he did not notice the approach of someone.

"Mr Edward Huntington, I presume," a booming male voice said behind him. Edward jumped up and nearly dropped his tool box.

A man in a dark blue coat and hat approached him, hand extended. Edward placed the toolbox on the cot and went forward to shake the man's hand. "Inspector Dudley Vickerson. Pleased to meet you, sir. I take it you are the missing Mr Huntington? Mr Fulton here said that you had been abducted by a satanic gang. It appears we have the bulk of it mopped up, sir. However, if you could shed some light on the extraordinary events we have just witnessed."

Edward swallowed. "Err...Fulton was quite right. I was taken against my will to assist in building that infernal machine. They sought to resurrect some ancient, evil being, using modern technology."

The police inspector chuckled, wiping his eyes with a handkerchief hastily drawn from his top pocket. The smoke within the warehouse had grown quite thick. "Hokum, I say, sir."

Edward could not stop his expression growing stern or hide his emotions, worn rough as they were by events. Why was this man not taking him seriously? Surely, he had seen with his own eyes the fantastic disappearance of Geneck and the girl.

"I am sorry to contradict you, Inspector. How I wish it was all balderdash and all that, but I am afraid it is not."

The Inspector jerked his head up at Edward's words, his beady dark eyes round. "It's not? My superior will have me in Bedlam if I wrote up a report along those lines."

Edward frowned, not liking that he had some sympathy with the Inspector's position. "They managed to summon something awful, Inspector. Something that owns the night and that will leave none of us unscathed. I suggest you prepare for the worst."

"Worst?" The Inspector's brows drew down, peering at Edward as if he was barking mad.

"I am no expert on these creatures, sir, but it has escaped. It is now free to roam, to rip out hearts and terrorise minds."

"What has escaped exactly? Some wild animal?"

Edward did his best not to lose his patience. He would speak the truth, but he could not make them listen or believe. That would come too quickly, when the streets were paved with blood and vampires stalked London. "It is a vampire, an old and powerful one."

A look of disbelief crossed over the man's features, which is what Edward expected, despite the evidence around them. Littered behind him were the bodies of the dead, throats ripped out, blood splattered on every surface.

The Inspector looked around him disinterestedly. "You jest sir. It is more likely some wild animal smuggled in from the Dark Continent. Why last week some fool let a lion out of his private zoo. Two people killed there. It is now a stuffed specimen in the police museum. Worry not, sir. We will catch it and dispatch it before long. We are fit for anything."

Edward did not know what to say. The Inspector seemed convinced that he had the answer. He could let the man continue to think it was a wild animal or he could try to convince the man of the truth.

Putting on his calmest and most reasonable voice, he said to the Inspector, "I know you think me quite out of my head, that I am spinning you some yarn. However, I beg you have a doctor go over the dead and you will see the injuries will resemble none that an animal can produce. Wild animals do not normally exsanguinate their victims."

The Inspector nodded his head and patted Edward on the shoulder. "Do not worry now, sir. We will follow strict police procedure. Best you go home. Take some rest and ease with your friends. I have your particulars. If I need further information I will be in contact with you."

The note of condescension in the police officer's voice irked him. It was pointless to argue now. "Quite right, yes. How silly of me." Edward bent to collect his tool box. "Perhaps after you have interviewed the survivors you will have a clearer picture. I will be happy to give you what information I can. If you no longer have need of me, we must return to Willow Park as soon as maybe."

The Inspector looked him up and down, noting the blood. His gaze slipped to Jemima behind, nodding to her as she clasped hold of Fulton. "I see you have been through a lot, sir. I suggest you make haste home. Willow Park is in Sussex is it not?"

Edward stuck out his hand for the man to shake. "Yes, it is." The Inspector narrowed his gaze at them. Edward felt impatient and wanted to slap the man, but that would achieve very little, except maybe incarceration. So he smiled and said, "We will make our way there immediately, I thank you."

The Inspector stood aside, clearing the way for them to leave. "Very well sir." He turned away then stopped. "Excuse me again, sir." Edward, who had turned to assist Jemima, faced the man again.

"Yes, Inspector?"

The Inspector nodded. "If you could humour me, please do not speak to the newspapers about this incident." He waved a hand in the general vicinity of the machine and the warehouse. "Bound to be a hue and cry over this, even though we are in the industrial area. We will issue a statement when we have further assessed the situation."

Edward nodded eagerly. "I certainly will hold my peace. I have no desire to speak to the newspapers. I have my young ward to protect. She has already been exposed to more than any gentle lady should. Now if you will excuse us."

CHAPTER 21

J emima thought it took ages to get out of the vast warehouse. Although, she was able to walk, Edward and Fulton decided between them that she should be carried. Her assertion that she could manage was ignored. Jemima decided it was better for their nerves rather than her own and acquiesced. Fulton took her in his arms and carried her tenderly. Despite his gentleness everything hurt, every footstep was agony. She rethought her position and agreed being carried was better than exiting under her own steam.

At that moment, she was still trying to digest that she was alive and the terrible scenes she had witnessed. Jemima winced as Fulton lifted her into the waiting coach and four. A driver in livery held the door for them. First Edward climbed in and sat beside her, carefully arranging the blanket and then reaching across her to draw down the blinds. Fulton was next, hastily pulling the door closed, after ordering the driver to depart. Then he pulled down the blind over the door window ushering in total darkness. The clopping of the hooves on pavement signalled their departure, as did the lurch as it surged forward,

Jemima did not like the darkness, the lack of ability to anticipate the lurch of the carriage or the turn in the road. Seeing nothing at all reminded her of that moment when she let herself go, when she felt her spirit fly: when she died. Hearing the contraption whirring in her chest brought out so many unnameable feelings. "This will not do. I cannot see a thing."

"I am sorry for the clandestine mode of travel. However, I think it best that we be private," Edward stated from next to her.

"I understand that, but it is early in the morning and no one is up and about and interested in this lumbering old coach. It feels so dreadfully horrid travelling in near pitch-black surroundings."

Edward felt for her hand, touching her leg before he found it. "The sun will come up soon and some light will enter then."

His touch was comforting as was the warmth of his body next to her. Even then, she found herself restless with questions. "Pray tell me, where are we going? Does David still hunt us?"

Edward grasped her hand, squeezing it tight before relaxing his grip. He then caressed her palm with his thumb, which she found mildly disconcerting. Edward was touching her as a lover would.

"That is one menace that will no longer plague us. I fear there is worse in store. Longhurst may be dead but his legacy is alive and well." Then drawing a breath, he added in softer tones. "At least you will have time to recuperate at Willow Park."

"David is dead. I...well... Am I not to know the how?"

Edward squeezed her hand. "At a later time, perhaps. It is all too new and real at the moment to talk about."

"Begging your pardon, Edward, but I have left Milly and Aunt Prudence at Hatfield. May I offer you both my hospitality?" Fulton's voice sounded different to Jemima, more cultured, more confident. Hatfield? What was that? It sounded stately. How Jemima wished there was some light in the carriage so she could see if there was a change in Fulton's countenance, so she could see for herself what alteration there was in her friend.

"I am not travelling anywhere covered in blood," she said, quite firmly. "We should go to our lodgings and refresh ourselves before going anywhere."

"Of course, you have lodgings. I did not consider. Can we enter discreetly?" Edward said from beside her.

"I think so, yes," Fulton replied. "We had paid for the rooms until the end of the month. There have already been such goings on that I had to slip the landlady a bit extra for her discretion. I also warned her yesterday that it was in her best interest to keep our business quiet as she needed to be mindful of her own reputation."

Jemima grinned to herself. "I suppose you have ordered some breakfast."

"Not yet, but it can be arranged quickly enough. I agree we cannot travel anywhere on an empty stomach. All your belongings are there, too, Jemima."

Edward let out a sigh. "I suppose it is all settled then. But then we must away by coach. I could not bear the public exposure involved in using the railway. Besides, I do not have a change of clothes waiting for me at your lodgings."

Fulton coughed. "Excuse my presumption. I thought it best to have your things packed up and shifted to our lodgings."

At this Edward chuckled. "You see...two inveterate organisers. I doubt I will get any peace with you around. We will stay long enough to wash and dress and eat a quick breakfast. Then we must leave."

Not long after they pulled up outside their lodgings. As they stepped down from the carriage, Jemima found the streets as empty as she had predicted. This did not stop Fulton from carrying her like a babe into the house. The landlady remained quiet when she let them in and let them pass to their suite of rooms. Fulton carried her inside and up the stairs to her room. Placing her gently on a chair he asked, "Can you manage? Susy is with Milly."

Jemima glanced at her mirror and pretended not to see the horrible state she was in. "Thank you, some warm water if you please."

At his departure, she looked around the room, hardly believing that she was there again in her familiar surroundings. Very shortly, Fulton arrived with a kettle and poured out some hot water into her wash bowl. Fulton lit the fire for her. "I will leave you to it then. Call out if you need anything."

As Jemima washed carefully, sponging blood from her chest and stomach, careful not to touch the ruby heart or let any moisture near it. In the mirror, she stared at her reflection, mesmerised by Edward's invention in her chest. He was safe now. They had saved him after all.

But now there were new difficulties. Her feelings were unchanged in that they were not shaken, rather events had caused her to wonder at him, at the secrets he had held so close and the wonder of his deeds. He had surely gone beyond science. It was magic and what did that mean? He was no sorcerer like David Longhurst. His tendencies were not vicious or evil.

The bowl of warm water was bright pink. Gingerly, she carried it to the window and tossed it out and refilled it with water from the kettle. Now she began again, soaping all of her person and then wiping it off. She had to be careful of her chest. The mechanism was exposed and vulnerable to water. Next, she went to her trunk and pulled out a dress. Her nightgown was in tatters and her outer robe too. These she kicked into the fire grate, watching them catch and burn. The flames reminded her of Fulton as he harried the vampires, with flame and electricity bringing him to focus. What Fulton had done in there against those vampires beggared belief. Her assessment of the leg mechanism certainly allowed for greater speed and power. She herself had tightened the springs. That he had an arm construct as well, was entirely a surprise. That he had hidden the fact was amazing to her. The gloves—he always wore a pair. So that was it! No wonder she did not notice.

How she wished for some time and privacy so that she could examine it. Her memories of their time together, her looking at his hands, her touching his hands or seeing them move as he ate. Surely his hand was real as he had been able to sew so perfectly. How was such a thing achieved with a construct?

Jemima took her time with her toilet. She had to fix her hair herself.

Fulton knocked on the door. "May I help you down the stairs?"

"I can manage quite well, thank you. I will be down shortly."

"Very well, be careful."

When she entered the sitting room, she sucked in a breath. Edward was clean and dressed, his expression relaxed now that he was surrounded by normalcy. Standing up, he could not keep his eyes from her. Awkwardly, he held out his arms inviting an embrace. She rushed to him, burying her face in his chest.

Fulton's cough reminded them of his presence and caused them to part. Shyly, she cast a glance at Edward and saw the warm look he gave her. Fulton urged them to sit and lifted the covers off the simple meal before them. He, too, had changed his clothes and put on some white gloves. Had she not seen Fulton in action herself, she would not have believed his ruthlessness and the courageous way Fulton had fought the vampires. She was sure that Milly never would.

They left for Hatfield in the afternoon. Again, with the blinds down. In the darkness of the carriage, the bright rays of her ruby heart leaked out. She had thought the dress had an ample bodice to hide it. "Could you pass me my shawl, Edward?"

Edward felt around for it and draped it over her shoulder.

A gasp sounded opposite her. "What an amazing device you have created, Edward. That ruby heart is difficult to hide, giving off so much light as it does." Fulton's voice conveyed awe.

Jemima looked down, considering the device inserted in her chest, ruining forever a near-perfect bust. "I do not think it is a heart actually, more like something that prompts my heart. You see no blood flows through it. It is not a pump." Jemima had been studying the device in the mirror as well of thinking of its creator.

"How very clever you are, Jemima." Edward gently squeezed her shoulders. He understood that she was still healing. In fact, her chest felt constricted with the device inserted and her chest was painful too. Each jolt of the carriage sent sharp stabs of agony lancing through her. However, she did not complain of the pain and was glad that the dim light in the carriage hid her expression.

"Are we to go all the way to Fulton's residence in this old coach?" Jemima asked.

Fulton's voice pierced the darkness once again. "Yes, it is the most private means. Why not try to sleep. The time will seem to pass faster then."

Sitting in the dark with Edward holding her hand, Jemima replied that she would try. Her head was too full of events, too stirred up by emotion to fully achieve true rest. She loved a man she hardly knew. She did drop off to sleep eventually, not realising until she found her head jolted from Edward's shoulder by the sudden lurch of the carriage.

Fulton lifted the edge of the blind and peered outside. He seemed normal with his head cleanly shaved and his clothing clean. "We have changed horses," Fulton said. "Take this. 'Tis but a sandwich but enough I hope to tide you over. It is near morning. We should reach Hatfield before dark."

Jemima thanked him and chewed on the food. Edward still slept beside her. In the dark of the carriage she dropped off to sleep again.

The sound of Edward's voice woke her. He was in deep conversation with Fulton. "We should not be on the road after nightfall. It is not safe."

"Where do you think the creatures will go?" Fulton asked.

She felt Edward's shrug. "I know not. The beasts cannot stand daylight and will need time to gather their strength."

"Surely, they will not attack us on the road tonight," Jemima added.

Edward shifted, perhaps to face her. "Yes, you could be right. It may be weeks yet before they again hunger. I fear what will come."

"As do we all," Fulton agreed.

Edward relaxed a little. "He has his daughter to keep him occupied."

Fulton shifted forward in his chair. Jemima heard the fabric of his coat rub against the upholstery. "You do not mean that it is the famous Geneck and his family?"

"Yes, none other."

Jemima exclaimed. "But you said you knew nothing of vampires, Fulton."

"I did not, but at your urging I undertook some research."

"Oh, I see."

The carriage lurched suddenly, and Jemima cried out.

"What is it? Are you ill?" Edward asked, fussing around her, hands pawing the front of her gown. She slapped his hand away.

"I am as well as I can be," she said in a gentle voice. "The machine is working fine. It is just that I suddenly remembered something important. I had a vision about Geneck and his family a few days ago now. I think it came from David because more than once he was able to enter my dreams and dictate their course. I had also read the account of them, so I am not so sure."

Jemima shivered, remembering the vivid account, it was as if she had been there in that Moldavian village more than a hundred years ago.

"How glad I am that Longhurst is dead, though I must admit, however reluctantly, that he did care for you in his way. Now that he is gone, his cursed spells should fade."

"With Geneck and his daughter loose, people will be helpless," Fulton said. "I read that when they first appeared, it was in a small village and, while their attacks were devastating in those surroundings, they were contained to that area. Think of what could happen in London with its large population."

"It is as I feared it would be," Edward said.

"It is not your fault, Edward. Please do not blame yourself. You could not control David Longhurst. Surely he would have found another way to...to..." Her voice trailed off when she could not come up with alternatives.

Edward replied. "Try not to worry. We must wait for news." His voice sounded light, but Jemima knew that he was worried.

She edged herself against him, letting him rest her head against his chest. She had not realised how broad-chested he was and how firm and muscled his arms. It felt good to be held in his strong embrace. "There you go. You are safe now. Ambrose and I will let no harm come to you."

With the sway of the coach, the dim light and Edward's warm embrace, she was able to let her eyes close. With the whir of her little machine in her ears, she slept.

Later in the day, she awoke with sunlight filtering through the blinds, illuminating Fulton across from her, sometimes in flashes. Jemima studied him. "Fulton, why are you so happy?"

Fulton shrugged, and grinned at her. "I have lots of reasons to be happy. You are alive. Edward is rescued, and Aunt Prudence is quite reconciled to my marrying Milly, with your permission, of course, Edward."

Edward sat forward, and Jemima could make out a smile. "Blessings to you. Excellent."

Jemima pursed her lips, considering her next words. "I supposed this reconciliation of ideas happened when she first caught a glimpse of your home?"

Fulton chuckled. "I do believe that did influence her somewhat. Our arrival is bound to shake her resolve. We must find some way of disguising your...um...mechanism before we enter the house. For while Milly is getting the used to the idea of my enhancements, I do not think she is quite ready for yours and all the explanations that it would entail."

Jemima glanced down. "As we will arrive after dark, I am sure they will be asleep."

"Perhaps," Edward said. "Her shawl will suffice to hide the glow of her ruby heart. Then we must expand Jemima's wardrobe. No more daring décolletage for you." Jemima detected uncertainty in his voice. Was he being Edward the guardian or Edward the suitor?

The lumbering old coach rolled through the gates of Hatfield and down the long driveway up to the house. Jemima could see little of it, except that its looming battlements would dwarf Willow Park. Only the porch light was lit, the rest of the many windows lay in darkness. With luck, she could slip upstairs to a bedroom without encountering anyone. Edward clung to her hand after they climbed out of the carriage, their feet crunching the gravel.

Fulton raced up to the door and knocked. The butler must have been waiting up for it opened just as they made the top of the stairs. The butler bowed quickly and went ahead of them lighting candles. He handed Fulton a lantern, which Fulton used to light their way to their respective rooms. He first entered one room, saw to it the trunks were placed by the footmen roused from their sleep by the butler, and then lit a few candles for her.

"I will put Edward near me. Milly is in the next room to this and Aunt Prudence is across the hall. If you need anything ring the bell. I am but four doors down; Edward is the next one over. Call out if you need anything."

"I will." Jemima surged forward, carefully hugging Fulton to her.

"Thank you for everything. You are a true and trusted friend, Ambrose."

Fulton blushed and after a quick glance at Edward moved down the hall.

Edward stood there staring at her. She lowered her lashes, unsure of what to say. So much filled her mind, she did not know where to begin. "Good night, Edward," she said rather formally. "Thank you for everything."

He nodded. She thought he was going to speak, but he stepped back and followed Fulton out the door.

She stood there in the chill night, bathed in flickering candlelight. Exhaustion and the aftermath of the horrible scenes in the warehouse must have been catching up with her. She felt numb and overwhelmed at the same time. Edward's actions confused her. After all that they had been through why did he hesitate to declare himself? Why did he hold back when she wanted to be held and comforted?

Her legs were as lead. She had to go to bed before she slumped to the floor where she stood. Finally, she rallied enough to undress and clean up. After a wash, she found a high-necked night gown in her trunk. This she climbed into quickly as the air was chill, before drawing back the bed clothes. She could not believe she was doing something so normal as sleeping in a bed. Her head felt like it was in a sack, jostled and filled with too many images. Every muscle in her body ached. She wished she had some laudanum to dull the pain. Once her head rested on the sweet-smelling pillow and the fresh sheets caressed her limbs, she found herself nodding off. The whirr in her chest worried her. How was she to disguise it? Another thing she had to put to Edward in the morning.

CHAPTER 22

J emima did not realise she had slept nearly the whole day away. The maid entered quietly replacing the jugs of hot water she had left earlier, which had gone cold. Even though Jemima was not fully awake, the maid curtseyed before leaving the room. Afternoon sun spilled in through the gap in the curtains. Jemima was stiff and sore, still, and was loath to move.

A soft knock at the door, heralded the arrival of Milly. "Are you awake?" she said in a near whisper.

"Yes, just." Jemima rolled over and smiled.

Milly's concerned expression transformed to a smile. "I am so sorry to bother you when you are still in bed. Ambrose said I should leave you and he and Mr Huntington have taken themselves off somewhere and I find that I could not wait. I had to see you, see how you were."

Another knock and the maid re-entered carrying a tray. Milly stood by the bed, an eager smile on her face. "Do forgive my presumption. I could not bear to know that you have had no sustenance all day. I asked for some tea to be brought to you. Oh look, the cook has put some fresh scones and jam on there, too."

Jemima sat up, with Milly leaning over her to plump up the pillows. Jemima was warmed by the woman's concern and care and tears pricked her eyes. "How silly of me," she remarked when Milly frowned at her.

"Have I hurt you? Are you in pain?" Milly asked handing her a handkerchief.

Jemima let her feelings flow for a short time and then tried to explain herself. "Oh, I am a little tired, but that is not it. I did not expect such a warm welcome after..." Jemima shut her mouth, lest she say more than she ought.

"You are family," Milly said. "And very dear to us all. Of course, we would welcome you back. Now, then, drink that tea and do justice to those delicious scones. I will leave you, but first I command you to stay in bed for the rest of the day. If anyone has need of you, I will personally escort them and preserve your honour."

Jemima slept and woke sometime after eight. Night surrounded her, except for the small lantern casting a warm glow across the bed. There had been no intrusions, no visits or enquiries from Edward or Ambrose, a fact which annoyed her. What were they up to taking themselves off? How could Milly bear not knowing what they were about? If Jemima had been in better health, she would not let them slink off without telling her first. Her anger, though, did not last and very soon she was fast asleep, waking a few times in the night disturbed by odd sounds in the house, creakings and sighings of the timbers and animal noises from outside.

Jemima was up and dressed when Milly quietly tapped on her door. "Oh wonderful. You are up. I shall dash below and let the others know you will join us."

Jemima nodded and finished dressing. She had a jacket on, with a frilly blouse underneath tickling her chin. Again, she could feel the machine inside her and worried at the sound it made. To her it sounded loud, but Milly had given no sign of noticing.

A footman stationed at the bottom of the stairs directed her to the morning room. Another opened the door at her approach. Her eyebrow rose. She had definitely made some erroneous conclusions about Ambrose. He lived in a style far superior to Edward. For Milly's sake she was glad of it.

Within sat Aunt Prudence and Milly. The younger woman came

forward and guided her to a chair at the table. Jemima glanced at Aunt Prudence as she sat down, expecting some dressing down or castigation. Yet she was unable to disguise her amazement at the aunt's manner.

"My dear girl. How good it is to see you up and around. Please, take some tea. Can I serve you an omelette? The cook here is divine, so light and fluffy you see, just the thing for one convalescing as you are." Before Jemima could make an answer, she dashed over to the sideboard and brought a serving over. Then after placing it before her, she stroked Jemima's hair softly before once again taking her seat opposite.

Jemima lifted astounded eyes to the older woman, who had always disdained her and saw nothing but sincerity in her expression. "Oh, my dear, how drawn you look, but considering what the doctor told us I can scarce believe that you are here once again with us. Perhaps in time your looks will recover." She paused to dab the corners of her eyes with a lace handkerchief. "My nephew tells me you are out of danger. I am so relieved."

Jemima detected a hint of the former Aunt Prudence and her malicious tendencies. However, there was no point in making a scene, given there was some improvement in the old woman's behaviour and any altercation would impact on Milly's and Fulton's domestic harmony. Jemima chose to busy herself in eating her breakfast. While Aunt Prudence still had barbs, Jemima experienced a sense of being home and had to work hard not to burst into shameful tears once again.

The rest of the morning was spent with Milly cosseting her, bringing her cordials and showing her books and other items of interest in the room. Aunt Prudence made regular pronouncements from where she reposed on the day bed. Milly's eyes often went to the door, perhaps expecting the master of the house.

Aunt Prudence excused herself. "I will see you later this afternoon perhaps. I must speak to the housekeeper and make sure there is something appropriate for you served for dinner. Some gruel perhaps."

The woman left before Jemima could protest that her diet was not so severely impacted. Milly said after Aunt Prudence departed. "I told you she was not that bad. How happy I am that she is reconciled with my marriage to Ambrose. He finds he can tolerate her much better when she is not scornful of him."

Jemima giggled. "I would have loved to have seen her face when he brought you here. I stupidly assumed he was a half-pay naval officer. I expect she thought him of even lower origins. Come to think of it, he did play the part a bit, you know. How evil of him to be laughing at us."

Milly chuckled, caught up in recollections. "I must admit to being fairly overturned myself because he had not warned me. You see he is a naval officer on half-pay. He was wounded and discharged. While he was recuperating, his older brother died after a hunting accident, leaving him the inheritance. I believe the associations of the estate are not good for Ambrose. His father ruled over them, spoiling the older brother, the heir and forcing Ambrose into the navy." Milly let out a sigh. "How happy I am that I have the chance to heal his heart and give him joy in life and in this house. It is way beyond my expectations."

Jemima let out a burst of laughter. "I will agree with you. What was he on about? Why did he not tell us who he was? Aunt Prudence was needlessly odious to him."

"I suspect he had his own reasons. The most important of which to be certain of my feelings. Given his injuries, he wished for someone to love him for himself and not his wealth."

"I would not have expected you to behave in any other way. You are too sweet and good natured to ever marry for money. However, I am excessively happy for you. I was sure that he cared for you and that you would be happy on fifty pounds a year."

"My expectations have never been high, although I would have preferred to be married and have a family without the old spectre of poverty looming over me."

"Well, that is secured now, and Ambrose is truly an excellent man. His manner is so pleasing and his temper so steady. I envy you—"

At the threshold of the open door stood Edward and Ambrose, both of them with pink stains on their cheeks. Jemima blinked and wondered how long they had stood there listening before they were noticed.

Milly went over and took Ambrose's hand. "Will you take some tea?"

Ambrose shook his head, his warm gaze fixed on Jemima. Edward came forward but did not approach her on the couch. He took up a chair at the table and sat silent and brooding. Jemima looked from Ambrose to him, her eyebrow raised. "Do I not even get a good morning? Where have you both been?"

Edward sat up straight and Ambrose led Milly to the couch. "Good morning," Edward said. "We have been busy."

Jemima nodded. "I see. We have been talking of Milly and Ambrose and their future domestic arrangements. Tell me, Ambrose, do you keep Aunt Prudence with you?"

He nodded. "Yes, I have already extended an invitation to her, and she has made inroads to making herself at home."

"So I noticed."

The conversation died off. Edward barely looked at her and Jemima considered that the presence of Milly may be what the issue was. Both of them reluctant to discuss matters which Jemima was keen to hear.

Jemima stood up and walked to the French windows, which opened to a lawn. It had been raining lightly but there looked to be a break in the clouds and there were ample paths to secure her a relatively dry outing. "Excuse me, Edward. Would you be so kind as to accompany me on a quick stroll around the garden?"

Edward leaped from his chair, his glum expression transforming. "It would be a pleasure."

Jemima waited by the door for Edward to join her and then arm in arm they took off. "Now, Edward. I would like to know what you have been doing since we came here. Why I have spent the whole time wondering what was going on, without any information at all to fill in the gaps. Is there trouble? Have you heard something? Why all these glum looks and strained silences?"

Edward looked disconcerted by her verbal onslaught. She could see each question register before he could speak and answer the previous. "I...err...I"

A lovely oak tree spread its vast branches over the path ahead, there Jemima paused and waited for Edward. "Well?"

"You are very direct, young lady. I am not sure it is a good trait in a woman."

"You will learn to live with it."

"I will?"

"Yes, most certainly. I have a precise recollection of you proposing to me. I gave you my life and now you are stuck with me. I will not be changing my mind, even though you are some strange creature I struggle to put a name to."

His eyebrow furrowed. "But I thought...I heard you...well, just now..."

Jemima sighed. "Really, I do care for Ambrose and I think him a marvellous human being, but I am not in love with him."

"You are not? I thought with you been thrown together so much that you...er...well you know."

Jemima glowered at him, not liking the thought of such an expression marring her fine features. "How can you be so odiously stupid? You, who are so clever in other ways. As if I would confess such a thing to his fiancé of all people. You will not get out of marrying me. I demand you marry me as soon as can be arranged."

Edward threw his head back and laughed. It was a joyous expression, relieving his face of much of the worry that had shadowed him. "Then it must be a special license because I cannot have you plaguing me daily, accusing me of trying to wriggle out of our bargain."

"Indeed." Jemima smiled and received the kiss that Edward bestowed on her. Not to be outplayed, she kissed him back, at first a light flirtatious peck, and then transforming it from something meek to something deep and passionate. She felt the change in herself and in Edward as he responded to her. His hands caressed her back, her hair as he let his feelings out, holding her to him, moulding himself to her body. Through the embrace, they had thrown off the barriers which had kept them from each other. Their passions and love came flowing over them, as wondrously they kissed, caressed and touched each other with a new-found wonder.

In that exchange, Jemima felt a release, a license to express the love and desire she had for him. "I love you, Mr Huntington."

"I love you, too, and I am very glad I am not your uncle." He rested his forehead on hers.

Jemima let out a laugh, remembered their first kiss. The rain decided to come down then and they hurried hand in hand down the path, taking shelter in a small pavilion. Jemima refused to let the pain in her chest mar this moment.

Again, she wondered how a person could love someone without knowing them completely. Huddling close to him, she asked, "What kind of man are you anyway?"

Edward reached for her and kissed the top of her head. "Why I am a magician did not you guess?"

Jemima shivered at the words. David had said he wanted to be one, yet he had turned out differently, darker, malevolent. Her thoughts must have shown on her face.

"What is it? What troubles you?"

"David told me when we were children that he wanted to be a magician. I...well...I thought for a moment."

Edward eyebrows cinched together. "Longhurst had some power within him certainly. His pursuits led him down dark paths. He was not like me. I am not like him. My arts use the light and the truth."

She looked up into his face. "I thought you were an inventor, even though some of the things you do seem to defy science as we know it."

"Well you see your father was a magician, too.'

"What? No."

"A fact I only ascertained when I inherited his estate and his laboratory. There among his notes, I found references to magic and he had left a message for me as well, telling me how to access the power within me.'

"But Papa was so normal seeming." She chewed her lip. "Except, now that I think on it, he did the mumbling and hand-waving things you do."

A smile lit his face. "I thought he was senile in the end, but something in his journals kept coming back to me and drew me to try the exercises he suggested. With practice, I was able to do the things he had described.

"Your father was good with animals, preferring nature above menial concerns. Me? I already had a scientific bent, making machines, experimenting with steam and electricity. So here before you is a result of that amalgam.

"As to what I have been doing, well I have some equipment here in Fulton's basement and I have been making a casement for your little machine. This I will fit straight away so we can seal it up and you can heal and live as normally as you can."

⚜

The private double wedding went off very well inside of a week. Edward and Jemima took the train to Sussex and then a carriage to Willow Park. It felt strange to be home again and as mistress of the house. They ate a light supper, Jemima feeling very conscious of her blushes, while she sipped the champagne. Edward reached for her hand and caressed her palm.

"I understand if you are not ready," he said, breaking into her thoughts. Jemima swallowed the last of her champagne and nearly choked on it. Using the serviette to cover her face, she thought of what she could say or do. They were alone, allowed to be alone and now she felt out of her depth. Setting down the serviette, she lifted her chin. "I am ready if you are."

⚜

Jemima woke early, the whisper of dawn a pale tendril of night beneath the curtains. Nestled in Edward's embrace, she smiled to herself, then a dark presence touched the edges of her mind, filling her body with cold fear.

The scar on her breast burned. "Geneck" she whispered harshly.

Edward jolted awake at her words.

A crash made them leap apart and up from the bed. The window smashed, throwing shards of glass in all directions, raining down on to the bed and the carpet. A round bundle, wrapped in bloody cloth landed in front of them, staining their still warm sheets. A shaft of light illuminated the severed head within the folds of fabric.

They stood dumbstruck for a second or two before Jemima screamed, and turned her face away.

"He's found us," Edward said, disengaging himself from her.

"No, he has found me."

Edward gaped at her and shook his head. "No, his hold was broken. I severed it. Stay here."

Edward patted her arm, then pushed his feet into his slippers. He went to the window, pulled the curtains open and peered outside. They were on the second floor, not an easy place to throw a missile and with so much accuracy. "Nothing. No one."

"I tell you, he was here. He was in my mind."

Edward thrust his arm into his dressing gown and crouched down beside the head to inspect it.

"Who is it," Jemima asked, her voice a trifle shaky. She kept her head averted, even though she was dying to look.

"That police inspector...Vickerson, I think his name was. The one who did not believe me."

Jemima sucked in a breath. "It is Geneck. He whispered to me. He is connected to me. It was my blood that was used to revive him."

She clutched her breast, remembering the stabbing pain just moments before.

"Yes, perhaps you are right. There is a blood tie, one that is not easy to break. If he has traced you here, then it has begun."

"We are going to fight then?" Jemima asked.

Edward nodded slowly, wiping his hands on his dressing gown. "Looks like we have no choice."

The End

ABOUT DONNA MAREE HANSON

Donna Maree Hanson is a traditionally and independently published author of fantasy, science fiction and horror. She also writes paranormal romance under the pseudonym of Dani Kristoff. Her dark fantasy series (which some reviewers have called "grim dark"), Dragon Wine, was first published by Momentum Books (Pan Macmillan digital imprint) in 2014. *Shatterwing*: Part One, and *Skywatcher*: Part Two, are now re-published independently in digital and print-on-demand formats. The next two instalments of Dragon Wine, *Deathwings* and *Bloodstorm*, were published in 2017. The final instalments in the Dragon Wine series, *Skyfire* and *Moonfall*, were published in 2018.

In April 2015, Donna was awarded the A. Bertram Chandler Award for "Outstanding Achievement in Australian Science Fiction" for her work in running science fiction conventions, publishing and broader SF community contributions. Donna also writes science fiction romance/space opera, with *Rayessa and the Space Pirates* and *Rae and Essa's Space Adventures* out with Escape Publishing. *Opi Battles the Space Pirates* was published independently in 2017. In 2016, Donna commenced her PhD candidature researching feminism in popular romance at the University of Canberra. Also available is her epic fantasy series The Silverlands: *Argenterra, Oathbound* and *Ungiven Land*. The Cry Havoc series is a steampunk-themed fantasy, with romantic elements, starting with Ruby Heart and Emerald Fire. It is based in Victorian England and features magicians and a very precocious Jemima Hardcastle. Another book, Amber Rose, is planned in the series.

Donna lives in Canberra with her partner and fellow writer, Matthew Farrer.

You can contact Donna or find out more about what she is doing on her blog http://donnamareehanson.com

Or sign up to her newsletter, Wing Dust

Or on Twitter @DonnaMHanson and www.facebook.com/donnamareehanson

NOTE FROM THE AUTHOR

Ruby Heart was a lot of fun to write. I have to thank my writer retreat buddies for their support. Way back in early 2010, the book was drafted over a two-week period in Oberon in New South Wales in the company of Kylie Seluka, Russell Kirkpatrick, Matthew Farrer, Cat Sparks, Joanne Anderton, Ian McHugh and Nicole Murphy. It was a record for me in number of words. Over the next year, I polished it and eventually gained an agent for it.

Alas, the powers that be in the traditional publishing world did not want my book. When pitching it we weren't allowed to call it steampunk either. It is very Victorian steampunk fantasy to my mind. Anyway, after about five years with my agent, I am publishing it myself.

Finally readers get to meet Jemima Hardcastle. I hope you like her. I think she's great.

If you had fun reading this book, please leave a review and let others know there is fun to be had with the Cry Havoc series.

I'm going off now to have a nice cup of tea and a sandwich or two and maybe some fruit cake.

Regards

Donna Maree Hanson

You can find out more about Donna on her website. Sign up to her newsletter Wing Dust for special deals, freebies and author news. http://donnamareehanson.com

On Twitter @DonnaMHanson

On Facebook https://www.facebook.com/DonnaMareeHanson/

ALSO BY DONNA MAREE HANSON

Cry Havoc Series (steampunk fantasy)

Ruby Heart, Cry Havoc Book One

Emerald Fire, Cry Havoc Book Two

Silverlands Series (Epic Fantasy)

Oathbound:Silverlands Book Two

Ungiven Land: Silverlands Book Three

Dragon Wine Series (Dark Fantasy)

Shatterwing: Dragon Wine Part One

Skywatcher: Dragon Wine Part Two

Deathwings: Dragon Wine Part Three

Bloodstorm: Dragon Wine Part Four

Skyfire: Dragon Wine Part Five

Moonfall: Dragon Wine Part Six

Love and Space Pirates (Science Fiction Romance-Sweet level)

Rayessa and the Space Pirates

Rae and Essa's Space Adventures

Opi Battles the Space Pirates

Short story collections

Beneath the Floating City: Short science fiction stories

Through These Eyes: Tales of Magic Realism and Fantasy

www.ingramcontent.com/pod-product-compliance
Lightning Source LLC
Chambersburg PA
CBHW021414110726
47901CB00008B/2162